Holybourne

The Magic of a Child

by

Carol Jeanne Kennedy

Vickie
Enjoy!
Carol Jeanne Kennedy
2019

Publication Rights

Dedications

To all my wonderful friends and family who helped me along the way in writing my novels. This book is dedicated to: Don Knight, Billy Miller, Jean Gess, Carol Silvis, and Mary Burdick. Also, special thanks to Hennie Bekker whose musical compositions *Algonquin Trails* and *Stormy Sunday* provided the creative spark for *Winthrope*, followed by the rest of my Victorian Collection.

Other Great Novels by this Author

Winthrope – *Tragedy to Triumph*
The Arrangement – *Love Prevails*
Bobbin's Journal – *Waif to Wealth*
Poppy – *The Stolen Family*
Sophie & Juliet – *Rags to Royalty*
The Spinster – *Worth the Wait*
Holybourne – *The Magic of a Child*

Links and Reviews

Visit the author's website: VictorianRomanceNovels.com
Like on Facebook: caroljeannekennedy
Follow on Twitter @carol823599

CHAPTER ONE

14 December 1861

When Mr O'Leary's carriage approached Holybourne, I hid. The odious gentleman owned the brewery, the inn, and just about everything else in town. He was the only pawnbroker for many miles around, and a nasty sort of man. Mama said he liked little girls.

Now that he was well down the road, I pushed my way through the creaking old turnstile and hurried to the Red Lyon Inn. Mama was the laundress there, and I helped her wash every noon. I dared not tarry for right this minute I could hear the noon stagecoach approaching. The coachman's shout, the horses' hooves, and the clang and squeak of the approaching *Londoner* arrived just as the town clock struck one, two ... then just as I turned the corner, upon my horror, I ran directly into Mr O'Leary.

"Well, well, Anne," he said and tweaked my cheek in rude fashion. Pressing his fat, sweaty body into me, he glanced around smiling. "Why, I don't see your mother." The stench of ale belched from his innards. "Have you been searching for me all by yourself?"

Flesh bumps crawled over my skin at his touch. "No, sir, I have come to help Mama." Just then the twelfth gong struck, and I struggled to enter the inn, but he blocked my way with his bloated stomach. The shiny buttons on his brown wool waistcoat pressed deep into my cheek. I tried to move, but couldn't. He lifted my chin, but I refused to look him in the eye.

Mr Ruther, who managed the inn for Mr O'Leary, grabbed my arm and pulled me inside. "Your mother is in the cellar falling behind in her work as usual. Hurry her along!"

I rubbed my cheek. Thankful to be away from Mr O'Leary, I nodded. "Yes, sir."

"Then hurry about it, girl! You're late again."

I hurried down the cellar's creaky roughhewn stairs. "Yes, sir."

I helped Mama gather up the dirty linen and ran back upstairs to fetch another armload, but first peeked to make sure O'Leary was gone. Satisfied that he was nowhere near, I hurriedly gathered more of the dirty rags, aprons, and tablecloths.

With nips of snow thick in the air, the patrons, motion-sick, muddy, and exhausted from their ride, crowded into the warm inn. Rubbing their hands briskly at the hearth fire, they spread the dreadful news about Prince Albert dying from the typhoid, and what a terrible disaster for the Queen—she so loved her Prince.

I listened to the news about His Majesty's death with sorrow and reflected that 14 December was an unfortunate day for the Prince, my Papa, and me. My eleventh birthday would not only be remembered as the day my Papa died, but now the same day our beloved Prince was, as the vicar would say, 'called to heaven.'

Ruther was watching me. I grabbed a dirty handkerchief from the floor and scurried down the steps to find Mama sipping from a gin bottle. "Mama, you mustn't. Ruther will catch you and ..."

"Catch her at what?" Ruther growled, coming up behind me.

"Prince Albert died, sir. I didn't want you to *catch* Mama weeping."

* * *

After Mama and I washed and hung the day's laundry, we left for home. It was almost dark, and Mama wanted to return by way of the sacred stream. Mr Braithwaite, the vicar, said that the pilgrims, on their way from Winchester to Canterbury, drank the blessed water. Mama said if it was good enough for the pilgrims it was good enough for her. Often at night she would walk along the banks and listen to the long-departed as they bemoaned their circumstances. Ruther told me that he often spied ghosts about the water, and once his dog chased one until the vision disappeared into thin air.

"Not tonight, Mama." I shuddered. "If I should stumble ... you know I can't swim."

She pulled her shawl up around her neck. "That was clever of you to lie for me in the cellar, Anne." She ruffled my hair. "You'll do well in life with your quick thinking."

"I only lied to protect you, Mama."

"As you should have, Anne, after all, I am your mother."

"I suppose now you will be doubly sorry when my birthday comes again, Mama."

"Indeed, what a burden it has become."

"The Queen must be very sad, Mama."

"The Queen." She sneered. "May she suffer as much as I have suffered with the loss of your father, then she'll know what real pain is."

"But, Mama, that was long ago. Surely you must forget."

She swayed and stumbled, and I felt disgusted at her drinking gin. Earlier, I had prepared a stew—bits and pieces of lamb, potatoes, carrots and turnips, but I knew she wouldn't eat.

"Mama, you've been sipping too much gin again. Ruther will be angry and find someone else to do the work."

"He won't find anyone else, my work is too good. Besides all that, I pay him for my gin, so never mind."

"But we have so little, Mama. Why is it always 'never mind,' Mama?" I covered my ears and quickened my steps. I hated the words *never mind*.

When we passed through our wobbly front gate, Mama sighed. "I suppose you must write to Her Majesty and offer our condolences."

"Very well, Mama."

"And you must mention how your Mama lost her beloved on the same day. Already I am tired of hearing how *she* will suffer. What about me, Anne? Who offers sympathy to me?"

"I'll write to her right off, Mama."

"Indeed you will." She entered the cottage muttering about the past. "At one time, Anne, your father mingled with wealthy royal society." She bumped into the table, found her chair and settled heavily into it. "Until I came along—a mere French governess."

"Yes, Mama."

The fire in the hearth had gone black, crusty, and cold. "I will rekindle the fire, Mama."

"Then be about it, girl. I'm chilled to the bone."

* * *

Morning came quietly through the low grey clouds half full of rain and snow. Fetching the morn's water, I felt the stiff brown grass crack under my footfalls. I lugged the sloshing bucket full of icy water into the kitchen. Mama sat in her rocking chair by the fire.

I poured the water into the old black kettle. "Bread, Mama?"

"A slice." She rubbed her head and moaned. Her hands trembled as she reached for her gin cup. "I'm not hungry, Anne."

"You must eat more than a slice, Mama. You know how your hands shake when you don't eat enough."

When she turned to warm her hands at the fire, I emptied half of her gin bottle into the wilting potted vine that had once grown so eagerly; now its flimsy brown tendrils reached thin for that little sliver of light at the window.

"If only he hadn't died, Anne, things would have been better."

"Prince Albert, Mama?"

"Prince Albert?" She flung a log into the fire. "Prince Albert? What about him? I'm thinking only of your Papa."

I never knew my father, and perhaps things would have been better had he not slipped beneath the wheels of the carriage on London Road the day I was born. "I know, Mama. Perhaps if he had lived, I would be happy." I dreamed of happiness as a day without the smell of gin.

She stopped her incessant rocking. "Why should *you* be happy?" Glancing at the last two logs sitting at the hearth, she grunted, "Humph, that's another one of your faults, Anne. You daydream too much and forget to bring in the wood."

Mama resumed her rocking, rocking, rocking. The smell of rancid gin, pungent and sour, was woven into the fabric of our days. I wondered why she could not see as I did—not just on my birthday, but each and every day—the glazed eyes, the twisted lips, the spittle-mixed words. Her sallow face and ashen complexion starved for the slightest stream of sunlight. Her dark dress hung on her body as though draped on a rack.

"I don't think Her Majesty drinks very much, Mama."

"Humph, from now on she will. I am very sure of it. How could she not? If you think about it, her cellars must be full."

"But if her children objected, Mama, they would shun her."

"Oh, they wouldn't dare shun their Queen. She'd lop off their heads."

Mama's thin, worn hand shook as she drained her cup. Wiping her mouth with the back of her hand, she smirked. "You wouldn't shun me, Anne?"

"No, it wouldn't matter, Mama," I whispered.

* * *

It was more than Mama's penchant to talk to the "bottle" as she so often did with teary-eyed fondness; in reverence, she prayed aloud for a word or two from Papa. Visiting with the mysterious fortune-teller, Madame Pinchot, was a Godsend to her ... or so she said.

Mr Braithwaite, the vicar, insisted such Godsends lay in God's house alone. But even before the church bell's peal on Sunday morning, Mama and I were on the well-worn path to Madame Pinchot's cottage to see if she had news from Papa.

"Mama, it will soon snow again."

"Indeed." She shoved me. "Hurry along then, Anne." As the snow, mixed with rain, fell heavily upon the leaves, Mama fretted. "Watch your step. You know how Madame fusses about mud."

I wonder why Madame Pinchot would worry over such a thing. Her cottage was much like ours, with heavy drawn curtains, except that Madame's candle nubs pooled hard to the dust-covered furniture; her hearth grates were broken and black, and soot thickened into cakes of unkempt char— why would she notice mud?

"Mama, while at the bakery just yesterday, I heard Mrs Braithwaite whisper to Mrs Pennyworth that Madame Pinchot was an evil woman who told nothing but bad fortunes."

"Hmm, what would she know?" Mama pulled her shawl tighter to her neck and gestured for me to hurry along.

"Yes, Mama."

With ease, I jumped over mounds of dirt and sidestepped every puddle. When we passed through the gate into the last meadow before The Road, I found a sparrow all aflutter, circling on the ground. It had a broken wing.

"Oh, Mama, it is hurt. A cat must have caught it." Holding it ever so close to my cheek, I felt its fragile warm body; felt its fearful little heart beat as if ready to explode. "We have come just in time."

"Let it go, Anne. It must survive on its own or ..."

I turned away. If Mama couldn't speak with Papa herself regarding her broken heart, then what could she know about my sparrow's broken wing? Sheltering my find, I insisted, "I'll ask Madame Pinchot what to do."

Mama coughed into her handkerchief and stopped for a moment to catch her breath.

We came to The Road, the London Road that Mama loathed.

"Make haste, Anne. You know I hate setting one foot on it."

This morning she even went out of her way to find the narrowest place to cross. My father died on this road. In his happy exuberance to hold his first born, me, my father failed to mind his step and slipped—his head was crushed between the wheel and The Road.

To add to the bitter irony for my mother, The Road led to London. It was there that my grandfather Holt declared his distaste for everything French, including Mama, and it was there where His Majesty, Prince Albert died.

I was told that my Aunt, Miss Alice Holt, lived there in a great chateau, Lesington Hall. According to Mama, it was also my Papa's childhood home. She said Aunt Alice was the one good thing to come out of London. She was wealthy and sent us money at Christmas, although she never answered Mama's letters.

Now approaching Madame Pinchot's, I sniffed the air. The smoke that escaped her crooked chimney did not smell pungent and sweet like ours. This wet morning I was careful to avoid the mud, but Misha, Madame's huge dog, greeted me with such wildness that I lost my balance and stepped into the muddiest of puddles.

Mama, too terrified to look the dog in the eye, grabbed my hand, trembling and said, "Come along, Anne."

Mama spoke French to Madame Pinchot, and that always made Madame smile. She charged Mama half of what she charged her other customers, and that made Mama smile. Everyone was smiling, except me. I was to remain sitting when I most wanted to be playing with the dog.

I was always fascinated with Madame Pinchot as she shuffled her faded and edge-worn cards. She called them her

Tarot cards. Putting her finger to her lips, she shushed Mama and me and began a mysterious chant over the fanned cards. I could hear someone trying to tiptoe in the room just above us. No doubt it was Monsieur Pinchot. Mama later insisted it was Papa's spirit.

A few of Madame's black curls strayed from the scarf knotted behind her head and dangled about her brow. Her squinty black eyes seemed always out of focus. Madame Pinchot wore all of her gold jewellery around her neck, on her wrists and every finger—even her thumbs. I thought perhaps she was worried about a thief in the night.

"Madame Pinchot," I offered in the eerie silence, "if you worry so about someone stealing your jewels, why not gaze into your crystal pebbles there and set Misha on the thieves before they come into your house?"

Mama kicked my leg.

Madame Pinchot ignored my most excellent suggestion. As her hands hovered over the pebbles, one of her long, claw-like fingernails tapped a tattered tarot card. She squinted at me. "Ooh, oui, Nana, someday you marry a man of great riches."

Mama smiled, easing back into her chair. "Did I not tell you so, Anne?"

"Oh, yes, Mama, you did. You did."

"You will be a great beauty." Madame Pinchot's lips were thin and red, thick with paint. Her eyes still squinted as she looked up at Mama. "You, Madame, must see that your daughter's hand is given to the proper man, for there are those who will seek it for ill favour."

"Oh, indeed, Madame Pinchot, indeed, I will hand her over to only the best." She winked. "Only the very best for my Annie."

"Given away, Mama?" I envisioned myself as a bottle of fine wine. But Mama would not give away any bottle of wine—let alone a vintage of 'great beauty.'

Madame Pinchot returned to her cards and waved me away with a dismissive hand. "I give your mother her reading, au revoir, Nana."

"Au revoir, Madame Pinchot." Removing myself to a stool in a quiet corner, I felt the flutter of my tiny captive yet in my pocket. "Oh, pardon, Madame Pinchot." I held up my bird. "It has a broken wing, Madame. How shall I care for it?"

"A bird?" She frowned. "You trouble me with a bird? C'est horrible." Glancing down at the Tarot cards, she hastily flipped one over.

Mama gasped. It was the death card.

Pinchot pointed toward the door. "Give bird to Misha." She cackled. "She know what to do."

I gasped, my warm breath whispering to the startled creature in my hand, "I won't."

To Mama's obvious relief, Madame gathered up the cards and reshuffled them. Glancing toward an open wine bottle sitting on the sideboard, Mama ventured, "On such a day as this, perhaps a petit glass of vin rouge, Madame Pinchot?"

Still busy with her cards, the fortune-teller chuckled, "Mademoiselle, you never see petit glass in your life."

Mama drew back at the insult. I knew she would not beg again. She was too concerned whether Madame had heard any words from my dear departed Papa. This time, she had not. Mama stood, not glancing for a third time at the vin rouge. "Very well Madame Pinchot, very well then, perhaps some other time."

Walking home, Mama squeezed the back of my neck. "You heard what Madame Pinchot said about marrying the proper man, Anne."

I squirmed away from her grasp. "Yes, Mama, I heard her words." It was now raining hard, and I snuggled the bird to my neck to keep it warm.

"Speak up, Anne, you mustn't whisper. I have been noticing of late how you whisper. It has become most annoying, girl."

"Yes, Mama." I tried to ignore her sharp tone. The fortune-teller's stinging rebuke had wounded her into another nasty mood.

"What?" Mama asked.

I spoke up, "We're coming to The Road, Mama." I wiped my eyes. "The Road."

As we waited for a carriage to pass, it stopped. The door opened. A man, sitting quite high and dry, called out, "Mrs Holt would you like a ride home?"

Mama lit up with a smile. Pulling back her hood, she nodded. "Oh, indeed Mr O'Leary; how very kind of you to offer."

He was never a polite gentleman and made no motion of helping either Mama or me up into the carriage. Rain pelted down upon us as I boosted Mama into the carriage. She tried hard to keep from splashing him, but with little success. I heard his impatient sigh.

When I attempted the first step, mud sucked the shoe from my foot. In my haste to retrieve it, I accidentally dropped the bird. Mama grabbed my hand and yanked me up into the carriage.

Mr O'Leary reached over to close the door. "Drive on," he shouted.

"Wait, wait!" I cried, "My bird."

Mama covered my mouth with her soaked glove. "Pay her no mind, Mr O'Leary, the simple girl found a nasty bird with a broken wing and ..."

As we lurched forward, I pushed past Mr O'Leary and scrambled out the door landing ankle deep in mud. "I'll walk home, Mama."

Rain pelted my woollen shawl. I heard the nasty whipcrack from the coachman as he cursed and whistled at the poor bedraggled horses, "Hup, hup."

Mud from the carriage wheels splattered my face. They left me in the middle of the road, but I couldn't leave my defenceless little bird behind. Being careful where I stepped, I searched the rutted brown ooze. Though I found my shoe, I never found the bird. I fancied she somehow hopped to safety. Perhaps her wing wasn't broken at all, and she had nestled beneath a bush being quiet and still, watching me. A chill swept over me as I felt the rain now soaking me to my skin. How fortunate for the bird, I thought—feathers never soak.

* * *

I took the long pathway home and stopped to pet Mrs Braithwaite's cow and her liver-coloured bitch, Pan. I then hurried along, convinced that Mr O'Leary would surely be gone by now. When I pushed through the turnstile behind our cottage, to my dismay, I spied his carriage. I had always detested him with his swaggering about our village of Holybourne, looking this way and that way, stopping now and again to voice his exalted opinion over things of little consequence.

I entered through the kitchen, quiet as a mouse. I removed my muddy shoes and drippy stockings and then tiptoed my way to Papa's room. It was a place forbidden to visit unless Mama was with me. I knew I could hide there until Mr O'Leary left, but when I opened the door, there he sat with Mama. Her face was red and her lip rouge smudged. She fumbled with her glass; an empty bottle sat next to a full one.

"There you are, my sweet. Why, I was just telling Mr O'Leary that if you didn't soon find home, I was going searching for you." Pushing back her wet, matted hair, she nodded with uncharacteristic sincerity. Her eyes could barely focus.

Mr O'Leary stood. "Indeed, Anne. Indeed, we were both going a searching."

"I could never get lost on the pathway from Madame Pinchot's. It is but a little distance." Thinking Mama would scold me for being late, I added, "I stopped to ... to pet a cow, and then a dog, and then I took a sip from the sacred stream."

Mr O'Leary drew back. His flabby pink chin hung well over his yellow stained cravat. "Well, well, the sacred stream. Hmm, such a heart you must have." He leaned toward me. "And you have such a way with words for a little girl. You impress me, child."

"Sir," I corrected, "I am not a child. I have a way with words because I read very much."

His brows raised; his lips formed a smile. "So you do, Anne. So you do." Patting the chair next to him, he invited, "Come now and sit with me, won't you, young lady?"

I obeyed, not because I wanted to, but because there was nowhere else to sit. He knew I detested him, though he continued to smile at me a great deal. I noticed his obvious interest in Papa's books, the wonderful leather-bound volumes stacked from floor to ceiling—the ones I wasn't allowed to touch, but often did.

My mother followed his gaze. "Mr O'Leary, this is my late husband's library. Oh, a few are mine." She flushed. "And with such books about us ..."

"Indeed they are, sir." I interrupted. "Mama was born in France, she was raised in France and became a beautiful governess. My Papa was a great man and lived in a great chateau in London." I nodded at Mama. "This room is where Mama had me write to Her Majesty to commiserate with the loss of her prince." I gestured toward Papa's desk. "And there is where Mama taught me to read a very long time ago and insisted that I learn to speak as the refined ladies do in the books, for no gentleman of importance and wealth would look my way if I spoke like a washer-woman with an ignorant tongue."

O'Leary clapped as he giggled. "Indeed not." Now leaning toward me, his face a deep pink, he ran his hairy fingers down my arm. "Dear me, Anne, you are shivering—you must change into something warm before you catch cold." He reached to help me remove my shawl. His touch sent chills up my spine. His breath smelled hot, his teeth yellow and crooked. I jumped up and ran to the door. "Mama, I shall change."

Sipping her gin, she ignored me and turned back to Mr O'Leary.

* * *

When I awoke the following morning, I recalled Madame Pinchot saying that I would marry into wealth, but would I ever be as happy as Mama and Papa once were?

"Anne," Mama called, her voice was hoarse and insistent.

I tossed off my covers, hurried to dress, and then hopped down the squeaky wooden staircase like a rabbit. I first stopped to look into Papa's room to make sure everything was in its place. I hated Mr O'Leary being in his room.

"Anne!"

"Here I am, Mama." The scent of Papa's books still hovered about me.

She sniffed the air, but apparently found nothing to light her eyes.

"Mr O'Leary is coming today. Tidy up now, tidy up."

"Mr O'Leary, Mama?" I shuddered, "but he was here just yesterday."

She eyed me with contempt. "He has promised to bring *you* a fine roast for supper."

Mama smiled toward the ceiling. Her eyes sparkled. "Mr O'Leary was very taken with you, Anne. You behaved quite proper last night." She gave me her most cherished handkerchief. "You may keep it, Anne."

"But Mama—"

"You shall receive many more presents, Love." She poured gin into her hot tea and sipped it. Her voice was now smoother. "Mr O'Leary hinted that you would one day grow into a beautiful lady."

Holding the lacy handkerchief with great apprehension, I thought of Madame Pinchot's prophesies regarding my face. I could feel my stomach lurch. "I don't want to grow beautiful just to please Mr O'Leary, Mama."

Her black eyes flashed in anger. "Anne, your Papa's purse is running low. Now, you must show the gentleman O'Leary what a good girl you are. Smile pretty for him." She took my chin roughly and moved my head this way and that. "There's a girl. Show your teeth for he has promised to take us to the fair."

*　*　*

Later that afternoon, as we walked about the great Fair with Mr O'Leary, Mama placed me in the middle. I wondered why she would punish me so. Long black hairs curled on the back of his swollen red knuckles; his fingernails were filthy. He would often pick his nose and then admire my 'sweet profile' by running his finger down my forehead, over my nose, across my lips. I grew to hate his hot foul breath when he would whisper the silliest secrets in my ear.

Though Mama walked with her head held high about the Fair's standing pens, jugglers, and food tents, tasting this and that, she was met with sneers. It was only when the bull-necked pawnbroker, Mr O'Leary, flashed his money about, that they stopped jeering.

Mama whispered, "You see Anne, how much respect he brings to our lives?"

His money does, I thought. We walked about, stopping once to poke our heads into a few tents, but then the rains came, and we boarded Mr O'Leary's carriage and returned home. Our splendid meal of roast beef was cooked to perfection. Indeed, I wondered if I would be roasted to perfection as well.

*　*　*

During breakfast the next morning, Mama poured gin into her coffee and cut into the leftover meat. "Mmm, my love, savour the taste. It's been a long time since we've eaten such a meal."

"Indeed, Mama, the roast was cooked to a turn."

"This morning we are to visit the brewery. You must wash your face, scrub your hands, and brush your hair to a sheen."

"But Mama, what about our work at the inn?"

"No, we will never be going back there again."

"Won't be going back there?" I frowned, "but, Mama, how will we buy our food?"

"Anne, you must do as you are told."

I pushed away from the table and ran to my room to put on my only frock. Such as it was, for most of my things were now coming from the vicar's wife. I had outgrown everything else. Indeed the money Aunt Alice sent was running thin.

Bounding back down the stairs, I found Mama dozing in her rocking chair by the fire. *What business could we have at the brewery? Why was Mama now not going to work?* Rubbing her shoulder, I woke her with a whisper, "You look pretty, Mama."

Standing up, she set her cup on the mantle and rubbed her arms. "Fetch me my shawl, my warmest shawl."

"Yes, Mama." I found it hanging behind the door on a peg, her bonnet alongside. Bringing them to my nose, I took in the scent of her hair. It was a warm, familiar scent, not flowery clean and weatherly like outside, but rather old hearth fire and dust. I handed Mama her bonnet and shawl.

"We are going to the brewery, Mr O'Leary's office, Anne. He will handle Papa's affairs from now on."

A deep sickening thought worked its way from my heart and inched up into my throat. I recollected the scheme in Mr O'Leary's eye last night as he perused Papa's handsome leather-bound books. Leather-bound black words lying face-to-face, touching on warm yellow paper, words combined to share truths. Perhaps those truths were the same for Queen Victoria, born in starry sparkles of wealthy heavens, as for those who lived in much worse circumstances.

I didn't want to cross Mama early on, but the disobedient words leapt from my tongue all the same, "Oh, I pray you aren't selling Papa's books, Mama." After the plea, I froze. *Had I planted a seed?*

"Nothing of that sort, Anne." She fussed with her bonnet. "Mr O'Leary will be handling your father's financial affairs."

"But I thought we didn't have any financial affairs, Mama."

"Mr O'Leary is quite adept at turning nothing into something, Anne."

"Will he handle Aunt Alice's Christmas money, Mama?"

She glared at me, her palsied hands shaking as she fluffed the bow beneath her sagging, yellowish toned chin. "Fortunate for us, Miss Chatter-Box, the kind Mr O'Leary has consented to handle those matters that I find most annoying. Your Aunt Alice's Christmas money doesn't annoy me. But regarding others—he will know how to deal with those sorts."

I was sure Mr O'Leary did know how to handle *those* sorts of people. His voice sounded smooth and narrow; his tongue sharp and pointed, and with such hairy hands, who would dare refuse him? He was the most powerful man for miles around. I was quite sure even Madame Pinchot would be nervous around him.

Now approaching the centre of the village, Mama took my hand. "Walk straight past the draper's shop, Anne. Don't glance in. We will not be stopping there today."

"Very well, Mama." I knew she was too ashamed to enter the shop. We owed them money too, but just as we were to pass his door, Mr Buffle hurried out.

Stepping in front of Mama, he nodded. "Good day, Mrs Holt. I saw you and little Anne crossing The Road yesterday. Hmm, pennies for Madame Pinchot, but nothing for me?"

Through Mama's yellow-grey pallor, her face splotched crimson. "In the future, Mr Buffle, Mr O'Leary will be handling our affairs. He'll soon pay our debt."

"Indeed." He backed away with a sneer. "So, you're now rich enough to have Mr O'Leary handle your affairs? Well, well, then. I shall look forward to his visit."

I could feel his gaze on us as we proceeded up the wooden walk.

"Impertinent man," huffed Mama. "Imagine accosting a widow and her daughter on the street in such a manner. Is there no shame, Anne?" She coughed violently into her handkerchief.

"Indeed, Mama." I patted her back. "Mistress Shrieve, the baker's wife, commented just yesterday as she handed me our bread saying that I had better bring money next visit, or she would soon put me to work."

Mama gripped my hand. "Such a nerve, Anne."

"But Mrs Pennyworth, who stood alongside, drew back, saying, 'Mrs Shrieve, where is your Godliness? You must never refuse beggar children bread.'"

"A beggar child?" Mama stopped. Her voice grew hoarse again. "She called you a beggar child?"

"Yes, Mama, and Mr Pennyworth gave me a slice of cheese, fresh from his wrapper."

"Well, well, Anne, on our way to the brewery this morning, you must curtsy as I showed you. Bow and nod, you'll soon learn to recognise those worth noting."

"Who might they be, Mama?"

"I will tell you, Anne." Adjusting her shawl, Mama lifted her chin quite high. "Indeed, tomorrow Holybourne's beggar child will be debtless. They'll then see who begs for bread." Mama stopped for a moment to catch her breath. After she dabbed her lips, we moved on. A group of ladies from the church approached. Mama nodded, but they ignored her.

"Why do they not speak to you, Mama?"

"I suppose they are heathens, Anne."

"But, Mama," I pulled my hand from hers, shocked at her appraisal. "Mrs Braithwaite is the vicar's wife."

"Going to church doesn't make one a saint, Anne. The sooner you find that out, the better your thinking."

I turned and watched the ladies scurrying up the path hovering and whispering. Glancing down at my ill-fitting frock, I pulled my shawl tighter about my neck. "But Mama, Mrs Braithwaite is the lady who gave me this frock."

"With mends, stains, and no buttons, but of course she would, my little rag and bone girl. Her Christian duty conscience nicely sorted out. I assure you, Anne, I will never wear a stitch from her or hers."

"Indeed, Mama."

* * *

I sat alone in Mr O'Leary's waiting room for what seemed an hour and wiggled one of my baby teeth loose from its socket.

Mr O'Leary's door opened.

"There now, miss," he glanced at me with a smile. "Come in, come in. What a pretty shawl you are wearing."

"Thank you, sir." I glanced at Mama feeling my tooth settle back in its gummy little socket.

"Well, well," he said, "come right over here to my desk, little miss. I have something I wish to show you." He pushed a few papers in front of me. "Do you know how to sign your name, little girl?"

I frowned. *Little girl? Did I know how to sign my name? Of course I did. I fancied my hand just as delicate as Queen Victoria's.* With indignation, I huffed, "Indeed I do, sir."

Tapping his pen to the bottom of the paper in front of me, he smiled. "Then let me see for myself such an exquisite hand as your mother has been bragging about."

Mama came to my side, gushing. "There's my girl. Sign your name, Anne. Sign it in your best, loveliest scroll."

I signed where she pointed.

"There now." She exhaled heavily and signed her name next to mine. "Your father's financial affairs are quite out of my power." She fanned her face with her handkerchief. "Oui, oui, it is over."

Smiling, Mama offered up her hand to Mr O'Leary and took my arm. "We must go now, sir, until tomorrow, then."

Stepping out into the cold noon air, I squinted up into Mama's face. She was humming. "You are now happy, Mama?"

"Oh, yes, Anne. My worries are over." She tweaked my nose. "As long as I live, I shall never have to worry over money for bread or cheese or ... ."

"Or gin, Mama."

"Speak up, Anne. You know how I hate it when you whisper." Smiling, Mama inhaled a deep breath and moved on toward home. And all the while, she did not find one person to whom I was to curtsy.

* * *

The very next day, Mama made me stand out in the cold and wait for Mr O'Leary's carriage. I was to alert her of his coming so she could better prepare herself. 'To look more presentable.' I knew the truth of the matter, she needed time to hide her bottle and then I was to run up the lane full of smiles and welcomes for the man. Oh, dread the moment. "But Mama, I assure you, I know when Mr O'Leary is coming, I do not need to stand and wait for him."

"Never mind, Anne, do as I say."

Indeed, Mr O'Leary's coachman seemed to delight in snapping the whip, cracking it just above the horses' ears, shouting and cursing so. I felt sorry for the poor creatures as their ears were twitching for the mean sharp snap of pain that seemed forever just a wrist flick away.

A rickety old cart followed directly behind Mr O'Leary's carriage. Miss Tilly Marvel, the Braithwaite's dairymaid, sat in it, crumpled up fat and tight. A sharp-boned cow was loosely tied behind. I knew something of Miss Marvel for she was always kind to me.

Climbing down unassisted, the heavy-set, yet agile Miss Marvel instructed the footman to carry the larger of her trunks into our cottage. Her puffy, red, pockmarked cheeks were in stark contrast to her black Irish hair twisted tight beneath her dingy white day cap.

"Anne," cried Mama, covering her cough, "you must come in now."

"You're coughing more and more, Mama," I said as I entered the cottage.

Her face coloured as Mr O'Leary stepped back, frowning.

"It's just a cold." Taking my shoulder, she whispered, "Do be a dear and show Tilly where she is to stay, Anne."

I didn't know where Tilly was to stay. There was just my room and Mama's. "Where, Mama?"

She gestured with her head toward my room. "Go along now, Anne, help our new maid with her things."

I led Tilly up to my room. Glancing around, she didn't seem pleased. My bed was small, and at present crumpled and soiled, filthy according to her. My basket of leaves and sticks sat next to the vacant black hearth. My wash-basin still held dirty water, and my chamber pot ... .

Frowning, Tilly straight away stripped the bed. "Filthy, filthy. I must wash this bedding before I sleep in it." She pulled my curtains from their hooks. Bright, bold snow light streamed into my little dark corner of the world. "Humph, filthy, as well." She cursed under her breath. "I've much work here, I can see that."

"I would help you, Miss Tilly, but Mama insists I act the lady and not callus my hands." Studying my palms, I closed my fingers to hide the calluses already there. "One day I am to marry a fine gentleman and live in London."

Slapping her hands on her ample hips, she shrieked through her gaping front teeth. "And," she bowed, holding the broom like a witch, "I will fly over the moon."

"I beg your pardon?" Mama stood in the doorway, her icy glare struck straight into Tilly's frilly day cap.

"Oh," said Tilly as she hurriedly gathered up the wash, "beg pardon, Mrs Holt."

Mama's face was draining pale again. "What is it, Mama?"

She waited until Tilly bustled down the hall. "Mr O'Leary has gone, Anne. You must write him a nice letter thanking him for bringing us a maid."

"But how are we to pay her, Mama?"

"Mr O'Leary is quite generous, Anne. He has lent Tilly to us for a time. Now be a good girl and show him your excellent writing." She patted my shoulder. "Just as you write to Her Majesty."

"Yes, Mama."

* * *

While Tilly unpacked her trunk, I began my thank-you letter to that odious Mr O'Leary. When Tilly laid a reading book on my bed, I glanced up. "Oh, I love to read, Tilly, is it a good one?"

"Lord, child, it is the Bible." She said it in such a tone that I felt my body tingle with anticipatory wonder.

Dropping my pen, I looked at her in wonder. "I have not read it, Tilly."

"Hmm." She folded her huge arms and squinted down into my face. "Nor have you ever gone to church, Anne." She took up the Bible. "The words in this great and glorious book, says Mr Braithwaite, will deliver you from evil."

My eyes stretched wide. I ran my hand over the Holy Black Book. "Indeed," I returned the whisper in awe. "Papa has such a book, but Mama said I was never to touch it."

Placing her large hand on my head, she glanced up to heaven. "But you may touch *my* Bible, Anne."

"Oh, Tilly, I do so wish to be delivered from evil. You must read to me every night."

The air of pent-up glory whooshed from her nose, her shoulders slumped, her face saddened. "But, but, I can't read, Anne."

I was dumbfounded. How someone could own such a book, recommend such a book, and yet couldn't read such a book? "How can that be, Tilly?"

"The vicar gave us all Bibles, Anne. Though I can't read it, I sleep with it every night next to my heart, so I do."

A grand and glorious beam from the author of such a holy book panged my heart with inspiration. Taking her plump red, rough hands in mine, and holding them to my heart, I offered,

"Don't fret, Tilly. *I* shall read to you." My chest swelled. "Together, we shall be delivered from evil."

I was not at all sure to what extent evil had penetrated my heart, and I knew nothing of Tilly's soul, as she was such a large woman, but I supposed the black book's words could add nothing but more good to her frame. As to Mama, perhaps when I was without evil, she might inquire as to my newfound character. I could then impart the righteousness of my ways and read to her as well.

* * *

Our reading became habitual as spring warmed into late summer that eleventh year of my being. When I could leave Mama in safety to doze, I would make my way to The Road and call out for Misha. Leaping, her tail jubilant, she yipped while licking my face in glee. Though I tried many times to make friends among girls my own age, I remained scorned and quite lonely.

But Misha loved me as I loved her. She was wild with God's speed when I'd toss a stick her way. When she was busy chasing a hare, I buried myself in stacks of hay and giggled as she barked and whined until she found me. We would then run to the sacred stream and lap up the fresh, sweet water.

Indeed, as the haymakers gathered and tied their bundles, as the leaves were raked and burned, as the fallen apples rotted, Mama rotted in her chair. Alas, she paid no heed to Tilly's and my righteous ways. Only rocking seemed the rhythmic solution to her nervous spells. On rare occasions, she stepped out to have a word with Ruther, who delivered her bottles of gin. But Mama's words were now more often than not slurred, and late at night, more shrill. She spoke more French than Tilly and I could ever understand.

Mama would always plead, "When Mr O'Leary comes to visit, Anne, you must promise to never forget how he has kept me alive for you; kept us with food, wood and coal to keep us warm. You must never forget what he has done for us. Promise me, Anne."

"I promise, Mama."

But when Mr O'Leary came to visit, Tilly always made me hide; assuring me it was God's will.

CHAPTER TWO

London, Lindon Hall

Mama had grown quite weak this summer even though Tilly and I did all the chores and cooking. I thought that by us helping it would have made her stronger, but she drank even more gin and her cough deepened, a swirl of yellow etched deeper into her face; her eyes sunk beyond despair into their black hollow sockets.

"Anne, come sit with me. I have something to tell you."

"Yes, Mama."

Tilly had left the room. Mama took her chair by the fire. I covered her thin little shoulders with her wrap and sat next to her on a stool. It was a cool early autumn evening as Mama remained silent staring into the fire, its flames glinted in her rheumy eyes. As I waited for her words, I tossed leaves into the fire, it was mesmerising to watch each leaf's last shrivel and hiss. How fast they curl in the flames. Not a speck of ash, not a hiss-spit, not even a thin leaf-stem left to sweep up. Their fiery little flakes of life once verdant and pliant have become simply a tidy vapour of eternity—much like my mother, consumed by the vice that, day by day, etched her life into nothingness.

"It is time, Anne."

"Time, Mama? What do you mean?"

"I have enough money saved for the coach. It is time you visit your father's sister, your Aunt Alice in London."

Frightened at such a prospect, I took her hand. "You will come with me, Mama?"

"No." She pulled her hand from mine. "You are old enough now, Anne, to make your own way."

I hid my tears. "Very well, Mama."

* * *

Traversing the narrow bridle path from our cottage to The Road, I clasped my shawl tighter; it was cool that day in autumn. With their chime-like tinny noise, the leaves broke free from their summer homes and fluttered atop Mama and me. She did not notice them, but only glanced at me now and again with a haunted, almost fearful look.

"Mama, don't worry, I'm coming back." The thought of visiting my Aunt Alice in London seemed exciting, but worrisome. I longed to see the world outside Holybourne, to meet the generous aunt who never forgot us at Christmas. Yet I worried about Mama and if Tilly would insist she eat a morsel or two. She so hated the gin Mama drank almost as much as she hated Mr O'Leary. And would Mr O'Leary continue to handle Papa's affairs?

Mama lifted her gaze toward the stark grey sky. "Hurry along Anne, it will soon rain." She stumbled over a little nothing, caught herself and moaned.

"Are you ill, Mama?" I put my arm around her scant waist with concern.

"No, no, child. It is just my old bones anymore. Oh, but they ache so."

"You must walk slower, Mama."

We stopped for a moment to greet Madame Pinchot as she emerged from the woods. Misha remained standing at a distance, hesitant. She barked at me, almost as if she were scolding me for leaving. I called out to her, but she wouldn't come. I ran to her, but she disappeared into the dark wood.

"Misha grieves, Nana," said Madame Pinchot. "She doesn't want you to go."

Monsieur Pinchot was burning leaves in his field and the smoke clung fast to my clothes. He waved good-bye as the London Coach squeaked and groaned to a stop. A man jumped down from the top box and opened the carriage door. Strange, unhappy faces peered out at Mama and me.

"Hurry 'bout it now, don't got all day," the coachman's voice was pebbly, moist, and harried. Holding shut his left nostril, he blew his nose. "Get on."

Mama deposited a few coins into his worn, mud-encrusted glove and handed me up into the crowded black box of dark trousers, muddy boots, and dresses with mud-crusted hems.

"There you are, off to visit your aunt." Clutching her brown wool shawl to her neck, Mama gave a nod to the coachman. Her eyes were teary as she turned away.

There was nothing to cry over, I would be gone only a fortnight. I heard Misha howling in the distance, an eerie feeling settled over me. All of a sudden, I was swallowed up by legs and hard boots. The door slammed and the coach lurched, nearly sending me sprawling.

"Sit, girl!" Ordered a fat lady wearing a dark blue frock with a white square collar.

Tasting her plump, nasty elbow, I obeyed and realised that the last of my baby teeth had given way under the jab. Deftly spitting it out, I clenched it in my hand hidden from view. I knew she would make me throw it away.

"Mind now and behave." She scowled, her jowls settling on either side of her thin pressed lips. "This is no place to spit."

"I wasn't spitting ..."

She huffed. "Impertinent little girl."

Impertinent little girl? As I held tight to my tooth, I glanced around at the icy stares from the others, but I had said nothing wrong. I sat against the hard seat and ignored them thinking only of Mama. *Maybe I could buy her something bright and pretty on my visit to London—a red silk ribbon, perhaps.*

* * *

Everyone in the coach sat so high and mighty that I couldn't see out, so I fell asleep. I was rudely awakened by the vicar who sat directly across from me.

He kicked my foot. "Wake up, little girl. We have arrived at the London Train station."

"Oh, but I am not taking the train, sir. I am to meet my Aunt Alice ... ." suddenly the coach stopped, the door flew open and I was promptly handed down. I brushed the dust and dirt from my frock and stood gawking at all the people. Could this be the place where I am to meet my Aunt Alice? Not knowing where to go, I clung to the skirt of the fat lady. She wouldn't feel my tug anyway.

Following her into the building, I let go of her skirt and stood in dumb awe. It was such a place—busy with coaches, luggage, bandboxes, men shouting, beggar children running, quiet people of sophistication moving here and there. The thunderous noise of the train reverberated through my thin soled boots.

Suddenly I heard my name called aloud. A man in a dark waistcoat waved a piece of paper in the air and called my name again, but I knew to remain silent until convinced that I was the correct Miss Anne Holt he was calling for.

When the irritable fat lady turned to leave, I prayed she wouldn't stomp on me. I prayed to hear the man call my name again, and he did. But this time the vicar and his sister who sat next to me in the coach, stepped in front of me. Squeezing between them, I heard my name a third time. I noticed a woman, wearing a dark taffeta frock embroidered with tiny red roses, standing next to him. A few strands of silvery hair curled from beneath her matching bonnet. I managed to squeak out, "I am Miss Anne Holt."

The woman in the taffeta dress took my hand and squinted down at me. "Miss Anne Holt, from Holybourne?"

"Yes."

She looked me up and down. Her gloved hand was firm and warm. Her other hand rested on her hip.

Could this be my Aunt Alice? I'd thought her grander.

"I am Mrs Mills," she said, looking deep into my eyes.

She exchanged a few words with the vicar and then led me away to her carriage—one far more comfortable than the London coach. Indeed, now I could look out the window.

Mrs Mills was quiet, so I remained quiet. Her jowls were not saggy like those of the woman in the carriage. At closer inspection, I realised she didn't have jowls; she had happy lines on her face instead. I expected she must smile a great deal. When she would look at me, I closed my eyes, fearful she might take offence that I stared at her with such great interest.

I tried hard not to kick her feet and annoy her, and worried that I had mud on my boots. Her gloved hands rested together in her lap; her dress was quite lovely, and to practice my numbers I tried counting the tiny red roses on her frock. I wanted to tell her she smelled like a rose, but thought wiser of the notion.

"Here we are then, Anne." Glancing about the carriage, she frowned. "Dear me, wherever are your gloves?"

"I don't own any, Mrs Mills." While looking up at her, I could feel my baby tooth folded securely in my handkerchief and wondered if she could remember when her baby teeth fell out. "Do you still have all of your teeth, Mrs Mills?"

Shaking her head, she stepped out of the carriage and reached back for my hand. "Come along, child." She shivered. "Oh, even through my gloves, I can feel your cold little fingers."

I breathed a long ohhh. Before me stood a home fit for the Queen. Mama would call it a chateau, that's French for castle. Aunt Alice's home appeared to be a magnificent castle indeed. I too shivered, not from the cold, but from the immensity of such a place. I was at once taken by its soot-blackened grey façade and mossy green crevices. In awe at its grandeur, I stared up at the black billowy smoke curling upward from its many chimneys. A blanket of wet glitter covered the slate roof. Fog and the heavy grey mist hung about the turrets and lead-veined windows. I could feel the invisible particles from the coal smoke settle over me. I sneezed.

"Dear me, I do hope you are not taking cold, Anne."

"No, no, Mrs Mills, the smoke tickled my nose."

"Very well, then, come along now." She moved ahead. "You must freshen up for supper." Glancing back at me, she added. "I suppose you are hungry?"

"I am very hungry, ma'am."

Whisking along through the gigantic house, I was thankful she didn't let go of my hand. I worried I would never in three lifetimes remember how to find the front door again. Up the stairs we swooshed down a great hall over five large carpets that I counted before we came to a glossy mahogany door.

"Here we are, Anne." She turned the knob. The door was so heavy it swung open by itself.

I stood there as a rush of sweet apple scent swirled about me. A wave of warm moist heat emanated from the cavernous white marble hearth where a fire, banked to perfection, blazed. In awe, I dropped my shawl to the floor, walked to the fire and envisioned Mama rocking right there. Oh, the size, the heat; she would never believe the size of this hearth. Why there was space for kettles and ... .

"This is your room, Anne." Mrs Mills stooped to pick up my shawl.

"My room?" I gawked. This room was bigger than our entire cottage in Holybourne. It was warmer and with very many windows, mirrors, crystal, and even an enormous bed. Tilly would truly marvel over it. White lace, draped over the top, cascaded like the holy waterfall Misha and I would visit on happy occasions.

There were six fluffy pillows scattered about the bedspread, shiny dark mahogany nightstands, and a step stool alongside my bed that I might climb to heaven to sleep. I didn't know what to say to Mrs Mills, but I heard my mother whisper to me, *Curtsy, Anne. You must show your pleasure at such a find.*

I curtsied, hoping my smile was bright, being careful to show my teeth, very much aware of the missing ones, however.

Mrs Mills laughed and brought me to her side, hugging me. She gestured toward the washbasin. "You may freshen yourself there." She moved toward the door and turned. "I shall return in one hour, Anne."

I nodded in awe. No stranger had ever hugged me before. I hurried to her side and hugged her in return. "Mrs Mills, are you my aunt?"

"No, no, child." She patted my head in such a kind way. "Why, I am your Aunt Alice's cousin—your distant cousin. I am a governess as well."

"Aunt's Alice's governess, ma'am?"

"Oh, my no, I am retired now." She brushed the tip of my nose with her finger. "I shall return for you at five o'clock, dear. Your aunt was called away unexpectedly, but she will return tomorrow. We shall dine alone this evening." She tweaked my nose.

"I should like that very much, Mrs Mills."

"Very well, then." Her smile lingered as she closed the door behind her.

From that moment on, I knew that Mrs Mills was a nice cousin. Her body was so soft to hug, no sharp edges like Mama's. Her eyes were soft blue, just like Misha's. Her cheeks were rosy, and there were no nasty vapours of gin seeping from her every breath.

Gazing about the room, I noticed the curtains moving. Behind them were doors left ajar. Walking out on the covered, grey-stoned balcony, I hugged myself thinking this a quiet cosy place. A cool strip of air moved about me as I caught a cluster of tinny brown and golden leaves; garnering them to my heart, I returned to my room. Surely Mama would be wondering about me before she sat down in her rocking chair. As I stood at the hearth, my thoughts were like the leaves I tossed into the fire—Mama loves me, loves me not, loves me, loves me not.

* * *

Three days had passed since coming to visit with Aunt Alice at Lesington Hall, and I had yet to meet her. She was delayed and delayed, but late one night Mrs Mills came into my room and informed me that I would take morning tea with her and Aunt Alice. I was to wait in the library.

The following morning Franklin, the butler, found me wandering the halls. I marvelled at his immaculate dress, not a wrinkle. He must sleep standing up.

"Lost, Miss Anne?"

Restless was more like it. I felt I could search this sprawling place for the rest of my lifetime and never see it all, but I kept my thoughts to myself. "I am to remain still and calm in the library, sir, until Mrs Mills should come for me."

And that was a difficult thing for me to do. It seemed all I ever did in this huge Great House was wait. Wait to have my curtains pulled back in the morning, wait until my basin was filled with hot water, wait until one maid chose what I was to wear, wait until another brushed my hair.

He bent over, his crisp demeanour softened with a conspiratorial whisper. "Miss Anne, you must call me Franklin. And do not worry, I shall be pleased to escort you to Mrs Mills."

Overwhelmed with his kindness, I seised his hand and kissed it. "Oh, thank you, Franklin. This chateau of Aunt's is really quite great. But for my part, I believe there are far too many halls."

"Very many halls, miss."

Glancing up at the row of portraits, I sighed. "Well, I suppose they had to have very many halls, Franklin, for all these paintings." I felt as though a thousand eyes followed me everywhere. Staunch and beady-eyed, stiff-faced men with nary a smile, wore curly white wigs, frilly collars and tight trousers. Somber, waxy-cheeked ladies were adorned in their brilliant shiny gowns. Even their dogs were groomed with clean, snappy, tippy-toed feet. I thought of Misha and her huge mud-caked paws.

"Miss, the 'hall' in the name of a dwelling such as this means that the house was centred on a great hall for entertainment, dining and ceremonial living on a grand scale. However, that has long since ceased at Lesington Hall."

"But why, Franklin? Why has it all ceased? Oh, I should love to see a festive occasion. All my life I've tended Mama with her gin, and endured the vile Mr O'Leary, and mourning for Her Majesty, and ..."

"Hmm." Walking past the ballroom, he paused. "If you remain still, Miss Anne, I will show you the grandest ballroom in all of London."

My heart thumped, I closed my eyes and squeezed his hand. I held my breath so as not to make one single noise. Hearing him open the doors, I felt I would faint with expectation.

"You may open your eyes, Miss Anne."

The curtains hadn't yet been pulled back and fastened. Morning's bright wash was shaded from this magnificent room, but I found it more than beautiful in its quiet closed shadows. Though I walked across the shiny floors silent as a cat, in truth, I wanted to shout the echo of my name—Anne, Anne, Anne.

A massive, ornately carved black walnut table sat in the middle of the room. A slight film of dust spread over it, dulling any opportunity of a passing fancy. High above the table hung a cut-glass chandelier. Its jingle muted and idle prisms seemed perplexed as to their purpose. Nay, not even one little sparkle escaped. Real beeswax candles sat white and straight and fallow.

Beneath the chandelier, beneath the massive table, spread a snow-white carpet. Along its borders, fan-tailed peacocks strutted on lush village greens, their brilliant green and blue-eyed feathers plumed, airy and gallant. Large white cockatoos, framed in royal purple boxes, perched high with their profiled head feathers spread like an open hand. Ivy covered their cages, and its pinkish-green tendrils curled about the edges.

I stepped onto the white part, feeling the power of whiteness soak into my boots; a whiteness pure, clean, and forbidden. Oh, now I know how the Eden apple felt hanging in the garden. A hum came into my throat as I scrolled my name atop the dust-laden table.

Peering over my shoulder, Franklin nodded with approval. "What a fine hand you have, Miss Anne."

"Oh, thank you, Franklin." I smiled. "Mama taught me to write just like Her Majesty."

He nodded amicably. "Oh, indeed, Miss Anne. I must say you have quite captured her flourish to a tee. Might I add that Her Majesty and Prince Albert once waltzed in this very room?"

My mouth gaped. "They did? Surely they couldn't have!"

"Oh, but it is so."

I shook my head. Just a few days past, I had wallowed in the middle of The Road, mud to my ankles, and now I stood where Her Majesty once twirled. "Franklin, did you know my Papa when he lived in this house?"

He took my hand. "No, Miss Anne, I have been here but a year."

I nodded as he led me from the room. "Thank you, Franklin, for showing me such a beautiful place." After a short pause, I took his hand. "Franklin," I said, hurrying alongside him.

"Yes, Miss Anne."

"I'm hungry, Franklin."

Stopping short, he put his finger to his lips. "If you promise not a word, I shall show you the secret way down into the kitchen."

Oh, a secret passage! I was beyond excitement. How I grew to love Franklin and his kind ways. He was so very handsome with hair dark as pitch, and he smelled of mint leaves and chocolate. He was tall as any statue in this Great House, and his wonderful wizardry at disappearing into the walls always delighted me.

"This way, Miss Anne." He pushed a wall panel, and it opened onto the top of a narrow staircase.

"Follow me, Miss Anne."

The staircase wound like the corkscrew Mama used to unplug her bottles. Franklin told me I must hold onto the handrails or I would fall. The passage smelled of things old and forgotten; its walls were cavernous and mysterious. More than once I felt Madame Pinchot's cool spirit whip about my neck. When we reached the bottom, Franklin pushed open another door, and we entered into a bright sparkle of bodies busy whisking about a white tiled kitchen.

My eyes gorged on the butcher's meat block, bloody and drippy. In the centre of the kitchen two girls stood kneading bread, flour sprinkled about as they chatted in happy, white powdery tones.

Franklin lifted me up and sat me on the stone sideboard. Everyone and everything promptly ceased. The dairymaid set down her milk, the cook turned from her copper stew pot, and the bread kneaders brushed the flour from their hands. The Housekeeper, Miss North's mouth gaped, and even the kitchen mouse stopped, sat up and twitched his nose. Indeed, everyone and everything stared at me.

Franklin smiled. "Allow me to introduce Miss Anne Holt everyone, and she is hungry."

Their eyes studied me up and down like the dead goose that dangled from cook's hook. I glanced from one face to the other. At least they were looking at me. So far, I had been invisible to everyone. Mary, who brushed my hair, only spoke to me when I addressed her first. And then she was abrupt and final as the vicar's wife, Mrs Braithwaite.

"Dear me, Miss Anne, you are hungry?" said Miss North. Her stern face broke into a kind, warm question. "Why, breakfast was surely brought to your room."

I had never eaten breakfast in my bedroom in my entire life. It seemed strange that maids were coming and going all hours of the night and day. One would tend my fire, pull my covers to my chin; one would lock my balcony doors; one would light my candles; another snuffed them. This morning one brought a food tray, but I didn't know it belonged to me. While the maid handed me my new clothes, I dressed in a flash because she said Mrs Mills was to see me in the library first thing. Since I didn't quite remember just where the library was, I left to find it.

"Excuse me, madam, but I didn't know the food was for me."

"So Franklin has brought you down the servants' steps, then?" Miss North glanced at him with a look as if he should not have done such a thing.

Now frightened to say another word, I nodded. My hands knotted in my lap. Everyone was still staring at me.

"Cook, how about a dish of warm plum pudding?" said Franklin. "Would you like that, Miss Anne?"

Plum pudding? I had only one helping of such a pudding before. "Oh, indeed, Franklin. Tilly saved a spoonful for me when she prepared it for Mama."

The bread kneaders giggled. I felt my spine unwind and eagerly returned their grins. At last, they seemed to be acting like real people, with real heads, mouths and happy glinty eyes.

"Well, the cook, Mrs Saveran, will soon see to that," said Franklin with a nod.

The cook smiled. One lazy eye remained on her kettle, the other on me. I unknotted my fingers and inhaled her delicious stew. "Oh, I love stew, too, Mrs Saveran. I make stew for Mama almost every day when she is sick. Once she found a spoon at the bottom of the pot."

Everyone laughed as Franklin lifted me down and seated me at the table. I noticed how his eyes sparkled as he spoke with Miss North. Though smitten with him, I could see his heart belonged to her alone.

Hearing a bell ring three times, Miss North hurried out of the kitchen. She soon returned. "Mrs Mills is in the library, Franklin. She wants to know if you have seen Miss Anne."

He nodded. "Very well, Miss North." Finding my bowl of pudding finished off, he smiled. "We must go now, Miss Anne."

I took his hand, first thanking everyone for the delicious pudding. I assured them if I could find my way back down into the kitchen, I would visit them often. But I was met with no more smiles, no more laughs and no more giggles. They had turned sullen once more.

The stiffness of the servants, Franklin explained, was reserved for the adults, and I would be unwise to break that familiarity. Servants must know their place, know what to expect. "We have all been trained not speak until first spoken to."

In one fell swoop, I was elevated to my aristocratic heritage. My kind didn't carry on conversations on an equal level with any servant, anywhere. Franklin explained that I must obey the rules; it was rather like a kindness shown them.

"But, Franklin, the vicar's old dairymaid, Tilly, is our maid and she is my best friend. She doesn't know of such rules, she can't read." I stiffened. "I will not turn away from her kisses and hugs when I return to Holybourne, I assure you." Wiping my eyes, I continued, "I so want to be kind, Franklin, but this somehow seems cruel, not at all in keeping with what I read to her from her Bible."

He chuckled. "I think you will have the wise heart to continue on as you have, Miss Anne." He nodded with a smile. "Indeed, city people are quite different from country people."

My spirits lifted. Very well, then, so the rules were different, but now living in the city, I was determined to learn city lessons as well as I had learned my country lessons.

* * *

Hurrying along the long hall toward the library, I noticed Franklin's manner had changed. He became a formal butler again. His shoulders were pulled back, his chest inched higher, his nose sniffed the air as Misha had done a thousand times. He seemed worried, and I scurried alongside him best I could. When he opened the library door, he stood back erect and motionless, stiff as Aunt's collection of knights in shiny armour. He nodded to Mrs Mills, and trying to be kind, I ignored him.

All of a sudden, I remembered my secret visit to the kitchen. My mouth must be purple with plum pudding. Franklin would be scolded. Had I wiped it? Yes, I remembered, I had. But a voice from within whispered, *Surely she will smell it on your breath.* I entered the library with hesitation.

"There you are." Mrs Mills peered over her spectacles. "I was just going to search for you."

Franklin walked past me. "I shall tend the fire, Mrs Mills. It is beginning to wane."

"Very well, Franklin." Looking at me again, she patted the seat next to her. "Come, now, Anne."

Walking with reverence over the beautiful carpet of deep red, blue, and green flowers, I sat down in the chair being careful not to utter a word, lest she smell my breath or ask to see my purple tongue. I pretended to admire the beauty of the carpet when Mrs Mills took my chin. She had found me out. I held my breath and closed my eyes.

"Before long we are to join your Aunt Alice in her study. Let me remind you that she does not tolerate loud chatter from children. Nor does she approve of children speaking before being spoken to. You must always remember that, Anne."

Though I'm tiny, I'm certainly not a child at eleven. She will see. I opened my eyes and smiled. Apparently, she found no trace of plum anywhere. Exhaling in great relief, I spoke, "Yes, Mrs Mills, just as I'm not to allow the servants to speak to me first." I felt proud that I had learned such an important kindness. I glanced over at Franklin who was busy making the fire. "That is a wonderful fire, Franklin." I, at once, added, "You may speak to me, Franklin."

Smiling, he nodded. "Thank you, Miss Anne."

Mrs Mills kept a watchful eye over me, it seemed. Indeed, I was afraid to ask her why she was still a retired governess to my Aunt since Mama had once called Aunt a spinster. I hoped Aunt Alice did not look, nor act like, an old spinster, shrivelled up with a pointy nose.

Hearing the soft tick of the clock works, I glanced up to discover the most unusual contraption. From a little door sprang a wooden bird singing, "Cuckoo-cuckoo!" In wonder, I moved just beneath its long hanging chains and sang in unison, "Cuckoo-cuckoo." When the door slammed shut in the bird's face, I jumped back, startled.

Half laughing, Mrs Mills touched my shoulder. "No need to be frightened of it, child. It is just a cuckoo clock. It was my father's, Anne, from the Black Forest." She smiled with a faraway look in her eyes, "but I seldom hear it anymore."

"Oh, it is a wonderful clock, Mrs Mills, but what does it cuckoo about?"

Franklin seemed to find humour in my estimation of Mrs Mills's clock because he chuckled as he swept up the ashes in the hearth.

"What does it cuckoo about?" She thought for a moment. "Oh, yes, dear me, Anne. Yes, of course, on the half hour the bird rushes out and cuckoos once. On the hour it cuckoos the time. Two cuckoos for two, three for three, and so forth."

Puzzled at why a tiny wooden bird would have to scurry in and out of its house, I asked, "Your Papa couldn't see or hear?"

Now standing at the open door, Franklin exchanged a knowing glance to Mrs Mills.

"Only when he grew old, Anne." Taking my hand, she squeezed it. "You remind me of your Aunt Alice, Anne, when she was your age." She chuckled. "That very clock intrigued her as well. You will brighten her day if you mention it to her."

"Oh, I tried to make Mama smile, Mrs Mills," I shrugged, "but she seldom did. Tilly always laughed, though, as I read silly stories to her. She said it made her work go faster." I sighed. "But, I could *never* make Madame Pinchot smile."

"Tilly? Madame Pinchot?"

"Tilly was our maid, Mrs Mills. Mr O'Leary brought her from the vicar's house. She had been their dairymaid, and Madame Pinchot was a Roma fortune-teller who read Mama's future, and sometimes spoke to Papa in heaven."

She frowned. "I see, and who is this Mr O'Leary?"

"He took over all of Papa's financial affairs, paid Mama's debts to the baker, glover, butcher, and to Mr Ruther, who brings Mama gin every day. Mama used to wash laundry at the inn that Mr O'Leary owns. I find Mr O'Leary odious, Mrs Mills—his breath is always hot and smelly. Mama wanted me to be happy to him, never to forget him, but Tilly made me hide when he would come to call."

Straightening, Mrs Mills nodded and shot a glance at Franklin. Her jaw set as she gestured toward the door. "Very well, then, Anne, soon the cuckoo bird will call out ten times. We must then go see your aunt."

Still enthralled at such a clock, I stopped her. "Where is the Black Forest, Mrs Mills? Is it always night time there? Is that why they call it the Black Forest, or do all the trees, flowers and grass grow black?"

When the kind Mrs Mills said I was an inquisitive young child, I corrected her saying I was no longer a child, for I was eleven.

She nodded. "You shall grow into a diminutive young lady, then. Not to be tall or robust, I would imagine."

"Diminutive?" I stumbled over the new word.

"Yes." She stood. "Remember, now, to mind your manners. You may address your aunt as Aunt or Aunt Alice, both being acceptable to her."

"Yes, ma'am."

Franklin walked ahead, tall and straight like my ancestors in the many portraits hanging on the walls. He turned to advise Mrs Mills that he had to rebuild Aunt's fire, too.

"Terrible weather anymore, Franklin," she said with a shudder.

"Is there no hearth in this hall, Franklin?" I asked.

"No, Miss Anne, there is not. Great Houses such as Lesington are glorious in the summer, but would cost a fortune to keep each room heated this time of year."

"Indeed a fortune, Franklin." Mrs Mills clutched her shawl. "I am chilled to the bone every day of life."

"Well," I added, lifting my chin, "the mornings are never this cold in Holybourne; I can assure you of that."

Mrs Mills laughed. "Oh, indeed, Anne, I take it Holybourne is summer all year round, is it?"

"Oh, no, Mrs Mills," I assured her, "our village gets cold, but never this cold, and we have a sacred stream. I drink from it often."

Smiling, she nodded. "Oh, indeed, a sacred stream, how nice."

Entering the room, I saw Aunt Alice at her embroidery, head bent, fingers busy, a shiny silver needle moving up, in, down; the pulling of pink thread, a knot. She didn't hear us enter the room, or else she concentrates very well. Just like when I was reading a book, I would never hear Mama shout for me.

Franklin went straight away to the waning fire, though the room smelled soft and warm to me. Older people chilled much faster than children or butlers, I supposed.

Letting go of Mrs Mills's icy fingers, I tiptoed to a chair and found to my delight a tea service arranged on a small shiny table with quaint little saucers with gold-rimmed cups and silver spoons. Oh, I had never seen such a ... I thought for a moment as to what exactly had intrigued me about a passage in *The Professor*. Oh, yes, the author described the scene as "a china tea-equipage." I counted a place setting of three, and a tingle enthused me to excite aloud, "Aunt, may I break the still air to wish you a very good morning?"

Aunt nodded as she gestured toward an over-stuffed chair. "Good morning, Anne. You may sit there."

"Thank you, Aunt Alice."

Taking her chair by the hearth, Mrs Mills suggested to Aunt that she deemed it appropriate that I should now address her as *Cousin Eleanor*.

"Very well, from now on, Anne, you may address Mrs Mills as Cousin Eleanor."

"I should like that very much, ma'am." I sensed that my new cousin returned my affections. Smiling up at her crinkling blue eyes, I felt a wonderful gladness fill my heart. Never had I felt such a kindness from someone so soon upon meeting, and to think she was my relative as well. "Indeed." I nodded. "I should love that more than anything, Aunt Alice."

Cousin Eleanor and Aunt exchanged wee smiles.

Before I climbed into the chair, I ran my fingers over the soft, warm cloth. Admiring the beautiful swirl of red, yellow and pink flowers, their stems arcing into giant palms, I envisioned living in a forest ... the Black Forest. "Aunt, I saw a cuckoo bird this morning."

Cousin Eleanor cleared her throat.

"Anne, you may sit now," said Aunt Alice brusquely.

That checked my enthusiasm, but only for a second. "Oh, indeed, Aunt, thank you." I climbed into the deep-seated luxury with pleasure. Leaning back into the plush softness, I sighed. "Beyond a doubt, this is the most comfortable and beautiful chair in Lesington Hall."

Aunt concentrated on her embroidery. But I chose to interpret her silence as focus, rather than reprimand. Studying her face, I was surprised and not displeased to see a small resemblance to myself. It was Aunt Alice's mouth that looked most familiar. Her lips hinted of a smile, even when not amused, and it appeared, she wasn't amused at the moment. We both shared freckly skin, pale eyes and red hair versus Mama's black eyes, olive complexion, and thick black curls.

Cousin Eleanor had cautioned me about speaking before being spoken to, and I understood her meaning exactly. Often my words would clamour from my mouth even before I knew they had escaped. Mama would never let me forget, though. She'd slap my mouth as a reminder. I glanced at Aunt's hands.

"Cousin Eleanor says one must not speak before being spoken to, Aunt Alice. If I do, will you slap my mouth?"

Cousin spurted tea down her chin.

"I'll fetch more coal, madam," Franklin announced, hurrying from the room as though a north wind nipped at his heels.

Putting aside her embroidery, Aunt stared directly into my eyes. "Holding one's tongue is an important lesson to master, Anne, but would I slap your mouth, never." She fidgeted in her seat. "Tell me, Anne, did your mother ever socialise in Holybourne?"

"Mama was reclusive, Aunt Alice, much like you." Now wasn't the time to mention Mr Ruther, washing dirty linens at the inn, and the bottles of gin or Mr O'Leary.

"Reclusive? Wherever did you learn the word reclusive? For a girl with little education, you seem to have command over words much bigger than even yourself."

I giggled. "Words bigger than myself, Aunt? Why, that is impossible."

Her mouth twitched, resisting my humour. "Tell me, Anne, where did you learn to enunciate so beautifully?"

"I don't know that I do, Aunt." I spoke the truth, because Mama complimented me on my speech only in front of Mr O'Leary.

"I am telling you so, Anne. One who speaks well must read well." She adjusted her spectacles and looked straight into my eyes again. "Did your mother teach you to read and write?"

"Yes." I couldn't help the modest glow kindling warm on my face. "Dr Benjamin Franklin says, 'If a man empties his purse into his head, no one can take it away from him. An investment in knowledge always pays the best interest.' " [1]

Cousin Eleanor laughed outright. "Excuse me, Alice." She placed belated fingers to her lips.

I was surprised to see Cousin apologise to my Aunt—she had done nothing wrong.

Not taking her eyes from mine, Aunt nodded. "I see."

"I would read every day, Aunt. I will read for you, too, Aunt, if you wish it."

"You have many books, then?"

Now I was the focus of the same tenacity that Aunt Alice had demonstrated on her embroidery. No, *I*, myself, didn't have the books.

"No." I could feel my face tighten like the thread Aunt tugged. My face turned warm—colouring perhaps like her red yarn. She would find me out—that I stole away in Papa's little room late at night. "Mama never questioned where I got the books."

I could almost sense Aunt's sharp silver needle jabbing into my tongue.

"No? So tell me then, Anne, where did you find the books to read?"

I resisted. "I found them, Aunt Alice."

"Yes, yes, but where did you find them, Anne?"

Crossing my fingers, I closed my eyes. "Mama must never know, Aunt Alice. I was forbidden to go into Papa's room alone, to touch anything of Papa's because ... because I think that's all she had left of him."

Aunt's 'Hmm' filled the silence I used to assemble my withering wit. She stuck her needle into the pincushion and put down her sewing.

"It was just his books that I disturbed, Aunt Alice," I confessed, "nothing more. When I was dusting, I broke a shelf." It wasn't quite the whole truth. I was dusting ... but the shelf broke as I pulled myself up to see the titles of the many leather-bound volumes there. "Papa's books toppled onto my head. I put them back, but when Mama got so sick one day, I took to reading them to her to get her well."

---

[1] Dr Benjamin Franklin (1706-1790) American statesman, author, and inventor, writing in *Poor Richard's Almanac*. Quoted from *Respectfully Quoted: A Dictionary of Quotations* by James Billington.

"Commendable, Anne, and what did you read to your mother?"

"*Evelina*, for one," I said, a rush of absolution calming my tumbling thoughts. "Oh, indeed, Mama would laugh as Evelina would escape one folly and then fall into another."

"Oh, yes, yes, of course," said Cousin Eleanor, who, it would seem, found the book as enjoyable as I had.

"Fanny Burney," added Aunt Alice, her face turning pink.

Encouraged, I counted with my fingers in an attempt to remember them all. When that failed, I glanced up at the ceiling as though the titles were etched more clearly there than in my mind. As though conjured by an unseen hand, they began to come back. "And then, Aunt, I remember *The Professor, The Vicar of Wakefield ...*"

"Hmm, Goldsmith, very good, Anne. Did you enjoy *The Vicar* as well as *Evelina*?"

"Oh, indeed I did, Aunt. Papa would have been so like the vicar in the book, Aunt Alice, had he only lived—priestly, a wonderful husband and kind father. It is all there, Aunt Alice. I shall read it for you if you wish."

Aunt studied me for a long moment. It dawned on me, then, that my papa was her brother. She knew him, but I didn't. Perhaps I didn't have the right to say those things about what I thought my Papa would have been like.

"Tell me, did your mother enjoy the books?"

"Well, I don't know if she did, Aunt."

"Why is that?"

Mama never saw things the same way as I saw them. "While I read to her, she would drink gin in memory of Papa, and then her head would droop."

"Hmm." Aunt exchanged a knowing glance with Cousin Eleanor, as though they understood Mama better than I did. "She drinks to him quite often, does she?"

"Oh, yes, quite often." I caught Aunt Alice's expression. Her mouth tightened, her chin lifted ever so, and I knew beyond a doubt that she wasn't pleased—that she didn't understand. "Oh, if only Prince Albert hadn't died, Aunt."

Her freckled brow shot up in surprise. "What has that to do with your mother's drinking?"

I couldn't have her thinking ill of Mama, even if it meant insulting my Aunt's integrity. "Well, that brought sadder memories back to her—the Prince died on the same day as Papa, and ... and all those who love the Queen honour her grief. Mama even had me write letters of commiseration to Her Majesty."

Again, my companions exchanged knowing glances that eluded my understanding. I couldn't help my sigh. "When she lost her love, she lost her life," I explained.

There was a long silence as the fire crackled. I could hear Cousin's soft breathing. Aunt Alice touched her fingertips together, saying, "A moment ago, Anne, you called me reclusive." She searched my gaze with a curious one of the same colour of blue, looking past it into the recesses of my soul. I had the feeling that I had somehow committed an irretrievable blunder. My thoughts tumbled like leaves in the wind, trying to salvage the damage done by my impulsive, well-meaning tongue.

Assuming my most gracious demeanour, at long last, I seised upon an answer with which I could find no flaw. "I suppose, after second thought, that I should get to know you better before I can say such a thing with all certainty, Aunt." I returned her gaze with the same curious blue eyes and checked her bewilderment with a knowing smile.

CHAPTER THREE

Soon I knew just about every room in the downstairs of this Great Hall. Franklin showed me where all the hidden doors were that led to the kitchen, pantry, cellar and beyond. Miss North, the housekeeper, showed me the intimacy of the servants' quarters. She showed me her quaint, cosy room with a single bed, tallboy, a nightstand, and a covered chair next to the little hearth grate.

Though each room was small, it was neat and clean; each had a window, a hearth and even gas lamps. Aunt detested the smell and the wavy black smoke that blackened and smudged the walls. Oh, I could not wait until I told Mama about such modern things.

And now, every morning after breakfast, Cousin Eleanor teaches me drawing, mathematics, history and French. I suppose they fancy me already well acquainted with things literary. Also, I was to learn etiquette; manners, dear me. Indeed my country manners must have been quite another thing entirely, since Cousin Eleanor insisted I concentrate upon the finer delicacies of being a proper young lady. I must admit I didn't take to mastering how to eat with sophistication. Goodness me, there were so many forks, knives, plates, glasses, and ways to unfold one's napkin. Well, I often wished aloud that I didn't have to learn such things.

Of course, there weren't many in Holybourne who had such a grand dining table where I might exhibit my new manners. Besides, I knew Tilly would only laugh at me, whereas Mama would, without doubt, show me off to Mr O'Leary, since he had such a fine table. The idea sickened me.

Cousin Eleanor would not be distracted, though I often tried. She was much too clever a retired governess to have anything to do with my contrivances.

One day, at long last, she complimented my diligence in tea service etiquette. "You now eat with your mouth closed, you chew your food properly, you dab your lips with dainty abandon ... yes, Anne, I will be proud to present you this very morning at tea with your Aunt." Cousin lifted her chin. Her eyes remained steady on my face.

"Oh, thank you, Cousin Eleanor." I was overjoyed at the prospect. I had been permitted only one such visit before. My manners must have been atrocious, for I hadn't been invited back. That one visit was an intriguing one. I had a glimpse of the real Miss Alice Holt, where she spoke less formally, even smiled, and chatted in happy tones with Cousin Eleanor.

When I swallowed my last bite of sweet cake, I closed my eyes and prayed it would slide down my throat without notice or else Cousin might postpone the happy event.

She giggled. Cousin Eleanor had actually giggled. I opened my eyes in wonder. Frowning, I gazed at her lips. Now she was laughing. Such unbecoming conduct; had I not been reprimanded only moments before for giggling when I, in a nervous flutter, poured the tea into the sugar bowl by accident?

"Come along, Anne." Cousin Eleanor, still laughing, ruffled the top of my head. "You are such a dear."

As Cousin opened the study door, I tiptoed alongside her. It was Sunday morning, and I knew how to walk with reverence on the seventh day. She had explained that lesson as well. I took my seat. Aunt and Cousin spoke about me as if I were not there. Though I felt like a fly on the sugar bowl, I remained quiet, often checking the front of my dress that my bows remained tied. I so wished to make a good impression on Aunt Alice.

As I poured tea, Aunt's occasional nod of approval made me smile. Soon her idle chitchat with Cousin afforded me the opportunity to sit back, feeling as if they rather liked me sitting with them. I marvelled at Aunt's sweetness to her cousin; they acted more like sisters. Now that I was allowed these intimate sittings, I saw Aunt as far more kind. Before she had seemed too far away, so aloof and distant that I feared she would never take to me. Perhaps she hadn't relished becoming too acquainted with me, since I would not be here with her for long ...

"Anne, you are humming." Aunt set down her teacup.

"Yes, Aunt."

"But, it is Sunday, Anne."

"I was making joyful noises unto the Lord, Aunt Alice."

Her face took on a magical transformation of sorts. One moment it was crossed with puzzlement, the next merriment, and the next a shroud of wonder. "Hmm, indeed, joyful noises, yes. Pour me another tea, Anne."

Cousin Eleanor kept her handkerchief to her lips; her eyes were watering. I knew she was laughing at me again, but I was at a loss as to why.

"Eleanor," said Aunt Alice glancing at Cousin, "be a dear and tell Franklin that the vicar, Mr Clarke, and his sister will be dining with us this evening, and I will not be receiving callers tomorrow."

Dabbing her eyes, Cousin Eleanor cleared her throat. "Very well, Alice."

Aunt, like Mama, had few callers. I thought of Her Majesty, alone, without her Prince. Mama said how she must hate to see happy couples coming to visit. I leaned back in my chair, much more at home now. "Her Majesty shuns callers, too, Aunt Alice." I nodded, growing more certain by the moment that I'd discerned Aunt's true nature from the beginning. "She rather prefers being alone."

Aunt glanced at Cousin and then to me. "Indeed, young lady, tell me again how you know Her Majesty's wishes that she prefers being alone?" She had that unravelling look again.

"Oh, Mama knew just how Her Majesty would suffer for losing her beloved Prince. Mama knew about the quiet solitude of pain, the vacant pillow ..."

"The vacant pillow?" Cousin Eleanor's lips quivered. Up came her handkerchief.

Aunt frowned. "Eleanor, please." She turned to me. "Anne, this morning, I will read aloud a few passages from the Bible." The room quieted. Aunt's breathing grew deep and thoughtful. She didn't turn a page; her eyes never moved.

"I know how that happens, Aunt."

I had learned there is a silent, reflective pause just before Aunt asks a certain question for which she must have an answer.

"How what happens, Anne?"

"Reading, but not really, in fact, reading." I sighed. "I know, Aunt. I find myself thinking about other things when I should be reading."

Franklin entered and bowed stiff as a board. "The church carriage, madam."

"Go on ahead, Anne. We shall be out directly."

Aunt Alice and Cousin Eleanor stood and watched as Franklin held the door for me.

I stopped at his side, and in my most eloquent voice said, "One more thing Franklin, Aunt will not be receiving callers tomorrow."

He nodded to Aunt Alice. "Very good, madam."

I turned and waved to them.

Aunt shook her head, Franklin closed the door, and we proceeded toward the carriage. I didn't receive a thank-you from Aunt, and this time Cousin Eleanor's face was blank.

"Dear me, Franklin, did I say something wrong again?"

We were standing at the carriage when he whispered, "Just continue to be you, Miss Anne."

But how could anyone be anything but himself or herself? I sighed in confusion with all these impossible ways of thinking.

As Aunt Alice took her usual place next to Cousin in the carriage, I breathed in her familiar scent of lavender. Her collars were always bordered with dainty lace, but on this chilly morning, she chose her hooded cape trimmed with fur. I loved to touch the soft fur, though I felt sad for the sacrifice of an animal. As our carriage ambled toward the church, Cousin Eleanor's Bible remained nestled in her lap, as Tilly's rested in her arms when she slept.

I marvelled at the idea of attending church for the first time. What would Mama think? Just wait until I tell Mrs Braithwaite. Oh, what a surprise that will be. I thought of Tilly, too, how her face will light up when I share all of my travels with her.

Our carriage stopped in front of St. Anne's Church. St. Anne's Church! Oh, how touched I was to know that there was a saint with my name. I didn't utter a word to Aunt over the stunning similarity, however. Sundays were not days one could muse without due consideration.

Stepping down from the carriage, I took in the London air. It was moist and heavy, and as the morning clouds hung grey and low about us, a woeful feeling rippled through my veins. Mama had mentioned once that she was not allowed to enter another church, if it wasn't of her faith. Though she never told me what faith she was. But soon I would know God for myself. I had Tilly's word regarding God's house.

I followed Aunt Alice and Cousin up the wet stone steps and felt people gather in behind us. They were whispering, I could feel their eyes searching me, hear their noses sniffing my air. I thought of Misha and how she snapped at the gawking hordes as they followed behind Madame Pinchot much the same way they were now herding me.

Entering the hushed silence of the church, I was first taken by the beauty of the windows: portraits of sad-faced people etched somehow in glass rather than on canvas; subdued colours of the rainbow veined with lead. There were green valleys, a shepherd's staff, birds, and what appeared to be kings and queens in prayerful assembly.

The ceilings were higher than Aunt's highest chimney. I was certain that I could shout my name and it would return a thousand times. Ornate chandeliers held tall, thick white candles, their flame waving yellow-white; it smelled like a chandler's shop.

Feeling a breeze wrap around me, I shivered and snuggled in my cloak. Hard shoes clunked about until everyone settled in his or her pew. A hush settled over the silver- bell singsong of the choirboys as the figure of a tall skinny man climbed the hidden stairs and flapped about the pulpit with great importance.

High and mighty he stood above us all, his shiny black sleeves billowed; his eyes cast down upon us sinners. That figure of a man, I recalled, was the very one who, with his sister, Miss Charlotte, rode the coach with me to London from Holybourne. Indeed, I frowned, the vicar, Mr Clarke Phillipps.

* * *

After church, as Cousin Eleanor, Aunt Alice and I were leaving Aunt's pew, the vicar bustled past us to the church door. With a *how-art-thou* smile, he patted my head.

"Good morning, Miss Anne. I hope you enjoyed this morning's service." He bowed just a little, his face pink and waxy. Exuding his pompousness toward Aunt Alice, he blushed, the pink turning to a deep rose.

"Sir," I replied, "I am sure it was a fine sermon, but in truth, I would not know a good one from a bad one, for I have never heard one before in my entire life."

Miss Charlotte Phillipps gaped at me. She stepped back into God's holy house and fanned her pointy nose with her handkerchief; her spiral curls wound about her face like clock screws.

Those standing about our circle moved a little distance away and glared. There were gasps and murmurs, directed at whom I was not at all sure, though I presumed it to be me.

Cousin whispered to Aunt Alice as the red-faced vicar bent over me again saying with a sour breath, his wiry nostril hairs pointing to heaven, "That cannot be, Miss Anne."

The vicar should have read my Aunt's expression and buttoned his lips.

"But," he repeated in a much louder tone, "it cannot be that you have never heard a sermon before in your entire life."

"Oh, but it can be, sir," I returned, every bit as loudly as he. "My mother has not allowed it." I glanced at Aunt, whose face drained. It was beyond me what all the fuss was about. I turned my attention to Cousin Eleanor, but she, too, turned away. I realised something was wrong. Did I not fit into their world of churches? Did my dislike for the vicar bubble from my brain and become all that obvious? Did I laugh when I was supposed to sigh? I was not at all sure what I had done, but I knew I would soon find out.

Aunt took my hand and squeezed it. I grimaced as I scurried alongside her to the carriage, my shoes skimming the pavement. Taking my seat, I waved goodbye to the vicar. He stood in his long black robe, shook his head and disappeared into the church with his yellow-haired sister in tow.

As our carriage lunged forward in rude fashion, my head hit the back of the cushion. "Goodness, me," I said aloud as I adjusted my bonnet, "the horses must be hungry."

Aunt Alice pinched her eyes with a gloved hand and sighed. It seemed she had a terrible headache. Then she lifted her chin quite high, swallowing hard. Here it comes—I was to soon learn my misdeed.

Speaking in her most stern voice, Aunt said, "Do not tell me, Anne, that your mother never took you to church?"

"I must tell you that, Aunt or I shall be a liar." Oh, if only Mama were here to explain the sordid details of what the church really stood for, the nasty people who congregated there, the snipes and stingy so and so's, but for all of that, I surely wasn't to be found at fault.

Cousin shook her head. "Lord, I do not believe my ears."

"Nor mine, Eleanor."

"The vicar will be coming to supper this very evening, Anne." Aunt dabbed her brow with the back of her gloved hand.

Cousin Eleanor pursed her lips. "And with his sister, Miss Phillipps, I presume?"

Still all aflutter, Aunt fanned her face. "You know very well, Eleanor, that his sister never leaves his side."

"Never leaves his side, indeed. Did you see how she grew faint when she heard Anne saying she had never gone to church? Oh, Lord, that skinny chicken will cluck the news high and low."

I wanted to interrupt, but knew to hold my tongue.

Aunt folded her fan. "So be it, Eleanor. It is too late to do anything about it now."

Cousin glanced down, fussed with my bonnet and sighed. "Miss Phillipps will peck your eyes out for never going to church."

"Peck out my eyes?" I blinked, I gulped. "Peck my eyes?"

Aunt Alice shook her head. "I had no idea you were ... ungodly, Anne."

Unfolding her fan, she waved it at her red, pinched face. I could feel the whoosh of cool air blow against my cheek and ruffle the blue satin ribbons tied beneath my chin.

"Eleanor, whatever am I going to say to them both? I shall be mortified."

"Indeed, Alice." Cousin rubbed a smudge mark on her gloves. "I never thought to ask the child about her religion. I just assumed, God in Heaven, I just assumed she had one. Now what are we to do about it?"

So that was what had them both so provoked; it wasn't that I had never stepped foot in a church, it was that they thought me a Pharisee. Looking at them, one to the other, I said, "I am not ungodly."

"Indeed and how can you now boast of such claims after you blasphemed yourself just moments ago in God's house, Anne?" cried Aunt.

"Aunt, you must calm yourself. To blaspheme oneself is to show irreverence to God. I did nothing of the sort. I said only that I had never heard a sermon before, and that is true, but I have read the Bible in its entirety. I'm not a lying heathen, Aunt."

Her mouth gaped. "Oh, I did not mean to infer ... ."

I took Aunt's hand. Her face was red. I realised then that I was different, but was being different bad? I had liked her church and the singing, making joyful noises unto the Lord, but I didn't think she understood Mama's wishes. "I understand, Aunt. I will remain in my room this evening and away from your company."

"No, no." Aunt folded her fan and tapped it on my wrist. "You shall do nothing of the sort, Anne. You are my niece and shall sit at the table, come what may."

Come what may? My eyes will be offered up as a sacrifice to the vicar's sister? How dreadful. I must awaken Aunt's blind eye to the possibility of losing my own. "What about the skinny chicken lady, Aunt? What about my eyes?"

* * *

Aunt and Cousin Eleanor sat with me in the formal dining room that Sunday afternoon as we took lunch. They explained where I was to sit, where I was to look. I was instructed to reply with a simple yes or no to any questions our company would ask. My head was full of all the do's and don'ts of polite conversation. I had thought I was polite enough. The poor dears, they must have been consumed with worry that I should embarrass them again. Oh, but I would not.

"Do not add anything, Anne, to the conversation. Remember, do not speak unless spoken to, and then answer with few words."

"Yes, Aunt." I smiled, confident that they could breathe easily, and that Aunt's headaches would never return on my account. Oh, indeed, I would be the perfect pupil. I wanted them to forgive me, to love me despite my odd ways.

"No more." Aunt added once more.

I nodded with enthusiasm.

"Very well, then." Cousin Eleanor took my chin and smiled, "Anne, you are a sweet child. You shall do very well." As if an idea swept over her, she added, "You know Anne, there are two angels who sit on each shoulder. One is the angel of evil who whispers bad things into your ear, and the other is the angel of good. You must always listen to the angel of good and act accordingly."

So that is who I so often heard whispering in my ear. Hmm, very well then, I must listen to only the good angel. I pressed my hands in supplication. "Thank you, Cousin Eleanor."

I so wanted to please them. After all, I might be allowed to sit with them every morning, becoming part of their conversations. I hoped to be allowed into their world, breathing the same air, devouring with glee the same little sweet cakes. Oh, I simply must heed their most excellent advice.

Franklin offered, "More tea, madam?"

Dabbing her lips, Aunt waved him off. "Indeed, Anne," she sighed, "I do hope you behave like the little lady you are meant to be."

* * *

Later that afternoon when Mr Phillipps and his sister were shown into the drawing room, I remained quiet and sat quite properly in my designated chair by the hearth, watching as tea was served, though not called upon once to pour. With my head quite full of Aunt's recommendations and my mouth firmly disengaged, I was now free to watch everyone titter and tatter, behaving their Sunday best.

But, something felt unsettling—a trouble deep within my heart. It wasn't where the bad angel perched, and for that I was thankful. It was regarding the vicar. For at closer inspection, I happened to notice a peculiar thing about him that I hadn't noticed earlier. Yes, the affection he had for my aunt became quite apparent to me. Every time he looked at her he blushed a deeper pink.

Though I didn't know at the time if Aunt returned the sentiment—I prayed she did not. I instinctively repelled his manner regarding me. I remembered him and his pious sister on the coach from Holybourne. Maybe he had smelled Mama's gin on my clothes, maybe the smoke from Holybourne's ashes lingered in his nostrils and he ventured me putrid to his Godly ideals, and more than once had Miss Phillipps' cruel glance swept over me. I sat up, breathed a sigh and wished away the nasty vision with a quick flick of the wrist.

Mr Phillipps noticed.

"So your niece is from Holybourne, is she?" he asked.

Aunt nodded with her usual aplomb. But she knew nothing of my little town with its sacred stream, more sacred than Mr Phillipps' entire church, more sacred than ... .

"Yes," returned the vicar setting down his cup and saucer, "I went to Oxford with a certain Jonathon Braithwaite now preaching in Holybourne." He smiled down at me. His nostrils twittered. "A fine fellow, I must say."

"Indeed, Mr Phillipps." Aunt smiled at the ceiling.

"Yes, mmm." He cleared his throat and glanced down at me.

I joined Aunt Alice in smiling at the ceiling.

"So, Anne," said Miss Phillipps, tapping my wrist with her fan, "you are *not* well acquainted with the Braithwaites, I take it?"

Hmm, not well acquainted? Why, the thoughtful Mrs Braithwaite gave me all her daughter's old things, but I rarely saw the vicar since Mama told him long ago to stop calling at our door. As I clasped my hands and sat up, I noticed the nervous motion of Cousin Eleanor's fingers, but I had to clarify Miss Phillipps' obvious misconception of my affiliation with the Braithwaites. "Indeed, Miss Phillipps, I spoke daily with the kind Mrs Braithwaite." Of course I did not need to mention it was on my way to the bakers for our daily bread.

"Is that so?" Glancing at her brother, she spread her fan quite supremely. A flutter of air whooshed up her nose.

"Well then," said the vicar nodding with a thin smile. "There is hope after all."

Just then Aunt Alice gave the rope pull two firm tugs. Within minutes Franklin ushered us into the dining room for dinner. Up until that time, Mr Phillipps' eyes remained cold, but after I took my place at the table, next to Aunt, his smile melted into cordiality. I knew that smile, for I had often witnessed that sort of patronising from that dreadful man, Mr O'Leary.

"Miss Anne?" His address pried my gaze from my plate up onto his face. "I will say grace this evening. Perhaps you could recite it aloud next Sunday in church." Smiling, he added, "I shall call upon you."

I returned my gaze to the china in front of me. True to my word, I didn't say one thing. I heard my Aunt exhale. She was, no doubt, proud of my obedient silence. She pressed my hand.

"You may answer the vicar, Anne."

Looking up, I nodded, distracted by his crooked yellow teeth. "Very well, sir. I shall be more than pleased to."

"Oh?" replied Miss Phillipps with a tilt to her head. "So, Anne has a good memory, does she?"

"A very, very good one, Miss Phillipps." I sat up straight. "I shall not forget even one little word."

Aunt patted my hand. "Very well, Anne. That should do it. I am sure Miss Phillipps is convinced."

The vicar's chest swelled at my braggadocios manner. I could see, flailing behind his beady black eyes a faulty ability to bring forth an exceptionally long prayer. When it failed him, as I sensed it would, he sputtered. "At any rate, I shall say this evening's offering of prayer." He tapped the table with his finger pointing at me. "Pay heed, Miss Anne."

Everyone's eyelids closed but the vicar's and mine. He began thus, "Lord God Almighty, creator of heaven and earth, and all those beneath your guidance. Oh, yes," he coughed, and while clearing his throat, hastily withdrew a little black book and read from it. " 'The world cannot show us a more exalted character, than that of a truly religious philosopher, who delights to turn all things to the glory of God; who, in the objects of his sight, derives improvement to his mind; and in the glass of things temporal, sees the image of things spiritual.' " [2] With great alacrity, he quickly stuffed the book back into his pocket. "A ... men."

Aunt lifted her head, cleared her eyes for a moment and gushed. "Oh, very good, Mr Phillipps. You have such a wonderful command of the language; such eloquence, sir, wonderful, indeed. However do you compose such perfect speech?"

"It is my business, Miss Holt." Beaming, he sniffed the air with renewed confidence. This time his nose hairs were pointing to Hell.

Miss Phillipps tee-heed again. I noted for the first time that her teeth, long and narrow, matched her brother's to a tee.

Cousin Eleanor nudged me with her foot and winked. I nodded. It wasn't such a long prayer that the vicar had spoken, without doubt I could recite it with ease.

---

[2] William Jones of Nayland (1726 – 1800) British clergyman and author. Quoted from *Many Thoughts of Many Minds* by Henry Southgate (1862). (*The Dictionary of Thoughts* attributes this quote to Venning.)

Cook brought in a tureen bubbling full of steaming turtle soup and set it on the sideboard. I glanced at Miss Phillipps, her bouncy spiral curls were long enough to droop into the broth. The prospect made me laugh aloud. I cupped my mouth—too late!

* * *

After bidding good evening to the vicar and his sister, Cousin Eleanor inquired of Aunt if she would like to take the air, a few turns about the garden perhaps. Walking in the cool evening air would do us all good, she coaxed. Aunt begged off, for it was too dark.

"Come along then, Anne. You will walk with me?"

"Oh, yes, Cousin." Thankful for the invitation, I took her hand.

Franklin had lit the torch; its snapping flames licked the chilly air as we stepped from the porch. We crunched about the pathway around the brown leafless shrubbery. The air felt cooler than I had expected and I quickly fastened the hook of my cloak tighter around my neck.

"Well, well, my dear, tell me, do you believe you can recite the vicar's prayer?"

"Oh, I think so, Cousin, though it would have been easier if I could have written down the words as he spoke them. But all the same, I think I shall do quite well."

"Hmm," she muttered, her white breath trailing about her mouth. "Your Aunt and I have noticed what an excellent memory you have."

"Thank you, Cousin." I blew my breath and watched its mystery disappear into the twilight of dusk.

"Anne, there is an Englishman's opinion whom I revere. I think you would enjoy reading his works—*before* your next Sunday's recital."

I squeezed her hand. "Oh, indeed, Cousin."

"And do look up the word plagiarism as well, Anne."

"Indeed, Cousin Eleanor, such a word." I smiled. "You know how I enjoy words."

Now feeling the cold inch about my hands, I dug my hands deeper into my pockets. I felt elated to be singled out for such a talk, for such attentions. "Yes, Cousin."

"Jones of Nayland is the author, dear. I shall place his book on your pillow tonight."

* * *

The following morning, in the library, I sat with Cousin Eleanor. Aunt had not joined us yet. I read Jones' essays. Cousin Eleanor pointed one out much to my astonishment. It was the very verse the vicar had used as Sunday's grace. The very one he pretended to think-up on his own. No doubt to impress Aunt Alice.

Such a thought made us laugh and giggle a great deal, but we knew well enough not to share what we knew with Aunt Alice. She would have nothing to do with our mischief plotting, bedlam, anarchy exposing Mr Phillipps as a copycat.

Next Sunday, while in church, the vicar promptly called upon me to recite his grace prayer. I stood and spoke to the congregation: "Not wishing to be thought a plagiarist, I must give credit to the author."

Smug and blushing, the vicar stood. He first glanced at Aunt, and then bowed to the congregation.

"Therefore, I quote the theologian William Jones of Nayland, 'The world cannot show us a more exalted character, than that of a truly religious philosopher, who delights to turn all things to the glory of God; who, in the objects of his sight, derives improvement to his mind; and in the glass of things temporal, sees the image of things spiritual.' " [3]

At its finish, I sat down. Cousin, along with Aunt, stared straight ahead. Miss Charlotte Phillipps, who had noticed the arrival of a handsome gentleman, smiled at him. I'm certain she did not hear a word I recited, but the vicar had.

Leaving the church in haste, and without bidding the vicar a good morning, Aunt decided to walk home. Did I wish to come along? We waved away Cousin Eleanor as her carriage lurched from the curb. Taking my hand, Aunt guided me across the street to the shadier side.

"Dear me, I must have left my parasol in the cab," she fussed. "The sun, you know, is not good for the skin, Anne."

I puzzled at her words. There was no sun this morning; it was grey and misty and cold enough to snow.

Taking my hand, Aunt Alice pulled me along at a brisk pace. She ignored the nods and smiles of passers-by. I remained quiet, thinking she must be annoyed with the

---

[3] Jones of Nayland (1726 – 1800)

plagiarising vicar. I dared not broach such a subject, Aunt was much too kind to think ill of anyone, much less say aloud what angered her that Sunday noon.

I noticed she was still holding my hand as we proceeded to the flower shop. Stopping and glancing at the flowers, she tried to catch her breath. Through the netting drooping from her hat, I noticed her complexion glowed like port wine; her lips still pressed together. The fur around her hooded cap sagged wet with mist. As I brushed the fur to revive its once soft fluff, I heard the wailing cry of a dog. I thought of Misha and remembered how her hair would lie when soaked with rain.

"Is it matted, Anne?"

"Just a wee bit, Aunt Alice." I blew on it, flicked it with my gloved fingers, but my coaxing did little to revive its once softness. "It would have matted on the dog too, Aunt, if she would be walking in weather such as this."

"A dog?" Aunt turned to face me. "But this is not dog fur, Anne, I assure you."

"What does it matter now, Aunt Alice? It is dead all the same."

She caught her breath, somehow stunned at my words. I must have said too much again. We resumed walking up the hill. Lesington Hall was not such a great distance, a half-mile at most. The echo of our boots on the pavement, the scratching of the leafless tree branches against the bleak grey sky reminded me of Holybourne.

Approaching Lesington's black wrought iron gates, I noticed Mose, the gardener, open the gate. He had wrapped himself in a long black, dark coat with a tartan scarf tied thick about his neck. He was kind and a good servant, often reminding me of Monsieur Pinchot. My mind returned to Holybourne once again and Mama. On such a day as this, she would be in her rocker in front of a warm fire. I had been here much longer than a fortnight; surely I would be sent home soon.

"Anne, I want to thank you."

Aunt's voice was soft and reflective. I glanced at her profile; her eyes were cast down. Her body moved in unison with mine, her step now slow and deliberate. "Indeed, Aunt Alice, and what have I done that deserves such praise?"

"For being a good little philosopher, my dear niece. You know you are quite bright for such a young girl."

"Am I like my Papa, Aunt Alice?"

Nodding, she dabbed her handkerchief to her nose. "In many ways, Anne."

My heart swelled. I wanted to know all about my Papa, this strange and dear man that I, in many ways, was like. I could feel Mama's grip on my heart. My breath caught. I know *how* he died. Dare I ask more?

"Afternoon, Miss Holt."

Mose's voice cracked the crystal air, startling me. Aunt placed a calming hand upon my shoulder as the gate clanged shut behind us. "Afternoon, Mose."

As we traversed the long twisting entryway, Aunt giggled. She sounded like Cousin Eleanor, I marvelled in awed wonder. "Aunt, what do you find so amusing?"

"The look on his face this morning."

"The gardener's face, Aunt?"

"My no, Anne, Mr Phillipps' face."

"Oh, indeed. Hmm, yes, it was puckered and cross."

"Indeed," she sighed. "Oh, the hypocrisy of our lives, Anne." She laughed again and ruffled my hair. "You are yet too young to realise the enormity of your innocent manoeuvres thus far, Anne. And how full your loving heart." Still giggling, she added, "How outrageous."

Outrageous? I knew what that word meant and cringed. "Dear me, Aunt Alice, I will try harder."

"No, no, you must be yourself, Anne." She hugged me with a giggle.

I felt her wonderful warmth, smelled her lavender scent; I marvelled over the familiar words, they were the same that Franklin had once said to me.

Entering the kitchen through the servants' quarters, we startled the help. They stopped their work and stood at attention like statues. Miss North hurried from her office. "Yes, madam, is anything wrong?"

"No, no, Miss North." She took my hand, smiling. "Anne and I just walked home from church. We shall have lunch now."

I glanced about the kitchen at the half-smiling anxious faces and beamed. "And I will never be called upon to recite one of the Vicar's grace prayers ever again."

CHAPTER FOUR

The second half of the second month of understanding Aunt Alice was spent on hallowed ground, the library. We read together every morning for two hours. Aunt Alice would read first. I was to interrupt when I did not understand a word, or a notion, or anything at all. Aunt read very well, better than Mama. I so loved these readings since she demanded that the room remain quiet, the fire always warm, the sofa always soft, the cushions banked against my back in perfect comfort.

The library smelled of wonderful old books, very much like Papa's. From floor to ceiling they sat on oak shelves, their stiff spines leaving nary a space for a thumb. Their arrangement situated neat and level, except where Aunt's books took rest. Her shelves were dishevelled; some books lay sideways, upside down even, I noticed. Ribbons hung over the brim of many—one even had three red satins dangling.

Aunt's books were read-worn, paper-edgy and yellow-thin. She read with great purpose. Her brows knit, her words triumphant and clear. Oh, if ever I should write a book, I hope she would be the reader—such a reader who would say aloud the words with vigour and proper interpretation. I was sure of it, and told her so.

One morning, just when my turn to read came, Cousin Eleanor entered. Glancing up, Aunt nodded. "Good morning, Eleanor."

Holding tight to her shawl, Cousin half-smiled. "Indeed, it is, Alice, a bit too cold for December, perhaps a little too snowy as well." She took her easy chair by the hearth.

"Yes, I do miss our morning walks," Aunt rubbed her arms briskly, "but the weather is too frightful to even consider a walk."

"St Paul's is having a Christmas recital, Wednesday next, the 14th." She nodded with certainty. "Yes, that is the date. What say we three go?"

Squirming with excitement, I looked up from my book, but knew well to hold my tongue.

"Hmm." Aunt glanced my way

I smiled from my toes up.

"Anne has never been there."

I dropped my gaze for fear of appearing too anxious.

"Very well then," she said. "It sounds like a festive occasion."

"Oh, festive, indeed, Aunt." For once, perhaps my birthday would be a festive occasion. I feared I would bubble over with joy any moment, like a teapot at full boil.

"Indeed, it is rumoured the Queen may attend," said Cousin.

The Queen! What would Mama think? That, perhaps, would put a smile on her face.

Aunt shook her head. "No, she remains in seclusion."

My whistling fancy quieted. Of course, I'd forgotten myself. The Queen would be too sad to venture out on such an occasion. The chance of Mama's smile faded. "Indeed, Aunt."

Cousin sighed. "She wears nothing but black."

Aunt nodded. "Bless her."

Guilt washed over me. Indeed, what right did I have to feel joy? "Oh, but I am a selfish, thoughtless subject."

"And why is that?" Aunt looked at me with a compassion that was nothing like her unravelling look.

"That His Royal Highness died, and that no one has taken a sip of wine in prayer to Papa and the Prince since I came here." I had wondered why she and Cousin Eleanor never lifted a glass of kindness in Her Majesty's honour.

"Rather than toast your Papa and Prince Albert with wine, Anne," she said with deliberation, "I think we should offer up a more meaningful condolence."

"But what could be more meaningful than the blood of Christ, Aunt?"

"The blood of Christ?" Cousin's intake of air was enough to reverse the draw of the hearth fire.

"Yes," I replied, no less aghast at the ignorance of these devout ladies. "Mama said ..."

Aunt Alice's face twisted pale. "Anne?"

"I know of the sacraments, Aunt, bread and wine. Mama told me."

"Prayer, Anne. I am certain your Papa from this day forward would prefer that his daughter prayed for him rather than drink to him."

"Indeed so," Cousin Eleanor huffed, "indeed so."

Now, why hadn't Mama thought of that? Prayer would not leave her so pale and wan, her head drooping as though her neck had turned to willow. "I must write to Mama, then, Aunt. She will know. She will feel it in her heart if we do not drink to Papa."

"Oh, indeed, write to her this afternoon. You may even use my stationary if you wish, our initials are the very same."

I gasped. "With Lesington Hall embossed on the envelope?" I wondered if my hand would shake like Mama's to write on such fine paper.

"Yes, and you may even say I suggested it. Calling it ..." She thought for just the right word, "a thoughtful, blessed change," she concluded with satisfaction. "And, I will send your letter by special courier."

A special courier to Holybourne? Did ever a girl such as myself know such privilege? Wrapping my arms around Aunt's neck, I kissed her cheek. "Oh, Aunt, thank you. What is more," I confessed with great relief, "I didn't like the wretched way wine made Mama feel."

Cousin wiped her eyes. "I am sure she will find that a good thing, child, a very good thing."

"Indeed." Aunt Alice dropped her voice to a discreet low. "And let this be our own secret ... just between us three."

"Us four, Aunt," I reminded her, counting Mama in on our secret.

"Oh, yes, just the four of us." My happy exuberance was too much to hold in. "Aunt, I'm most certain Mama will be relieved to substitute prayer in place of that drink which makes her feel so wretched."

Aunt Alice drew me to her in a tight embrace. "Indeed, Anne." She kissed my forehead.

Although slender, Aunt had no sharp edges like Mama. Pressed to her softness, I inhaled the lavender scent of her soap and thought to myself that this must be the feel and scent of love.

* * *

After a while, I began to feel acceptable to Aunt Alice. Having memorised all the rules at Lesington Hall, I tried hard to obey them, but I worried more and more about Mama, and I wondered if she still coughed a great deal. Would Tilly have caught Mama's nasty cold? Misha would not remember me, of that I was sure. Madame Pinchot had no doubt cast me out in one of her spells. Indeed, I would have to break a rule and insist I go home.

I was beginning to feel too attached to this wondrous, beautiful world at Lesington Hall. Of its teas, walks, book readings, sachets of summer flowers hanging about, my new frocks, warm bed covers, Franklin, and warm porridge covered with cream. I sighed as I entered the library and joined my Cousin Eleanor. This morning I would break the rule about not asking when I was going home.

Sitting next to her, while we waited for Aunt, I reached for the dictionary. It was always to be found open on the table. Words seemed to intrigue Aunt as they did me; though I found them a pathway of conversation and acceptance to Aunt Alice, they did little for me now as I sat fidgeting in my chair.

I thought about how I would broach such a subject without sounding ungrateful. Thumbing through the dictionary, I decided the right time would present itself at any unsuspecting moment. Glancing down onto an open page the word "grandmother" caught my eye. Sitting up straight, holding my finger on the word, I hemmed, "Cousin Eleanor, do you have a grandmother?"

Twisting toward me, she frowned. "What a question to ask, Anne. Why, heavens no. My grandmother died many years ago. I do not remember her at all."

"I do not remember my grandmother, either, but I remember my mother. Plain as day, thanks to the burning leaves."

She turned to me. "Yes, we have noticed that you collect them in your little basket, but you toss them in the fire. Why is that, Anne?"

"The smell of burning leaves reminds me of Mama, Cousin." Withdrawing my neatly rolled handkerchief from my pocket, I held it out for her inspection. "Riding in the coach from Holybourne, I found some leaves in my pocket. It was a blustery day when Mama put me on the coach. The leaves must have found their way into my pockets. The fat lady on the coach told me to throw them away, but I didn't. I rolled them in this handkerchief," I explained in a whisper.

At last, I had found courage. Retying my handkerchief, I looked up. "Cousin Eleanor, I must go home."

Her grey eyes were teary and squinty, her brow furrowed. She dabbed each corner of her mouth. "Anne," she pressed my shoulder, "you must speak with your Aunt regarding such matters."

"I am sorry if I have made you sad, Cousin. But ... ."

"Anne, you must not question your Aunt's authority. You are much too young to know of the consequences. You must not seem ungrateful."

"Oh, I do not wish to be ungrateful, Cousin Eleanor. It is just that Mama must need me by now."

Her look softened. She took my hand. "Look, child, at that portrait hanging there." She pointed.

Placing the dictionary on the table, I glanced up at the painting of an elegant lady sitting with a big black dog at her side. "Yes, she is pretty." I had admired that portrait often.

"That lady, Anne, is your grandmother. Your Aunt Alice's mother, she was my second cousin. She too had a most unfortunate beginning, but she had faith and trusted in God, as you must. You must not upset your Aunt. She knows best."

I lowered my head and thought perhaps some other time. "Very well, Cousin Eleanor."

At that moment Aunt Alice entered the room and smiled up at the picture. "That woman is your grandmother."

"She is as beautiful as Queen Victoria," I said.

"Oh, indeed." Aunt brought her handkerchief to her lips.

I admired the dog standing on its hind legs and resting its front paws on Grandmama's lap in the portrait. Pointing to it, I asked, "Aunt, do you know the name of the dog?"

"Holly," she said in a low tone. Her gentle nudge moved me along. "Come now, Anne, I have another portrait I wish to show you."

"The dog's name was Holly, Aunt?"

"Yes, Anne."

"Hollyborn, Holly, Holybourne."

"What a coincidence, dear." She placed her hand on my shoulder. "Come along now."

"Indeed, Aunt." I missed Holybourne. I missed drinking from the sacred stream. I could feel Misha's heart beating inside mine; I could hear her soulful cry.

Moving through the Great Hallway, Aunt Alice came to the portrait of a man sitting on a great white horse. There were so many hunting dogs mingling about that they hid the horse's feet.

"That handsome man is your father, Anne."

Stunned at such a declaration, I stared up at his face, but I didn't see myself in his expression. His hair was dark like Mama's. His brown eyes gazed out, a faint smile on his lips. Perhaps his slipping from the carriage and dying so young broke Aunt's heart, too. Maybe that is why she could not speak about him. Feeling his mystery move warmly through my body, I wanted to ask her about him, about everything, but I knew I must not.

"Is there a portrait of Mama?"

"No, Anne, there is not one portrait of your mother hanging in Lesington Hall. No need to watch for it, search for it, or ask about it."

"Very well, Aunt Alice." I lowered my head. Something dreadful happened here regarding my mother and father—of that I was sure. It was in Aunt's voice, the way in which she stood, solid and quiet. Now was not the time to press. Perhaps before I returned home, she would tell me. I did not want Aunt Alice out of humour with me so early in the day. So, in a happy voice, I pointed back to Papa's portrait, counted aloud twenty-five dogs, and giggled. "Oh, Aunt, do you know all their names?"

"Dear me, Anne, that was so long ago." She removed her spectacles and leaned closer to the oil. "Hmm, let me see. Well, I can name but a few." She pointed. "This one is Suzie, this one is Blue Sky, and there, by your father's boot, his favourite, Rusher."

"Rusher?" Oh, indeed. Such a powerful dog would rush about chasing hares and foxes. "Misha is as big and powerful, Aunt Alice. At night, just as I close my eyes when the walls creak and the floors settle, when the wood in the hearth pit drops into glows, I hear her cry." I lifted my head and just when I was forming my lips to howl for Aunt Alice, she took my hand. "Yes, Anne. I can imagine. Come along now."

Glancing back now and again, I felt Papa's gaze on me as we continued down the hall; his eyes never left me. Rusher was standing proud, his long pointy tail straight and taut. We continued down the hall as Aunt pointed out one great-great Grandfather after another and great military leaders, too, like my Uncle, Admiral Kerr. There were hundreds of portraits of my long-ago family. Moreover, I was fascinated to see the name *Anne* oft repeated on the brass nameplates.

"Aunt Alice, I see that there are many grand ladies with my name. Why is that?"

"The name carries a long history of great ladies in our family, Anne. It is because you were first-born, and therefore, given the name."

"But your name is Alice?"

"My older sister was first-born, Anne. She died when she was three."

"I am sorry to hear of it, Aunt Alice, but I know about death. In Holybourne hardly a month passes that someone buries her baby."

"Indeed, a pathetic thing it is."

That vision of Holybourne haunted me. Since first coming to London, I had not heard a word from Mama, and though I was not a baby, I did cry myself to sleep at night sometimes. Weeping helped block out the thought of Mama's constant rocking. I missed throwing sticks for Misha and kissing her soft sweet muzzle. I missed helping Tilly cook dinner. Then there was the dastardly Mr O'Leary coming and going. I shuddered, feeling not at all sure that Tilly would be in the best of moods anymore. Would she have found work elsewhere, leaving Mama alone to tend herself?

Now standing at Aunt's favourite hall window, long and bare, we stared out onto the shrubbery maze below, leafless and brittle. Thick black clouds rolled above the distant emerald-coloured meadow. A white cow lumbered awkwardly toward the pasture gate; I could hear the far-away clang of her bell. The field grass was frozen a deep green, almost blue. My eyes did not need to squint today, for the sky was grey and deep purple all around us.

"Aunt Alice, many fortnights have come and gone. I worry about Mama being alone with only Tilly. And then with Mr O'Leary—well, I was wondering when I may return home?"

Putting her arm around my shoulder, she pulled me close and whispered onto my forehead. "When your mother wishes you home, Anne, she will send for you."

"But, Aunt ..."

"Come along now, dear. One must not stand so very close to the window when it storms."

* * *

It was a mild late February day, months past the fortnight I was to stay at Lesington Hall, I had received only three letters from Mama. Her hand was scratchy, and many of her written words did not make much sense, and still she had not beckoned me home. If Tilly could only read and write, I would send her a letter asking about Mama's health. I could have her carry water from the sacred stream for Mama. My heart grew more anxious by the day. I knew I must return home soon, but how?

I loved Lesington Hall, loved Aunt Alice, Cousin Eleanor, and dear Franklin. Shopping with Aunt Alice and Cousin in London afforded me all the best clothes, frocks with dainty satin bows, thin frilly petticoats, and silk stockings. Indeed, I enjoyed going to theatres and glimpsing once at Her Majesty as she passed our carriage on Threadneedle Street. Oh, yes, I also enjoyed the grand and glorious British Museum where Mr Dickens had once sat and read books.

At St. Anne's Church on Sundays with the odious vicar and his sister, I prayed for Mama under the great arched ceiling. It was a place that seemed to welcome my prayers, and so I begged God to watch over Mama. Even with all this joy and goodness abounding, I ached to go home; Mama needed me.

One Tuesday morning, as Aunt Alice and I sat in her study reviewing my French lesson, I was in the midst of forming the French words to express my heart's aching for Mama when we heard hooves crunching the stony bridle path. It was a fast approaching rider, I mused.

Glancing out the window, Aunt Alice squinted. "Why, it is a courier."

I sprang from my chair. "It is a letter from Mama! It is from Mama! At last, she has sent for me!"

Cousin Eleanor entered, carrying a black-edged letter. Peeling it open, Aunt read it to herself and then handed it to Cousin.

"Anne, let us bundle up and take the air."

Skipping along the shovelled pathway, I jumped ahead of Aunt humming as I carelessly disturbed the snow piled high along the narrow verge. The air was crisp, the sun was shining, the sky was a brilliant stark glaze of frozen space. Beneath the hawthorn, laden with tuffs of puffy white sparkles, I spied a small cache of dry leaves. I had gathered five fine large ones when a sparrow suddenly flitted from her recluse. I heard Aunt sigh. Holding the leaves to my heart, I inquired, *"Qu'est-ce qui ne va pas?"*

"Oui, Anne, there is indeed something wrong." Glancing into the cloudless sky, she prayed aloud, "Dear God, I only wish this day was dark, cloudy, frigid and bitter." We walked on a few more steps. "Anne, your mother has died."

A sharp, icy pang pierced my lungs. "Mama?" The bright glare of stark whiteness scorched my eyes; tears trickled thickly down my face onto the bonnet-ribbons tied beneath my chin. Rolling the dry, broken leaves in my hands, I stuffed them into my muff and thought of the cold, rough wooden box where Mama would be—like all the Holybourne babies. Would anyone have remembered her shawl?

Venturing into the crisp, deep snow, I soon came to the verge of a silent meadow and knelt. Cupping my hands to my face, I inhaled a deep breath and caught the shadow of Aunt Alice lingering over me.

"I will never see her again, Aunt." I closed my eyes and tried hard to picture Mama's face, but only a moss-stained, warped grey coffin lid came into my view. "I cannot remember her face."

Pulling me up from the snow, Aunt hugged me. "We will bring her home, Anne." Kissing my brow, she smiled. "I know of one portrait of her, Anne. Perhaps you would like to have it."

I nodded. "I must pray for Mama."

"Do you wish that I leave you in privacy, Anne?"

Taking her hand, I held it firm. "Oh, no, no." I tried hard not to cry, but I couldn't help it. "I must write to Tilly," I pleaded. "Oh, but she cannot read, Aunt."

Chafing my cold hands, she smiled warmly. "She will find someone to read it to her, of that, I am sure."

"Oh, Aunt, I pray Mama had a soft, warm fire and that she was not alone."

"We are taught that we are never alone, Anne."

* * *

The deepest part of winter turned severe; moreover, its bleakness lasted well into April. A constant worry tormented my heart, for there were no flowers to lay upon Mama's grave. Would she be pleased with my simple wreaths of holly? Oh, if spring would only come. Bundled in my blanket, I sat at my window-seat and stared out at the bleak, foggy morn.

Mary, the chambermaid, entered. She always had a cheerful voice. "Good morning, miss. I'll have your fire rekindled in good time."

"Oh, Mary, spring will never come."

"Have faith, Miss Anne," she said poking the fire.

I wrote the word "Faith?" on my frosty pane of glass, and while I peered through the wavy letters, tiny streamlets of moisture pooled on the bottom sill ... along with my faith. "No," I sighed, you are wrong, Mary. Spring will never come."

Crossing herself, she smiled. "You must have faith, miss."

Watching Mary cross herself, I was pulled back in time, sitting with Mama next to Madame Pinchot as both of them did that—crossing themselves before Madame held her séance. What could it mean?

"Mary, what is that you do with your hand?"

"It is the sign of the cross, Miss Anne."

"And it works for miracles?"

"Oh, indeed, but you must have faith."

Of course it would work miracles. Mama spoke with Papa, or at least through Madame Pinchot, did she not? I realised having faith was the hard part. What had faith brought me thus far?

Before closing the door behind her, Mary winked and left me to my faithless visions. The fire grew fine and hearty. I closed my eyes and crossed myself repeating the word "faith" many times over. Opening my eyes, I saw that I had fretted for nought—the sun broke through. The word "Faith" that I had squeaked on the windowpane now glistened around the edges. I crossed myself again, and then ran to Aunt Alice's bedchamber door where I knocked loudly and shouted for her to come. Hearing her faint reply to 'Come, come,' I dashed in— breathless. "Oh, Aunt, look! Look!"

Startled, she sprang from bed and grabbed her robe. "What is it, Anne?"

Pulling aside her heavy curtains, I stood awash in the rays of bright sunshine and twirled around like a ballerina. "Oh, Aunt, spring has finally come. To think, I had nearly lost my faith. We can now plant flowers on Mama's and Papa's grave."

* * *

Aunt Alice, Cousin Eleanor and I stood watch as Mose, the gardener, hoed with great care around the base of Mama's and Papa's gravestones. I envisioned a troubling scene. Taking Aunt's hand, I asked Mose, "How deep do the roots of those flowers go?"

Aunt Alice put her arm around my shoulder. "Oh, but an inch, Anne—but an inch."

I wiped my eyes as a blanket of warm sun spread across Mama's grave, its rays resting atop the soggy, rough, black soil. "Oh, look," I sighed, running my hands over the words etched on her granite headstone: *Catherine Hiriart Holt—In Loving Memory.* "How the letters sparkle."

Aunt kissed my temple.

Cousin hugged me. "Indeed, Anne, they sparkle like your eyes."

"Thank you, Cousin Eleanor."

I sighed. "Now Papa will never be left alone again. Thank you, Aunt, for bringing Mama here to Lesington Hall so she can be with Papa."

Turning away, Aunt Alice bid Cousin and me to walk with her. "Come along with us, Eleanor."

"Excuse me, Alice, but I have letters I must answer."

"Very well, then."

I took Aunt's hand, anxious that the flowers just planted on Mama and Papa's grave would flourish—I so wanted a blanket of beauty. It had been a long winter and I prayed not much damage had been done to the soil.

I must keep my faith. Glancing about, I was reaffirmed to my vow for this glorious spring afternoon came in waves of warm fresh air. Fresh green shoots along the shrubbery borders broadened quickly under the sun's coaxing. The birds, out in great numbers, fluttered, swooped, and sang in delightful chirps. Tilting my face to the sun, I took Aunt's hand and fondled the rings on her fingers. "Aunt, tell me about your rings again."

"Anne, you are the most inquisitive little creature I know." We walked on a few steps. "Very well, then." Removing the thumb ring, she said, "This one was your Grandmother Foyle's."

I examined it, finding it nice enough, but plain. "Oh, yes, go on."

"This one was ..." she removed a silver braided ring that I had not seen before, "this one belonged to your uncle, Sir Charles Holt."

"Of Chittingdon House, Aunt. His portrait, with you and Papa, hangs in the library."

"Yes." She brought the ring to her lips. "On his deathbed, he gave it to me."

I felt sad for Aunt. How she had suffered, losing her sister, her brother Charles, her mother and father, and my Papa— what heartache must abound within her. Though I too felt sad, I did not want to make her more so.

"It is a beautiful ring. It must be your favourite, Aunt."

She stopped by the fountain and ruffled my hair. "*One* of my favourites, Anne."

"How many favourites, Aunt?"

"I wear them all, Anne."

She lifted her baby finger to show me a thin gold band.

"Hmm, it is plain, Aunt, but, I do like it ... if you do."

She smiled and brought it to her lips, kissing the ring. "I have never taken it off."

I thought of Mama. Now buried deep in God's earth warm and comfortable, I imagined, coddled in soft cushions. Her gold wedding band must still wrap around her finger. "Oh, yes, Aunt, Mama never removed her ring either."

Her smiling countenance settled upon me as I gazed up into her face and smiled. As we continued to walk about the garden, Aunt would now and again lift the little gold band to her lips. Because she seemed far away in thought, perhaps even melancholy, I did not question her about who had given it to her, some other time perhaps.

Swinging our hands, I whispered, "Thank you, Aunt."

"Hmm, for what, Anne?"

"You are very kind to me, kind and brilliant."

She laughed. "Not so very brilliant, child, no, not so very brilliant."

Nodding, I assured her that she was. "But, I fear, you have much locked up in your heart, Aunt ... riddles, family dilemmas ..."

"Riddles and dilemmas?" She squeezed my hand. "To be sure, Anne."

Thus far, Aunt Alice had spoken only a few words regarding my Mama. Today, I hoped, she might impart a little more about my Papa.

"I never knew my father, Aunt Alice, but I know his name was James Andrew Holt. I read that on the gravestone, and it was written in his books; it was on his nameplate."

Rolling a ring around her finger, she nodded. "Indeed, it was. He was our eldest brother." She sighed. "I cannot satisfy you, Anne. Regarding him, you must not ask me questions. When you are older, perhaps, I will share more with you."

The tone of her voice stopped the begging question. "Mama seldom spoke about anyone in our family until she became weak with cough, Aunt, and only on the very day I was put on the coach to London did I learn I was being sent to you.

"I remember holding her hand as we made our way to the London Road from our cottage. 'Mama,' I said, 'you are coughing more at night, it seems. I wake and hear you.'

" 'Aye, Anne, it wakes me, too. Too much rain, I think.'

" 'But, Mama, why is that so? I do not cough from the rain.'

" 'Oh, I suppose it is the dampness, then, that pushes my chest.'

" 'I think it is the gin, Mama. You must not drink it anymore.'

" 'No, no, Anne,' she argued, 'you are quite mistaken. It is but a heaviness that tires me.'

" 'Is that why I'm going to Aunt Alice's, Mama?'

" 'Until I feel better, child. A fortnight should do.'

" 'I should stay here then, Mama, and care for you.'

"She didn't answer me, Aunt Alice. She just gripped my hand as you are now doing."

Loosening her hold, Aunt Alice cleared her throat. "Indeed, Anne. It would be difficult to see you leave."

After a quiet moment, I continued, "We came upon Madame Pinchot. Monsieur Pinchot was raking leaves. It was there where Mama and I helped him—where the leaves must have found their way into my pocket.

"Mama smiled at him, a little out of breath, coughing again as she told them I was going to London to visit with my aunt, Miss Alice Holt—a fine lady."

" 'Anne, so you are going to London?' Monsieur Pinchot looked impressed. 'What a traveller you will be. Misha will miss you.'

"He was a kind old man, Aunt Alice. His hair was white as snow, thick and wiry. His hands were cracked and calloused, but the handle, Aunt, on his rake, was shiny and smooth.

"He smiled at me as I gathered a pile of leaves and scattered them to the wind. Laughing, I slipped my hand in Mama's, and we were off again to the exact place where the coach would stop on The Road.

"Later, sitting in the coach, I was pinched between two ladies. One extremely fat and the other, Aunt Alice, was Miss Phillipps, the vicar's sister. It was hard to see out, and it was very smelly with stomach rumblings of all sorts."

Aunt Alice smiled. I took it as encouragement.

"I reached into my pocket and found some crumpled leaves." I paused in my narration, remembering how I had rolled them in my hands back and forth—smelling them, thinking fondly of Mama.

"Miss Phillipps was mightily disgusted with me; she told me to brush my filthy hands. I sensed she was not pleased about the dirt clinging to my clothes. In haste, I emptied the leaves into my handkerchief—saving the precious leaves of Holybourne. Fearful she would force me to discard them I closed my eyes and pretended to sleep.

"The vicar and another man, a kind older gentleman with a long grey beard, sat across from us. Their idle conversation turned from me to the weather; I could smell the heaviness in the air and wanted to smell my leaves again, then it began to rain hard. I wanted my Mama, and when the fat lady drifted off to sleep, I pretended to pray in order to smell my hands. I knew not to cry, though. That would not do, and I remained quiet.

"At each stop, not wanting to be left behind, I followed the ladies, keeping mind to behave. Not having any money, I declined to eat. Miss Phillipps shook her head saying, 'Very well, starve, you picky thing.'"

"I only took food from ..."

Aunt smiled. "Oh, yes, Mr Phillipps would offer such a kindness."

"No, Aunt, he did not. The bearded gentleman handed me some bread and cheese. Mr Phillipps would not look at me.

"After travelling down the road a little ways, we stopped at an inn. I thought of our beloved Queen and asked how many pints they drank to Her Majesty's good health."

"Oh, Anne ... surely you did not?"

"The bearded gentleman laughed aloud. 'Twas an *act of parliament*,' [4] my dear." He explained. 'I had five pints o' beer.'

He tweaked my nose. 'Aye, and tasty ones at that, Minikin. Aye, years ago when I was a soldier it didn't cost me a shilling. Indeed, then a landlord was obliged to give to each of us, gratis, five pints o' beer.' He laughed jovially, 'but 'twas long ago.'

"The vicar glared at us both. Had it not been for the kind old man, I know Mr Phillipps would have snatched my bread and cheese and tossed them out the window."

"Oh, Anne, you quite mistake the man."

"Oh, I assure you, Aunt, I do not. What is more, Miss Phillipps said I was an ignorant little girl and unable even to make polite conversation. 'Such are the ways of country people,' she said, sniffing the air. I was not spoken to again for the remainder of the trip to London."

"Dear me, Anne."

"When we arrived, I was shoved out of the coach, but the kind bearded gentleman helped me up. I thanked him for helping me, and for toasting Her Majesty. I said I would write and tell her of his goodness."

"And what did he reply?"

"He patted my head, Aunt, saying to make sure I spelt his name correctly."

"And?"

"Sir John Barleycorn, [5] Aunt."

"I see," said Aunt Alice shaking her head with a giggle.

"I believe Sir John Barleycorn to have made the better vicar, Aunt Alice."

---

[4] Act of Parliament (Quartering Act – circa 1765) A landlord was obliged to give to soldiers 5 pints of beer gratis.

[5] John Barleycorn is a British folksong, dating back to the *Bannatyne Manuscript* of 1568. Robert Burns published a version in 1782. There are several versions. The character "John Barleycorn" in the folksong personifies alcoholic beverages made from barley.

CHAPTER FIVE

The spring winds blew hard and gusty. I worried greatly for the safety of the starlings and sparrows. Oh, how they struggled to build their nests, only to be blown about at each venture. Hearing the flapping and pitter of one bird, I watched in awe as she chose the hidden recess of our drawing-room window ledge for her nest. Oh, clever girl.

When the mother bird left her three eggs snuggled in a copse of twigs and straw to forage for food, I sang to them in tune with Cousin Eleanor's clock, "Cuckoo, cuckoo."

One morning, when I was so engaged, Aunt Alice entered the room. "Anne? Is that you?"

Peeking around the curtain, I held my finger to my lips and whispered, "Aunt, a bird has built her nest. Come, see." She tiptoed to my side. I slowly pulled back the curtain. "There, you see?"

"How dear," she whispered. "I used to watch them too, Anne, when I was your age." She smiled. "I had nearly forgotten." Her chest swelled.

"I can't wait to see the babies, Aunt."

"Nor, I, Anne, you must tell me when they hatch."

Franklin entered. "Madam, Mr Phillipps and Miss Phillipps have come to call."

"Very well, Franklin, see them in." She smoothed her hair.

I wrinkled my nose. How could I endure another gruelling hour with the black-coat clackity-clack? "Must I stay, Aunt?"

"You must."

Franklin showed them in.

Aunt smiled. "Good morning, Mr Phillipps and Miss Phillipps."

I certainly didn't want to smile or encourage any sort of friendship with either of them. The vicar, no doubt, quite adept at reading minds, singled me out.

"Good morning, Anne."

"Good morning, sir." I noticed his sister was her usual dull-witted self. She probably could not, or cared not to, read my mind, or for that matter, I thought unkindly—her own. She did, however, nod my direction with a stiff smile. Turning from her gaze, I spied a mouse scampering toward them.

I jumped up and pointed. "Oh, look, Aunt, a mouse!" I captured the frightened tiny creature between Miss Phillipps' frayed hem and the vicar's muddy black boot. I held it by its warm, heart-thumping, little grey body. Lifting it nearer Miss Phillipps than her brother, I was met with a hiss.

I glared at Mr Phillipps. "It followed you in, sir."

Aunt's face turned ashen. "Take it out, Anne."

The vicar shuddered. "I should have the filthy thing stepped on ... squashed immediately."

Holding a handkerchief to her nose, Aunt sank deeper into her easy chair.

Before I left, I called back, "I shall do quite well by it, Aunt, do not fret. When at Holybourne, I captured many. They are quite friendly, actually."

I ran to the coach-house. There I found a suitable stack of hay, made a suitable door and deposited my little find at the threshold. Then, noticing a cat's tail twirling about my leg, I realised my predicament—actually, the mouse's predicament.

"There you are, Miss Anne." Franklin towered over the three of us. "Your Aunt Alice wishes your immediate return."

"I caught a mouse, Franklin and hid him in there." Glancing down at the hay mound's front door, I added, "I do hope Cat does not snatch him for dinner."

"Gilbert is blind, Miss Anne."

Petting the old fellow, I felt sad at that bit of news. "Oh, how sad, Franklin. Why have I never seen him before? How does he get about? How does he eat?"

On our way back to the Great House, Franklin explained that the dairymaids feed the old boy. "He is a fat one, Miss Anne."

"Yes ..." I glanced back as he followed behind us, stumbling and bumping into things, "yes, he is quite fat alright."

Entering the drawing room, I was happy to explain about the blind cat and the safe deposit of the mouse into its mouse house.

Miss Phillipps fanned her face. "Disgusting, why the cat should have been left to do his duty," she said flatly.

"But, he is blind, Miss Phillipps." I smiled with confidence.

Snapping shut her fan, she glared. "Even a blind cat has a *nose*, Miss Anne."

"And ears," added the vicar with a twisted smile.

"But, our fat cat is *never* hungry."

"That will do, Anne." Aunt took in a great breath. "I think we have heard quite enough about mice and cats."

"Indeed, Miss Holt." The vicar brushed a bit of lint from his trousers.

Cousin Eleanor entered. Squirming in my chair, I smiled up at her. I couldn't wait to tell her what had just transpired.

"Eleanor," said Aunt, "Mr Phillipps and his sister have invited us to accompany them to the South of France on holiday."

"How very kind," Cousin responded, "the South of France, indeed. Hmm, how nice."

I prayed fervently that Aunt would not go anywhere with them—the two most boring bodies in the whole of England.

Aunt glanced at me. "And Anne has never been there."

"Oh, Aunt, I am too young to travel such a great distance."

Mr Phillipps cleared his throat. "Indeed, Miss Holt, Miss Anne is welcome to stay at the parsonage with Mrs Mahoney."

Breathing relief, I crossed myself.

Turning purple, Miss Phillipps gasped.

The vicar and Aunt were still in conversation when Cousin Eleanor injected, "Alice, it would not seem like a holiday without Anne. We couldn't possibly leave her behind."

"You may leave me." I closed my eyes, crossed my fingers, and prayed they would.

"You are right, Eleanor. Anne needs to see new and different things."

"I just saw a mouse, Aunt, and a blind cat. Is that not difference enough?" I'm most certain my voice held a tinge of hysteria.

Alas, the clack herself, Miss Phillipps, spoke up, "Yes, Anne, you simply must come, for I do not have a travelling companion." I glared at her pouty face.

I sank low into my chair. Visions of angry mice and fat blind cats flitted before my eyes. I muttered, "Indeed, strange animals seem to find me."

Aunt Alice cocked her ear. "Speak up, Anne."

I sighed aloud. "You would not wish to hear it, Aunt."

"Come, Charlotte," said the vicar as he stood, "good morning, Miss Holt, Mrs Mills, Miss Anne. I have a meeting with the squire yet this afternoon." He nodded. "Until the Sabbath then."

We all followed along and just as Mr Phillipps removed his hat to enter the carriage, a mother bird deposited a snowy gift upon his shiny bald spot.

"Oh, dear me," cried Aunt, all aflutter as she rushed to his side with her pocket-handkerchief.

Cousin and I, flustered to glee, turned and hurried back into the house giggling.

* * *

Later that afternoon as Aunt, Cousin Eleanor and I sat in the study, I had little success convincing Aunt that I preferred to stay in the parsonage with the housekeeper, Mrs Mahoney, even though I had never met her before in my entire life.

Aunt held a peculiar smile. "Nonsense, Anne, Miss Phillipps needs a companion, someone just like you."

"Needs *me*, Aunt?" I half closed my book, *Emma*. "But, Aunt, I do not think she likes me."

"You are very right, Anne."

I glanced at Cousin Eleanor in hopes she would come to my rescue, but she held her *I am not going to lend you aid today* look. Franklin was no better. At Aunt's nod, he traversed the wood floor, picked up her prized world globe, a marvellous ball of greenish brown bumps, and placed it next to us.

Cousin Eleanor spun it. "I just enjoy watching it twirl." She sat back gazing as it wobbled and creaked in a brownish, greenish blurry whirl.

Watching it spin, I marvelled. "Oh, such a round ball." Examining it more closely, I stopped it with one finger and spun it in the opposite direction. "La, what a fine trick it is."

"Anne, the globe is not a trick." She touched the tip that sat in its ornately carved crescent-shaped pedestal. "This rod holds the globe beginning at the South Pole and emerges at the top ... at the North Pole, as you can clearly see."

Rarely had Aunt seemed so engrossed in anything as in this silly ball. Peering at the sphere before me in amazement, I listened as she pointed out the various countries and the oceans. "I love the globe, too, Aunt."

"Oh, you love everything."

I giggled. "Aunt, you are laughing."

She stood erect, her hands resting on her hips. "So, you think me devoid of humour, then?"

"Very near it, ma'am."

At that, Franklin teetered, pouring my tea into the sugar bowl. Thank goodness no one noticed. Grabbing up the bowl, I handed it to him giggling. "More sugar, Franklin."

He winked. "Very well, miss, at once."

Returning to the globe, I pointed to the Nile, Greece, and the Alps, but I could not find Holybourne. Aunt must have been reading my mind.

"Anne, the globe is too small to show every town in the world. You must first understand that."

"Yes," I pointed, "there is England, Scotland, and Ireland." It spun at the slightest bit of air—even as I whispered, "If ever I own a globe, I shall have someone paint Holybourne's name upon it."

"The continent, Anne, is where we shall be travelling."

"Hmm, yes, with Mr Phillipps *and* his sister." My heart sank.

Aunt Alice ran her finger from London across the sea to France. "Look here, Anne. Along here, I would suppose, is the way we shall travel, almost to the Pyrenees Mountains. I am going to discuss with Mr Phillipps about staying in the small town called Issor. It is where your mother's family is buried."

"Mama's family?" How intriguing the thought was to me. I didn't know just where Mama's family lived or where she was born, but I knew she came from far away from *the continent* as they called it.

"Issor, France, Aunt? That is where Mama's family lives?"

"Where they are buried, dear. I was told you are the only one left on that side, other than possibly a few distant cousins."

"But you are alive, Aunt Alice."

"I am on the other side of the family, dearest."

"Well, then, Aunt Alice, I am most thankful that I am on your side."

She half-laughed. "Indeed, and so am I."

I somehow dreaded the thought of Mr Phillipps sharing in my newfound family, even if they were dead and buried on the other side. Such a moment of discovery did not belong to him or to his sister. Perhaps Aunt might change her mind, and we could go alone.

"Must Mr Phillipps and his sister come along, Aunt Alice?"

"He was gracious enough to invite us to accompany them, Anne."

Cousin Eleanor hemmed. "Your tithing will no doubt finance the entire affair, Alice."

"Curates earn very little, Eleanor. We must be charitable."

Cousin flushed. "Well, I do suppose it was cruel of me to have said such a thing."

Coming to her defence, I offered, "Maybe not so cruel, Cousin Eleanor. Perhaps it is not the tithing that is odious, but the recipients who are the rub."

Aunt's face wrinkled. "Recipients who are the rub, Anne? What on earth?"

Cousin covered her face with her hands. "Oh, God forgive me, but I must laugh."

Picking up her Bible, Aunt thumbed through the pages and then stopped. Handing it to me, she pointed. "1 Peter 3, please read Chapter 3, verse 8, Anne, aloud."

"Very well, Aunt. 'Finally, be ye all of one mind, having compassion one of another, love as brethren, be pitiful, be courteous.'"

"Was your comment courteous, Anne?" She glanced at Cousin Eleanor, who pretended to be concentrating on her embroidery. (She peered over at me only when Aunt was not looking.)

"No, Aunt it was not, but, Miss Phillipps carries such an air of conceit. And what is more, what is there about her to command such conceit?"

"There is nothing, Anne, and I have a mind to work upon it." With a faint smile, she bid me off to sleep. "Good night now, Anne. Pray forgiveness for your unkind words."

"Yes, Aunt, good night." I lowered my head. I knew my unkindness was merited. I sighed. Dear Aunt, how forgiving she was.

"Bid goodnight to Cousin Eleanor."

"Good night, Cousin Eleanor."

"Good night, Anne."

"Before I go, Aunt, may I have one more question?"

"Go on, Anne."

"Sometimes you call Cousin Eleanor, Mrs Mills, but she does not have a husband."

"A title of respect, my dear," she said.

Cousin smiled. "If it is permissible by your aunt, you may call me Cousin Elly."

"Oh ..." I replied smiling, "May I, Aunt?"

"I suppose you may. But in public, you must address her as Mrs Mills, or Cousin Eleanor."

"Indeed I will, Aunt."

"Now, you must go to bed; it is late."

Cousin Elly smiled. "Come then." She set aside her sewing. "My eyes have failed me again." She took my hand. "I will walk with you to your room. Good night, Alice."

Aunt Alice laid down her Bible. "Anne, tomorrow at breakfast, there will be an envelope at your place."

"An envelope, Aunt?" I so loved surprises. I searched in my mind what I had done to deserve an envelope. I frowned. But maybe it wasn't a present. After all, I had been naughty just moments ago.

"There is something in it that I wish for you to have. In the morning we shall discuss it."

"Indeed, Aunt, I can scarcely wait." I kissed her cheek.

"Good night, Anne. I will see you for breakfast."

Cousin Elly and I ascended the stairs. "Aunt Alice comes into my room late at night, Cousin. I pretend to be asleep. She stands over me for a long time and then kisses my brow. I do believe she is fond of me. Maybe not so much as Mama, but I feel that she does in my heart."

"Anne," she whispered, "your aunt adores you. Though, it has taken her time to ... to accept you."

My heart leapt in my chest. "She adores me? She has told you, then, of such feelings, Cousin?"

Elly put her fingers to her lips. "I have spoken too loosely, but, rest assured, she loves you."

"Did she love my mother?"

"Your Aunt spoke little of your mother, Anne. I came to Lesington Hall years ago to help dear Alice care for her ailing mother and father. Your grandmother passed away shortly after my arrival. When your grandfather Holt died a year ago last June, Alice convinced me to remain. She and I being the only Holts left, except of course for you and your mother.

"The first I knew of your coming was when she shared with me your mother's letter requesting that you would be allowed to come to Lesington Hall for a visit. It was a great surprise ... ah, a wonderful surprise. Your Aunt's exact words: 'Eleanor, I would wish for you to fetch my niece, Anne Alice Holt. She will be riding the Winchester coach from Holybourne. She is due in at twelve of the clock tomorrow.' That is the whole of it, Anne."

We could hear Aunt coming up the stairs, and we scurried to our rooms. I put on my nightgown and climbed into bed. A gnawing ache swelled in my heart. Hugging my pillow, I cried, *Oh, Mama, I miss you.* I reached beneath my pillow, found my old handkerchief of crushed Holybourne leaves and pressed them to my lips. *I shall never forget you, Mama.*

* * *

The next morning a shiver of great expectancy ran through my body. I was anxious to see the surprise Aunt Alice had promised to be sitting at my plate. I hurriedly dressed and ran down the stairs. Oh, a glorious sun shone through the tall undressed windows of the morning room and spread across the table like melted butter. Spying an ivory coloured envelope resting against my water glass, I twirled in happy exuberance.

"Good morning, Aunt Alice." I nodded. "Good morning, Elly." The sound of *Elly,* so personal an address to my cousin, warmed my heart. I must be becoming endeared to them. My heart was as happy as the chirping birds.

Acting the little lady, I took my chair and sat. Spreading my napkins on my lap, I stared at the envelope—my name written in Aunt Alice's exquisite hand. I dared not touch it until she nodded, but I did once or twice lean in to sniff it. It smelled of Aunt's lavender. I had to move it. "Aunt, hot wax is dripping all over it."

Looking up at the antique chandelier, she frowned. "Dear me, we cannot have such a thing happen."

"No, indeed we cannot." I picked away the clumps of warm wax and replaced the envelope.

"Once you remove the wax from your eggs, Anne, you may open it."

Elly scolded with a laugh, "Oh, Alice, you are too cruel."

I slipped my fingers beneath the seal. A locket and chain slid into my hand. "Oh, Aunt." I closed my eyes and held it firm. "It is Mama. I can feel her." I opened it and found a miniature portrait of Mama on one side and Papa on the other. "Oh, yes, it is her—the same black hair and black eyes. Oh, Aunt." I hurried from my chair and hugged her. Wiping my eyes, I kissed her cheek. "And a portrait of Papa?" He looked so young. "Where did you find such a thing, Aunt?"

"It was in his vest pocket. When ... when your father was brought here." Her lips were pressed thin. "I completely forgot all about it, putting it away for safe keeping. My, but that was years ago."

"He died on the day I was born, Aunt Alice." I fondled the locket.

Aunt swallowed hard. "We know."

I knew that by her set jaw and by Elly's glance at the ceiling that was the end of the explanation. "Hmm." I nodded. "May I wear it now?"

"Yes, Anne."

All through breakfast, I remained quiet, listening to Cousin Elly and Aunt Alice talk. But most of all, I felt one with Mama and Papa for the very first time. I felt the coolness of the locket touching my throat; felt the chain catch at the nape of my neck ... *I love you, Mama.*

* * *

I wore the locket around my neck everywhere, taking it off only to cleanse myself. After church one Sunday, while Aunt and Elly were conversing with a few of their lady friends, Miss Phillipps pulled me aside.

"I see you are wearing a piece of gold jewellery, Miss Anne."

Her eyes glued onto my locket, its fine gold chain glittering like the sun. Might I add, sparkling my heart with song. Miss Phillipps seemed to find all things that glitter to be gold, but my locket was no concern of hers.

"Oh, yes, quite an important piece from my Aunt's vast collection of 'ojects d' art," I said with such an air. I did not lie, for I had just learned the expression in my French lesson—'Ojects d' art in French meant any collection of things ... thimbles, vases, glasses, even old buckets ...

"Indeed," she fawned, "it is quite delicate." She reached toward it. "May I?"

To open it and show her Mama and Papa's picture would only lead to more questions I could not answer. "No."

A soft gasp escaped her as she quickly withdrew her hand. "Well, then."

Her face flushed; her spiral curls hung long and pointless. I had wounded her pride. A pang of guilt tapped my heart. There I stood on sacred ground, as Aunt Alice called it, and I had caused someone pain. I recanted. "Very well, then, Miss Phillipps you may *look* at it." I begrudgingly held it out.

"Your aunt has a vast collection, does she?" Fondling my locket, she sighed. "My brother put away *my* finer pieces for safe keeping." Lifting her chin, she added, "Until I marry, of course."

"Of course." I felt like saying that turkey-necked spinsters do not wear jewels when another pang hit me, this time deeper into my heart. I shook my head. That nasty evil angel sitting on my shoulder, I supposed, was at work. I glanced up at Miss Phillipps, her eyes taking in my locket, as if to memory. "You may open it, Miss Phillipps, if you wish."

She placed it back at my throat. "It would not concern me one way or the other to view someone I do not know." With that, she turned and joined her brother. She whispered something to him. Immediately his eyes cast toward my locket.

Aunt pressed my hand. "I noticed Miss Phillipps viewing your locket, Anne."

"At first, I was most rude to her Aunt Alice. I did not want her touching my locket. I refused to let her touch it, but then I felt it too mean a thing to do and changed my mind. But she said the picture inside did not concern her in the least."

By then our carriage arrived, and we settled ourselves for the ride home. Pulling away, I waved goodbye to Miss Phillipps, but she did not wave back. She only gathered up her dull, plum coloured taffeta skirt and followed her brother back into the church.

"Aunt, I told her of your vast collection of 'objects'd art." I giggled. "Perhaps I spoke out of turn. She said her brother was holding her jewels until she married. Can you believe such a thing? Haha."

The netting on Aunt Alice's hat lay about her collar in soft folds. "Anne, if we are to travel to France on holiday with them, you must soon make friends with Miss Phillipps. Today being

Sunday, Anne, I would have expected more from your sweet nature."

My heart thumped in my throat. It did not take much of a scolding to embarrass me. "Perhaps I might invite Miss Phillipps to luncheon sometime then, Aunt Alice."

"That would be a kind gesture, Anne." She exchanged glances with Elly. "Send an invitation first thing tomorrow. Perhaps Tuesday will suit her." Aunt smiled. "Indeed, we shall entertain her in the garden."

Elly lifted the lace veil from her hat and dabbed her lips. "Hmm, that sounds the best of plans."

"The garden? Oh, indeed, just the place. Miss Phillipps should be pleased to sit amongst the pink hydrangeas. Thank you, Aunt Alice."

* * *

On Tuesday morning Aunt advised me to send a carriage for Miss Phillipps.

"Ladies, Anne, are not to walk alone such a distance." Adjusting her shawl, she glanced out the window. "And besides, the air is a little misty."

"Indeed, Aunt Alice. Mose said it would clear by noon. May I ride along to the parsonage, Aunt?"

"Very well, Anne."

How grown up I would look sitting all by myself nodding to the passers-by as my carriage bumped along the street. Perhaps, I might even be seen stopping to buy a nosegay from the flower girls.

I climbed into the carriage and sat back as we wound our way through the tight alleyway next to the church. Miss Phillipps stood waiting on her step. I could see the vicar peeking from behind the curtain. He quickly disappeared when I waved to him.

Miss Phillipps settled into the seat next to me, nodding. "Good afternoon, Miss Anne."

I took in the scent of something that smelled rather ancient. There draped over her shoulders was an old fur cape with little white patches of scaly dander where hair had moulted. I shuddered. Perhaps in the dim light of the parsonage, she could not see how worn it was. And there she sat acting like royalty in all her splendour. I sighed.

"Drive on," she called out.

I sat up, *but this was my carriage. How dare she command it so?* I sat back looking at her stupid snake-like relic wrap and thought of what I would say next. "Aunt Alice and Mrs Mills will be joining us in the garden, Miss Phillipps."

Her nose wrinkled as if sampling the air. "I shall look forward to that."

"Yes, you and I shall take a turn in the garden, perhaps. I have memorised all the names of the flowers and shrubbery." I felt quite proud of my accomplishments thus far.

"How very nice for you, then." She resumed staring out the window.

"Indeed, Miss Phillipps." I glanced again at that thing wrapped about her shoulders. I dared not sniff the air for fear its remaining fur would fly up my nose. We were soon delivered to Aunt's revered garden. Stepping from the carriage, I felt the warmth of the sun beat down upon my face. Outstretching my arms, I stood and welcomed the wonderful warm splash of sunshine.

"Really, Miss Anne, your nose will freckle."

She pumped up her well-worn parasol. A piece of fringe came loose and dangled quite stupidly behind her head. "Freckles, what do I care? Not two straws, I assure you." Stepping alongside her, I smiled. "Come along then, Miss Phillipps, we are to luncheon in the garden."

She moved ahead of me. "I know the way, Anne. I have been coming here longer than you."

My heady enthusiasm wilted like a day-old daisy. "Indeed." My words came more like a whisper than a mutter. I followed behind like a puppy.

"I suppose this is where we are to be entertained?" Without waiting for reply, she pulled out one of the white wicker chairs and sat. She then hastily flung her hairy serpent wrap onto the chair next to her.

Sitting at the table, Miss Phillipps and I remained quite sullen, all in all. I hated being sullen, but there was something about her that elicited such reactions. But if Aunt joined us and found such a dull table, she would not be happy with me.

"Miss Phillipps, I do like your dangling earring, all a sparkle and everything."

She touched it. "Oh, yes, they were my ..." she felt for the other, but it was gone. "Oh, dear me!" She scooted back from the table looking around. "It is gone. Oh, I have lost my mother's earring."

I was now on my hands and knees patting the grass. "I do not see it anywhere." My head hit Mose's flower-cart. "Ouch."

"Dear me, Miss Anne," said Mose finding me crawling about. "What seems to be the trouble?"

Rubbing my head, I grimaced. "Miss Phillipps lost her earring. Please do look in the carriage, will you? Perhaps it fell there."

Still on my hands and knees, I crawled back to our table and stood. "It must be in the parsonage, Miss Phillipps." I brushed the soil from my grass-green stained frock.

"Oh, I hope not, Clarke will be furious ..." She put her hands to her mouth.

"Why would he be furious? It's *your* jewellery, and you lost it quite by accident."

"Oh, I shall never find it." She dropped her head in her hands, her lips quivered.

I felt sorry for her. I fondled my locket and knew if I lost it how devastated I would be. But surely Aunt, unlike the vicar, would not be furious with me; after all, accidents do happen. I patted her shoulder, but she abruptly pulled away, and her *lost* earring dropped onto the table.

By then Mose returned with the maid, Mary. "I am sorry Miss Anne, but I could not find it."

"We just now found it, Mose, thank you. All along it must have been hooked on Miss Phillipps' collar." I judged her most undeserving of such luck.

"Very good, miss." He nodded and left.

"Shall I bring the lemon water now, Miss Anne?" asked the maid.

"Thank you, Mary."

Now dabbing her nose with her handkerchief, Miss Phillipps huffed to the maid, "Lemon water? No, no. I wish to have coffee, very hot coffee."

Coffee? Oh, indeed, I reasoned she never had coffee at home. It was too expensive.

Shielding her eyes from the sun, Miss Phillipps glanced toward the house with a sigh. "I wonder when your aunt will be joining us?"

"I would hope she and Cousin Elly will not be too long in coming." I suppose she thought it beneath her dignity to be entertained by someone my age. But it was she who needed a companion to travel with. "Tell me, Miss Phillipps, why would

your brother be furious with you for losing an earring? Surely
he has misplaced things."

"Did I say furious? Dear me, so I did." She examined the
smudges on her gloves. "I suppose he realises how precious the
stones ... they could never be replaced you know."

"Indeed not. They must have cost a great deal."

"Oh, mind, it is not the money, I assure you. It is only that
the stones are very old. They are heirlooms from our family,
actually."

Watching the earrings dangle and sparkle, I clasped my
locket and felt its coolness. Just then I spied Aunt Alice step
from the house and walk toward us. Anxious to be away from
my droll companion, I ran to her. "I have a present for you,
Aunt." Glancing around I asked, "And where is Elly? Oh, and
Miss Phillipps and I have been having a very nice time."

"Child, child, do give me a moment to answer."

"Aunt, please, do not call me *child*."

"Very well, Anne. Well, where is my present?"

When we joined Miss Phillipps, I presented Aunt with the
nosegay that I had picked and arranged for her earlier that
morning.

"Oh, it is lovely, child ... ah, I mean, Anne, how very
thoughtful of you." Sniffing the petit flowers, she smiled. "So,
how is your brother, Miss Phillipps? I do hope he is in health
since last Sunday?"

"Oh, indeed, Miss Holt." She sipped her coffee.

Aunt fidgeted for something more to say, "So, we shall
soon leave on holiday to France. Have you ever travelled on the
continent, Miss Phillipps?"

She drew back, fanning herself. "Dear me, yes, yes of
course. Why, we travelled quite extensively when I was a child,
near Anne's age."

I wrinkled my nose. *When I was a child, near Anne's age?
Humph.*

When Elly joined us, Miss Phillipps was speaking in such
a flutter that I forgot to warn Elly where *not* to sit, and she
chose the chair where the serpent cape was coiled. Sitting
down, she touched it and gasped. I giggled loudly. She
promptly tossed it onto Aunt's prized pink hydrangeas, where
it hung lifeless and stupid—its once vicious snarl, now a
twisted sort of rigour mortis. I burst out laughing. Miss
Phillipps' face became a kaleidoscope—mainly crimson.

Aunt Alice frowned. "Anne, advise Mary that lunch may be served—at once."

CHAPTER SIX

We arrived in France by steamship, and straightaway, Mr Phillipps hired two coaches to travel inland to Issor. One carriage was for us, and the other was for him and his sister. Abigail, our maid, rode atop with Gunderson, our groom.

Entering the small village of Oloron-Ste-Marie, we found a very nice inn. Aunt at once deemed it "clean and tidy, just the place to stay the night until resuming our journey. Before we had the luggage delivered to our rooms, Aunt insisted we consult the vicar—allowing him his opinion.

He nodded. "A fit and fine place to sleep."

Within a short while, we were escorted to our rooms. I thought it a novelty that I did not have to climb endless steps to my room. Aunt and Elly shared accommodations, and I lodged with Miss Phillipps, her brother took a room down the hall.

When first entering our room, its sweet, snug warmth welcomed me. The walls were whitewashed and clean. Sitting upon my bed, I found it soft; however, Miss Phillipps complained of hers being too hard.

"You may have mine, Miss Phillipps."

"Yes, thank you, Anne, I think I shall."

Pointing to the open doors, I commented, "I think I see a water garden just outside our room."

She sighed, tossing her bonnet onto her chair. "A frog pond, no doubt."

"Frogs?" Oh, how I loved slimy little creatures. I remembered hearing them croak when nearing Madame Pinchot's. "Indeed, Miss Phillipps. Come then, we shall see for ourselves."

"I think not," she snipped.

I hurried out into a beautiful garden and found that each room opened onto the same courtyard. Walking about, I met Aunt Alice.

"Oh, is this not quaint, Aunt?" I twirled around in the soft patches of sunlight beaming through the lush overhead grape vines. Great clusters of fruit, deep purple and plump, intertwined along the white wooden trellis atop and alongside the courtyard garden.

"Look there, Aunt Alice." We both stood in the centre of the garden staring up at the grapes. Picking a few, I popped one into my mouth. "They are delicious, Aunt."

"Be careful, Anne, they will stain your fingers and your mouth. And be mindful where you step." She plucked a few grapes from my hand. "Mmm, they are tasty. Even without my spectacles, I can see that."

"Aunt Alice, look there, a passage." I pointed. A glint of sunlight streamed over her shoulder.

We entered the moist stone tunnel and soon exited into an open meadow. Walking a little distance, we stopped amongst the tall field-grass. A spectacular valley spewed lush and green before us. Gnarly vines strung with processions of grapes entwined one another forming arrow-straight rows. Tall wispy-thin trees swayed as they lined the dusty blond roads; a soft, warm breeze feathered our lace collars.

"It is beautiful here in France, Aunt." I steadied my summer bonnet from loosening. Glancing at her, she had closed her eyes. Her sun-hat sat tight, its ribbons, tied loosely beneath her neck fluttered in the warm breeze. A strand of her thick red hair lay twined upon her shoulders.

Smiling at the charming scene, I fondled the curled spring of her hair. "Aunt," I giggled, "you are becoming someone quite different."

She inhaled with a sigh. "Mama could smell the seasons before they came."

From the corner of my eye, I watched her study the magnificent terrain before us. Standing in silence, I too, squinted at the purplish coloured mountains that loomed far off in the distance. The tall green field-grass swayed like rippled pond water. The sky was a stark, crystal blue such that an artist paints on canvas. White clouds, now stretched and pulled apart, left mere hints of their once voluminous canvas-dabbled assembly.

Aunt sighed again. "Aah, the clouds are scattered into a meagre flimsy scene, Anne, no cluster remaining." She took my chin. "So it is with families."

I lifted my eyes to the heavens. The sky was expansive, massive, and powerful. It made me dizzy. Closing my eyes, I steadied myself upon the spongy soil. I felt the soft grace of the field-grass brush my fingertips. "It is so peaceful, Aunt."

"Yes, quiet and beautiful."

Removing her bonnet, her lustrous red hair unfurled. Soft, shiny long curls brushed her waist as she tied the ribbons of her sun-hat to her wrist. She meandered into the field. Patches of red, blue, and white scattered far out and beyond— peasants farming, I supposed.

I returned to the courtyard to leave Aunt with her thoughts. I found Miss Phillipps sitting at a white wrought-iron summer settee taking tea. Enormous clusters of grapes dangled above her head.

"And what do you make of the fruit, Miss Phillipps?"

"Well, truly I say, I have never seen so many growing in such abundance."

"Have you eaten any?"

"Oh, dear me, no. I should think it improper—it would be stealing."

"Stealing?" I shook my head. "Indeed." She was more of a prig than I had first imagined. "Aunt and I ate an entire bunch."

"Indeed not, you silly girl," she scoffed.

I stuck out my purple tongue.

She glared at me. "Oh, forevermore, Miss Anne, how uncouth."

I was happy that she was repulsed by my childish antics. "Indeed," I giggled, "I will pick some for you." Standing on one of the chairs, I reached for a lovely clump when I heard a man's voice.

"Allow me, miss."

Turning, I found a handsome gentleman standing next to me. The colour of his hair reminded me of sand. He had soft dark brown eyes, his breath was sweet. He held out a white cloth and deposited the grapes onto it. Smiling, he handed them to me. I noticed Miss Phillipps' face gather into a pink bouquet. She was alive after all.

I curtsied. "Merci beaucoup, Monsieur."

Miss Phillipps smiled as she nodded to the gentleman. "Indeed, sir." She plucked a grape and popped it into her mouth, smiling up at him, her cheeks a warm pink.

Speaking English, the gentleman pointed at the grapes with his walking stick. "I have found the fruit here delicious and the wine spectacular." Glancing at me, he added, "Je ne parle pas francais, mademoiselle?"

"I understand it, but speak only a very little. I am a new student in French. Again, I do not speak it well."

He nodded. "Perhaps someday you shall." He bowed toward Miss Phillipps. "Allow me, mademoiselle. My name is Dr Hathaway, from London."

I smiled. "Sir, I am Miss Anne Holt."

Studying my face, he repeated, "Holt?"

Charlotte nodded. "Sir, I am Miss Phillipps, from London as well."

He glanced about the small courtyard. "Quaint little inn. I stay here now and again in my travels. He helped me down from the chair. "Au revoir, ladies." He bowed and left the courtyard.

"Imagine meeting a gentleman from London, Miss Phillipps."

"I suppose so."

"He is handsome." I sighed. Turning, I gestured about the area. "Not a frog in sight, miss."

Elly stepped out from her room. "Frogs?"

"Miss Phillipps does not care for the courtyard, Cousin Eleanor."

"Oh? And why is that, Miss Phillipps?"

Wrinkling her nose, she half-laughed. "It is just that I cannot imagine a French courtyard without at least *one* frog hopping about, which I detest."

Shrugging, Elly glanced at her watch pendant. "Dear me, I wonder what is keeping your aunt? She misplaced her spectacles, and I have been helping her search for them, but for the life of me, I can't find them."

"Oh, Aunt is just out taking the air. She doesn't need them. Come, let me show you where she is."

Pulling Elly along through the cool stone tunnel, we soon broke out into the warm, breezy meadow. "There," I pointed, "there she is," I shouted and waved.

"She won't be able to see you without her spectacles, Anne."

Aunt Alice turned toward us. Her hair and frock moved in unison with the grass and trees. Then, quite out of nowhere, a large black dog bounded up to her and paused by her side. I could hear her cries of excitement as she ruffled the dog's head. She threw a stick for it to fetch.

I thought of Misha, yelping in excitement. "Come, Cousin, let us go and pet the dog."

"I shall remain here, Anne. Big dogs frighten me."

Miss Phillipps remained alongside Elly, frowning. "I do not like big dogs either."

I shrugged. "Very well." Running to greet Aunt Alice, the dog broke from her side and ran to me. "Hello there, girl." I petted her soft, sun-warmed coat with great affection. She didn't look like Misha, but her smile was hers exactly—her eyes sparkled the very same.

"I cannot tell you how she found me," said Aunt catching her breath. "By all appearances, she is well cared for." The dog remained heeled by her side. "And look how obedient she is."

"She likes you, Aunt. Look how she chooses to sit at your feet; how she gazes up at you with such fondness."

As I was teasing Aunt over the obvious affections of the dog, I caught her gaze move over my shoulder.

"Dear me," she gasped and plunked on her bonnet, stuffing her hair up into it.

Turning to find the matter, I spied the kind English gentleman, Dr Hathaway, approaching. The dog whined, bolted from our side, and leapt by bounds toward him. We watched the hound frolic about him.

"Well now, certainly the animal belongs to the gentleman," said Aunt, squinting.

"Obviously, Aunt Alice, and lucky for the dog, such a pity if she were lost."

Dr Hathaway fastened a leash to the dog and left. Aunt and I met Elly at the stone tunnel.

Shielding her eyes from the sun, Elly shook her head. "That was a very large dog, Alice."

"It belonged to Dr Hathaway," I replied.

"Dr Hathaway?" Aunt's brows arched. "How could you know the owner?"

"He was kind enough to pick a bunch of grapes for us earlier, in the courtyard while you were in the meadow."

"Yes, indeed," said Miss Phillipps. "He seemed quite the gentleman."

"I have been gone but an hour and already you have made acquaintances?"

"Yes, Aunt, he was quite the gentleman and a handsome one." As we entered the courtyard, I added, "*And* he shares this quaint courtyard with us."

"Anne, without a proper introduction, it is wiser to remove yourself from such company." She eyed Miss Phillipps as if she should have known better.

"My very thoughts, indeed, Miss Holt," said Miss Phillipps, sniffing the air.

"Very well, Aunt, I shall be more mindful in the future."

"Eleanor, did you find my spectacles?"

"I did not, Alice."

Aunt shrugged. "Very well, then, I will search for them myself." She went back into her room.

Miss Phillipps watched her leave. "I must ready for supper, excuse me."

I waited until she left. I was anxious to share my plan with Elly. We both disliked the vicar, and I had hoped Aunt might find a gentleman of *our* choosing. "Elly, maybe the handsome gentleman, Dr Hathaway, will return when Aunt joins us for tea. I shall introduce him."

"Oh, Anne, I think not." Her nervous eye twitched.

I held my most pitiful look.

Dabbing her brow with her handkerchief, she looked at me. "Why the pouting?"

"I shudder to think of Mr Phillipps and his sister sharing Lesington Hall." Elly was about to laugh, but she caught herself.

"You are never one to mince words, Anne. That I share my opinion on who your Aunt chooses to marry would not be appropriate."

"But you are her closest confidant, Elly. You know what an ignoramus he is."

Trying to calm her twitching eye, she sputtered, "Ignoramus? Why, Anne, how unkind."

"But he is, Elly. He is not fit for Aunt's company, let alone to marry her. Have I not a claim to an opinion?"

"Dear me, Anne, you are much too young to have such strong opinions."

"But I am not too young to know she does not love him, nor do I think she will ever love him."

"Sad to say, Anne, love is not an essential ingredient in marriage. Besides all that," she sighed deeply, "you do not even know if this Dr Hathaway is married."

The sudden thought sank into my stomach like a sour plum. "Oh, I would know if he were, Elly. I would know."

* * *

It was unfortunate that my plans for a nuptial arrangement between Dr Hathaway and my aunt did not take place that very day, for we did not see hide nor hair of the handsome gentleman for the remainder of the afternoon. Besides that, I had to discover if he had a wife. Disappointed to be sure, I settled into watching Aunt Alice and the others play cards until my eyes waxed heavy and I went to bed—in the wrong one.

When Miss Phillipps came in, I was shaken awake and straightaway sent to my own bed. Falling back to sleep, I was once again nudged.

"Anne, you must wake up. I thought certain your aunt's maid would come to help me, but alas she has not. Now, be a good girl and untie my corset."

Yawning, I stumbled to her side. "Very well, miss."

"There now, fetch me a basin of water. There now, hand me the towel ..."

Just as I laid my head upon my pillow, I felt a nudge. "What is it?"

Aunt held a candle to my face. "It's first light, up you come, dear. It is rainless and quite a beautiful morning to travel."

"But Aunt, I have only now closed my eyes." Sliding deeper beneath the covers, I mumbled, "Surely you mistake the time of day."

"Come, come now. You have been sleeping since 10 o'clock last night. Awake now. I shall dress your hair. We must be sitting in the coach by half past, or the Phillipps' shall leave without us."

My eyes sprung open. "They would leave without us, Aunt?" Glancing over at the snoring Miss Phillipps, I nodded. "I shall dress right away, Aunt, and I shall come to your room to have Abigail comb my hair."

I tiptoed out of the room in silence, gently closing the door behind me, hoping Miss Phillipps would not waken.

Skipping down the hall, I thought of Elly's wonderful clock and cuckooed along at the thought of travelling with just Aunt and Elly.

All of a sudden the cribbage-faced vicar stuck his head out of his room. "Good morning, little girl, and where is my sister?"

"Back there." I pointed toward our room and continued skipping. "Cuckoo, cuckoo." I knocked on Aunt's door. "Hurry, open."

"Come," she called.

I rushed in, exhaling a great breath as I closed the door behind me.

"Well, dear, what was that all about?"

Glancing at the ceiling, I shrugged. Though I hated my hair braided for all the twisting, pulling and knots, it was faster which meant we would be on our way—without the Phillipps. "Braids, Aunt. Pretty braids wrapped and joined in the back with maybe a blue ribbon on the top?"

"Hmm, braids? You do not like braids, Anne."

I rubbed my nose. "This morning I do, Aunt."

"Very well."

Abigail began weaving my hair, and within a few minutes it was done.

Elly sipped her morning tea sitting by the window. "We should reach Issor by noon. That is, if we get off on time."

I began to hum. "Then we should leave now."

"Anne, was Miss Phillipps dressed when you left the room?"

"She was dressed in her nightgown, Aunt."

* * *

The morning dew made everything wet and drippy and cool. The sun planted its foot solid upon every dark corner, and in particular, I rightly supposed, Miss Phillipps' bed. Being the last to leave Aunt's room, I watched as her brother knocked loudly upon his sister's door. Lingering around the corner, I heard Miss Phillipps open the door, and I hurried away.

As Aunt, Elly and I waited in the coach, I offered, "I do not think they are coming. Perhaps we should move on, Aunt Alice."

Sitting atop the carriage, Abigail cried, "Here they come, Miss Holt."

Leaning her head out the window, Elly grunted. "Miss Phillipps looks a wee disconcerted, her curls are not quite so springy this morning."

I leaned back in my seat, shaking my head. Defeat at every turn. Folding my arms, I shrugged. "I was her maid last night, but decided this morning I would have nothing of the sort."

"Her maid? Whatever do you mean?" Aunt frowned.

"Miss Phillipps thought you would share Abigail with her; to help her undress, fetch her basin, water ... ."

"And you did all those things, Anne?"

Did all those things? My fingers felt as if they would bleed at any second. "All except wake her this morning, but she didn't tell me to."

"Indeed," Elly murmured, "no wonder she looks a fright."

The coachman stepped up into the carriage. "Shall we depart, madam?"

Just as our coach pulled away, I caught a glimpse of Dr Hathaway out walking his hound. "Look, Aunt." I pointed and smiled. "It is the handsome gentleman, Hathaway, and his dog."

Elly leaned forward, blocking Aunt's view. "Oh, my yes, indeed, I should say, fine looking."

Aunt tugged on her sleeve. "Elly, really now, that is most unladylike."

"I was commenting about the dog, Alice."

"Oh, right you are." Aunt squinted in his direction. "But Eleanor, you do not like dogs, and blast that I cannot see one foot without my spectacles."

"Well, Aunt. He is tall, with sandy-grey hair, brown eyes and very distinguished— unmarried," I would think.

Leaning back, Aunt spread her fan. "That is quite enough, young lady."

Elly was still gazing out the window. "It's not that I am not fond of dogs, Alice. It's that I sneeze so when around them."

"Oh, I am happy that I don't sneeze around them, Elly. Someday I wish to own a beautiful dog like Misha, or perhaps a beautiful black dog like the one in Grandmother Foyle's portrait."

Sitting awash in morning's warm yellows, Aunt glanced back at Dr Hathaway and his dog. "I once had such an animal."

"Did you, Aunt? And what did you call him?"

"She, I named her Holly. When she was a wee pup, I found her nestled in a holly bush. She died on the thirty-first of March. She would have been ten on the twelfth of October."

"I am sorry, Aunt," I said, pressing her hand.

* * *

As we travelled the dry, dusty roads—passing villages and farms—our guide Henri issued directions in a thick French accent. Henri was a wandering star, I fancied. He seemed happy and proud of his beautiful French countryside. I could hear him singing atop the carriage *'Aqueros mountagnes, qui tan haoutes soun, m'empechon de bede mas amous oun soun ... .'*

"Aunt," I exclaimed in awed wonder, "I remember Mama humming that very tune to me. And now, to hear the words ... ." Humming along, smiling I fondled the locket at my neck. *I miss you, Mama.*

All of a sudden, Henri's singing gave way to whistling and shouting.

"Aunt, what is he doing?"

Leaning forward, she shook her head. "He must be greeting friends or family. I cannot tell."

Our carriage stopped in front of a church, a Catholic church, Iglesia San Juan Evangelista. Henri helped us down. It felt good to stretch my legs and move about the breezy, dry air. I skipped along the cobblestones and found we were on a little hill. Spread out in front were clusters of red-headed little houses hugging the road as it wound in and around rolling hills at the base of the Great Pyrenees. Sheepherders waded through streams as they tended their flock. "So this is my ancestral village, Issor."

Now standing in the shadow of the church, I felt a chill and walked around the side of the small structure where I smelled the warmth of the dry grass and let the sun's hot rays settle upon me. The heat felt soothing, though Aunt would be displeased, for the rays were full upon my face now. She thought freckles were nasty marks, and my nose would be splattered with them, but I didn't care. I walked through a gate to find everyone surrounding a grave.

Coming upon the reverent gathering, I read the name chiselled on the headstone: Catherine Hourcatte Chaldu and then Jean Chaldu.

"Here lies your grandmother and grandfather, Anne." She touched another headstone. "Your aunts, uncles, cousins ... ."

"Oh, Aunt Alice, I wonder why Mama never told me." Glancing about, I found Marie Chaldu Bidalot, her husband Pierre Bidalot, their children, Simon, Philip, Marie. Domingo Hiriart was not here.

"Indeed." I said a prayer for each of them, that they were safe in heaven. Would Mama have preferred being buried with her family? No, she had loved Papa too dearly.

Mr Phillipps hemmed. "I did not realise you were of Catholic descent, Miss Anne, but then, of course, you are French, I might have known."

"Indeed, Mr Phillipps." Aunt straightened. "Anne's proud heritage begins with Saint Peter."

Miss Phillipps dabbed her brow with her handkerchief. "Well," she sniffed, "shall we move on?"

"Indeed we must." The vicar took her elbow and whisked her away to his waiting coach.

Leaving the churchyard, I noticed Henri sleeping atop our coach. I was excited to share my ancestry with him. "Monsieur Henri," I called, "Monsieur Henri ... ."

Springing from his post, he adjusted his soft cloth hat and rubbed his eyes. "Oui, mademoiselle?"

"Monsieur Henri, my mother was born here in Issor. My grandparents and cousins—all are buried here."

He puffed his chest. "Oh, yes there is one man I met from this little place long ago. A Monsieur Pierre Lonne ... a sheepherder." He glanced up at the mountain. "He's probably up there with his flock, and there is another family, a young girl, Josy Mondet."

I followed his gaze. "Oh, someday when I return I will search for them, Henri."

His eyes smiled; his manner became even more congenial. And when I told him I remembered my Mama singing the very song he had sung, he tweaked my nose. "Oui, mademoiselle," his eyes twinkled, "it is very old music—from the mountains."

Henri smiled. "The name Hiriart is Basque. You must visit Saint Pee Sur Nivelle, where many Basque were born."

"Oh, Henri I will ask Aunt if we will go there, I do not know of the Basques, Henri."

"They are an ancient people, long before any places had names. Many do not speak French, only their own words."

He pointed toward the Pyrenees and spoke in broken English. "We must go now. You chateau only a little distance away."

Mr Phillipps approached us with a furrowed brow. "No time for idle chit-chat. If we are to be settled at the chateau sometime today, we must move along."

Scurrying atop the coach, Henri stared straight ahead. "Oui, monsieur."

As we clopped and clattered along the dry, dusty road, barely more than a donkey path, I watched the church slowly fade into a soft little speck of grey stone, its steeple sharp and obediently pointing to heaven. Henri was singing again. I joined in, suddenly proud of my new-found French heritage, untouched by the vicar's rebuke.

Glancing down at my hands, I traced the long blue veins tunnelling toward each finger. The blood that filled those veins was the very same that had run in the veins of those buried in that old graveyard—my grandmother, grandfather, aunts, and uncles. At one time they danced and celebrated on that very square, in front of the church. Imagine the stories they told.

I sighed looking back at the church. There was no family left in Issor to greet me. No one I could run to, laugh with, hug or love. Their stories are silent.

CHAPTER SEVEN

It was only a little time until our carriage turned off the wider road onto the narrower, shrub-lined entry. Taking great care not to scratch his coach, the driver pulled the horses to a slow walk, but a bush must have scraped the cab, and he cursed—Aunt covered my ears.

"But, Aunt, it is in French, and they are not such bad words ... ."

"And how would you know that?"

As the carriage broke into a small meadow, I stood and leaned past Aunt to see the chateau. "Oh, it is so charming, Aunt."

Chateau Labrucherie was more than a great castle—almost grander than Lesington Hall's romantic balconies and mysterious turrets. I anticipated many wonderful hiding places in those cavernous towers. "Oh, I cannot wait to explore it."

"Perhaps to find a frog or two?" Elly waved away an errant gnat with a smirk.

Henri opened our door with a smile. "Qui, mademoiselles, welcome to Labrucherie." As if he owned the chateau, he bowed low. "Welcome."

After securing us, he half ran up the entry steps and disappeared. Soon servants scurried all about, helping with the trunks, bandboxes, and our packages. We were escorted up a long set of immaculate white stone steps to a grand porch which offered a magnificent view over the entire valley.

It was beginning to rain, and I took a chill. Once inside the chateau, I was in awe of its elegant French grandeur, the spaciousness and colourful warmth of the red carpets, shiny dark mahogany tables, and there in the wide vestibule, a blazing fire. I moved toward it when Aunt caught my arm, "Wait, Anne, someone is coming."

A short, heavy-set woman, of middle age, approached and spoke in a thick accent, I could barely understand her.

"Oui, Madame, I have been told by my nephew, Henri, that you are English ladies. You are very welcome. I am Madame Loubet, Housekeeper of Labrucherie."

Aunt nodded. "We are with another party as well, Madame Loubet. Mr Phillipps and his sister, Miss Phillipps, accompany us." She glanced at the open door. "They should be here any moment."

The housekeeper, her dark hair pulled tight beneath a clean, stark white cap, nodded. "Very well, Madame." A gold watch hung from a chain pinned high on her bodice. About her waist chimed a huge dangle of keys.

"In any case, Madame Loubet, we expect to stay a week," offered Aunt Alice speaking slowly and repeating herself often. "We would need three most excellent rooms—close together—and good accommodations for the servants."

Presently the vicar entered. His sister swooped in like a giant crane and fluttered to my side.

"Mr Phillipps," Madame Loubet smiled graciously, "Madame Holt informs me she will need three good rooms."

"Yes," interjected Miss Phillipps, "Miss Anne Holt and I," she took my hand, "are to lodge together."

"I am not a fussy lodger," added Mr Phillipps, "being a man of the cloth and of modest means."

The housekeeper nodded. "Oui, sir, I have just the room for you. Oui, Par sue vue pleas."

We followed her to the grand staircase and at the top—but a few doors down—were our rooms.

Madame Loubet fidgeted with her keys and gestured to Phillipps. "Monsieur, this way."

They disappeared up another flight of steps.

Aunt first inspected her room then followed to find Ellie's room to her liking as well. My feathered friend and I entered *our* room. Miss Phillipps straightaway rang for fresh water, cleaner towels, a softer pillow … .

One maid arrived to start the fire, another unpacked our things. Miss Phillipps instructed the hotel maid to have her things pressed … before supper.

Slipping out the door, I hurried to Aunt Alice's room and tapped.

"Come," I heard her soft, familiar voice.

Glancing around, I rather liked her accommodations. "Aunt, how do you find your room?"

"It is nice enough, Anne." She exhaled. "However, I do hope Miss Phillipps is kinder toward you, dear. Do forgive me."

"Indeed, Aunt, nothing to forgive. She is not of your doing."

"Well, Anne, I know you will make the best of it."

"I suppose I must." Glancing around her room, I sighed. "Miss Phillipps has already ordered fresh water, fresh towels and more fluffy pillows."

"Yes, I do believe she would."

"She acts very rich, Aunt, but her brother says he has very little."

"They did have a great deal of wealth at one time, Anne. His older brother, however, squandered the family fortune. Miss Phillipps was forced from his protection to the austerity of her brother's parsonage. You will keep this intimate conversation to yourself, Anne."

"Yes, Aunt, I will." Walking about Aunt's room and inspecting each closet, I settled at the window, the rain began to slow. I felt a pang of pity for Miss Phillipps. Gazing out, I sighed, "Aunt, I would much rather have been poor first, rather than rich first and then poor."

"I quite agree, Anne. But for my part, I would much rather be born rich and remain rich."

"I suppose I must return to my room and claim what little space is left. I do hope I am allowed to sleep in one of the beds."

Aunt laughed and kissed my forehead. "You will find your way, Anne."

"But will Miss Phillipps?"

* * *

"Oh, there you are," Miss Phillipps cackled. "I wondered where you ran off to, Anne. Come now and fluff your pillows. I ordered them special for you."

"Thank you, Miss Phillipps, how thoughtful of you."

"Yes, I suppose I am ... thoughtful."

"Not too thoughtful, though." I patted my pillow, set it cosy against the headboard and watched her face turn pink. I was hoping she would inquire into my meaning, but she did not.

"Well, I am famished. I do wonder when we shall eat." She plopped down on her bed and rubbed her stomach.

"You may eat any time you wish, Miss Phillipps."

"You may call me Charlotte. After all, we are friends now—roommates that we are."

I thought her a different sort of species, for she had often taken the liberty of addressing me as Anne. "Then I am expected to say you may continue to call me Anne?"

"Well ... ." she stammered, fanning herself, "what does it matter?"

Listening to her stomach growl, I sighed. "Come, we must go find something to eat."

"Yes, I am really very hungry, but we must first wait for your aunt and my brother."

"Oh, come along. They will be forever situating themselves."

Walking sensibly down the hall, I noticed how Charlotte swooshed alongside me. "You walk as Madame Bovary would have walked, Charlotte."

Her mouth gaped. "Madame Bovary?" Frowning, she whispered, "Anne, you must not say such things."

"And why is that?"

"Why, Madame Bovary was a ... a naughty woman."

"So, you have read the book?"

"I have *heard* of the book, Anne." She pursed her lips.

"All the same, I think you walk as she would."

"I walk nothing of the sort." Her face turned sour.

Coming to a great hall, I thought of Franklin and the mysterious passageways at Lesington Hall, some even with pictures hanging on them—secret doors that he pushed open to my delight. Surely Labrucherie would have the same.

Madame Loubet caught me pushing against one of the walls.

"Mademoiselles, may I help you?"

"Oui, Madame Loubet," I said, righting a statue I had tipped. "We wish for breakfast."

Frowning, she shrugged. "You cannot walk through walls to find breakfast."

I elevated my chin. "At Lesington Hall I did it every day."

Charlotte Bovary shook her head.

We followed the housekeeper into a spacious dining room. The soft rain slid down the mullioned windows. Tables draped in elegant lace stood near a large carved marble fireplace, blazing bright. We were seated. I spotted two young gentlemen dining alone a few tables away beneath one of many sparkling chandeliers. There was another couple just behind us.

"I shall order for us, Anne. You are much too young to know of these things."

"Well, I knew enough to find the dining room."

"Indeed, pushing walls, nearly upsetting Venus."

"Venus?"

"The statue, Anne." She squirmed in her seat trying to settle. "You gave a fright to Madame Loubet. You would do well to listen to me in future."

I watched as she ordered this and ordered that, prepared this way and that way, poured this way and poured that way.

"Those gentlemen are watching you, Charlotte."

"They are?" She blushed as she peeked over her menu at them.

"I think they find you enchanting."

"Really?"

I nodded. "Perhaps they watched you enter. You know the way you walk."

She glared at me.

"I am only teasing, Charlotte. You must learn to laugh more. You are far too stuffy, and with little reason for it."

"You have an impertinent air, Anne."

"Impertinent air?" I shrugged. "Well, I suppose that is not so terribly bad."

"It is not so terribly good, either." She huffed and bit into her soufflé.

"They are still watching you, Charlotte."

Shaking her head, she would not look their way.

"Yes, they are definitely intrigued."

Peeking around our candle centrepiece, she spied them. "Well, they are not watching me now."

"But just wait ... now, now Charlotte, look up at them and ... smile."

She did.

They stood and walked toward us. I giggled. As they neared our table, Charlotte set down her fork demurely, fluttered her eyelashes, and smiled up at them. They passed us by for the couple sitting behind us—old friends apparently meeting, of all places, in the South of France.

"Oh, well, Charlotte, forgive me. I thought they were staring at you."

She finished off her soufflé, drank her tea, and silent as a dormouse, stood. "I will return to my room."

"Well, it was not that you are not attractive enough, Charlotte." I tried to soothe her wounded, snubbed feelings.

"Really, Anne, I would rather not discuss it. I don't think they were watching me at all."

"You think I made it up, then?"

"I believe you find delight in tormenting me."

"If you were not so prudish, Charlotte."

"Prudish? Earlier I walked like Madame Bovary, and now you call me prudish. I can scarcely wait for another insult."

"Let me see ... ."

"Keep them to yourself, if you please."

"But if I promise to say only nice things from now on?"

"You are too silly, Anne."

We entered our room, and I sat on the edge of my bed. "From now on I will say only nice things about you ... if I can find any."

Instead of blushing and hissing at me, Charlotte laughed. It was a spontaneous, happy laugh. Tickling my sides, she cried, "You are, indeed, a wicked little imp!"

"You see, Charlotte," I cried, "you can laugh, after all."

There came a knock at our door. "Come," I called, still giggling.

Aunt Alice and Elly entered. Looking surprised at our jovial setting, Elly smiled. "So, we have interrupted a joke, perhaps?" She sauntered about. "This is a nice room, Anne."

"Oh, yes, Cousin Eleanor, *we* find it quite acceptable."

Charlotte fastened a few stray hairs into her bun. "Yes, Miss Holt, it is a fine room." She nodded. "And how do you find your accommodations?"

"Oh, much like yours," said Aunt still perusing our room.

Elly glanced at me. "I am famished. Come, you must eat with us. You both must be starved."

"Oh, I am not hungry," I said, patting my stomach.

"Why, yes," said Charlotte. "I should love to come along, though I will have only tea."

"Very well," said Aunt looking at me, "we will leave you, then. If you change your mind, Anne, come."

The hotel maid entered as they left. Watching as she brushed the ashes on the hearth, restacked the wood, and kindled the fire, I commented, "You fix a delightful fire, miss."

Pretending to understand me, she curtsied. "Oui, mademoiselle, merci." She bowed from the room, smiling. I caught her glance just before she closed the door, and I waved.

Even though the fire caught on quite nicely, the room seemed somehow vacant and hollow. Opening the wardrobe door, I found hanging on one hook Charlotte's meagre wardrobe and her tattered and oft mended stockings. About halfway down, sitting on a sturdy, but stained shelf, sat the chamber pot. It was white with blue flowers. I did not want to pee in such a lovely pot. To my dismay, I found that the washbasin and pitcher sitting on the toilet-table were of the same pattern. "Oh, dear me," I said aloud. "What if, in my sleep, I use the wrong one?"

Hearing a clap of thunder, I retreated to the bed and climbed atop. My eyes felt heavy. Curling into a ball, I reached for a cover and watched as lightning zigzagged about the room—flashing on the walls. I lay back, adjusting the soft, fluffy pillows, and within seconds I drifted off to sleep. When I awoke, the room was dark. My fire had been tended again. I was warm and comfortable. The mantle-clock chimed six, the curtains were still open, and I could see on my balcony a torch burning. The rain had stopped. Before splashing my eyes, I made certain—yes, I was using the correct bowl.

Opening the balcony door, I stepped out into the warm evening air. Glancing over the rough, shiny wet stone balustrade, I saw, to my astonishment, Dr Hathaway and his dog, they were down one level. "Bonsoir, monsieur." I waved and smiled. Remember me, sir?"

"Bonsoir, Mademoiselle Holt."

The dog's ears perked at my voice as she whined and jumped.

"What is her name, sir?"

"Berry, Miss Holt."

"Hello, Berry girl." The dog barked up at me. "She is a beautiful dog, sir."

"Thank you," he replied as she tugged at her leash. It began to drizzle again. "It rains like this at home." He smiled up at me, his eyes blinking from the rain.

"I say it does, sir. Aye, it does remind one of England, a very little bit, though."

"Oh, a very little bit, Miss Holt."

Berry began to pull him away. Chuckling, he called up, "I must go now; please excuse me."

Leaning over the railing, I watched them leave.

"To whom are you speaking, Anne?" said Aunt as she joined me.

"Dr Hathaway, Aunt. But he had to go." I motioned to the level below.

"I see." She glanced over the balustrade. "Really, Anne, I must warn you about speaking with strangers."

"I am sorry, Aunt Alice. I think I startled him by hovering over his head. I merely bid him good evening."

"All the same, child."

Elly came through my room and out onto the balcony. "Well, here you are, both of you." Squinting in the rainy mist, she adjusted the scarf around her head. "It is near seven and time for supper. Shall we go into the dining room?"

"Oh, yes, now I *am* hungry, Elly." I glanced around. "Where is Charlotte?"

"She decided to remain with her brother. He met some colleagues when we were at lunch this afternoon. They are in the library."

* * *

Descending the grand staircase, I noticed an old-fashioned chandelier with wax candles dripping, pooling on the floor. "Oh, Aunt, do be careful." I picked a dab from her shoulder.

"Oh, a sign of luck, Alice," said Elly.

With a wry smile, Aunt returned, "I am glad to hear it, Eleanor."

"A sign of luck, Elly?" I had never heard that before.

Continuing down the steps, Aunt shook her head. "Anne, pay her little mind, she made it up."

Henri met us at the dining room entrance and held the door open. "Bonsoir, mademoiselles, bon appetit."

It was the same room where Charlotte and I had eaten breakfast, but this evening it was empty. "There are no diners, Aunt."

"It could be that we are early," said Elly.

Sniffing the air, I closed my eyes. "Mmm, something good is simmering."

Henri led us toward the large hearth. "Perhaps you would feel more comfortable by the fire."

Carved into the oak mantelpiece, a ferocious wolf-like creature stared at us. Passing it by, I shuddered as its eyes seemed to follow my every move. We sat. Two long loaves of hard-crust bread wrapped loosely in white linen lay next to a shiny silver compote. Our waiter with a crisp neatly folded white napkin draped over his arm bowed and prepared to pour wine.

Aunt covered her glass. "Pardon, we wish to drink only tea." She glanced at Eleanor—unless *you* wish a wine, of course?"

Elly nodded to the waiter. "A small sip, s'il vous plaît."

"Qui, Madame." He poured an ample glassful, to her obvious delight.

"Careful, Eleanor, you will become a wild imbiber."

"I hardly think under *your* watchful eye, Alice."

"Anne?"

"Non, merci, Aunt. I prefer eating grapes to drinking them."

Turning toward Elly, Aunt nodded. "You see, what a wise young lady ..."

As if struck dumb, Aunt's words froze; her cheeks burned red. Fumbling with her handkerchief, she looked down. "Anne ... Eleanor ... please move the candelabra. Will you? The fumes are most annoying." Removing her spectacles, she dabbed at her eyes.

"Aunt, is there something in your eye?" I took her chin and examined them. "Nothing, Aunt. I cannot see one thing."

Hearing someone approach, I glanced up and found Dr Hathaway walking past. I smiled at him.

He nodded, "Good evening, Miss Holt."

"Good evening, Doctor." Turning back to Aunt Alice, I said in a loud tone in hopes he would stop. "Oh, Aunt, perhaps some drippy hot wax has found its way into your eye."

He stopped and turned back. "Is there a problem?" he asked. "I am a physician ..." He looked concerned. Taking Aunt's chin, he gaped. "Miss Alice Holt?"

Aunt blinked several times and drew back. "Anthony ... Hathaway?"

"Alice Holt? *Miss* Alice Holt?"

"The very one, sir," she said.

His voice softened, "Why, it has been many years, Alice."

I was astounded at their familiarity. He was calling Aunt by her given name, and she returned the intimacy. I settled back and watched as she dabbed her eyes, behaving quite uncharacteristically nervous.

In a near whisper, she gestured with her hand. "Dr Hathaway, this is my niece, Miss Anne Holt."

He looked startled. "Your niece? Why, one would think she was your daughter, Alice, she is your very image."

"Thank you, sir." Aunt smiled at me.

I smiled at Aunt, pleased all the more, for I thought her beautiful.

Elly sipped her wine, watching.

Still near whispering, Aunt introduced Elly. "Anthony, this is my dear cousin, Mrs Eleanor Mills. Do you remember her?" Aunt dabbed her eyes again and took a deep breath. "Well, perhaps not. It has been a long time."

Elly extended her hand. "No, sir, I do not believe we have met. Though, I have been at Lesington Hall for a number of years." She glanced at Aunt. "Before that, I was a governess. Our family is a small one, sir. After my dear cousin Holt past on, I remained on with Alice."

"My belated condolences at the passing of your father, Alice, and your beloved mother," he said solemnly.

Behind his kind regards, he seemed familiar regarding our family, and yet Elly did not know him.

Aunt held his gaze. "Thank you, Anthony."

He turned to Elly. "Do you still teach, madam?"

"My, no, sir, I am now retired, and we travel about very much," said Elly, smiling.

Dr Hathaway studied Elly's face. "Indeed, I recollect seeing you at the Abbeville Inn where we lodged last night." He smiled and nodded at me.

Elly nodded. "Why, yes, we were there."

He sighed deeply. "I was busy with my disobedient dog."

"Oh, yes, yes, the very large black one."

"Indeed, she is a handful, madam." As if trying to make additional conversation, he continued on, "Tell me, Mrs Mills, do you now instruct Miss Anne?"

I sat up. "Oh, indeed, sir, Cousin Eleanor wishes to polish me to gleam."

Elly laughed. "A gleam? Dear me, what a thought."

"Anthony," said Aunt, "Mrs Mills does very well at instructing Anne, being an excellent governess. But in actuality, she is more my companion and confidant. It's the season of her life to retire and enjoy travelling."

"Indeed, the august season of my life," replied Elly as she motioned for the waiter to bring more wine.

"August season? There now, Mrs Mills, you will have many more seasons before august."

"Thank you, sir. I pray so," she said looking smug at the compliment.

He turned to Aunt. "Alice, are you staying here long?"

"We are staying the week, Anthony."

"I see. I am travelling from holiday in Marseille and on to Paris tomorrow, a physician's conference."

I could not help but become infatuated with the man. He was kind and exceedingly handsome. His hands were soft, well-formed, and expressive. I had never seen Aunt so taken or flustered before. Elly and I, of course, knew at once of her obvious affections for the gentleman. We simpered and smirked in her direction.

Dr Hathaway made more idle conversation, but soon seemed to run out of anything more to say. Aunt, still in a fluster, could not join sentences long enough to hold a gnat's wing from flapping, but I saved the day. "Sir, you are quite welcome to dine with us."

He smiled. "How very kind of you, Miss Holt." Returning his gaze to Aunt, he shook his head. "Thank you, but I am not travelling alone. I really must go." He nodded to Elly and me and back again to Aunt Alice, but she still didn't say a word. "Well, I must go now." He straightened. "Alice, I will be in the next dining room if you experience any more trouble with your eyes."

Standing erect, he glanced once at us and then again to Aunt Alice.

I felt sad that he would be leaving and I kicked Aunt's foot hoping she would say something. He nodded again to Elly and me, and then to Aunt. "Alice, my practice is still in London, if you are ever in need." He bowed.

I kicked Aunt's leg again, but she could only say—in a whisper, I might add, "But of course, Anthony, if there is a need, bonsoir." Her eyes never left his.

He remained a few seconds holding her gaze and finally nodded. "Bonsoir."

I waited until he quitted the room. "Aunt, why did you let him go? Why didn't you insist he stay?" I glanced at Elly for help, but she was busy pouring another glass of wine, the bottle was now near empty.

Aunt Alice grabbed Elly's glass, and in one gulping motion, finished it off.

My jaw dropped. "Aunt, I am amazed." Turning toward Elly, I added, "And Elly, you drank the entire bottle?"

Rolling her eyes, she patted my hand. "Not all of it, dear. Not *all* of it. Besides, it is only fermented grape juice and nothing more. It rather soothes my nerves. Altogether, I would not put too much into it."

"I do not understand, Elly."

"Someday you will, Anne."

I shrugged and turned to Aunt. "Please excuse me, I want to find that other dining room. I want to see who Dr Hathaway is dining with." I smiled. "Do you think he's married, Aunt?"

She blushed. "It matters not, Anne. Please sit down. Do not embarrass me by snooping."

I knew very well she was just as inquisitive as I. "I shan't be long."

I found Henri in the vestibule. "Monsieur Henri, I have been told there are two dining rooms in Chateau Labrucherie. We are in the larger one?"

He nodded. "Oui, mademoiselle."

"Is there a proper way to look into the smaller dining room without being seen?"

Henri seemed puzzled, but after a few seconds smiled. "Oui, this way if you please."

Following him back into the dining room, I smirked at Aunt and Elly as we hurried by, waving before disappearing into a side room. We were in the kitchen, Henri nodded to the chef.

"Mademoiselle, this way." He walked down a small hallway. "We do not *spy* as you say, but only watch the tables to anticipate needs, nothing more." He bowed, and leaning into the wall, pushed up a tiny wooden knob. He put his eye to the hole and peeped. "Ah-ha, very good. If you will, mademoiselle, see for yourself."

I peeked and found him sitting with a party of distinguished-looking gentlemen. "Oh, that's good. At least Dr Hathaway isn't with a lady."

"No, mademoiselle, he is forever alone. The gentlemen with him are doctors."

"You know them then, Henri?"

"Oui, I do. They travel here often, and we are grateful."

"Grateful?"

"Oui, mademoiselle, we are grateful that if my family is sick, Dr Hathaway makes them well."

"I see, and you say he is forever alone? He is not married?"

"I do not know so much of his personal life, mademoiselle." He dabbed his brow.

"Oh, Henri, please. He is an old acquaintance of my Aunt's. And she has not seen him in a very long while. We, I, was curious if he was married and nothing more."

"Hmm, very well. He say to me, one day his wife die, mademoiselle—but he have two sons."

* * *

Swooshing back into my chair next to Aunt, I had much to tell them. "He was not dining with a lady."

Aunt inhaled deeply. "Indeed, Anne. What a little spy you are."

"Well?" inquired Elly, "Is that all you learned?"

"His wife ..."

"There you are," said Mr Phillipps holding Charlotte's arm as they approached our table. He nodded. "Charlotte and I first knocked upon everyone's door and found no one at home." He chuckled.

"What is the humour in that?" I asked.

Aunt stepped on my toe. "Well, Mr Phillipps," she gestured, "do join us now."

"Very well." He motioned for the waiter to bring more chairs. Before sitting, he eyed the empty wine bottle, Elly's smudged glass, her purple lips ...

Charlotte stood like a little statue next to him, boredom written on her pale face. Earlier she accompanied him to meet a few of his colleagues. I wondered if she found any of them handsome. "So, Charlotte, tell me, were there any *particular* colleagues of your brother's that you found to your liking?"

The vicar hemmed, his pink, sleep-caked eyelids squinted as he leaned into me. "The gentlemen are professors of music, Miss Anne. It was not for my sister to enjoy their company." Adjusting his tight cravat, he continued, "I found an excellent book in which she became instantly engrossed."

"Ugh!" I clapped my hand over my mouth, but too late.

"Anne," said Aunt, "that is quite enough." Turning to Charlotte, Aunt smiled. "And what book did he set you down with, dear?"

"Ah ..." she replied, blushing, "I do not remember, exactly."

CHAPTER EIGHT

Just moments before the cock crowed, I was awakened by Charlotte's snores. She drew in great gasps and then rattled off, drew in, then rattled off ... dear me. I tiptoed to her bed, being careful not to disturb her and studied her nose. Just as I was peering up her nostrils, her eyelids flew open.

"What?" She sputtered, sitting up still flustered. Drawing the coverings to her chin, she huffed. "What are you staring at?"

"There is something stuck up your nose." Rubbing my eyes awake, I frowned. "Such a racket, you woke me."

"I did not hear one thing." Yawning, she dangled her bare feet over the side. "What time is it?" She sniffed the air. "I smell coffee."

"Perhaps a breakfast tray is coming."

"But we did not order a breakfast tray, Anne."

While I slipped on my frock, Charlotte pulled the window curtains aside. Squinting in the bright morning light, she sighed. "I suppose it is time to rise anyway. It is good you have not left me on my own, Imp. I cannot fasten my corset without help." She brushed back her long yellow hair. "There now, pour my water ... ." She caught herself. "Forgive me. I shall pour my own water. But, please, Anne ... will you help me dress?"

I studied her newfound politeness. No, I thought, it was not kindness, but an awakening of some sort of spirit, though I was not at all sure she would not go back to her snippy ways. I would, nonetheless, help her. "I will, of course."

"And then I shall help you," she said.

"But I am dressed."

She held the hand-mirror to my face and smirked. "What about your hair?"

"Hmm, very well," I conceded.

After Charlotte had smoothed and braided my hair, and while she fussed with her face, I ventured out onto the balcony. Morning shadows of cool purple stretched to the balustrade where I stood. Rubbing the flesh bumps on my arms, I chattered aloud, "Ooh, it is too cool; the sun will not reach this side until noon."

Glancing down, I hoped to see Dr Hathaway's dog, but they must have already departed. I ran back to my room and grabbed my parasol and wrap. "I will first find Aunt and then return to corset you, Charlotte."

Hearing carriage wheels crunching over the pebbly roadway, I walked around the balcony and to the great promenade out front. The sun, full on this side of the Chateau, felt soothing on my shoulders. At least I had remembered to bring my parasol. Aunt would be pleased.

"Anne."

Turning at her familiar voice, I waited for Aunt Alice to join me.

"I spotted your parasol, dearest." She nodded. "Up early, I see." She inhaled, sampling the fresh, crisp air. "I have been out taking the air this morning. Have you seen Cousin Eleanor?"

"No, Aunt Alice, I just got here. But the table outside our rooms is set for breakfast."

"So I noticed, Anne." Squinting into the bluish-yellow sunrise, she said, in a disappointed tone, "I was hoping to eat, again, in the dining room."

And see Anthony once more, I mused. The sound of a carriage moving below our terrace piqued my curiosity. Peering over the railing, I watched it amble out onto the main road.

"Pity." I exhaled, certain it was Dr Hathaway's.

"Pity? Pity for what, Anne?" Aunt braced herself on the balustrade, never taking her eyes from his carriage.

"Dr Hathaway always being alone."

"And how would you know such things?"

"Henri told me last night, in the kitchen. He said the doctor travels here often and helps the sick. He travels alone, or with other physicians, Aunt."

Coming up behind me, Elly spun my parasol.

I giggled. "I knew it was you, Elly."

"You are a natural born magician, my dear."

"Careful, Eleanor, she'll make you disappear."

Giggling, I thought of Madame Pinchot.

Elly held her head. She looked a little peaked. "Oh, if she could only make my head disappear."

Aunt smiled smugly. "Fermented grape juice will do that, Eleanor."

"I had a few sips, Alice. Let us not make a fuss over little things."

"As you will, Eleanor."

We glanced out again, watching Dr Hathaway's carriage wiggle its way through the narrow opening and disappear into the thick grove of poplar trees.

Following our gaze, Elly asked, "Did you see someone off?"

I sighed. "No, we were just watching Dr Hathaway's carriage amble out of our lives." Spinning my parasol, I watched the fringe flap, and then I flapped, "Probably forever."

"Indeed." Elly stole a glance at Aunt Alice's sad face.

* * *

Returning to my room, I helped Charlotte dress. "Oh, you look charming, Miss Charlotte." I lied.

She twirled about the small room. "I have only two frocks." Picking at the folds in her skirt, she offered with a sad sigh, "I have mended this one so often."

"I wouldn't have known unless you told me where." One would have to be half-blind not to have noticed. Though my voice was most sincere, my eyes must have belied my words.

"Here," she gathered up her skirt, "you see ..." She glanced up at my examining eye and laughed. "Oh, you are a clever little imp to expose my vanity."

Feeling the truest sort of sincerity in her manner, I took her hand. My heart went out to her; this time I was sincere. "I would not call it vanity. You simply do not wish to look slovenly."

"Indeed." She nodded.

"After breakfast, we are to go to the famous Issor Music Festival. Aunt says the musicians are some of the finest in the world." I felt a chill and sunk back into the easy chair by the fire. "I have been told it's held outside." I chaffed my hands at the fire.

"Outside?" Miss Charlotte frowned. "Oh, I pray no rain. I do not have a decent umbrella to my name."

I wanted to say something to cheer her, part of which was not so cheery. "Your brother will accompany us."

"Oh," she murmured and lowered her head.

"But," I infused with a happy note, "he has invited those two handsome gentlemen you met most recently to come along."

She lit up with a smile. "Really, Anne?" Then she sobered. "Oh, what does it all matter, I am quite the bore."

"Oh, if you would shine more, I believe they would find you less boring."

Looking into the mirror, she shook her head. "Shine?"

"Well, yes Charlotte. You ought to shine more and smile. Intrigue them. You appear much too haughty and with little reason for it."

"It is an air, Anne. Ladies must carry themselves with a certain mysterious air."

"But you seem altogether too mysterious; your aim is quite off."

She snuffed her candle and walked to the window. Closing her eyes, she asked, "And how should you know of such things?"

I didn't have the heart to tell her what a spinster she looked and acted like. Her brother was well pleased with her dowdy appearance. But I suspected she savoured the attentions of men. "Well, I have never seen a gentleman on your arm."

"Indeed," she said tersely, "who should want me?"

Handing her my prized lace handkerchief, I put my arms around her waist. "I am sorry if I hurt your feelings, Charlotte. But ..."

"No, no, little imp, it is my false pride." Her voice faltered. "We were rich once. Very wealthy, but now no man will look my way. I must remain at my brother's beck and call. I have no place else to go, or I shall starve."

Taking her hand, I placed it to my heart. "I understand, Charlotte. If it weren't for my aunt, I would have nowhere to live either." I patted her shoulder and kissed her cheek. "Come now," I led her to the door, "let us eat a hearty breakfast, go to the Music Festival and listen to music—that will cheer you."

"I used to play the piano. It was my passion, but Clarke sold it." She sighed deeply. "But I am grateful for the provisions he affords me."

Understanding perfectly, I nodded, remembering well the favours of Mr O'Leary and the sickening letters I was forced to write him. Oh, yes, thanking him for our bread and butter, all the while eating my supper in revulsion. "Oh, yes, the unfortunate business of preventing starvation, Charlotte."

"Yes." She nodded. "I steal away at night to play the piano in the church. Imagine, at one time I preferred music even to food."

"Well, now that you prefer food to music, you may come to Aunt Alice's and play her piano anytime you wish."

"Mmm." Taking my chin in her hand, she smiled. "That is kind of you, Anne. Thank you. I should wonder, however, if your Aunt would take to such an idea." She shook her head. "No, it is not an easy thing to adjust from abundance to nothing."

"I would find that a very cruel misfortune, Charlotte."

She stared at me for a moment. "Yes," she tilted her head slightly, "I believe you would." Wiping her eyes, she hugged me. "You are more than kind, Anne. Can you forgive me for being so rude to you?"

"It was only because I did, indeed, torment you in return, Charlotte." Giggling, I added, "And ... you never walked like Madame Bovary."

* * *

Entering the thick-treed park, we spotted the Issor musicians tuning their instruments. They were sitting on a most unusual, but very pretty octagon shaped stage. It was open on all sides, with white lattice pillars supporting grapevines that had grown quite wild. The vines had reached atop the roof and dangled about each side.

Mr Phillipps chatted amicably with Aunt and Elly as we were escorted along the grass. We were situated in the first row, directly in front of the stage. Our chairs were lovely white wicker.

"Oh, how fortunate, Aunt, that I do not have a fat head in my view."

The vicar frowned and removed his hat. "Indeed, Miss Anne."

Aunt was quiet; Elly was quiet; the vicar squirmed in his seat, glancing now and again at Charlotte's mended dress. The poor dear, forced to wear such tatters. Though his trousers were shiny, *he* did not suffer from bumpy knots and threadbare cuffs. Charlotte kept her chin high.

Glancing around, I spied the vicar's gentlemen friends coming toward us. I waved excitedly.

"Anne," Aunt Alice tugged at my sleeve, frowning. "Waving in such grand excitement is unbecoming of a lady."

"Oh, forgive me, Aunt."

Charlotte nudged me. Cupping her mouth, she whispered, "Thank you, Imp."

The music was quite nice. The mild afternoon belied the bilious clouds that were gathering. Now and again a bright splash of sunshine spurted, washing everything a warm yellow. Sunbeams pierced the thick grapevines and illuminated the shiny oboe one young musician played. A patch of soft yellow lay gently on the black shoulder of his waistcoat.

At the conclusion, the orchestra bowed to our warm applause, and we silently watched them pack their instruments. One by one, they removed from the stage.

I had witnessed Charlotte's sway to the music; heard her silent hum; her ladylike clap at its end. Taking her hand, I pulled her to the stage. "Look, the piano is abandoned, Charlotte. I would love to hear you play."

Her eyes darted to her brother who had turned away chatting with Aunt and Elly. She took in a great breath and smiled. "Very well, Imp."

Laying her hands atop the ivory, brown-streaked keys, she looked heavenward and smiled softly. I glanced over at Mr Phillipps, who was now watching us—his pinched face was red. Aunt and Elly looked pleased. I sat next to Charlotte on the piano bench as she began playing.

Her music mixed beautifully with layers of sweet-scented French country air. Tears streamed down her face; never once opening her eyes, she played from her heart. Even though her summer shawl fell to the floor, she played on. Finally finishing, she lifted her fingers and turned to me. "Thank you, Anne." She kissed my cheek.

No doubt mesmerised by her beautiful playing, the audience had returned. Applause rang out.

"Really, Miss Phillipps," clapped Aunt, "that was quite beautiful."

Professor Mandeville, one of the gentleman friends of the vicar's added, "Mozart would be proud, Miss Phillipps." His face shone. Turning to the vicar, he commented, "Why, Phillipps, you failed to tell me your lovely sister played so excellently."

"I, I ..." he mumbled, "I suppose it has always been her passion."

Professor Mandeville continued to clap as he returned his attention to Charlotte. "Obviously as religion has been yours, sir."

"Mr Phillipps, why, I do not believe you have a piano in the parsonage," said Aunt. "How does she practice?"

"She cannot, Aunt," I said, "her brother sold ... ." I covered my mouth. Charlotte gasped. I prayed for a diversion, rain came to mind. As if on cue, it began to drizzle.

"Oh, dear me." Charlotte fretted. "I didn't bring my umbrella."

"Not to worry," said Professor Mandeville as he deftly stiff-armed his umbrella." He smiled as it whooshed open into a cavernous black, snuggling place. "This way, Miss Phillipps, allow me to escort you to your carriage, if you please."

The vicar touched Aunt's elbow. "Humph, I will speak with Charlotte on her lack of propriety." He shook his head. "Imagine exhibiting in so public a place. I have forbidden her playing in church for such self-aggrandising." He hurriedly pushed open his umbrella. "Come along now, the carriages are waiting."

Aunt's face sobered, she did not stand under his umbrella. Her voice was firm, "Really now, Mr Phillipps, I find nothing in her display to suggest any sort of wrongdoing."

I was very proud of Aunt at that moment—sassing the vicar. "It's raining on your hat, vicar," I giggled. Elly took my hand, pinching my thumb. "Ouch."

We all scurried to our respective carriages as Charlotte and Professor Mandeville made their way to her brother's waiting carriage—by the longer pathway, I noted.

Watching the couple hunch close together, I remarked to Aunt Alice, "Professor Mandeville carries an awfully small umbrella, Aunt."

Elly leaned over my shoulder and whispered, "He is only making it seem so."

* * *

When we arrived back at the Chateau Labrucherie, Aunt rang to have tea in her room. Elly wanted to roam about the many shops. The rain had stopped, and through Aunt's window, as we sipped our tea, a beam of streaming gold sunlight carried onto our table. Millions of tiny yellow-white dust specks floated within the narrow beams. Enchanted at their odd beauty, I stuck my finger into one of them—seeming to disrupt the flecks, but alas, they milled around my finger.

I caught Aunt Alice watching me. I smiled at her pretty blue eyes, her silky red hair glistening in the sunlight. She then touched the tip of my finger with her own.

"Aah, Aunt," I giggled, "the magic is in you now."

A light tap came to our door. Half-laughing, Aunt called, "Come."

"Mademoiselle, your English tea and crumpets," said the soft-voiced waiter as he entered pushing a teacart."

"Mmm, delightful," she nodded with approval, "tea and crumpets, how divine."

Our table sat next to the window. Trees swayed softly; people strolled about the French chateau's gardens. "Oh, Aunt, are not these Frenchmen clever at building wide open spaces for their gardens?"

"I must show you Versailles someday, Anne. Hundreds canter about those gardens, open, airy, spacious. Their gardens are meant for walking, whereas our garden paths are meant for intimate conversations, delicate teas and whispers. Indeed, deliberate and smallish—meant for strolling, Anne."

"Oh, Aunt, I cannot wait." I noticed a carriage moving along the road. "Look, it is Mr Phillipps' carriage, Aunt. I should wonder why it has taken them so long in returning from the music festival?"

"One can only wonder, Anne." She squinted out the window. "There, I see another following it."

"Aunt, it is Professor Mandeville's carriage and look who is sitting with him. Oh, how daring Charlotte was to accept a ride with him. Her brother will be quite provoked."

"Aah, yes, Professor Mandeville seemed quite taken with Miss Phillipps." She stirred her coffee. "I have noticed you have warmed to her, Anne."

"She told me a little of her tragic past, Aunt. I do feel quite sad about it, actually."

"And you imparted a little of your own, Anne?"

I slid a sweet crumpet onto my plate, "Oh, I have you, Aunt, whereas Charlotte has only her stuffy-headed brother—I dare not complain."

* * *

The next several days, between jaunts to local shops, evenings at the theatre, and walks in the wood, the vicar entertained us with sermons and great quotes from his little book, and he seemed careful not to reprimand Charlotte in front of Aunt Alice anymore.

This being Sunday, and as we all sat quite solemnly in the library, Mr Phillipps reached for his prayer book for another sermon, I supposed.

Elly winced. Pinching the bridge of her nose, she stood. "Excuse me, Alice," she interrupted. "Excuse me, sir. It seems I have developed another nasty headache."

I kicked her foot.

Taking my hand, she added, "Come along, Anne; you shall help soothe me."

Leaving the library, I glanced back and waved goodbye to Aunt Alice, Charlotte, and the back of the vicar's prickly-haired bald spot. Now sitting out on the balcony, I poured Elly a cup of tea. "I think Mr Phillipps knows you are fibbing about your headaches, Elly."

"I do not care, Anne."

"Oh." I giggled.

She shuddered. "If I hear another sermon on ..."

At that moment a dog bounded up the steps and headed for us. "Elly, it looks like Dr Hathaway's dog, Berry." I pushed back from the table.

"Anne, do be careful."

"It *is* Berry, Elly." I stroked her head as she licked my face. "Berry girl, how are you?" Her leash dangled about her feet. "Dr Hathaway must have come back, and Berry must have somehow gotten loose. I will take her back downstairs, Elly." A vision of him running up the steps searching for Aunt Alice flitted through my head. *Oh, dare I believe such a love story?*

"Very well, Anne, but do be careful."

"I will, Elly." Taking her leash, I walked toward the stairs. *Indeed, Dr Hathaway decided he couldn't live another moment without Aunt Alice and had come back to claim her as his own.*

Skipping down the hall, humming, I found Henri standing not far from the library where Aunt, Miss Charlotte, and the vicar were situated. "Henri," I whispered, "has Dr Hathaway returned?"

He shrugged. "Mademoiselle, follow me. I will see."

We tiptoed down the hall.

We found Dr Hathaway's carriage near the coach-house, and that's when all the trouble began.

Berry's ears perked. She must have taken in Dr Hathaway's scent for she suddenly lunged, pulling me along at great speed, I might add, down the hall.

"Oh, no, girl," I shrieked, "not so fast!" But Berry had her own mind.

I was pulled helter-skelter along the shiny, slippery floors, swooshing past statuary pillars with the likes of Napoleon, Plato, and David when suddenly I crashed into Louis—the Roman numeral XIV King. His pillar toppled sending his splintered head rolling down the hall nicking Plato's nose.

"Dear me," I cried, lying on the floor trying to undo Berry's leash tangled about my ankles. All the while she whined and barked, licking my face in apology. But the more she licked, the harder I laughed.

Henri threw his hands in the air muttering, "*%#&!"

"It is not nice to curse, Monsieur Henri."

Madame Loubet and Dr Hathaway rushed to my side all aflutter.

"Dear me, Miss ... Miss Anne." He knelt by my side trying to untangle the leash, but Berry kept whining, wiggling and licking his face, too.

Madame Loubet, with her hands resting on her ample hips, scanned the hall in dismay. "Oh, oh, where is Louis's head?" Tears slid down her olive-skinned cheeks. "C'est horrible!"

Leaning on one elbow, I pointed.

Aunt Alice rushed up looking quite mortified at the carnage. "Who, in God's name, lost his head?"

Finally, Dr Hathaway loosened the leash. My ankles were red, chaffed, and bleeding just a wee bit. "Come, dear girl." He lifted me up. "I must examine your legs."

Madame Loubet noticed the blood and hurried alongside, "Oh, this way, doctor, this way."

Carefully stepping around the tilted chairs, scattered rugs, and shattered statuary, he carried me into Madame Loubet's office. Berry pushed ahead of us all, panting and whining. I leaned over, giggling as I stroked her head.

"Anne," scolded Aunt, "it is not a laughing matter to have brought such chaos to Chateau Labrucherie." She took my hand and pressed it to her cheeks. "Oh, that your legs will be bruised and sore."

Berry barked. Reaching down, I petted her nose again. "I simply got tangled in her leash, Aunt. She must have taken Dr Hathaway's scent for she dashed away, pulling me along ... at great speed. She meant no harm."

Dr Hathaway removed my boots and stockings. "Alice, it is my dog's fault entirely. I assume complete responsibility." He ordered a basin of warm water and a clean cloth.

Dabbing at the welt marks on my legs, he shook his head. "I am terribly sorry, Miss Anne, but I am afraid my dog has quite taken to you."

"I have a way with dogs, sir." I glanced down at Berry. "But no matter, sir, I do not hurt ... all that much."

"Stand then, that I may see you can walk," he ordered in a gentle tone.

Now barefoot, I tiptoed about the room. Aunt looked pale. Mr Phillipps and Charlotte crowded into the room; his face was sour.

"Devastation along the halls, shrieks and laughter, and on the Sabbath." He shook his head gravely. "How did I know you were involved in the folly, Miss Anne?" He glanced at his sister. "Did I not tell you, Charlotte, that this looks the work of Miss Anne?"

Dr Hathaway glanced up, arching his brows. "Indeed, sir, perhaps you have a bit of clairvoyance running in your veins."

Phillipps' face burned red. "That, sir, is the work of the devil."

Mumbling, Hathaway returned his attention to me.

Charlotte put her arm around me. "Lean on me, little Imp. I shall take care of you."

Aunt hemmed. "Thank you, Anthony. It seems Anne will survive quite nicely." Holding his gaze, her face shone like the very sun.

"Doctor?" I asked, "I thought you had gone. Aunt and I watched your carriage leave the Chateau."

He smiled at Aunt Alice. "You did?"

She blushed with a nod.

"Well, yes," he said, "my carriage stopped just the other side of the groves. One of the horses went lame, and while I examined his leg, Berry escaped. It appears that she could not find me and ran back here and ... found you, Miss Anne." He tweaked my nose.

Stroking Berry's head, I giggled. "She's a strong one, sir."

"Indeed, and also a naughty one." He looked down into her round soft brown eyes and shook his finger. "Well, then, Anne, I must see that you are able to walk on your own before I go."

"Oh, no," blurted Aunt Alice, "Ah, why, well ..." she glanced at me. "Indeed, Anne must be able to first walk *by herself.*"

I knew the look. "Oh, but I feel faint, Dr Hathaway."

"Faint?" He steadied me. "Mr Phillipps, be good enough will you, and take her other arm."

The vicar's bushy brows gathered into an even row along his furrowed brow. "Indeed, sir."

Berry growled at his closeness.

Aunt Alice hemmed. "Please, take her to my room." She hurried toward the door, "This way."

Laying me down atop Aunt's bed, Dr Hathaway stood back, chin in hand, looking at me soundly. "Hmm, and how do you feel now, Anne?"

"Ah." Aunt propped pillows at my back and felt my brow. "Oh, I still feel dizzy, sir. Perhaps I shall faint at once."

"Very well," he said. "I will stay the night and leave in the morning."

I glanced at Aunt, her face still aglow. "Oh, but what if I am not well by then?"

Charlotte sat on the bed. "Oh, my little Imp," patting my hand, she cooed, "you must get better; you are my chaperone." Leaning in, she whispered, "Professor Mandeville wishes to take me riding tomorrow ... you *must* come along as my chaperone, or I shan't be able to go."

Dr Hathaway nodded. "I will return later, Miss Anne." Turning to Aunt Alice, he smiled, gesturing toward the balcony doors. "Shall we take the air, Alice?"

She smiled. "Indeed, sir."

Mr Phillipps hurried to her vacant side.

"Oh, Mr Phillipps," I called, "do stay and say a prayer for my healing."

"What?" He turned, looking confounded. "Come again, Miss Anne?"

"Do come and pray over me, sir." I sighed and dropped back rather dramatically, my head swooning about the pillow as any great actress would, I must say.

Watching Dr Hathaway and Aunt Alice hurriedly close the balcony doors behind them, the vicar hemmed. His lips pursed; his face puckered; he drew out his little black prayer book. Licking his thumb, he flipped through one hurried page after the other.

"Something lengthy this time, sir. Something I can delight in memorising ... again." I grimaced and patted the bed that Berry would jump up and lie next to me. "Come girl." Now lying contentedly, I petted her silky black, happy head—no matter a little drool here and there.

"Oh, yes, Clarke," added Charlotte smiling at me with a wink, "Anne must be fully recovered by morning ... or at least midmorning."

Mr Phillipps read many fine prayers, but none that suited me. "Very well, Mr Phillipps, at least you tried. Thank you, sir. Already, I feel quite blessed."

"That is very good news, Miss Anne." He inserted his little book, patted his vest pocket, and glanced at the balcony door. "I wonder what is keeping Miss Holt and Dr Hathaway? Well, well, I shall just go and see for myself."

CHAPTER NINE

Now back in London from our French holiday, Elly and I waved at the vicar's carriage as it turned down Elizabeth Lane and on toward the parsonage. I thought again of Dr Hathaway and how right he seemed for Aunt Alice, and how *wrong* Mr Phillipps' intentions. I knew the light in the doctor's eyes shone only for Aunt Alice. I remembered Hathaway's soft voice, his words exactly, 'My office is still in London if ever you need me, Alice.'

"It has been a delightful holiday, Aunt."

She leaned back, gazing out the window. "Oh, yes. All the same, it is good to be home."

Elly shifted in her seat. "Indeed, it is Alice, my bum is numb."

I laughed. "You are a rhymer, Elly."

Aunt giggled. "What am I to do with you two?"

As we pulled under the carriage-porch, Franklin stood attentively.

Aunt removed her gloves. "Well, Franklin, is everything in good order?"

"Indeed, madam," he glanced around the foyer, "everything and everyone is in excellent order."

Aunt nodded. "Very well, I will be in my room."

"Franklin, how is Gib, the old barn cat?"

"Oh, yes, miss. He meowed to me first off this morning inquiring when you would be home, and I told him you should be returning this very day."

"I will share with him that I met a big beautiful black dog, Franklin."

"Oh, Miss Anne, such news would surely break his heart."

Aunt stopped midway up the stairs. "Come away, Anne or I will speak with the cat myself."

* * *

The following morning was Sunday. Lying in bed, I listened to the birds squabbling over what I could only imagine was a fat worm, and I thought of Mr Phillipps. Then to my dismay, I remembered I was to recite a passage in Sunday school, but which one? I decided to ask Aunt.

After dressing, I hurried to her room and knocked softly. She bid me enter. "Aunt, I must recite a passage this morning in Sunday school, but I do not know which one to memorise."

She glanced about her room. "I must have left my Bible in the study. Bring it up, will you?"

Stepping lightly down the stairs, I hurried into the study and found her Bible lying next to her sewing basket. In my haste, I dropped it. Papers flew about the floor. Gathering them, I noticed they were news clippings. One was a yellowed clipping of a wedding. I read the words:

Mr Anthony Hathaway betrothed to Miss Helen Marie Sloan. I glanced through the papers and found an obituary. *Dying suddenly, Mrs Helen Marie (nee Sloan) Hathaway, leaving two sons and beloved husband, the prominent surgeon, Sir Anthony Hathaway, London.*

I folded the clippings and slipped them back into the Bible. Feeling wonder and puzzlement at such a find, I slowly returned to Aunt's room. She had known all along that Dr Hathaway was a widower.

At my knock, she looked up from her desk. "Thank you, dearest. I have been thinking of an appropriate verse ... . " She must have read my mind. "What's wrong, Anne?"

"I am sorry, Aunt. I dropped your Bible."

"Well, accidents do happen." She looked it over. "It is not damaged, Love. Do not worry over it."

"Some papers fell out, Aunt."

"Papers?" She stood and walked to the window. "Newspaper clippings, Anne?" Gazing out, she gestured for me to join her. "You once asked about this ring, Anne." She lifted her baby finger and removed the golden circlet. Sighing, she laid it on the windowsill and stared out into the flower garden.

"Yes, Aunt, your very favourite ring."

"I have loved him all these years, Anne. No other man, no other has tempted me."

I remained silent, staring at the gold band.

Standing at the window, her features softened. "Anthony proposed to me, out there in the garden many years ago, under the Yew."

I squeezed her hand.

"We were engaged, Anne."

I felt her trembling and hugged her tighter.

"Papa banished Anthony from Lesington Hall, Anne." With a weary sigh, she whispered, "I have tried these many years to forgive Papa."

I sensed she wanted to impart something more, something sacred, but she pulled the mask of secrecy over her eyes once more. I dared not ask why such a good man as Dr Hathaway was banished from Lesington Hall. Perhaps my grandfather Holt was as severe as the vicar. I shuddered.

"I am sorry for it, Aunt." Oh, it was terrible to see the pain in her face. "It is not too late, Aunt, if you still love him—if you should want to marry him."

She shook her head slowly. Tears slid from her eyes. "It is too late. I, I, I am an old spinster."

"Not a very old spinster, Aunt Alice. You have a handsome face. I see how men notice you, but you never look their way." I conceded. "Even Mr Phillipps finds attractiveness about you."

"Oh, Anne, he is so harsh a man."

Indeed, far more cruel and harsh than she had the heart to ever suspect. In a distant way, very much like Mr O'Leary. "He is cruel to little creatures, Aunt. Remember the day he wanted to step on my little mouse, and ..."

"That will do, Anne." She hugged me. "Be about your memorising. We shall leave for church at ten o'clock."

As I was about to leave the room, she stopped me. "Anne, this shall remain between us."

"Indeed, Aunt." I left her room, my head low, my heart low—poor, dear Aunt Alice. But I would not abandon my good intentions for her happiness. I would not surrender so easily as I had when Mama put me on the coach to London, or when she bade me write to that nasty fellow O'Leary. No, I would not give up until I secured for Aunt her heart's true love.

* * *

After church Aunt, Elly, and I walked in silence past the graveyard to our carriage. The birds strutted about the walk in front of us, chirping, darting this way and that. Glancing up, I stopped, startled, for there, not twenty feet before me stood, I was sure of it, Mr O'Leary. In haste, the man pulled his hat down around his ears and hurried away. I was not at all certain it was O'Leary, but all the same, a terrible feeling seised my soul.

Elly nudged my shoulder and half-laughed. "Move along now, you won't step on them."

"I did not stop for the birds, Elly." I watched the man hastily move through the cemetery gate and disappear.

"That was a fine Biblical passage you read this morning, Anne," said Elly, climbing into the carriage, setting her Bible next to her.

"Very," added Aunt Alice in a subdued whisper.

Listening to the sharp peal of the bells, I glanced back at the church as our carriage rounded the corner. Glancing up and down the street, I didn't see the dark figure of a man who had evoked such terrible memories. *But what a startling similarity to O'Leary*, I thought as I lowered my head, fighting off the thought of him. *Surely I must have been mistaken, for what would he want in London?*

"Charlotte looked pretty today." Aunt Alice brushed my cheek in a kind gesture.

"I nodded." I returned her smile, my anxious, dark feelings had returned to normal. "Aunt," I sat back, tugging at my gloves, "Charlotte said if it were permissible she would be delighted to give me piano lessons."

Elly nodded. "Well now, music lessons. That sounds like a good thing."

Aunt nodded. "If you wish it, Anne, she does play most excellently, and without having a piano in the parsonage, it amazes me how well she played at the Faire in France."

"I believe she is trying to escape from her brother," I said matter-of-factly.

The silence of midnight settled in our cab.

"Escape from her brother?" Aunt Alice spread her fan. "Whatever do you mean, Anne?"

"He sold her piano thinking it sinful to exhibit God's talents in a show-offish manner. All along she was led to believe they needed the money for food. If Charlotte comes to teach me, it must be kept secret from her brother, Aunt."

"Well then, indeed, it shall."

Elly huffed up. "What a nasty thing to do to the poor dear. Why, I have never heard of such narrow-minded flummery, and only think how he flaunts himself. He's constantly quoting this and quoting that—so pompous a man."

"Indeed, he is strict, Eleanor. No doubt about that."

"I knew it from the start, Aunt. Anyone with three great vertical ridges hovering at the bridge of his nose is ... ."

Aunt frowned. "Anne, must you?"

"Vertical ridges?" Elly faced me. "What on earth are vertical ridges?"

"You don't have them, Elly. Neither does Aunt. Only mean people get them." With my fingers, I pushed my forehead to make the ridges. "Like this ... you see!"

Aunt and Elly leaned in to inspect my ridges.

"Hmm." Aunt resumed gazing out the window.

Elly nodded. "Ah-ha, yes, it seems we have a monster in the monastery, Alice."

"Indeed, and to think all along, the vicar quite fancied himself a Gentile."

"Not gentle at all, Aunt Alice. Sir Anthony is gentle and kind. There are no ridges on *his* forehead, only crinkly little lines when his eyes laugh. Oh, perhaps a few lines around his mouth, but they only deepen when he smiles. Did you see how happy he was when Berry licked his face? Not once did he shoo *her* away." Sighing, I added, "I would love to see Berry again, Aunt."

I gazed out the window. It was a wispy summer day; children skipped along with their mothers and fathers. One lady held a pug in her arms, her husband the parasol. With my nose to the window, I stared at them as they jotted merrily down the street. "If I had a puppy, Aunt, I should name her Holly Berry."

* * *

The very next Tuesday morning, Miss Phillipps entered the music room a few minutes over ten o'clock, the scent of summer lingered everywhere she walked. Her yellow hair was pulled back and arranged quite nicely beneath her sunbonnet which held pretty paper daisy greens sprinkled along the brim. Aunt Alice bid her welcome.

"Good morning, indeed, Miss Holt." Glancing about the room, Charlotte gave me a little wave and removed her bonnet. "I cannot thank you enough, Miss Holt, for allowing me the privilege of teaching as well as playing ... and earning some money." She lowered her head, fumbling with her bonnet.

"Charlotte, the pleasure is completely ours. To be honest, Anne is beside herself with the idea of learning to play. I had no idea you were so accomplished."

"I played at an early age ... three."

Aunt drew back. "Three?"

"Yes, ma'am, Mama and Papa saw to it that I received the best instructions. And then ... well, I was left to play on my own."

Aunt nodded. "Yes, Charlotte, I must say you have done exceedingly well." She gestured toward me. "So, here sits your first pupil." Turning to leave, she said, "I will be in the study."

I smiled, wiggling my fingers over the keys.

"Today, Anne, we will start with exercising—proper fingering."

Our lesson lasted one hour. My brain was full of scales and the do's and don'ts, notes, do ra me fa so la ti do's, ups, downs, back again. Fingers in, out, over ... flap, flap ... sit straight ... I exhaled and wiped my brow. "Very well, Charlotte, such an hour I shall never forget."

Tweaking my nose, she smiled. "That is precisely the plan, little imp."

Franklin set down the tea tray. I was happy to engage my fingers on something other than ivory. "I may learn to play, but I doubt I shall ever play as well as you."

"You are only twelve and just beginning. Don't forget, I was a wee thing when I began to play." She lifted her teacup and blew at the steamy vapours.

"Oh, yes," I exhaled, "you must have been playing the piano before you were born—inside your mother's stomach."

Her mouth opened in awe. "Playing inside my mother's stomach?"

"Indeed, on her rib cage, perhaps."

She gasped, blushed, and laughed, spilling her tea. "Oh, you are an odd little imp, Anne."

Her laugh was delightful. Her face broadened, her teeth, not yellow at all anymore, glistened.

"It is good to hear you laugh, Charlotte. Does your brother ever laugh?"

"Oh, my no, there is nothing that he finds humour in." She shook her head. "I was becoming the same way until ..."

"Me, Aunt, and Elly."

Cocking her head, she nodded. "Yes, I suppose so ... though, when first coming to the parsonage, I laughed a great deal. But Clarke soon put a stop to all that. 'Charlotte,' he would say, 'to cackle like a scullery maid is most unbecoming.'"

I passed her the plate of sweet cakes. "When we were in France, I noticed Professor Mandeville laughed a great deal."

Her face coloured. "Yes, and so did I, when we were together." She set down her cup and walked to the window. "My brother does not approve of musicians calling. He says they are not proper and fit company for a lady."

"But Professor Mandeville is a professor. Is that not gentleman enough?"

"I would have thought so." Tears dripped down her cheeks.

Aunt entered. "Well, I didn't hear the piano ... so you have finished your first lesson, Anne?"

We both turned.

"What is wrong?" Aunt hurried toward us. Taking my chin, she searched my face, and glanced at Charlotte's teary eyes. "Goodness, me, was Anne that pathetic?"

Dabbing her eyes, Charlotte smiled feebly. "No, ma'am."

"Oh, Aunt, a terrible tragedy has befallen us." I sighed deeply.

Aunt led us to the sofa. "What tragedy, pray tell?"

Charlotte dabbed her eyes with her lace handkerchief. "Oh, Miss Holt, I am in love with Professor Mandeville."

"Well, that is not such a tragedy." She paused. "Unless he is ..."

"Oh, no, Miss Holt, Professor Mandeville is free. It is just that my brother Clarke does not approve of him. He thinks musicians are not fit for the likes of a lady like me."

Aunt puffed up. "Well, we'll just see about that."

* * *

Later that evening, over supper, Aunt Alice and Elly were discussing schools, girls' schools in particular.

"Yes, indeed, Alice, Miss Pramm's seems just the place. Such a coincidence, for just this morning I spoke with the governess of Mrs Tell's daughter, and she recommends the school."

Aunt spooned into her soup. "Mmm, yes, and Mr Phillipps finds it to his liking, thinking it a fit and proper finishing school for a young lady."

I kept my head low, sipped properly, and did not interrupt one time. Having just finished *Jane Eyre*, I had a deep rumbling suspicion that I would be sent off to Lowood Institution. Oh, God, I prayed, *can there be two Mr Brocklehursts on the earth? Yes, of course, Mr Phillipps. What have I done that they are sending me away?*

"Aunt, I do not want to be sent off to Lowood Institution. Just because Helen Burns died, and not Jane Eyre, doesn't mean it would not be my turn to die next."

Aunt tapped my wrist. "I don't mean to send you away, Anne. There is an English law that children must attend school at your age. I am thinking of enrolling you in a day school, not far from here, Miss Pramm's School for Girls."

Tapping at her soft-boiled egg, Elly nodded. "A proper school."

"Indeed, a proper school, where I am hoping you will meet other young ladies your age. Elly and I have quite kept you to ourselves. I am afraid that will do you no good in proper society, Anne."

"But Mademoiselle, I already know how to read and write, do mathematics, and ..."

"It is a finishing school, dearest, where you learn the finer arts."

"Refinement, Anne." Elly spooned into her gummy egg. "Refinement."

"To act like a lady?" I sighed. "I know I can do that."

Patting my head, Aunt smiled. "Very good, Anne."

I thought of what my first day in school would be like. Indeed, skipping down Lesington Hall's long driveway to the black wrought iron gate where I would squeeze through the bars with ease, and onto the street past the flower girls. How smart I would look carrying my books, my braid dangling down my back with a smart bow tied at the end. Oh, indeed, the shopkeepers would know me as Miss Anne Holt from Lesington Hall. How the greeters would nod and smile as I walked past them.

"If Miss Pramm's is not far, Aunt, may I walk?"

"No, dearest, I will have the carriage take you to and fro. School is Monday to Thursday."

I took in a great breath. My grand spirit visions disappeared more quickly than I had envisioned them. "Very well, Aunt Alice." I shrank in my chair. "I think I shall like going to school. When do I begin?"

"Next Monday I shall enrol you. Together we shall tour the school and meet the other young girls over tea. It seems a delightful gathering, all in all."

* * *

Aunt Alice and I attended Miss Pramm's tea that very next Monday as promised. Oh, the delightful gathering, all in all, went quite well. No one simpered and smirked at me like I had imagined.

Aunt and Elly seemed cheery and relieved that I was at least attending a school. But, watching the other girls and studying the teachers, I was not at all convinced this was the place where I belonged. However, I thanked God many times over, that it was not the grey, harsh, freezing *Lowood* institution of *Jane Eyre's* era. Nevertheless, the first day, being *sent off*, did not start off as well as I had wished.

Waving goodbye to Aunt and Elly, my carriage lunged quite rudely toward Miss Pramm's School for Girls. Yes, I was a girl, but I wondered where boys attended. It was little time when the carriage stopped, and the door opened. I scooted farther back in my seat.

Franklin chaperoned me, but he had dozed off. Perhaps I should tell the driver to return home. Miss Pramm would not even miss me. "Drive on!" I shouted. Franklin startled awake. The carriage had not moved. I was just about to repeat myself when Miss Pramm opened the door and leaned in.

"Well, well, Miss Holt, is it? Come along, now."

Franklin smiled as he waved goodbye.

Settling myself at the curbstone, I eyed the other young girls, some of whom I had met at the tea. They nodded and smiled at me. I felt better; at least they had not sneered. Perhaps they thought me a lady already. Oh, indeed, a young lady coming for a last-minute polish. Why not? I asked myself.

"This way, Miss Holt. Now since this is your first day in school, you will be doing sketches. Oil paintings, or watercolours, or charcoals ..."

"I love drawing, Miss Pramm. Actually, I do quite well with charcoal."

"Is that so? Your Aunt did not mention that. Well, then, you are in luck. Your class is doing charcoal this very moment."

Of course, Aunt never mentioned it to her, for I had never mentioned it to Aunt. I had supposed everyone sketched, as I had drawn flowers on Madame Pinchot's garden wall many times.

Miss Pramm escorted me into the art room and to an empty desk. "This will be your seat. The paper and supplies are over there." She gestured toward a bench piled high with paper, canvases, bowls ...

"And the hearth?" I asked.

"The hearth?" Turning, she pointed.

While I gathered sticks of burnt wood from the hearth, I heard giggling. Standing, I turned to find everyone staring at me.

"What are you doing?" inquired one girl in particular.

"Gathering charcoal with which to draw." By then my hands and the front of my frock were filthy black. "What else?" I asked.

"Indeed," the girl's lip curled, "what else would one expect from a clod-hopper from Holybourne." She sniffed the air. Whispering to the others, she glanced back at me.

A tall, young girl, approached. "Hello, my name is Miss Katherine. We do not use *that* charcoal to draw with." She took my hand. "Come, you must wash your hands."

The others were still giggling. I was warm with embarrassment, but managed to tell Miss Katherine my name.

"Come along, Miss Anne." She glanced over at the giggling students. "Don't worry over them. Margaret is the devilish one; she's to be avoided at all times."

"But how did she know I was from Holybourne?"

Katherine shrugged. "Her mother knows everything."

Just then the teacher entered the room. I curtsied. "Excuse me, madam; may I be excused to wash my hands?" She ignored me.

Katherine stifled a giggle. "Mrs Heath cannot see without her spectacles. She won't even know we are gone." Careful to avoid the black smudges on my frock, she took my sleeve. "When we return, I shall show you the pencils, the *charcoal* pencils." Giggling she pulled me into the hall. "Oh, I, too, was stupid when I first came to Miss Pramm's, Miss Anne."

I could feel my face turn warm. I had always prided myself on my adaptability and intelligence. Surely a simple drawing class on my first day in school would not be my defeat. "But I'm not stupid, Miss Katherine."

She wrinkled her nose. "I don't like the name Katherine. My brothers call me Kate, but while at school we must say Miss Katherine—and I never for a second thought you were stupid."

My heart warmed. Her manner was pleasing, and I liked her directness. No, I am not stupid. "Very well, Miss Kate, I shall remember your preferred name."

"Now," she directed me to the washbasin, "when we return, just do as I do."

"Thank you, Miss Kate." I remembered how unclean Mr Braithwaite found me and forbade any association with his daughter. I hoped to impress my new found friend. "I do quite well at literature, mathematics, geography, French ..."

"Oh, we do nothing of those things, Miss Anne." She handed me a towel.

Alarmed, I dried my hands and followed her back into the art room. "No literature. No numbers. No French?"

Sitting next to me, Kate occasionally glanced at my work. "That is a very good cat, Anne."

"But it is a dog." I shook my head. "Where do we go from here, Miss Katherine?"

"The walking, sitting, standing class—deportment."

"Hmm, and then?"

"Facial gestures, hand gestures, elbows, feet."

"What gesture is your favourite, Miss Katherine?"

"Arching my eyebrows." She hesitated and then added, "And I have learned to blush on command."

"I cannot wait to tell Aunt and Elly."

"Who might they be?"

"My aunt, Miss Alice Holt and my cousin, Mrs Eleanor Mills."

"You live with your aunt, then?"

"Yes." I was abrupt in my response in hopes she wouldn't question me regarding where mama and papa were. Thank goodness, she did not.

* * *

Over supper that evening, as Aunt Alice and Elly chatted over this and that, I was a little disappointed neither had remarked how well I had done in school. Then a spark of notice ...

Aunt set down her fork. "Anne," she said, "ever since you have come home today, you have been making faces."

"Allow me to correct you, Aunt. They are facial expressions."

Still chewing, Elly glanced at me over her spectacles.

I dabbed my lips with my napkin. "Indeed, today I learned to be expressive. 'One should be able to read a lady's face from a distance and ascertain her pleasures or displeasures and respond accordingly.' " Arching my eyebrows, I extended my baby finger. "Did you never learn that, Aunt Alice?"

She exchanged glances with Elly. "You have not come to the subtleties portion of the class, Anne."

"Aunt, I have a question."

"Yes."

"What is a clod-hopper?"

Both Elly and Aunt frowned. Aunt set down her cup. "Well, I would suppose a clod-hopper is one who hops over clods—dirt clods."

"A farmer," said Elly.

"Today in class Miss Margaret North called me a clod-hopper from Holybourne. Miss Kate says that Miss North's mother knows everything about everyone. But Mrs North must not be so very brilliant, Aunt, or she would have known that I no longer hop clods."

"Indeed you do not, Anne."

Sitting straight and proper, I smiled, making sure my teeth showed.

Looking away, Elly shook her head.

"Since you are doing so well in school," Aunt added, "I have a gift for you."

I showed my teeth in grand appreciativeness.

Aunt laughed. "In the music room, Anne."

"I know what it is, Aunt."

"No, you do not."

Pushing from the table, I nodded. "Pardon, mademoiselle, but I do." I knew it was a puppy. Rushing into the room, I searched around the floor, behind the door, under the sofas ... I stopped to listen for its whimper and whine, but found only silence.

"Give up, Anne?" Aunt and Elly stood in the open door.

Shrugging in disappointment, I muttered, "I thought it was a ... ."

Aunt brought her hand from behind her back, holding a leash. Rushing to her side, I followed it—and there at Aunt's heels sat a fluffy black ball.

"A puppy! A puppy!" Kneeling down, I gathered her up into my arms and buried my face into her soft, warm fur. "I love her, Aunt. I love her already." While I cradled the small bundle, the puppy licked my face. "Thank you, Aunt ... thank you, Elly."

Aunt wiped her eyes. "You must remain a good girl, Anne. Do well, and life will be kind to you."

I kissed her cheek. "Thank you, Aunt Alice. I love you."

"Come then, let us sit in the study that you may fondle your pet."

"May I name her, Aunt?"

"I believe you already have."

* * *

The very next morning, excited to share the news of my puppy, Holly Berry, I stood in front of Miss Pramm's School for Girls and patiently waited for Miss Kate's carriage. It was little time when I spotted it and hurried to the street.

"Miss Anne," her smile broadened as she stepped down. "Good morning."

"Good morning."

"Kate," said a young man who stepped from her carriage, "remember now, we shall meet for lunch."

"Very well, Charles, I shall remember."

The young man whispered to Miss Kate. "Where are your manners, silly girl?"

"Charles," she giggled, "please meet my school friend, Miss Anne Holt. Miss Anne Holt, my brother, Mr Charles Hathaway."

He nodded. "Pleased, Miss Holt."

The school bell rang, and Kate grabbed my hand. "Charles, we must go. I will see you for lunch."

Hurrying up the steps, I tugged on her sleeve. "Miss Kate, I didn't know your name was Hathaway."

"Well, it has been for a very long time." Just before entering the glee club room, she turned and giggled. "It has been Hathaway all my life."

"Your brother is handsome, Miss Kate."

"He is soon to be married and," she lowered her voice, "I do not like her."

"Then, neither do I."

"Come along with Charles and me for lunch, Miss Anne. Miss Pramm will not miss us."

Thinking of her very handsome brother, I nodded. "Very well, I should like that."

* * *

I could not believe my good fortune at having such a friend, going out for lunch without Aunt and Elly and all on the same day. My heart overflowed. How truly grown-up I really was. Oh, how wise Aunt Alice was for sending me to this great and glorious school.

As lunch approached, I was almost giddy standing next to my friend, Kate. We were to meet her brother in front of the school. How handsome Mr Hathaway was, and I wondered if they were related to *the* Dr Hathaway.

When Charles approached, I did not see any resemblance to Sir Anthony, however, Charles being such a handsome man, I was flustered when he spoke to me. I could feel my face burn. We were escorted into a lovely little shoppe and were seated very near a huge open hearth. The aroma of baking bread wafted about mingling with warm spiced apples.

"Miss Holt," he inquired politely, "you have not been enrolled long at Miss Pramm's?"

"Only a month, sir."

"And how do you like it?"

"Hmm," I thought for a moment, "well, sir, I have learned a great deal already."

"Is that so? And what have you learned?"

"How to hold my finger when sipping tea; how to enter a room with great dignity, how to sit ..."

"Well, yes," Charles dabbed his lips with his napkin, "right into the meat of things, I see."

Kate giggled. "You see, brother, what we are to become?"

"Indeed, Miss Kate," I sighed deeply. "But nothing the likes of Dickens would care to bite into, I would imagine."

"Dickens? Mr Dickens, the author?" said Charles. "Bite into?"

"Bury his teeth to the bone, Mr Hathaway," I said.

Kate nodded in sympathy. "But, we are to read *Flora's Lexicon* this afternoon, Miss Anne."

I nodded. "Yes, I suppose an added dimension of *The Language of Flowers*—bouquets of words and so on."

Charles laughed. "So, you read Dickens?"

"He is one of my favourites, sir."

"Kate, you should introduce Miss Holt to Edward. He is acquainted with Mr Dickens. I do believe he is to visit him soon."

I sat straighter. *Could this be possible? Oh, my good fortune.*

Charles resettled his cup onto the saucer. "Indeed, Miss Holt, Edward would be happy to introduce you to Mr Dickens."

Smiling, Kate nodded. "Very well, brother. If not, I shall."

The café clock struck one, and Charles stood. "Come along now, you must not be late returning to class."

Standing on the school steps, Kate kissed her brother good-bye. I nodded adieu.

"Nice meeting you, Miss Holt. You must come to visit." He put his hat back on and sauntered up the street, melting into the crowd.

"Who is Edward, Miss Kate?"

"Our cousin."

A thought suddenly burst into my brain. "Is his father the great surgeon?"

She smiled. "You know of my uncle, Dr Hathaway, then?"

Her uncle? I nodded feeling giddy at such news.

"Oh, I suppose you would. He is quite prominent in the news. Papa has me cut the clippings from the paper. At the moment, Uncle Anthony is travelling in Brussels."

"Edward is his son?"

"Uncle has two sons, Edward and John."

CHAPTER TEN

When I joined Aunt and Elly at dinner that evening, I was past all excitement. Oh, my heart thumped with such news of the day, but I knew well not to mention that I was the best of friends with Miss Kate, Sir Anthony's niece. I must keep that secret in my inner sanctum for at least a little while. I believed Aunt would be more than upset if she knew I plotted to bring Sir Anthony back into her life—into our lives. What a happy assembly it would be to have such an uncle. I so yearned for the kind family affections such a man would bring to Lesington Hall.

"Well, well, my dear. You look absolutely thrilled. You must tell us what new things you learned in school today."

"My friend, Miss Kate—you met her, Aunt, in the 'how to properly serve tea' rehearsal last week."

"Yes, dear, I faintly remember her."

I squirmed in my seat. "Well, her cousin, Edward, may introduce me to an acquaintance of his. Oh, just imagine, being introduced to Mr Charles Dickens."

Elly smiled. "Ah, yes, the clever writer, Dickens."

Cutting into her ham, Aunt inquired, "And what prompted that association, Anne?"

"Oh, it was during lunch today with Miss Kate's brother, Charles, that I happened to mention that I respected great authors."

"You had lunch with your friend's brother, Charles?"

"Yes, Aunt, Miss Kate and I ate lunch with him. He is to be married next year. Of course, Miss Kate and I do not like her."

Aunt raised her eyebrows. "You do not like the bride-to-be, Anne?"

"Yes, Aunt, that is correct."

"Who is she?"

"I do not know, Aunt Alice."

Now that I was aware of the subtleties of being a lady, I noticed at once the facial and hand gestures of my adult company. I thought Elly did well with her sighs, and Aunt's frowns prompted me to explain: "You see, Aunt Alice, I have read exactly your gestures already. You are puzzled at how I could dislike someone I have not yet met."

Elly shook her head. "Well, Alice, the child is learning."

"Go on, Anne."

"My friend, Miss Kate, doesn't like her."

Setting down her cup of coffee, Aunt nodded. "Thank you, Anne. It's all quite clear now."

* * *

It was Friday, my piano lesson day. Aunt had made arrangements with Charlotte to arrive near ten in the morning. Sitting on the grass in the warm sun, I patiently waited for her. We couldn't send the carriage for her, since her brother was not to know she was teaching piano. I rather thought it a fine joke and relished in the thought that women, banding together, could succeed quite nicely at most anything they chose.

Holly Berry rolled and stretched as I rubbed her soft taut belly. I glanced up and spied Charlotte rounding the corner. Skipping out to greet her, I waved. "Good afternoon, Charlotte. I have been practising my piano lessons every day after school, just as you instructed."

Very well, then, come along and let me hear you play."

I fingered the keys up and down, calling out each note, the sour ones as well, until she was convinced of my well-spent labours.

"Very well, Anne. Now, today we are going to practice a small ..."

Holly Berry tugged at her hem.

We both giggled.

"Oh, Holly Berry," I scolded, "you must behave."

"What a sweet name." Taking the pup into her arms, Charlotte cuddled her. "I noticed that Professor Mandeville will be conducting *Symphonie Fantastique* by my favourite

French composer, Berlioz." [6] She sighed deeply. "But, I cannot go."

I read the sadness in her eyes; her voice flat and final. "Your brother will not permit it."

"Oh, no, never." She snuggled Holly Berry closer. "Clarke quite refuses even to discuss Professor Mandeville, and he detests Berlioz, calling him noisy and preposterous. So I have not mentioned the symphony."

Oh, the thought of her losing the love of her life, the kind Professor Mandeville, sent me into tremors. A burst of bright designs encroached upon my brain. An uncontrollable blurt escaped, "Perhaps Aunt Alice and Elly would take us both. Your brother need not know. It would be an outing where just the four of us would attend."

Now that I was getting on with the gestures and lady-like signals, I interpreted Charlotte's with perfection. Her eyes lit up; her cheeks burned red. She straightened her shoulders and cried, "Oh, if only she would."

Just another example of how well women work together in the advancement of their heart's desires. I further explained, "Aunt and Elly are away this afternoon. When they return, I will ask permission, Charlotte—I will drop you a note."

She kissed my forehead. "Oh, happy days, Anne, but let not a word be spoken in case it should it reach Clarke's ear. If he found that I disobeyed him, why, I believe he'd have a stroke. The performance is to be held at the Royal Albert ... Wednesday next, eight o'clock in the evening."

* * *

Later that evening I jotted off a note to Charlotte.

Evening - Lesington Hall
Dear Miss Phillipps,
    It is with great gladness and cheer that I inform you that you must accompany Miss Holt, Mrs Mills, and me to a "lecture" at the Royal Albert Conservatory, Wednesday, eight o'clock, alone. A refusal is not

---

[6] Louis Hector Berlioz (1803-1869) French composer, born in La Cote-Saint-Andre, Dept. of Isere.

*acceptable to the ladies mentioned above. Aunt will send
our carriage to fetch you. We will be in it.*
        Your friend,
        Miss Anne Holt

Sealing the envelope, I sighed. "Oh, thank you, Aunt. You
will make Charlotte very happy."

"Well, I certainly think Charlotte should be allowed to
pick and choose which musician she prefers." Aunt lifted her
chin, a defiant sort of lifting. I noted it with glee and clapped.

Elly nodded in obvious agreement. "Indeed."

Squiggling about, I dreamily prophesied, "Professor
Mandeville just may propose to her very soon."

"I hope for her sake, she accepts." Aunt rubbed the vacant
space on her finger, where the gold band had once twirled.

I touched my heart.

Elly pursed her lips white. "And, I suppose, her brother
shall be quite outraged over her choice."

Aunt shrugged. "*If* he discovers our deed … so be it."

Picking up Holly Berry, I ruffled her head. "I dare say we
shall be in the very centre of the scandal."

"I hope we are," said Aunt. "A woman her age should have
the right to do as she pleases."

I thrust my arm in the air and shouted, "A woman at any
age, Aunt!"

"Dear me, Alice," Elly chuckled. "I do believe Miss Pramm
will faint straight away when she finds what a hell-cat she has
in her *lady-making* school."

* * *

Charlotte was more than excited to accept our invitation
to join us that following Wednesday. She showed her brother
the proper invitation, and he gave his approval *with* the
understanding that she was to be home before midnight.

Of course Aunt gave the assurances that we were all very
well chaperoned, even if we should arrive home the following
morning. The vicar did not reply to Aunt's note.

Wednesday came, and as our carriage approached the
parsonage, Aunt instructed our footman, Wallace, to ring the
doorbell and escort Miss Phillipps to our waiting carriage. We

watched as he rang the bell. Their door opened and out came Charlotte with her brother. He insisted upon escorting her to our carriage himself. Nodding to Aunt Alice, he held his sister's hand until she was securely situated inside next to me. Aunt held a slight smile, Elly stared straight ahead.

Our groomsman whistle-clicked to the horses and we were off without a hitch. Sitting backwards in the carriage, I watched the sour-face vicar as he remained at the curb watching us until we rounded the corner of Snitchfield and Voltaire.

Entering the Royal Albert Conservatory, I nudged Charlotte. As we took the programs from the ushers, her face was already a deep rose, and even before Professor Mandeville glanced her way. "He spied you, Charlotte."

"Do not make a spectacle, Anne," she whispered. "I will act as though I do not see him." She casually thumbed through her program.

"Certainly I will not make a spectacle, Charlotte. Why, Miss Kate and I just learned the Art of Allurements today. Oh, imagine the coincidence," I sighed. "And to think, just this very day, I learned the invaluable lessons ... the very principal." Exhaling lightly, I said, "Watch this."

"Anne," Aunt Alice laid her hand on my shoulder, "I would wish it very much if you did not apply your *art of allurements* on Professor Mandeville this evening. You must promise me."

"But Aunt ..." I knew the look. "Very well, Aunt." Cupping my mouth, I whispered to Charlotte, "You will have to do your own allurements this evening."

Professor Mandeville approached us. Aunt took my hand and pulled me beside her. His face was flushed; I noticed right off the telltale signs of being in love. The trembling hands, glassy eyes, one glove on, one off. Mismatched shoes ...

"Good evening," the Professor greeted us. "What a pleasant surprise." He quickly glanced at Aunt, me, and Elly. "If you do not already have your seats, I would be honoured if you sat in my box."

Aunt Alice nodded. "Oh, how very pleased we would be, sir."

"Indeed," said Elly, "what an honour, sir."

Charlotte beamed, but remained speechless.

Professor Mandeville cupped her elbow. His eyes canvassed her entirety. "Come, Miss Phillipps." He gestured to us as well. "Please, sit in here. It is far more comfortable."

I smiled broadly. "Professor Mandeville," everyone's breathing stopped, "you are glowing."

He tweaked my cheek. "I have every right to glow, Miss Holt. I must thank you for the note you dropped me announcing that *all of you* would be here this evening." He glanced at Charlotte and seemed to have melted under her gaze. "This evening's music is in your honour, Miss Phillipps."

She nodded, fanning herself demurely. Her thick dark eyelashes fluttered like a butterfly. "Thank you, sir."

Tears welled in her eyes. Tears welled in Aunt's eyes, Elly's eyes, my eyes. I squeezed Charlotte's hand. Allurements actually worked.

* * *

Now more than ever, I was impressed with Miss Pramm's School for Girls. My visions and plans of matrimonial bliss for Aunt Alice and Sir Anthony had become firmly lodged in my heart, and I would soon find a way for them as I had for Charlotte and the Professor.

That very next morning, while riding in the carriage heading for school, I squirmed in my seat anxious to hear more stratagems on becoming the skilled, artful lady I was meant to be. Finally arriving in front of the school, I opened the carriage door myself and jumped out. Oops! I missed the steps entirely, but caught myself and found that no one, including the snobbish Margaret North, noticed my unladylike faux pas.

"Miss Katherine," I cried, scurrying to her. "We must hurry along." I took her hand. "We cannot miss one minute of class."

"You are certainly spry this morning, Miss Anne," noted Kate.

"Oh, Miss Kate, last night at the conservatory, during the symphony, I witnessed Miss Phillipps and Professor Mandeville seal a love pact."

She wrinkled her nose. "A love pact? Why, how wonderful for her."

"And this morning Miss Pramm is to instruct us on the *How and When to Weep* segment. Ah, elocution, I believe."

Entering our classroom, we anxiously took our seats, and within a minute we heard the familiar creak of the doorknob. The class grew silent. Miss Pramm, wearing her wooden-heeled boots, entered. I noticed at once that her left sleeve was much puffier than the other.

Standing at the lectern Miss Pramm wrinkled up her face, and in a high-pitched whine, greeted us. "Good morning, ladies."

I covered my ears. "She sounds like our cat."

Kate giggled through her fingers. "Oh, Anne."

Miss Pramm squinted and grunted and then stuck out her left arm. "Young ladies," she sniffed, pulling out a beautiful lace-edged handkerchief from her cuff, "you must always carry a delicate lace handkerchief up your sleeve." Dangling the beautiful hanky, she continued, "There will come a time, many times actually, when you must shed tears in order to get your own way."

*   *   *

Later that evening at dinner, no one commented on my delicate lace-trimmed handkerchief stuffed up *my* sleeve.

"Very well, Anne." Aunt Alice set down her knife and fork. "Please explain to Elly and me why you keep your prized lace-trimmed handkerchief dangling from your sleeve."

Elly stared at me. "We simply must know, Anne."

I sighed deeply. "I thought you two would never ask." I brought my handkerchief to my crinkled face and wept. Holly Berry ran to me whining and pawing at my skirt. Aunt and Elly pushed from the table and hurried to my side.

Letting the handkerchief flutter atop my mashed peas, I looked up dry-eyed and smiling. "You see, Aunt Alice and Elly, I did quite well in the *How and When to Weep* class today. Tomorrow we are to discuss *Making Feet for Children's Stockings* [7]... ."

Aunt gasped. "Anne, wherever did you hear that vulgar phrase?"

"Making feet, Aunt?"

---

[7] Make feet for children's stockings: metaphor for procreation. Quoted from *A Classical Dictionary of the Vulgar Tongue* by Francis Grose (1796).

"That is quite enough, young lady," she fumed. "Again, explain where you learned such language."

"Miss Katherine and I were in the library when Miss Margaret North and two other upper-class students were giggling. They told us that making children's feet would be tomorrow's lesson, and we must be prepared, since Miss Pramm herself would be teaching the class. Is something wrong, Aunt?"

"Make such a fuss, Alice," said Elly as she returned to her seat, "and Anne will surely make more of it than necessary."

"I will speak with Miss Pramm then." Aunt resumed her chair, somewhat in a huff, I noticed.

Elly smirked at Aunt. "Well, I really think you need to speak with Anne first."

"Speak to me about what, Aunt?"

* * *

Making feet for children's stockings was just one of the crude phrases I would pick up along the way at Miss Pramm's. Oh, yes, I would be thirteen come next December, but all the same, I would rather not have learned how children's feet were made. As for the silly girls at school, well, I should soon scold them. One must not trifle with children's feet.

My first stroll in the garden with Aunt Alice since learning about *mating* left me feeling quite odd and very circumspect. My arm entwined with Aunt's, we strolled the crunchy path. I exhaled greatly. "My perspective on life has now changed, Aunt."

"Well, now, what brought that on, Anne?"

Removing my arm from hers, I gestured. "My dear friends about the garden," I pointed, "the butterfly, the bird, the sweet little hare are now animals to be viewed quite differently."

"Is that so? Why, I see no difference in anything at all, Anne."

"It is *how* they got here, Aunt. Therein lies the difference."

There was a reflective silence as we continued on.

"Actually, I am quite put out over the affair."

"Dear me, Anne, you must explain your meaning."

"Well, I know baby birds come by an egg, the butterfly by its cocoon, and the bunny comes wrapped in fur, but we come naked, crying, bloody ..."

"Yes, indeed. We do come a different way. I would suppose we are delivered ignorant, naked, and alone—perhaps to be prepared for life by caring hands. Much as the mama bird teaches her young to leave the nest at the proper time, we are advanced, complex creatures who need an extra amount of time to be nurtured, fondled and prepared for the world clothed. We cannot fly away from danger like the bird, nor can we flutter our wings so demurely as the butterfly, nor outrun the fox."

Approaching the fountain, Aunt placed her hand under the soft trickle of water. "Cowper most recently said, '... and God gives to every man The virtue, temper, understanding, taste, That lifts him into life, and lets him fall Just in the niche he was ordain'd to fill.' " [8]

"Hmm, Aunt." I sat on the stone balustrade and glanced up into her face—now rippled by the watery shadows of the fountain, the sun full on her shoulders. "I wonder what Mama's niche was?"

"We are all quite different for good reason, Anne. I do not have all the answers. I, like you, am learning new things every day of life."

"I think perhaps Mama's niche was marrying Papa and delivering me into your caring hands, Aunt."

"Oh, how dear your thinking." She kissed my forehead. "Come, love, let us walk on a little more."

Stopping at the sweet briar, the eglantine vine, Aunt took my chin in her hand, her breath as sweet as its fragrant leaves.

She began:

" '*A sweeter spot of earth was never found.*
I look'd and look'd, and still with new delight;
Such joy my soul, such pleasures fill'd my sight;
And the fresh eglantine exhaled a breath,
Whose odours were of power to raise from death.' " [9]

I kissed her hand. "Thank you, Aunt. That is a beautiful poem."

---

[8] William Cowper, from "The Winter Evening" in *The Poetical Works of William Cowper*, by Cowper (1843).

[9] John Dryden (1631-1700) English poet and author. From "Tales from Chaucer" in *The Poetical Works of John Dryden*, published by John Alden (1883).

* * *

Something warm and caring entered my heart that morning as I clasped Aunt's hand. Her kind words seemed to release the sadness in my heart. I had thought about Mama and her purpose on earth many times since learning about life's purposes and how we are supposed to contribute to the world and not take too much away without replenishing it.

What is more, I finally realised it would not do to question God on His plans beforehand. It was much too complicated, what with all the foreign languages in the world, I knew it would be my luck that He would speak to me in Chinese.

Something else entered my body later that afternoon. From a child, I emerged into Aunt Alice's study a puzzled and a nervous Anne from Holybourne. Entering slowly, I eased the door closed behind me. Pausing, I found Aunt busy with her embroidery—her shiny silver thimble all a glittery. Franklin had built a warm fire.

Setting down my petticoat on the footstool next to the hearth, I stared into the flames and wept. I could not control my tears, nor had I prophesied their arrival.

Aunt Alice dropped her sewing. "What is wrong, Anne?"

I held up my bloodstained petticoat—my face felt as hot as the blazes in the fire pit. "I am sorry, Aunt. There is something very wrong with me."

"Oh, Anne." She knelt at my side, wiping away my tears. "Dearest." She hugged me. "Calm yourself. There is nothing wrong with you." Folding my petticoat, she took my hand, "Come, love, with me."

Aunt took me to her room, and while I sat behind her privacy screen, she handed me fresh under things. Once I was clean, she led me to her sofa by the hearth. I watched as she searched through her bookshelf.

"Yes, here it is." She sat next to me. "Remember our last lesson?"

"Making feet for children's stockings, Aunt?"

She shuddered. Opening the book, she cleared her throat. "Anne, this is a book on the human anatomy."

Peeking at the open page, I spied a pen and ink sketch of the body of a naked woman standing with her arms straight down. Millions of blood vessels were running up and down her body. I covered my eyes and listened to yet another strange account of how young girls, in one glorious instant, became young ladies.

"Well, Aunt," I shook my head, "I can assure you, I do not feel glorious."

She patted my hand and kissed my forehead. "No, Anne, nor do I."

* * *

All during that following autumn, I watched my breasts grow and found little red hairs sprouting on the dark corners of my body—just as Aunt had predicted. I kept her and Elly informed of all the changes taking place. True to her book of anatomy, my little girl body was fast dissolving into a form quite like Aunt Alice's.

While taking tea with Aunt and Elly one gloomy Sunday afternoon, just before Mr Phillipps was to call, I sighed. "At night, just before I fall off to sleep, I can feel my breasts growing."

Elly shook her head laughing.

"Really Anne," Aunt moaned, "one cannot *feel* their breasts grow."

"Oh, but I can, Aunt. And I can feel my legs stretching longer, my feet ..."

Franklin entered. "Miss Holt, Mr Phillipps."

"Thank you, Franklin. Ask Abigail if the vicar's favourite sweet cakes are ready."

When Mr Phillipps entered the room, his hair was sticking straight up where his hat had been. He looked quite silly, all in all. But then, he always did look ...

"Good afternoon, Mr Phillipps," smiled Aunt.

Elly nodded. "Tea, sir?"

"Why, yes, thank you." Taking his usual place, he hemmed, indignation clearly embossed on the pattern of his façade. "Miss Holt," he said to Aunt Alice, "I most recently discovered that my sister attended a *symphony* at the Royal Albert." He cleared his throat again.

Aunt regarded him innocently. Elly tugged the rope pull for Abigail. I was fidgeting with the rings on Aunt's fingers. When she did not respond to his obvious concern, he continued.

"Yes, well, imagine my surprise when I discovered it was not a lecture at all, but a symphony with a former colleague of mine."

Abigail bustled in with the tea tray and sweet cakes.

"And?" inquired Aunt Alice. "What of it?"

The vicar first requested two more sugars. He held his cup up to Abigail, "Yes, yes, that's it." Clinking his spoon about the cup for what seemed an hour, he continued, "Professor Mandeville led his students over a Berlioz composi ..."

Aunt interrupted, "It was marvellous, sir. I enjoyed it with immense pleasure." Sitting down her tea, she lifted her chin and, still eye-to-eye with the vicar, smiled.

The wrinkle on his nose reddened. "I do not approve of such music, Miss Holt. It is the devil's work."

"I do not find it so, sir." Aunt's chin lifted just a little higher.

His face grew a deeper red; storm ridges gathered over the bridge of his prominent, pocked-marked, nose. Holding the cup to his chin, he inhaled, steamy vapours disappeared up his nostrils—something was brewing.

"I shall make myself quite clear on the subject." He pursed his lips. "I forbid my sister, henceforth, from attending any lectures or symphonies when Professor Mandeville is in attendance." He frowned, emphasising again, "I forbid it. Certainly I cannot instruct you, Miss Holt, but as your moral counsellor, your ..."

"Mr Phillipps," Aunt straightened in her chair, "I have every intention of listening to whomever and whatever, whenever I wish—and with whomever I wish."

Excited over Aunt's grand stand, her sass, I jumped up and felt, for the first time, my little breasts jiggle. Awed at the sensation, I giggled.

Mr Phillipps glared at me.

Aunt turned to me. "Anne?"

"Excuse me, Aunt Alice." I closed my mouth and my eyes.

The Vicar's hand shook as he withdrew his spotted handkerchief and dabbed his brow. "Hmm." He stood. "Excuse me, Miss Holt, Mrs Mills." He nodded at me. "I have the sick yet to visit. Good afternoon."

The room remained quiet. Elly stood at the window, peeking around a bit of lace, whispering, "He's gone."

"He loses at every turn, Aunt." Glancing at Abigail's tray, I added, "and he didn't even take a sweet cake."

Returning to her easy chair, Elly picked up her knitting. Cushioning it on her lap, she sighed. "Well, he is at least constant."

"Who said, 'Tis is often constancy to change the mind?' " [10] Aunt glanced at me. "Anne?"

"Hmm," I leaned back, staring at the ceiling. "I am quite certain it was not Miss Pramm."

*   *   *

Mr Phillipps continued to pay his dutiful visits to Lesington Hall, and this afternoon Charlotte accompanied him. Sitting at his side, she held a delicate love-filled smile. Thoughts of the Professor, I was quite sure of it. As we entertained them in the sunroom, the vicar sat awash in the sun's yellow rays. I actually found him not quite so pallid. I had learned so much about skin tones, light and tints and how to judge one's character by his cheek and brow. Madame Pinchot had once said something about lumps and bumps on one's head, but I would never touch the vicar's prickly head—never.

And now, with a great deal of Miss Pramm's schooling, I felt I could show Madame Pinchot a thing or two. Indeed, I fancied myself quite perceptive. Pulling Charlotte aside, I inquired, "You have been smiling a great deal this morning, Miss Charlotte."

Blushing, she whispered, "I received a letter from Professor Mandeville, Anne—while, thank God, Clarke was in his study."

"Well, then," I raised my voice for her brother's benefit, "you must play the piano for us."

"Oh," she glanced at him, "Oh, yes, of course, if you insist."

He grunted, but made no comment.

As we scurried to the music room, Charlotte withdrew the well-worn letter from her bag. "Hurry, Imp," she said breathlessly, "read it while I play."

---

[10] Pietro Metastasio (1698 – 1782) Italian poet and opera composer. From "Siroes", Act 1, scene 8 in *Dramas and Other Poems of Abbe Pietro Metastasio*, translated from Italian by John Hoole, Vol. 3 (1800).

"Oh, Charlotte," I giggled over her shoulder, reading it aloud as she stumbled on the keys. "He loves you. Maybe soon, by Christmas at least, he will ..."

"Who loves whom?" Her brother loomed in the doorway.

I hid the letter behind my back. Holly Berry guessed at the game and ripped it from my hands. She ran willy-nilly about the room with the letter dangling from her mouth.

Charlotte immediately stood from the piano and faced her brother. Her face was flushed.

"Holly Berry," I called, "naughty girl, come, come, now."

Aunt and Elly entered the room. "Oh, that troublesome pup," said Aunt, half-laughing. "What has she in her mouth, Anne?"

"Papers, Aunt."

"I can see that, but what papers? Pray tell, it is not Charlotte's music lessons?"

Charlotte's face turned pale, Aunt apparently realised her error and moved toward us. Her brother had been successfully kept in the dark regarding Charlotte's music lessons and the little money she received.

"Charlotte's music lessons?" boomed Mr Phillipps. "Are there two Charlottes in our neighbourhood?"

I caught up with Holly Berry and salvaged the letter—now soggy, ink-stained, and raggedy.

Taking Mr Phillipps arm, Aunt flashed a sweet alluring smile. As she worked her charm to remove him from the room, he blushed, obviously forgetting even the time of day. "Come, come ... sir," she whispered, "I have something I must show you."

Blubbering a sentence or two, he finally managed a few coherent words, "Oh, indeed, Miss Holt."

Elly followed pulling the door closed behind her.

Charlotte brought her hands to her face, fretting, "Oh, Anne, Clarke will surely question me about the music lessons when we return home."

"No, Charlotte, I think not."

"Why, what do you mean?"

"It is the art of allurement, Charlotte. Aunt Alice will smooth everything to perfection." Folding up her soggy letter, I returned it to her. "More to the point, Professor Mandeville loves you. So, what are you to do about it?"

"I have not the slightest idea, Imp."

"Oh, if only Aunt could find a way."

"Your aunt has such a way with Clarke, Anne. I am certain one word from her and Professor Mandeville would surely be permitted to call on me."

"Then you must speak with her, Charlotte, and soon."

"Very well, Anne, tomorrow when I come for your piano lesson, I will purport my dilemma."

* * *

The next day just before my lesson, I situated Charlotte in the red velvet chair by the window seat. Holly Berry lay curled by the hearth, asleep. Charlotte looked nervous and tinged with lovesickness. I was sure of it.

"I shall find Aunt and bring her here, Miss Charlotte. Once you share your dilemma, then perhaps you shall feel better for it."

"Oh, thank you, Anne." She shuffled her music sheets and sighed. "I think I just may."

Oh, I could not bear it that Charlotte would shed one more tear at separation from her true love, her heart's desire. And I went searching for Aunt. I found her alone in her study. I begged a word with her.

"Come, come, Anne. What do you mean you wish to *beg* a word with me? No need to beg. Come, now." She patted the cushion next to her. "Is your piano lesson not going well?"

"I love my piano lessons, Aunt Alice." I took in a breath. "But not as much as Miss Charlotte loves Professor Mandeville."

Aunt studied my face for a moment. I could see her lips quiver; she either wanted to laugh or scold me. "Well, I do not know that she loves him more than you love your piano lessons, Anne."

Putting on my best-begging face, I pleaded, "Oh, she *loves* him more, Aunt Alice. I assure you of that."

"Anne, you must not pry."

"Please, Aunt Alice, Charlotte needs your most excellent guidance."

"Excellent guidance? Why, whatever do you mean, Anne?"

"She is in the music room, Aunt ... with Holly Berry."

Aunt took my hand. "Come along, then."

We huddled together with Charlotte on the red velvet sofa. Holly Berry would lift her head, peruse us, and flop back down stretching and yawning, soon to resume her snoring.

"Miss Charlotte," said Aunt, taking her hand, "Professor Mandeville is quite sincere, of that I am convinced. But I hesitate at becoming involved ... I do not wish to make enemies with your brother."

"Oh, Miss Holt," she brought her handkerchief to her eyes, "Clarke would never become enemies with you. He finds you, ah, excuse me, Miss Holt, but my brother certainly admires and respects the Holt family." Her face flushed. "If I only knew *why* Clarke does not approve of Professor Mandeville."

"Well, I could surely find *that* out." Aunt inhaled a conspiratorial breath.

"I would be much obliged, Miss Holt." Charlotte wrung her hands. "Clarke refuses even to discuss him."

"Indeed." Aunt pursed her lips. "Give me a little time, Miss Charlotte." She gestured toward the piano. "For now, you may continue your lessons." She stood, glanced at me and smiled, then quitted the room.

"Oh, Anne, I cannot tell you how grateful I am for your Aunt's assistance."

Holly Berry nudged my leg. Petting her silky head, I sighed, thinking of Aunt Alice, yet unmarried. I thought of her obvious love for Sir Anthony and how soon it could once more fade without my intervention. No, no one should ever squander love into a faded memory. I broke from the daydream and fretted, "How dreadful the idea of becoming an old maid, Charlotte."

"Oh, indeed, but I am twenty-two, and you are just twelve."

I puffed out my budding little chest. "Soon, thirteen." I studied her sad face and imagined spending an eternity in the parsonage alone with her brother. "I certainly would not like to live in a church all the days of my life."

"Surely not, Anne." She frowned. "One can scarcely breathe for the rules."

"Not to forget the clangour of bells, the brattle of candles ..."

CHAPTER ELEVEN

Spring 1864

That following spring, my dearest friend Kate was to return to Miss Pramm's from a long time travelling with her family. Just as I was to enter the school, I heard her familiar voice. "Miss Anne!"

I hurried back down the steps. "Miss Katherine!" All aflutter, I rushed to her. "Oh, how I have missed you." Kissing each cheek, I hugged her. "Your letters were delightful. How did you find Brussels, Liverpool? How was your holiday at Bath?"

Hugging me, she shook her head. "Oh, Bath does wonders for Mama. She waded in the waters every day. Liverpool is Liverpool." She shrugged. "Brussels is pleasant enough. Papa always has much business there. I quite dislike being away for so long."

"Yes, and I have been so bored without you."

"Did you get my card for your birthday? And how was your Christmas holiday? Oh, I have been too long absent from Miss Pramm's."

"Indeed, you have missed much."

Walking down the noisy hall toward the art room, I recollected one session in particular. "We learned how to recover from a fainting spell with the utmost decorum, Miss Kate."

"Indeed." She wrinkled her nose into a question mark. "How does one fall gracefully?"

"Oh, one never falls, one slopes, slouches, or folds up."

She giggled. "Then soon you must demonstrate for me, Miss Anne."

Reaching our art class, we took our seats at the easels.

"Miss Anne, I am having a party next month. Just this morning I sent you an invitation. All my family will be there, and I will introduce you to my cousin, Edward."

My scheming little heart fluttered. Sir Anthony would be there. Oh, great and glorious were my visions to have love abound in Lesington Hall once more. Moreover, I would meet Sir Anthony's son, Edward—or was it John?"

Kate blabbered on with high-toned enthusiasm, "And my cousin, Edward, the one who was well acquainted with Mr Dickens, will be there. Oh, and by the way, Mr Dickens has been invited. You must come."

"Oh, Miss Kate." I twirled. "I will, I will."

* * *

The following morning, waking from a sweet dream, I pondered how I would conduct my love schemes for Aunt Alice at Kate's party. A sudden dark blanket of shame spread over my good intentions. Aunt was a proud woman. Had I betrayed her loyalty by befriending a Hathaway for such purposes of igniting an old love with Sir Anthony?

Though I loved Kate as a sister, I also wanted to have Aunt happily married, and not to be ignored, I would be situated in the very middle of such happiness. Could this wish be selfish? I knew I must confess to Aunt my affiliation with the Hathaways and speak to her about Sir Anthony. Surely bringing two lit candles together to form one glorious flame was not sinful.

Knocking upon Aunt's bedroom door, I listened for her call. "It is I, Aunt Alice, wishing a moment of your time."

"Come, dear."

"Good morning, Aunt. It is a sweet morning."

Bundled in her white morning robe, Aunt sat in her cosy sunlit alcove—sipping tea. The silver tea service gleamed in the soft morning light; a small antique silver spoon lay near hidden by the crystal vase crowded with ferns and yellow daisies.

"What brings you to my room so early, Anne?"

Taking the red velvet cushioned window seat, I spied the gold ring still lying on the sill. "I have been invited to a party, Aunt. It is from a schoolmate."

"How nice." With both hands around the dainty white porcelain cup, Aunt inhaled. "Miss Katherine, is it?"

"Oh, yes." I smiled, nodding. "Miss Katherine Hathaway, Aunt." Again I glanced at the ring. "Her uncle is Sir Anthony Hathaway."

Aunt's hands did not tremble; her brows did not lift, nor did her face colour. "She is a kind and humorous friend of mine, Aunt Alice. Already I love her dearly. I do hope you do not find my friendship with a Hathaway disloyal."

She set down her cup. "Disloyal? Dear me, Anne. Indeed not. Do not think for a moment that my history with Sir Anthony should in any manner interfere with your friendships."

Relieved, I leaned back against the cool window pane. "Kate has promised to introduce me to her cousin, Edward. He is great friends with the author, Mr Dickens, Aunt—and to think he will be at the party."

"Indeed, then you must go. You are quite fond of Dickens. Yes, I shall have Elly accompany you."

Since she had not offered to chaperone me, I knew not to ask. A silence settled in the little alcove. Aunt's face did colour just a little, but I couldn't tell if it was from the excitement of my meeting Mr Dickens or my meeting Sir Anthony again.

"I do hope his dog, Berry, will be there, Aunt."

A smile curled her lips. "Berry is a beautiful dog, much like your Holly Berry. You must tell Sir Anthony how she got her name, Anne. It will delight him to hear of it."

"Oh, yes, Aunt. I shall tell him." I prepared to leave and paused. "But, Aunt, perhaps someday soon you might enjoy telling him the story yourself."

She crossed her hands, rested her chin atop them, and glanced up at me. "You are a clever little cupid, my dear."

There was that faint smile at the very tip of her mouth that I loved. That slight, simple gesture eased my troubled heart, assuring me I was not a wicked person after all. I was, in her eyes, acceptable and wholesome. My thoughts were never purer than at those moments of acceptance, of being loved and valued, when only goodness floated about my heart. Then, sun-filled visions eased the darker moments of my reflections: Mama lying spent in her airless wooden world heaped with black dirt; the vile Mr O'Leary's hairy fingers; Madame Pinchot's Tarot death card; Misha's mourning cry. Indeed, everything was right in the world. Certainly, I could meld two burning candles into one.

* * *

I waited for Kate's party with glad expectation. Aunt, Elly, and I went shopping for the latest fabric for my new frock. I had grown a little since my last social gathering, and Aunt Alice insisted I should look quite the darling. I was more than anxious to meet Mr Dickens, and more to the point, to see Sir Anthony again. Oh, happy stratagems, oh such happy stratagems. Yet, I must be patient. To try too hard at Aunt's reconciliation might put a knot in the very weave of destiny's fabric.

* * *

The day of Kate's party arrived. As I twirled in my new dress, Aunt looked me up and down one last time.

"Very well, Anne," she cocked her head and nodded with that ever-discerning eye, "You will do."

"You know very well, Alice, that Anne looks beautiful." Elly poked a loose flower back into my braided hair. "Indeed she will do."

Hearing the chain works from the cuckoo preparing itself, I puckered my lips to sing in unison with my wood-headed little friend. When he sprang from his little chalet, I mimicked, "Cuckoo, cuckoo, cuckoo."

"Kiss your Aunt, good-bye, Miss Cuckoo, we must be going."

I kissed Aunt's giggling lips.

"Do enjoy your party, dearest," she smiled.

"I will, Aunt Alice. I will."

I would mention her to Sir Anthony; I sensed she knew that I would. Elly and I met Franklin in the vestibule. Holding the door open, he stood stiff and formal.

"We shall not be late in returning, Franklin," said Elly.

"Indeed, ma'am."

The petticoats under my satin skirt crinkled like sheets of fine paper. Touching my elbow, Franklin helped me into the carriage. "You look just as stately as Her Majesty, Miss Anne."

I lifted my chin, settled into my seat and waved away his words. "Oh, indeed, Prince Franklin, indeed I must."

Elly shook her head and muttered, "You are both cuckoo."

* * *

In the entrance to the Hathaway House, there was an enormous, round-faced oak grandfather's clock. Its long brass pendulum flashed brassy streaks as it swung silently within its thick glass case.

Kate hugged me. "I am so happy to see you, Miss Anne."

As the clock strained four tinny strokes, I introduced Elly. "Miss Katherine, I am pleased to introduce you to my dear cousin, Mrs Mills."

"So very pleased, ma'am," said Kate. "Miss Anne has told me such kind things about you and Miss Holt."

Elly nodded. "We have heard nothing but high praises about you as well, Miss Hathaway. It is my pleasure."

Kate guided Elly and me through the throng of guests to meet her parents.

"Mama, Papa," said Kate, "Please meet Miss Anne Holt and her cousin, Mrs Mills."

"Miss Holt." Mrs Hathaway took my gloved hand. "Pleased, my dear. Katherine speaks warmly of you."

"And often," laughed her father. He bowed over Elly's hand. "So nice to meet you, madam, though not advertised, it is Kate's birthday."

"Oh, la," I kissed Kate's cheek. "Happy birthday, you are ten and four then?"

Kate smiled broadly, "Yes."

"Ugh," I moaned, "I must wait another eight months."

Elly shook her head. "Pity the more."

We moved along mingling in the crowd. Eventually, Elly found the side room where tables were laden with food. Meats, cheeses, sweets, apples, and other assorted fruits were arranged on silver tiered plates.

"Oh, Lord, child," she dabbed her lips, "stand right where you are. I just spotted the cookies."

"And over there," Kate pointed, "is the lemonade."

Elly hemmed. "But right *there* are the cookies."

Elly whispered to herself at every sweet-tart design; examining every bit of fruit; every little brown upturned pie corner; every petit lace doily; each exquisite dish. "Oh, a splendid table, Miss Hathaway."

"I am glad you find it so, Mrs Mills, and please, you must call me Katherine."

The music was not of my choice, and I thought of Charlotte. *If I ever have a party, I shall have her play her heart out to everyone's delight, and I shall invite Professor Mandeville and his students and ...*

Tugging at my elbow, Kate leaned into me. "When Cousin Edward comes, I shall straightaway introduce you."

"I cannot wait, Miss Kate."

"Excuse me, Papa is motioning for me."

Turning to Elly, I said in a low tone, "I am sure Aunt told you Kate is Sir Anthony Hathaway's niece." She nodded continuing to nose about the food. "Well, she is going to introduce me to his son, Edward." My chin went up. I was feeling very smart indeed. "Do you know that Sir Anthony has two sons, Elly? Yes, and today I am to meet one of them—Edward Hathaway."

Elly held a delicate berry tart in her hand. "Yes, I am aware of his two sons."

My self-esteem vented. I was not quite as all knowing as I had thought. "At any rate, Edward keeps good company, Elly. He will introduce me to the author, Mr Dickens, this very evening."

"Oh, right, your favourite writer, how fortunate for you, dear."

"Miss Anne," said Kate tugging on my sleeve, "Edward has finally arrived."

Moving through the crowded room, I held her hand tight. She approached a thin, handsome young man; his eyes were a warm dark brown, his thick black hair parted crookedly in the middle. He was fair in complexion with a fine straight nose.

Kate nudged me. "Cousin, please meet my dearest friend, Miss Anne Holt."

"Miss Holt," he half-bowed, "pleased."

I curtsied. "Sir."

"Edward, Miss Anne is the friend of mine who is so very fond of Mr Dickens ... you must introduce her to him."

"Oh, yes, now I remember." He glanced about the room. "I do not believe, Cousin Kate, that Dickens has arrived just yet." Turning back to me, he smiled. "But, Miss Holt, when he does I shall find you promptly." With that, he excused himself and took the hand of a pretty girl who stood behind us.

Turning to a familiar voice, I found Sir Anthony directly behind me. I could see how Aunt had fallen in love with him: his warm brown eyes seemed to be able to read one in a second; sandy coloured hair set him apart from the others. No one else had such a colour; his smooth clean complexion crinkled when he smiled; his voice cheery, serious, calm—a mixture of good breeding and natural kindness, I supposed.

"Oh, Uncle," Kate took his hand, "please meet my dearest friend, Miss Anne Holt.

Standing back, he eyed me soundly. "Why, I know you. Yes, Labrucherie ... France. You are Alice Holt's niece."

"Yes, sir, I am pleased to meet you again, sir."

He glanced over my shoulder. "Did your Aunt Alice come along?"

"No, sir, she did not. My dear cousin, Mrs Mills, accompanied me instead." I looked around but could not find her. "She is probably nibbling at something, somewhere."

He nodded with a half-smile.

"I have healed, sir." I gestured toward my ankle. "Not a mark remains."

Kate's brows lifted. "Marks?"

Sir Anthony shook his head. "Berry took her for quite a jaunt down the halls of Labrucherie, an inn in France. I was passing through, travelling on to Marseille, when we met."

I explained how her uncle and my family met while on holiday there.

Sir Anthony smiled. "Tell me, Anne, is your aunt in good health?"

"Oh, she is very well, sir. Mrs Mills and I just left her."

"Before the evening is through, I shall speak with Mrs Mills," he said.

"And how is Berry, sir?"

"At this moment I do believe she is wading in the fountain just out front."

Kate nodded. "You must have guessed by now, Miss Anne, at how spoiled she is."

"Indeed, but she is a wonderful dog." I smiled remembering how playful she was.

Just then Edward Hathaway approached with a familiar looking gentleman. "Father, I promised Miss Holt I would introduce Mr Dickens to her."

The famous author took my trembling hand with kindness. "A pleasure, Miss Holt."

"Oh, sir, I cannot tell you how I love your books, especially *David Copperfield*. It was masterful, sir."

"Masterful?" he smiled. "For one so young, you are very generous with your praise."

"Oh, sir, I know my own mind."

Sir Anthony laughed. "And so you do. Come along now, you shall have Mr Dickens quite conceited before he leaves our company."

Curtsying, I smiled as Edward led Mr Dickens back into the crowd. "Oh, thank you, Miss Kate. Shall I now demonstrate how one swoons gracefully?"

Sir Anthony dabbed his brow. "Shall we step onto the balcony for a little air? Come along, ladies. You may do your swooning there," he laughed.

We followed him out onto the balcony. For late March, it was unusually warm. Glancing down, I spotted Berry resting on the cool spring grass. The purple shade of the Hathaway House hovered over her.

"Uncle, please excuse me for a moment. I must remind Mama of something." Kate then hurried away.

Sir Anthony turned to me. "Tell me, Miss Anne, is your Aunt Alice well?"

"Oh, very well, sir." At this very moment, I felt, with a few well-placed words I could quite possibly have a hand in awakening a long overdue love. *Let me see now … .*

He glanced over the crowd in the ballroom. Returning his gaze to me, he smiled. "And you live with her, do you?"

"Yes, sir." My mind raced to find something, anything to rekindle a vision of Aunt Alice: *She is very beautiful, my Aunt. The vicar admires her … no, no, that would never do.* I wracked my brain, willing the pieces to fall into their correct places, but I had no pieces with which to work.

"In London … Lesington Hall, is it?" He asked.

"I beg your pardon, sir?"

"You live with your aunt at Lesington Hall?"

"Oh, yes, yes, sir."

"Hmm, so, ah, have you lived with her all your life?"

"No, sir, only since I was eleven years of age." Of a sudden, my plans to further Aunt Alice's cause melted away, dissolving into a blank slate, dark grey, and silent. Then I blurted, "I must explain myself, sir. Before Mother died, she sent me away to my Aunt Alice. I was born in Holybourne, 14 December, 1861."

"Oh, dear me, how unfortunate ..." he hemmed, "Ah, forgive me, Miss Anne, I meant how unfortunate your mother's death, not that you were born, of course."

Relaying certain oddities of my life to him, I could feel his gaze steady upon my face, that familiar expression that Aunt, Elly, and Franklin, all of them held when I spoke of Mama.

His face, indeed, held a sorrowful expression. "I am sorry to hear of her passing, Miss Anne. Truly I am. I remember your mother and how she loved to dance." He looked up into the heavens. "But that was long ago."

A spark of wonder raced through my body; my throat went dry; my heart pounded, much the same as when I touched Aunt's gold band on the sill. "Then you must remember my dearest Papa, as well?" My breathing seemed to stop. At last, perhaps, I would learn from him what no one else had ever shared with me, things about my father.

"Oh, Uncle," said Kate as she took his hand. "Come, hurry, will you? Mama is with another nasty headache."

"Excuse me, Miss Anne."

Oh, I was so close to learning about Papa. I didn't want to lose such an opportunity and followed them through the birthday revellers: past the musicians blowing their horns, plucking their strings; past the butlers balancing trays of tall crystal glasses full of sparkling juices. Then I followed them down a wide hall where they hurriedly disappeared into a room. Stopping at the door, I thought it wise to wait just outside. But, becoming weary, I returned to Elly's side.

Setting her empty dish on the side table, Elly hemmed, "We must soon be off, Anne. Your Aunt will wonder if we have left her for good."

Just as we were putting our shawls on, Kate found me. "Dear me, Miss Anne, I have been searching for you. I thought you left without saying goodbye."

"We were just now leaving, Miss Kate." I took her hand. "You must come to Lesington Hall and visit with us."

"I will, I will, but first come now and say good-bye to Mama and Papa."

"And Sir Anthony?" I asked, hoping for another word with him.

"Oh, I am sorry, Anne, he was suddenly called away."

* * *

I waved good-bye to Kate as our carriage left the Hathaway House. Thinking about her superb party, I watched Elly fuss with her berry stained gloves and I wondered in amazement at the new secret passage of my life.

"My, but you are sighing a good bit, my dear. Did you not find the party to your liking? Oh, I know, you didn't meet your revered author, Mr Dickens?"

"Oh, but I did, Elly and it was a wonderful party. It was just that I am caught up in yet another one of life's mysteries."

"Caught up, are you? Well, mysteries are often easy puzzles to solve, my dear." She tweaked my nose.

"Oh, Elly, I think not such an easy puzzle shall be solved." I shook my head in the dusky expanse of our cab. "Aunt told me I was not to question her regarding my father—at least not until I am older. And I don't know how much older I am supposed to be."

"Yes, I know, dear," she pressed my hand, "so, what brought on the mystery regarding your father?"

"I was speaking with Sir Anthony Hathaway. He said he remembered my mother. I inquired regarding my father. Oh, I am most certain he was to impart something, but he was suddenly called away."

"Anne, I cannot be disloyal to your aunt. You must understand that."

Dusk was pulling a purple curtain about the city; it had begun to rain again. As we passed Covent Gardens, the street lamps cast a warm glow about the shiny pavement. Turning his back to the wind, a lone policeman held his hat. Lucky for the street urchins, who hid amongst the gate vines that they would not get wet. With my nose pressed to the carriage window, I watched the little beggars until I fogged the window. "Pity them."

"Pity who, Anne?"

The carriage was now quite dark inside. "Pity and bless the beggar children, Elly. If not for Aunt Alice, I should have become one of them." My heart, heavy with remembrances of my own dark past, was equally perturbed that I had squandered my opportunity to ignite Sir Anthony's passion for Aunt.

* * *

The following morning, as I snuggled with Aunt in her window alcove, she seemed her usual self while I relayed the particulars of the party. "I met Mr Dickens and Sir Anthony. But Sir Anthony was called away, Aunt. There was not time enough ..."

"Anne," she put her finger to my lips, "do not worry. C'est la vie."

"Oui, c'est la vie, Aunt."

Later that afternoon, alone with my thoughts, my mind raced with Aunt's 'C' est la vie: 'that's life; that's how things happen.' But I would not give up so easily as she. I must find a way for her ... and him.

* * *

The next day, in school, the older girls' drama class was to perform Shakespeare's *Much Ado About Nothing*. Just as I entered the theatre, Kate tapped my shoulder.

"I got your invitation to tea, Miss Anne."

"I addressed it myself," I said proudly.

She smiled. "Hmm, indeed, I guessed as much. Such a dainty scroll, if ever I saw one, dear."

I smiled. "There is much more, Miss Kate." I raised my brow, lifted my chin. Though she was my dearest friend, I dared not tell her about *everyone* I had invited. I kept that secret to myself.

"I must know, Miss Anne, what have you planned? I would suppose tea, sweet cakes, fortune tellers, and perhaps a reading from your most famous Madame Pinchot?"

I teased her all the more. "You shall never guess, never." I pinched my lips and closed my eyes.

"Anne, you are vexing me again." She begged. "Come now, you must tell me." Tickling my sides, she clamoured, "You must tell me the secret."

The lights in the small makeshift theatre dimmed. Frowning, Miss Pramm shushed us. Two students pulled the heavy green velvet drapes apart. I was unable to hold the secret longer and whispered to Kate, "We are to have a live monkey at my party."

"A monkey?" cried Kate out loud, disrupting the play.

Miss Pramm promptly escorted us from the laughing crowd. "Monkey, indeed, Miss Hathaway." She gripped my hand. "And, Miss Holt, what part have you in the folly?"

"Miss Pramm, it is only that I am to have a live monkey at my first tea."

"A monkey? Indeed not, for I have never heard such a shocking thing." Tut-tutting in obvious disgust, she scolded, "Have you not learned one thing from the tea class? Of course you have not. I will certainly speak with your aunt, Miss Holt. And Miss Hathaway, I will speak with your mother."

"Oh, thank you, Miss Pramm," said Kate exhaling in such a breath. "Mother is just the one to scold me. Papa is far too severe."

Kate was a clever girl, I reasoned, for Mr Hathaway was the more jovial of the two ... and always quite forgiving of his little darling.

"Hmm." Miss Pramm muttered, "Perhaps then a silly, giggly girl of your making deserves the attentions of a male persuasion."

"Oh, please, Miss Pramm, not my father."

Taking in a great air, Miss Pramm sighed. "I am afraid I must. It is all in your best interest, Miss Hathaway."

Scurrying down the hall, we followed Miss Pramm into the art room where she hastened together two paper cone hats. On both she wrote in thick black India ink: "Monkey Mannered."

I was positioned in one corner of the room, Kate in the other. We had to bear the humility of wearing the hats the remainder of the day.

* * *

When I came in from school, I found Aunt in the study. I had thought and thought how I was to explain to Aunt about Miss Pramm's written notice of our ill-manners. I was forced to carry home, and hand deliver, my *monkey mannered coned hat*. But how was I to do such a thing? Just simply place it near her salver and hope she forgets to look? I had never been disciplined before in school. What might Aunt say?

"And what did you learn in school today, Anne?"

"That monkeys are stupid little creatures, Aunt Alice."

Elly mimicked my words, "Stupid little creatures?"

I was not amused.

"I cannot believe such a change in my strong opinionated niece. One who simply insisted upon having a monkey spoon the sugar," said Aunt Alice.

"And pour the cream," added Elly with a nod.

"From this, Anne, am I to understand you do not wish to have a *real* monkey at your first tea?"

"That is right, Aunt." I handed her my cone hat and a note from Miss Pramm. I sat on her foot stool, staring up into her face.

Aunt read the note and then handed it to Elly.

"But you were so excited at the *Monkey* prospect," added Elly.

I found them exchanging glances. They knew, and now I knew they knew.

Shaking my head, I said, "No, monkeys will simply not do."

Aunt set down her book. "I think that a very sensible plan, Anne."

Elly nodded, with a poorly disguised snicker for a yawn.

* * *

Today was my first formal afternoon tea party. The guests were chatting amicably as they strolled from their carriages toward the garden. And, I noticed with relief, that the horses were all tethered behind the coach-house. I had worried that Gib, our beloved blind barn cat would become confused again at all the people and somehow stumble into the path of a careening carriage. But my worst fears were alleviated when I spied the old fellow had found the fish platter ... much to Abigail and Franklin's dismay. Gib was hoisted into the arms of the milkmaid and promptly whisked away from the food table and safely deposited into the mews.

Holly Berry was content to teethe on the corners of Aunt's white, hand-woven table linen that hung, useless in Berry's opinion, over the serving table. Spying the raggedy gnawed edges, I knew Aunt would not be pleased.

With little trouble, Aunt secured Professor Mandeville and his students to play at my tea. At noon they were busy tuning their instruments; spearing the air with his wand, the professor frequently glanced over his shoulder, no doubt searching for Charlotte.

"Anne," said Aunt, as she touched my shoulder, taking in the air, "what a perfect day for your first tea party. I see your guests are now arriving. You have invited eleven?"

"Yes, Aunt." I smiled.

"I take it someone will come alone, Anne? Eleven is an odd number."

"The *odd one* is the vicar, Aunt Alice."

Kate entered the garden with two young gentlemen at her side. Franklin took her umbrella.

"Aunt, come with me and meet Miss Kate." I led her to the fountain. "Aunt, may I introduce you to my good friend, Miss Katherine Hathaway."

Aunt seemed proud as she took Kate's hand, smiling. "So very nice to finally meet you, Miss Hathaway."

"Good afternoon, Miss Holt. So nice to meet you as well."

Aunt smiled at the two young men who stood next to her.

"Oh, Miss Holt," said Kate, "please meet my brother, Mr Charles Hathaway and my cousin, Mr Edward Hathaway."

I was intrigued to meet Sir Anthony's son, Edward. I watched Aunt as she appeared to be studying Edward as well. Both young men seemed taken by Aunt Alice's comeliness, for their faces coloured just a tinge.

Charles glanced around at the grounds. "Lesington Hall is more than beautiful, Miss Holt."

Edward puffed up. "Indeed it is. Upon occasion, Father and I have driven by, and I have often wondered what lay behind the walls; what might the gardens look like, and what sort of fountains would adorn the grounds." He nodded, looking impressed. "I am not disappointed. This is a splendid garden, indeed."

"Thank you, sir." Aunt continued to study his face.

"Come along everyone," I directed, "when we sit, you must use *this* table." I gestured to the crescent-shaped table situated in the shade. "You must sit under Aunt Alice's ancient yew."

Edward eyed the massive tree. "Oh, yes, this *is* an old fellow. I venture to guess 500 years, at least."

Aunt stood next to him looking up at it. "Why, that it is, perhaps, or very close, at least, Mr Hathaway. How clever you are."

"It is your favourite tree in the garden, I can tell." Edward smiled.

"Yes, Mr Hathaway, it is."

Now Aunt's face coloured. Her smile seemed ironical in a way, for that was where Edward's father, Anthony, had proposed to her years earlier. Glancing up to Aunt's window, I spied the little gold ring still sitting on the sill. My plan was formed.

Just then the garden gate clanged, and I found that it was Miss Pramm and Mrs Bleecher, our instructor in art—I had to invite Miss Pramm, of course. Her signature and that of Mrs Bleecher's were required on my diploma. I happily situated them very near the food table.

Charlotte and her brother arrived, but they chose to come through the house rather than the gate. Stepping from the side porch-door, Charlotte took my hand and whispered, "I spied Professor Mandeville first off. Oh, Anne, I cannot thank you enough."

"It was Aunt's idea to invite him, Charlotte." I squeezed her hand.

She exhaled, glancing up to the heavens. "I shall fade into oblivion when he turns and looks into my eyes."

"Do not fade until *after* tea, Charlotte. Miss Pramm will not approve."

Charlotte's brother stood on the porch and hemmed until he secured Aunt's attention.

She nodded. "Mr Phillipps, sir, a very good day to you. Excuse me, but I did not see you come through the gate."

"Charlotte and I entered through the front entrance, Miss Holt." Squinting in the sun, he ran his finger around his tight collar and glanced around with a frown. "But, I do not know where she has gone off too, however."

I paired off the vicar with Miss Pramm and Mrs Bleecher, all three were gluttonous over one thing or the other. My guest's names were etched in a handsome scroll sitting at their designated place at the table, and I situated the vicar with his head facing away from our table. Amen.

There seemed to be no limit to the ideas and inspirations that spring, sprang and sprung from my ingenuity. Oh, the novelty of it all. I was feeling quite dizzy with "the power" until Mr Phillipps offered to say grace.

I could feel something vexatious bubbling about my brain area—a few trickles began draining from my cunning pool of power when he stood. He soon noticed Aunt sitting at our table under the great yew, a vacant chair next to her. I had reserved *that* chair for Professor Mandeville. Charlotte would then be positioned next to him. It was broad daylight, and anyone with an open eye could read the handsome place setting scroll: *Professor Mandeville*. Surely he would not take the professor's chair, but I've been wrong before.

Charlotte preened as she waited for Professor Mandeville to take his chair. The vicar inched his way toward my fatal error—the vacant chair error. *Will my plan unravel?*

Mr Phillipps, now smiling down at Aunt Alice, slid the chair back, and in the process, raked clumps of Aunt's revered virgin grass into lifeless little dirt clods. Glancing up into the outstretched limbs of the Great Yew, he seemed absolutely assured of his place at Lesington Hall. He patted his vest pocket. I will just take this chair, Miss Holt." He patted his vest pocket again. "Dear me," he frowned, "I seem to have misplaced my little book of prayers."

Glancing down, I heard Holly Berry gnawing on something ... oh, how unfortunate. "Excuse me, Mr Phillipps." I snatched his little black prayer book from her jaws and waved it. "Here it is, sir."

"Why, thank you, Miss Anne." He glanced heavenward. His head jiggled, no doubt in humble thanks to the Holy Father, for all things missing shall be found for the glory of God. When he tried to open the little black, half-chewed, soggy, common book of prayer, his beady black eyes cast downward at my puppy—creature from hell. "Oh, so be it." He fumed. Now refraining from licking his thumb, he squinted, searching ... but the corners, home to the page numbers, were gnawed away.

Clearing his throat, he found the passage now hidden behind his curly thick black eyebrows. Sticking his little book back into his vest pocket, he gestured for all heads to bow, all eyelids to close, and all chewing noises to cease. "Today, dear Lord, we ..."

There was a most peculiar noise just before the branch from the yew tree left its socket and conked Phillipps directly on his brittle head. Yes, it was akin to a little zap of lightning— well, perhaps not quite as loud.

Nonetheless, the vicar, staggering under the leafy assault, fell backward.

Aunt rose from her chair, all a flitter. Elly sprang from her seat like Gib after fish tails. Edward and Charles hurried to him, calling for a pillow.

Edward ran his nimble fingers over the vicar's prickly haired head. "No blood," he said as he shook his head. "Head wounds would bleed excessively. I cannot see a severe wound, thank goodness."

Charles called for Franklin to bring a plank. "So as to convey this limp form from under this present danger," he said, glancing up.

"Oh, take him into the house," said Aunt, pointing. "Dear me. Oh, how dreadful. Take him into the kitchen." She glanced at Edward for approval. "That is, if it's the proper place?"

"Indeed, ma'am, and we will need hot water. Do you have a physician?"

"Why," she looked paralyzed, "why, no, I, we have never ..."

"Fetch my father, Kate," said Edward. "Make haste."

Franklin, Mose the gardener, two grooms and a stable boy hauled the groggy Phillipps into the house. Now sitting up, he seemed quite dazed and silly. His black eyes blinked trying to clear them. He mumbled something about 'where am I?' and 'what happened to my head?'

"Sir," I offered, "you were conked on the bean by a yew branch. Had you only not left your designated place at the table with Miss Pramm things may have ..."

"Anne," said Aunt, "*your* designated place is with your guests."

Charlotte hovered over her brother as he attempted to sit up. She held a moist towel to his head. "Oh, dear brother," she soothed, "how are you?"

"I am, Sister, by the grace of God, alive." His eyes were all *roll-about* as he went limp again.

Edward consoled Charlotte. "Just a knock to the noggin, miss. He shall recover quite nicely. I am sure of it."

"Why, sir, you are indeed the youngest doctor I have ever met."

Edward blushed. "Thank you, Miss Phillipps, but I am not a doctor. I have, however, learned much from my father. He is the physician. My cousins, Charles and Kate, went to fetch him."

My mind whirled under the prospect. Imagine, Sir Anthony here? Under the yew? Oh, how my heart fluttered. I took Charlotte's hand and pulled her outside. "Come along, Charlotte, your brother will be fine, perhaps a nasty headache in the morning."

Glancing back at him, she sighed. "Indeed, Clarke does seem to have recovered."

"Professor Mandeville must be worried sick. Indeed, wondering what has become of you."

She nodded. "Oh, indeed."

When we stepped back into the garden, Professor Mandeville rushed to her side. With utmost concern on his face, he took her hand and led her to an empty table next to the flowering rose. Condoling with her, he gushed, "Thank heavens it was not you, Miss Phillipps. Begging your pardon, how *is* your brother?"

Not waiting for her reply, he continued, "Why, however should I conduct a symphony again as long as I live knowing that such a sign from God Almighty—a falling branch—should thwart my advances." He shook his head. "No, no, I could never twirl a wand again knowing any harm should befall you or yours in my presence."

Charlotte nodded, dabbed her brow and sighed, "Really Professor Mandeville?"

Presently I heard the clatter of hooves crunching and clattering along our entryway. The gate clanged and in rushed Sir Anthony with Charles and Kate at his side. I pointed toward the kitchen. "He is in there, sir ... and still breathing."

Sir Anthony nodded, concern etched on his physician's face. "Thank you, Miss Anne. You are, beyond a doubt, very brave."

As he hurried past and entered the house, I shrugged with a whisper, "Oh, not so very brave, sir."

Miss Pramm and Mrs Bleecher stood at my side. "Oh, yes, my dear," preened Miss Pramm, "you were very brave, indeed. We saw the whole unfortunate incident. Oh, had the vicar not left his designated place at our table ... why, the branch would have fallen quite harmlessly behind your aunt."

"Well," commented Mrs Bleecher, "I didn't witness the branch strike his brain, but I definitely heard the thud, watched him stumble, moan, and ... Oh, my, how he cursed the devil."

"I did, too," cried Kate holding a high and mighty face. "Such cursing I shall never forget."

"Curse the devil?" Miss Pramm drew back. "Curse the devil? Why, I heard nothing of the sort."

"You were busy eating, Miss Pramm. Of course you did not," said Kate, "lucky for you."

I left the two in heated discussion as Mrs Bleecher stood and pointed toward the half-eaten pork pie still sitting on Miss Pramm's plate. Gib was inching his way back to the fish platter, his nose all a flitter. Elly, frowning, withdrew her prized fringed parasol and hurried toward him.

Kate cried out, "Do be merciful, Mrs Mills."

"Oh, indeed, dearest." She shook her parasol. "Perhaps a little shade for the ol' boy."

I scooped up Holly Berry and kissed her cheek. "Poor dear puppy." I stroked her shiny little head and thought of Mr Phillipps' chewed prayer book. "Your tummy must be full of paper prayers, Holly."

It was little time when Aunt and Sir Anthony emerged from the house, side by side, talking in hushed tones. Mr Phillipps, walking and wavering behind them, had Edward and Charles to hold him up.

Someone called out, "Steady as you go, Vic!"

Holding Holly Berry to the nape of my neck, I smiled at Sir Anthony. "Sir, this is my puppy, Holly Berry."

His face lit up. "You don't say? Why, what a treasure you have there." He patted her head in great affection.

"Oh, indeed." I smiled up at Aunt. Her face seemed to glow even in the shade of the Great Hall's covered rose trellis.

"Holly Berry, is it?" He tapped her nose with affection.

"I named her in honour of Aunt's dog, Holly, of years' past and Berry, in your dog's honour, sir."

"Why, I am truly touched, Anne, truly." He glanced at Aunt Alice. "I remember your dog Alice. Holly was a fine hound."

"Sir, you must bring Berry to visit and play with Holly. There," I pointed, "under the yew."

He nodded and shot a quick glance at Aunt. "Perhaps, I shall."

Glancing up at Aunt's windowsill, I could not see the gold band. Do I have the right window? Indeed I had, but the band was gone.

"Oh, Miss Holt," mumbled the vicar as he held his head, "I fear I must leave your party ... can you forgive me?"

"The forgiving is Anne's, sir. This is her party."

"Oh, Mr Phillipps," I nodded, "do go, and do not think for a moment of apologizing. Make haste, sir. Tomorrow is another day."

"Another day?" He thought for a moment, scratched his bony head and winced. "Well, yes, I suppose that is right." He nodded to Aunt. "Good day, Miss Holt. Thank you, Dr Hathaway."

"Father," said Edward, "Charles and I will accompany Mr Phillipps to the parsonage."

"Oh, that won't be necessary, my sister will," said Phillipps, and glanced around for Charlotte.

"Mr Phillipps," said Elly, twirling her new fringed Chateau Labrucherie parasol, "Miss Charlotte is in the house fishing a bone from Gib's throat. Franklin will see her home."

The vicar's eyelids fluttered in obvious confusion. "Gib? Gib? Is that not the blind cat, Mrs Mills?"

* * *

Later that evening, I curled up with Holly Berry in my lap—Gib purred on the back of my over-stuffed easy chair. My eyes waxed heavy; the fire crackled and hissed. "Oh, Elly," I yawned, "what a wonderful tea party."

"Indeed. It was your first party, and I must say, well done at that. Oh, a few minor mishaps, but Miss Pramm left Lesington Hall quite proud of herself. She and Mrs Bleecher were all smiles as they wistfully closed the garden gate behind them."

"Really, Elly?"

"Oh, I watched it all."

"What do you suppose happened to the gold ring, Elly?"

"The one on the sill?"

CHAPTER TWELVE

Franklin entered the study, holding the mail salver. "A letter from Holybourne, Miss Anne."

I jolted. "A letter from Holybourne, Franklin? But, I know of no one who should write to me." My heart fluttered. Could Tilly have learned to write? Madame Pinchot?

He smiled. I took the letter.

"Open it then," said Elly, setting aside her sewing.

I examined the address. "Hmm, it says, Miss Anne Holt, Lesington Hall, London." Bringing it to my nose, I sniffed it. Glancing up at Elly, I frowned.

"Perhaps *you* would open it, Elly?"

"Bring it then." She turned it, held it up to the light, and then handed it back to me. "You open it, Anne."

"Maybe I should wait until Aunt returns from Liverpool."

"Oh, goodness me, Anne, that could be several days. Come now, here, use my little pocket knife. It may be an urgent notice."

I read it aloud.

"10 August 1864 - Holybourne
Dear Miss Anne Catherine Holt,
    I have long since pondered the thought of some day returning your father's library, a collection of rare books. And now that I am approaching the mighty age of eighty-six, it is time. My eyesight is failing and the books will do me no good now. I bought the entire collection from a local businessman, Mr O'Leary. I remember your father, and I send my condolences at the passing of your dear mother. I just recently returned to Holybourne to

die myself. Pardon my joviality of death, but so it is an
inevitable aspect of life.
   Miss Tilly Marvel, our maid, passed on your
address. She sends happy tender blessings that you are
well. Happy I am at the prospect of reuniting my beloved
collection of books on to you. Dear me, why it never
occurred that you would refuse them. Oh, I dare say, you
surely must have your father's flair for the written word.
   If I should die before this finds you, little Wicket,
Miss Marvel assures me that she will hold them for you.
Until sometime in the future,
   Samuel Pettibone Grinby

"Oh, my Tilly, how I wish to kiss her cheek once more!"
Then dropping the letter to my lap, I felt a cold shudder run
through my body. "Mr O'Leary?" His vision became vivid
again. "How he comes in unexpected ways to haunt me, Elly.
What can you make of it?"

"Bless the old gentleman, Mr Grinby, then. But, I must
say, how did that awful Mr O'Leary learn of your father's
books?"

"He must have bought them from Mama or taken them."
Brushing his nasty vision away, I begged, "We must not tarry,
Elly, but leave soon. Oh, that Mr Grinby would die before I had
a moment with him." My eyes filled with tears. "Oh, Elly, we
simply must go at first light." I inhaled and felt the old
gentleman Grinby to be floating to heaven that instant.

"Dear me, child, what is all the worry? Calm yourself."
Elly put her arm around my shoulders. "We have time, Love.
Your Aunt will be home within the week."

"We cannot wait a week, Elly. Mr Grinby will be dead and
Tilly will be sent away."

"Oh, I think not, dearest." She hugged me. "He said the
books will be in her care if something should happen to him.
What fear have you over it?"

Oh, it was not just about the books. I wanted to know
about my father. Despite the off-chance of a meeting Mr
O'Leary, I wanted to hear about Papa and what happened to
him? Why is it forbidden to discuss him at Lesington Hall? I
wanted to see Tilly once more. "Oh, Elly, please, what harm
should come from it with just me and you to Holybourne?"

I pulled out my handkerchief with my Holybourne leaves rolled in it, and holding it to my nose, inhaled the fading scent and prayed that Elly would ...

"Very well, Wicket." Elly shook her head. "We shall leave in the morning."

I put my arms around her. "Oh, thank you, Elly. Thank you." Still hugging her, I wondered aloud, "Why do you suppose Mr Grinby called me *Wicket*?"

"I am quite sure Mr Grinby meant to write *wicked*, my little imp." She tickled my ribs with a laugh.

* * *

It was dawn when Elly, Franklin, and I climbed into the carriage. Franklin, who insisted upon accompanying us to Holybourne, glanced out. "The highway is rife with scoundrels anymore."

Elly seemed quite nervous over his declaration, but a few miles down the road she regained her sensibility and seemed to feel quite safe once more. Skimming along the London Road, I recognised most of the names on the fingerposts, but not the pathways, not the trees, not all the cottages and inns we passed. It had been several years since I had last been this way. "How long do you think it will take us to get to Holybourne, Franklin?"

"Oh, four hours at the most, Miss Anne—barring rain." He straightened and looked out. "A fair day, Miss Anne, Mrs Mills, no rain. We should be stopping at the Inn Farway for a stretch; we can rest the horses and then soon be on our way again."

"Franklin, however shall we find Mr Grinby?"

"I shall locate him, miss. Do not worry over the matter. I do not think Holybourne is such a large place."

"No, not so very large." I closed my eyes and prayed Franklin would not go to O'Leary's brewery for directions. I felt the warm touch of Elly's hand and opened my eyes. "Elly, perhaps we could drive by where I was born—where Misha and I played. I could show you the sacred stream."

"Lord Bless you, child, perhaps another time, when your aunt comes along."

I nodded. "Yes, I understand."

* * *

Franklin found the Grinby residence. It was a far superior house than where Mama and I had lived. I thought the roads and trees looked familiar, but felt strange that I could not remember any one particular cottage thereabouts. Surely we must have travelled a way I had never been before.

Mr Grinby's house was very beautiful with its thick thatched roof, and even the outbuildings were thatched. Large yellow roses grew in abundance over the entire front of his house. Hedgerows stood guard against the north winds; a seeping well to our right fed a small pond where fishes darted about. I could hear a dog barking somewhere from deep within the house. Elly drew back.

"Oh, do not fear, Elly. It is only a dog."

"Only a dog?" She frowned. "You know how dogs frighten me, Anne."

Remaining in the carriage, Elly and I watched as Franklin conversed with a lady at the cottage door. I grew anxious. "But where is Tilly, Elly?"

"Do be calm, dear, she is probably hard at work somewhere abouts."

"I suppose so." Sniffing the air, I nodded. "Oh, yes, this is Holybourne, but I still cannot recognise just where my cottage is." Pointing through a patch of green meadow, I said, "Maybe across that field, Elly."

Raindrops began to pitter on the pond water.

Holding an umbrella, Franklin helped us from the carriage. "This way, Miss Anne, Mrs Mills. Do mind the broken steps just ahead."

"Franklin, did you inquire about Tilly, too?"

"Yes, Miss Anne."

The servant at the door introduced herself, "I am Mrs Brunti, the housekeeper." She glanced us up and down in a kind manner. "Mr Grinby is out at present. Do come in from the rain." She gestured us into a hallway. "I will take your things. Mr Grinby received your letter and was expecting you."

Handing her my shawl, I smelled stale tobacco smoke. As Franklin and Elly removed their wraps, I noticed the ceilings were low and whitewashed clean. *Neat as a pin.* Anxious to see Tilly, I blurted, "Is Tilly about?"

"Oh, yes, I will send her in."

"Oh, thank you, thank you," I said in a most gleeful tone.

The maid exchanged glances with Franklin and Elly. Smiling, she escorted us into the parlour. "Mr Grinby will be home shortly. Please comfort yourselves. Tilly will be in with the tea."

I warmed my hands before the delightful hearth fire, anxious to once again see my friend. In nervous chatter, I said, "It is a small hearth, Franklin."

"Not as great as Lesington Hall, but I wager just as warm, Miss Holt."

"Indeed, Franklin. Why, yes, it certainly is." On the mantle sat a picture of Her Majesty, in mourning. Black crepe hung on her and swirled about the floor.

Glancing up, I was met with a stuffed pheasant hanging above the hearth, his wings spread in early flight. I sighed, but not early enough, old boy. Moving on, I glanced back at its beady eyes and shuddered. It reminded me of a certain vicar.

Bustling in with a china tea service, Tilly was smiling ear to ear. "Oh, bless me, child!" She cried, nearly upsetting the tea tray. "I had no idea you were coming *today*."

Hurrying to her side, I wrapped my arms around her thick waist and hugged her. "Oh, Tilly, I have missed you so." Tears slid down my face.

She held me out and spun me around. "Oh, look now how you've grown." She tweaked my cheek. "Aye, rosy cheeks, sparkly eyes, a little meat on your bones." She glanced up at Elly and stood straight, wiping her eyes with her thick, red calloused hands. "Beg pardon, ma'am."

Elly smiled. "Oh, do not apologise, Tilly. Anne speaks highly of you. Thank you for informing Mr Grinby of her whereabouts."

Hugging Tilly again, I said proudly, "Mrs Mills is my cousin."

"Indeed, madam." Tilly curtsied and smiled at Franklin.

"Franklin is our Butler—a very good butler."

"Oh, indeed." Now highly jubilant, Tilly fussed about the tray. "Oh, here now, let me pour you all a nice cup of tea. You must be all done in. Please take a seat anywhere you wish."

Suddenly I heard a dog whimper. "Is the poor creature hurt, Tilly?"

Checking the sugar bowl, she resettled the lid softly. "Ah ... yes, Miss Anne."

"She sounds pitiful, Tilly."

Elly hemmed. "Anne, one must not be rude."

"Oh, excuse me, madam," Tilly curtsied, "but Miss Anne is not rude at all. Why, the dog was put in the cellar. She's limping about so. Mr Grinby does not have the heart to ..."

"What?" I blurted, "Put it to the good earth?"

"Well, just this morning, from out of nowhere, the pitiful creature appeared at the doorstep yelping, begging for a scrap or two." Tilly dabbed her eyes with her apron. "Oh, bless Mr Grinby. He can't see one thing suffer. He brought her in, fed her, and hearing her whimper from being pulled about so, gently carried her down into the cellar to bed atop warm straw. He's in hopes to ease her misery a bit. I was just finishing my noon work and was going to look after her myself."

"Oh, how kind of you, Tilly, may I come with you?"

Elly shook her head.

I took her hand. "Please, Elly, just a peek. What is the harm?"

Franklin nodded. "Indeed, Mrs Mills, what is the harm?"

She sighed. "Very well, Anne."

Tilly smiled a thank-you to Franklin. "This way, Miss Anne." She led me through a very excellent kept kitchen. There was a maid scrubbing the floor, I nodded and smiled, but she ignored me.

"Here we are then." Tilly lit a candle. Holding it high, she slowly opened the cellar door. There at the threshold were two soulful eyes, a bedraggled emaciated body—a sickly creature, trembling. As Tilly held the light closer, I whispered through tears, "Misha!" I knelt by her side and gently put my arms around her. She licked my hand; her breath was hot.

Tilly gasped. "Misha? Why, that can't be ... that looks nothing of the great dog I remember at Madame Pinchot's."

I glanced over her once magnificent body. "She has been abused, Tilly—terribly abused."

When I tried to move Misha's head onto my lap, she whimpered. "Oh, dear me, girl, I am sorry. Please, Tilly, the candle, if I may."

"Oh, but of course." She carefully handed it down.

Having situated Misha's head upon my lap, I felt her legs. Aah, there was the trouble. "Her leg is injured, Tilly. I will wrap it, like you taught me."

"Well, well." I heard a gentleman's voice over my shoulder, "What have we here?"

Tilly gushed, "Oh, Mr Grinby, sir, this is Miss Anne Holt—from London. She has come for her father's books, sir."

I looked up.

"Indeed." He nibbled on his pipe. "It looks as if I have found the best sort of little lady to return the books to."

I beamed. "Oh, indeed, sir." I kissed Misha's head.

"You wrapped the dog?" He inquired squinting through his pipe smoke.

"Mr Grinby, sir, I learned this trick from Tilly. You gather four corners of a cloth and tie a sling."

With an admiring glance at Tilly, he smiled. "Hmm, quite marvellous."

I stroked Misha's head. "Yes, sir, Misha belongs to the fortune teller Madame Pinchot and ..."

"Burned out," he interrupted, "some angry townspeople on a religious roil routed them gypsies all away." He patted Misha's head. "She hung about an old abandoned shack near the sacred stream."

"Oh, indeed, sir, that is where Mama and I lived."

"Mean spirited children from the rag-and-bone yard threw stones at her. Probably how she got her leg injured."

I pulled Misha to my heart. "Oh, sir, she is hungry."

"Indeed." He glanced at Tilly as she hurried to a cupboard, found a saucer and filled it with milk.

I begged, "She could use a little mush, sir, if you please?" For sheltering Misha as he did, I knew he would not refuse me.

"Oh, very well, then."

We watched as Misha gulped every morsel, licked the plate clean. "She is full, sir." I smiled up at the man who smelled greatly of cherry tobacco.

"Come then, Anne, into my study." Glancing over his shoulder, he added, "You may bring the dog. That is, if she will follow with that bad leg."

"Oh, thank you, sir."

Mr Grinby winked at Tilly. "You may come too, Tilly."

"Oh, indeed, sir, I will tend the fire." Tilly bustled down the hall ahead of us.

As we walked past the parlour, Elly and Franklin shook their heads as Misha hobbled behind me.

"Now then, Anne, I shall show you your father's books and a little something more I discovered."

"Something more?"

Mr Grinby patted Misha's head. "I could not have given the books to a better human being on the face of this good earth. I can see that now."

Cocking his pipe, he puffed and spurted as he forged his way down the dark hall leaving a stream of smoke curling about his shoulders. Speaking between his clinched teeth, he said, "Come along now, miss."

Following the elder gentleman, I waved away the churlish cherry smoke that stung my nose. Filling the doorway, Mr Grinby nodded. "Here we are, then." He pointed to a large chair by a crackling fire. "You may sit there."

Tilly stood at the hearth; her hands pressing her apron in nervous fashion.

"There now Tilly, the fire is a good one. Come sit with your friend, Miss Holt."

"Mr Grinby, sir, do you have fires in *every* room?" I was astonished. Tilly scooted next to me, beaming with her fire-flushed cheeks aglow.

"I do." His bones creaked as he eased into his chair. "At my age, and with few things to give me comfort, I insist upon it." His glance softened as he spied Misha curled at my feet.

"Sir, you wrote in your letter that you might die before I came. Well, sir, you do not look as if you would die today."

Tilly tried to stifle a giggle.

"Perhaps tomorrow then, Wicket." He laughed as the smoke rings circled the warm air just above his fine, white hair.

"Oh, no, sir, I meant only you do not seem very old at all. How well you walk and talk."

"Hmm, yes, for that I am thankful." He tapped his ashes in a thick-glassed amber bowl. "While I was packing your father's books, I came across a chest that I had not noticed before."

"Oh, indeed, Mr Grinby."

"I was a professor at Cambridge, my dear, and never paid much mind to fancy wooden boxes. Books were my concern. However, the chest is just there." He pointed with his pipe. "There, on the shelf. It was placed amongst the books, perhaps in error. It was your father's."

I rose, careful to not disturb Misha and took hold of the chest and set it on Mr Grinby's desk. I ran my fingers over the shiny burnished wood. It felt warm. "Oh, sir, a very handsome chest it is."

"Hmm," his eyes narrowed, "perhaps a treasure chest— open it, my dear."

I unlatched the gold filigree clasp on the front. Though old, it was solid and easy to open. I ran my hand over the burnished wood again. This had been my Papa's ... perhaps inside were gold coins, diamonds, a tiara, like Her Majesty's.

I opened the chest. There wrapped with a purple ribbon were ... "Letters, sir?" Pulling the ribbon apart to release the letters, I found the top one was addressed to *Miss Catherine Hiriart* ... from *Mr James Holt*. Glancing back to Mr Grinby, I smiled in awe. "These are letters to my mother, sir, from my father." I brought them to my heart and closed my eyes.

"I thought you should own them." Grinby's grey eyes glittered beneath his bushy eyebrows.

"Miss Hiriart was my mother, sir." Fondling the letters, I brought them to my lips. "Did you know her, Mr Grinby?"

"Oh, my, no, my dear, I have been gone from Holybourne over forty years ..."

"But my father, surely you knew him?"

"Met him at Cambridge, an excellent young man. Bright, well on his way to a brilliant career in medicine, if I recall correctly." He leaned back in his chair, tapped his pipe with his finger and looked up at the ceiling. "As I recall, there was another young man, quite prominent. Hmm, Oh, yes, a Mr Anthony Hathaway, they were good friends."

I stood motionless, holding the letters to my heart. I was afraid to ask a question fearing perhaps Mr Grinby would stop talking. Tilly put her arm around my shoulders.

"We met one evening, as I recall, in the dining room at University ... yes, the two of them, serious, studious—scholars usually are, my dear. I mentioned I was born in Holybourne and one word led to another and we became friends.

"Then, later when I was on holiday here, I ran into a prominent businessman in town. I told him I was a Cambridge Man. He said, 'Well then, such a learned man would certainly be interested in a learned man's library.' He looked to be an unsavoury sort of fellow, but at the mention of books, I agreed. He led me to his office, and when I opened the first book, I noticed its owner to be Mr James Holt, London. I bought the entire room full."

I glanced up at the kind professor and nodded. Tilly pursed her lips and glared at the ceiling. I knew the *unsavoury sort of man* he bought the books from had to be Mr O'Leary.

"The long and short of it, Miss Anne, every book is now boxed and ..." he glanced out the window, "being loaded onto your coach this very minute."

I swallowed hard. "You never heard from him again, sir?"

"The businessman who I bought the books from? Why no ..."

"No, sir, I mean my Papa?"

"He came once to my cottage here, years ago. I remember it well, for I was on holiday and here only for a few weeks when we rediscovered one another. I did not meet your mother, I am sorry for that. A short time ago, I learned that she had lived here in Holybourne, as well, and had been for several years." He smiled at me. "I hope I have pleased you with their letters, my dear."

"Oh, thank you, sir. I shall treasure them my entire life."

Just then Misha laboured to rise. She looked deep into my eyes nudging my leg with her nose.

"Oh," Mr Grinby glanced at her, removing his pipe, "I do believe she has some business to do."

"I shall take her out, sir." I stopped. "That is, if I may?"

"Of course, Miss Anne, and if Mrs Mills approves, you may take her home with you." He stood and chomped nimbly on his pipe stem. "You call her Misha?"

"She belonged to the fortune tellers, Professor. Misha and I played together when I lived here." Now on my hands and knees, I kissed Misha's head. "I love her so, Mr Grinby. When Mama put me on the coach for London, Misha did not want me to leave Holybourne."

"She is yours."

"Oh, sir, thank you, thank you." I kissed his cheek. "Aunt Alice will at first say no, but like butter, she will melt."

"I am sorry not to have met your Aunt, Miss Anne."

"At the moment, sir, she is in Liverpool. A friend's mother died quite suddenly. ..."

"Dreadful."

"But sir, you must come to Lesington Hall sometime." Holding Tilly's hand, I added, "and when you do, you must bring Tilly. Please, sir."

"I will, I will. When next in London we shall look you up."

* * *

Kissing Tilly goodbye, I wiped my eyes. "I shall write to you."

She waved a gallant wave. Even from afar, I could see her bottom lip quiver as she turned and hurried back into the house.

I sat in the carriage, my treasure chest on one side, my faithful friend on the other with her head resting in my lap. We proceeded to Lesington Hall in haste. To linger in the village at Holybourne, according to Franklin, was not wise.

Franklin glanced out the window. "What with the gathering storm, poor roads ... no, no, Miss Anne, perhaps another day when your aunt accompanies us."

"Indeed, Franklin," Elly patted my hand. "Another day, Anne."

I ran my hand over the warm, wooden chest sitting snugly to my side. "Very well." I glanced out the window. "I cannot recollect right-off where our house was anyway, Franklin."

Peering between Mr Grinby's cottage and his row of wind-block row hedges, I spied a pathway through the meadow that looked familiar. But then as we wound our way onto the Winchester-London Road, *The Road*, every meadow seemed to have familiar looking pathways.

It was now raining quite dismally and the carriage was slipping and sliding down the last narrow road that joined the main highway when Elly grabbed the carriage banister. "Dear me, Franklin!"

With his head jiggling in sway with the carriage, he smiled. "Oh, I've seen worse, Mrs Mills."

I sighed. "Pity the driver and footman; pity the horses."

As we drove on, the rains eased, and the closer we got to Lesington Hall the roads improved considerably. Franklin, however, never seemed to doubt for a moment that we would arrive unharmed and in good time.

Lifting his watch from his vest pocket, squinting at the timepiece, he said, "By my watch, we should be arriving well before supper." Sliding it back in place, he sighed, "*If* we can stay ahead of this rain shower."

"Oh, yes, enough of this slip-sliding for me," said Elly.

"I do hope Mr Grinby, the polite and generous scholar, remains dry."

"A scholar you call him, Anne?" said Elly.

"He told me he was a professor at Cambridge." Running my hand over Misha's head, I wondered why Elly had not sneezed—not once. "I do hope Aunt warms to Misha, Elly."

"Well now," she said, still not willing to touch the dog, "I think not."

"Oh, dear me, Elly."

"The less fuss we make regarding the dog, the better the outcome."

"Oh, yes, yes." I snuggled Misha and kissed her muzzle. "Holly Berry will love you too, girl. She may be jealous at first, but she will keep you."

As we jiggled along the squishy highway, I could hear the mud slapping the bottom of our carriage and dreaded when Misha would need out. With care I moved my hand over her injured leg and wondered, with no money in my purse, how I could have it mended.

Turning onto Regent Street, Lesington Hall's chimneys were streaming with thick black smoke curling heavenward. "Home, Misha." She raised her head and sniffed the air.

Pulling under the alcove, we were met by Abigail, Aunt's maid. Franklin stepped down from the carriage and took Elly's hand and settled her. Reaching back, he took my treasure chest with one hand and helped me down with the other.

Aghast, Abigail drew back, staring into the carriage. "Goodness me, what is it?"

Turning, I smiled. "Misha, she was Madame Pinchot's dog, Abby."

"Doesn't look too friendly ..."

Just as I climbed the last step into the house, Elly took a tumble.

Franklin and I hurried to her.

"Oh, dear Elly, are you hurt?" I cradled her head with my hands.

"Oh," she moaned, "it's my leg," she pointed. "I believe it's my ankle or my foot."

With great care, Abigail removed Elly's boot.

"No, no," she cried, shaking her head, "the other one, the other boot."

Abigail had my luck.

We all followed Elly as she was carried up to her room by the footmen. Entering Elly's room, Franklin set down Misha and I held Holly by the collar. Mrs Saverin rushed in and immediately tended to Elly's covers. Abigail fluffed her pillows. I covered her with a quilt. "We must call for a physician, Elly."

"Indeed," she grimaced, "and you prefer ... ?"

I lit up like a gas lamp, smiling. "Oh, of course, Dr Hathaway, Elly."

She nodded. "I thought as much."

Franklin bowed. "Indeed, Mrs Mills, I shall send for him at once."

Pressing her hand, I frowned. "Oh, let us pray he is not out of town, Elly."

Abigail stuck her nose in the door. "I shall bring you tea, Mrs Mills."

"Indeed, and bring the sherry, too." Elly winced. "Bring the entire bottle."

Cook, sniffing the air, pushed them all aside as she headed for the kitchen. "Smoke, smoke! I smell smoke. Oh, my bread, my bread!"

Sitting at Elly's side, I noticed she was still wearing her gloves. "Dear me, Elly, your gloves—they are filthy with mud." I gently removed them.

Misha hobbled in a circle, grunted and lay down at my feet. With a puppy bow, Holly sniffed her. Misha curled her lip and Holly scurried into the corner.

I tossed Elly's gloves onto her bedstand.

"Thank you dearest." Chaffing her hands, she nodded. "Yes, that feels much better."

I could feel tears well in my eyes. Elly's face was now a blur, my voice faltered, "You must recover, Elly."

Propped up on pillows, her foot up in the air, she shook her head. "Oh, I rather doubt that I shall live, Anne."

Misha lifted her head and licked Elly's drooped hand.

"Why," Elly raised her brows, "why," she laughed in disbelief, "that dog licked my hand."

"Misha has taken to you, Cousin."

"Nonsense," she glanced at her, "dogs don't take to me."

"This one has," I assured her.

Elly ran her hand over Misha's head. "Which leg is broken?"

"Oh, I don't know if it is, Elly ... but I think the back left one."

She sighed. "Just like mine."

Suddenly, we heard a gnawing, ripping sort of noise.

I recognised, right off, the familiar sound. "Rats, Elly."

"Rats?" She stiffened in fear. "We don't have rats at Lesington ..." Leaning on her elbow, she glanced down at the floor. Settling back on her pillows, she closed her eyes and exhaled. "Oh, yes, a very large, black rat, at the moment, is chewing on my favourite travelling boots."

"Are you sure those were your very favourite boots, Elly? Yes?" I grabbed Holly's collar, "I really must put her out ..."

CHAPTER THIRTEEN

After settling Misha on a warm wool blanket, just off the kitchen, I assured Cook that I would diligently attend the injured dog every minute of the day. "She will be no trouble, I promise, Mrs Savarin. I am in hopes that Dr Hathaway will set her leg to right."

"Very well," she replied, her one lazy eye on the dog, the other on me. "But, you know how busy we are near supper time, Miss Anne."

"Oh, yes, of course I do." Patting Misha's head, I smiled up at the cook. "Might you have an extra bone, Mrs Savarin?"

"Hmm." Turning, she reached up and lifted from a hook a mangled bloody stump and tossed it wildly onto the butcher's table. Raising her whacking knife, she plunged it deep and violently into the roast. Thunk! Thunk! Thunk! Even Misha winced.

I squinted, focusing only at the neatly-tied apron bow at Cook's back. Turning, she dangled a bone with what looked to be an eyeball hanging by a ... a thread?

" 'Twas for the soup, miss, but the hound can have it."

My stomached turned. "Ah, *my* soup, Mrs Savarin? The soup we all slurp?"

She nodded.

"I shall never have soup again in my entire life."

Laughing, her belly jiggled, much as my breasts do upon occasion—but now was not the time to dwell ...

"Well, when you get hungry enough, child, you'll eat just about anything. Come along, then, give this scrap to the wolf. She's drooling ..."

"Wolf? You know it to be so?"

"Saw one at the Faire once," she said matter-of-factly. "A long time ago, but that one there is half wolf anyways."

"Then Aunt will surely not approve, Mrs Savarin." I lowered my head.

"She don't know wolf from mutt, missy. Come now, take this and give it to her."

"Yes, ma'am." In relief, I took the bloody little bone with the dangling eyeball and handed it to Misha.

"You see," smiled Mrs Savarin, "she'll not starve."

I hugged Mrs Savarin. "Thank you, cook. Oh, thank you."

Setting down her oaken bucket, Nancy, the milkmaid, cooed at Misha, "Oh, what a dear she is."

"Thank you, Nancy. She has an injured leg, and Dr Hathaway is coming soon. After he fixes Elly's ankle, I pray, he will set Misha's."

Nancy shook her head, licked her thumb and pasted it to the palm of her hand. Smiling, she winked. "For luck, I learned that gesture years ago, it works, miss."

"Oh, I use this, Nancy—only for miracles, though." Closing my eyes, I whispered a prayer for Elly and Misha and crossed myself.

Looking bewildered, she shrugged. "Well, crossing oneself ought to do it, miss."

Nodding, I bid my retreat. I found the housekeeper in the hall. "Miss North, has Dr Hathaway arrived yet?"

"Oh, yes, Miss Anne. He is with Mrs Mills this very minute."

I bounded up the steps and tapped at her door.

"Come, come, Anne," said Elly.

"Good evening, Miss Anne," said Dr Hathaway, glancing over my shoulder.

I knew he was looking for Aunt Alice. "Good evening, sir." Taking Elly's hand, I sighed. "It is a pity, sir. My Aunt Alice is away."

"Away?" He set down his black case. "Hmm, well." His broad shoulders slumped.

"A funeral, sir," said Elly as she held her pitiful look.

"I do hope she will not be long away ..." He hemmed, as if catching himself, and moved to the foot of Elly's bed. "Hmm, what have we here?" He stared at her ankle for a moment. Opening his black case, he removed some shiny tools and wiggled each toe with great tenderness.

Reliving the event and how she fell, Elly exhaled, "Oh, in my hurry to stuff my face at dinner, I missed a step."

"We must count our blessings, Elly." I reminded, as I glanced at her swollen ankle. "At least you did not slip at Professor Grinby's cottage."

"Oh, yes, yes." She nodded with her eyes closed. "Thank you, Anne. I had quite forgotten to count that one."

Dr Hathaway looked up smiling. "I once knew a Professor Grinby while at Cambridge." He sighed, "But that was years ago." He continued to examine Elly's foot. "Does this hurt, Mrs Mills?"

"Yes," she grimaced, "forgive me, sir, but it even throbs when you breathe upon it, sir."

"Perhaps when the doctor wraps it tight, Elly, it will not ache so."

He glanced up at me. "Indeed, Miss Anne, you know something of medicine then?"

"Just from watching Tilly Marvel wrap injured animals, sir." Moving to the end of the bed, I bent over and sniffed Elly's foot.

Her face coloured. "Oh, please ignore the girl, Dr Hathaway, sometimes she behaves like a dog."

He patted my head. "Then you shall help me wrap her foot, Miss Bow Wow."

After Elly's foot was wrapped and elevated, Dr Hathaway gathered up his things. "You are going to live through this one, Mrs Mills."

"Quite sure, are you? Well, I must be able to curtsy to the Queen, you know."

He shook his head. "No curtsies, madam, for at least a month. I do not believe it is broken, but sprains are sometimes just as troublesome. Do be careful, now. I shall come again tomorrow." He smiled, his eyes crinkled as he patted her hand. "Her Majesty will, no doubt, understand."

"Anne, do see Dr Hathaway to the door."

"Certainly, Elly."

Holly Berry waited at the bottom of the steps. I had tied her with a leash to the banister.

"Well, now, what is this? Holly Berry in restraints?" he said in mocked surprise.

"A naughty girl, sir, she has been chewing again," I sighed.

Holly rolled into a little ball, head down, tail curled beneath her. "Oh, she knows she has been a bad girl."

Reaching down, he patted her and smiled as he felt her sharp baby teeth. "It's not her fault to chew. Be patient Miss Anne, I had the same vexations with Berry."

Heading for the door, I hemmed. "Excuse me, Dr Hathaway."

"Yes?"

"Could I trouble you, sir, for another great favour?"

"But of course." He must have read my face. "Whatever is wrong?"

"Please, sir." I gestured toward the kitchen. "My other dog, I believe she has injured her leg."

Kneeling by Misha's side, and with gentle hands, he unwrapped her leg. "Hmm, she has the disposition of an angel, I see." He smiled with relief. "That is a good thing. This sling is very well done, Anne. You did it?"

"Yes." I could feel my face burn with pride.

"I am not the expert on animals, Miss Anne. My son, John, is studying to become a veterinary surgeon. I would wish that he be allowed to examine her."

"Oh, indeed, sir, I have met your son, Edward, but I have not the pleasure of meeting your other son."

"John has been away at school. What luck, he is home on holiday. When I come tomorrow, I shall bring him."

"Oh, Dr Hathaway, thank you, sir."

Patting my head again, he smiled. "You are very welcome, Miss Anne." Just as he was to step into his carriage, he turned. "Miss Anne, it will be late tomorrow before we come. I have a previous engagement that I cannot postpone."

"Indeed, sir. I will tell Elly. I do hope Aunt Alice will be home as well."

* * *

The next day, as I was reading *Emma* to Elly, Holly suddenly jumped to the window—her tail wagged.

Elly's eyes sprung open. "I hear your aunt's carriage, Anne."

Scampering down the steps, I flew open the door. "Welcome, Aunt Alice! We did not expect you back so soon." I hurried to her, hugging her, kissing her cheek. "Oh, how we have missed you, Aunt."

"Well, well," she smiled, holding her hat, "and how I have missed you."

"You will never imagine what happened to Elly yesterday, Aunt." I turned and pointed to the place where she fell.

Aunt frowned. "What happened to Elly?"

"She fell and hurt her ankle, Aunt."

Pulling off her gloves, she handed her wrap to Abigail. "She is in her room?"

"Oh, yes." As we ascended the steps, I apprised her of the happenings. "You will find her quite contented, Aunt. All snug, propped with fluffy pillows. Two of which are mine ... ."

"Two of yours, Anne?"

"Oh, indeed, Aunt, I brought them from my room. Just now, one is at her back and the other at her ankle. And, I am sorry to say, a big black rat gnawed on her favourite travelling boots. Indeed, quite ruining them."

Tapping lightly at Elly's door, Aunt entered. Holly lay snuggled before a warm fire. She shook her head. "Yes, there lies the little rat now. ..."

Elly stiffened. "Well, I have been called many things."

Aunt stopped dead in her tracks. "What is that ... dog doing on your bed, Elly?" Moving closer she recoiled. "Why, it looks a little wild ..."

I hurried to Elly's bedside. "She has a kind disposition Aunt, please love her."

Misha's tail wagged.

Elly smiled sheepishly. "She has quite taken to me, Alice—broken leg and all."

"I thought it was your ankle that was broken?"

Elly chuckled, "Oh, my no, dear. Why, it's Misha's leg that is broken." Gesturing toward the chair, she sighed. "Do sit down, my poor dear, Alice. How confused you look."

Removing *Emma* just before Aunt sat, I nodded. "You do look weary, Aunt. Perhaps the long drive has done you in."

Aunt sat, shaking her head. "I have been gone only four days ..."

"I told you, Aunt Alice, you would not believe all the happenings."

Removing her hat pins, she nodded. "You are very right, Anne. Tell me, Elly, of all places, how did you fall from the porch?"

"Yes, well dear, we had just returned from Holybourne. It had been raining; the drive was a long one, stepping from the carriage there, wafting about was the aroma of Cook's soup, and in my haste to sample it, I somehow slipped."

Aunt frowned. "You just returned from Holybourne? And why is that?"

"Professor Grinby wrote to me, Aunt Alice. Imagine my surprise at receiving a letter. Tilly Marvel, you remember her, Aunt Alice—our maid, well, she informed Mr Grinby of my whereabouts."

"And who might Professor Mr Grinby be?"

"I shall show you his letter of introduction, Aunt."

Closing her eyes, she nodded. "Very well, Anne, but ... right now, I am exhausted. May I read it later, Love? After I have cleansed myself, changed, and eaten supper?"

"But of course, Aunt."

Aunt Alice kissed Elly on the cheek. "I shall send for a physician, Elly." Glancing at her ankle, she asked, "Do you think it ..."

"Oh, Alice, you are too late. The good Dr Hathaway has already been here." She gestured toward her propped up leg. "Wrapped it snug with a splint, so he did. I can't curtsy for a month, imagine? But, he said I would live another day."

Pushing her hat pin, Aunt pricked her finger. "Ouch!" She put it to her lips. "I will never leave Lesington Hall again."

"Dr Hathaway is coming back this very evening, Aunt Alice."

Puffing up, she forgot her finger entirely and tried to hide a smile. "Really?"

"Indeed, he is to examine Elly again, and he is to bring along his son, John, who has been away at school studying veterinary medicine."

Elly stroked the dog's head fondly and smiled up at me. "To set Misha's leg to right, Anne?"

"Oh, I pray so, Elly."

Aunt turned, shaking her head. "There cannot be a thing more to rouse my astonishment. Excuse me ladies, I shall go to my room."

I remembered my treasure chest and just as Aunt was to close the door, I called, "Only one more thing, Aunt, I have something that just may astound you more."

She covered her ears. "I will not hear it, Anne. Please, dearest, after supper?"

"Yes, ma'am."

The door closed.

Elly glanced at me.

"My treasure chest, Elly."

* * *

Aunt ate supper in Elly's room. I ate with Holly and Misha in the kitchen. Abigail found me sitting in the servant's quarters.

"Miss Anne, your aunt wishes to see you now. She is in her boudoir."

"Hmm, thank you Abigail."

I fetched Professor Grinby's letter and my Papa's treasure chest, and quickly decided to visit with Elly first. I knocked gently on her door.

"Come."

I showed her the chest and waved the letters. "Aunt wishes to see me now, Elly."

She nodded. "Leave the door open. I will listen ..."

"Very well, Elly."

Tapping on Aunt's door, I heard her beckon me come. Entering, I smiled. "Oh, Aunt, you look rested now. Not in the least weary for such a long ride."

"Thank you, dear."

Aunt wore her newest frock, her favourite lavender silk— and the gold band. Her shiny red hair was down, tied back with a velvet ribbon. Dr Hathaway would swoon when first he sees her. We sat in her window seat. It was pitch outside. The wax candles reflected warmly about our little place. A quaint three-log fire burned in her ornate white marble hearth. Tea and sweet cakes had been arranged for us.

Glancing at the chest, Aunt inquired, "And what have you there, Anne?"

"May I first read the letter from Mr Grinby, Aunt, and then explain?"

"Certainly, dear."

Hearing a ruckus at the door, Aunt frowned. "Pardon the interruption, dear, but what could that scratching be?"

Holly Berry slid in. Wiggling and hopping in glee, she hurried to welcome Aunt.

Smiling, Aunt let her hand drop. "Very well, Holly. Oh, yes, yes, I missed you too." Furling the hair on her head, she weakened. "Oh, Anne, I suppose she must stay with us." Holly licked her hand.

"She missed you so, Aunt. It is kind of you to allow her in your room."

"You know very well I cannot stand to hear *anything* whimper."

I giggled. "Yes, Aunt Alice, we know."

"And this Mr Grinby gave you his dog?" She glanced around. "And where is this dog?"

"In the kitchen, Aunt Alice—temporary quarters, I assure you."

"And Mrs Savarin allows it?" She asked with raised brow.

I nodded.

"Franklin tells me the dog is injured and that you cared for it quite like an expert."

"Oh, I simply wrapped its leg, as Tilly would have."

"I see." She added sugar to her tea, and while stirring, nodded. "You may continue reading Mr Grinby's letter, Anne."

Reading the last of it, I smiled up at her. "Now you must see why I was so excited to tell you about the astonishing events."

"Indeed, you found your father's books astonishing, did you?"

"Oh, I have not had a chance to see them, Aunt. Mr Grinby had them packed already. And while we ate lunch, they were loaded onto the carriage. I have been so busy with Elly and Misha that I have not had a moment to touch them." I squirmed. "But, Aunt, the astonishing thing is—he gave me this." I set the chest proudly on my lap. "It is a real treasure chest, Aunt Alice. It belonged to Papa."

Aunt's brow knitted—a worried sort of knit. "By my word," she shook her head. Reaching out, she ran her hand over the smooth, oiled wood. "It is a familiar looking one ... have you opened it?"

"Oh, yes, Aunt. Mr Grinby gave me permission to do so at his house in Holybourne."

"And?"

My mind stopped for a second. I closed my eyes, my heart was full. I took in a little breath. "These are letters to my mother, Aunt Alice, from Papa."

I held it to my heart. Closing my eyes again, I wondered what love letters and wonderful things Papa had written to my mother. Perhaps I would be mentioned—and, oh, maybe how dearly he loved me. I could feel the soft, warm burnished wood. The tiny gold filigree clasp at its front was easy and well worn. I snapped it open and then closed it, then opened it. I inhaled its sweet wood—Holly Berry began to chew on my toe.

"Ouch!" I opened my eyes. "No, Holly Berry. No."

Aunt Alice remained passive, her gaze returned to the fire.

"May I read one, Aunt?"

I could see her soft breathing, her eyes closing slowly. Her left hand clasped the arm of her chair. "You may remove *one*, Anne."

I reverently opened the chest. A warm, old hum wafted all about me, inhaling, I felt Papa. There were at least twenty crisp-edged folded letters tied with a thin purple silk ribbon. With great care, I untied the ribbon. Closing my eyes, I withdrew one letter and held it in my lap.

Looking at me, Aunt said in a low tone, "Is it addressed to you, Anne?"

Looking down at the neat, masculine hand of my father, I saw that it was addressed to my mother, *Miss Catherine Hiriart*. I ran my fingers over the dry, black ink. "No, ma'am," I whispered.

She resumed watching the flames. I returned the letter to its place and retied the purple ribbon. Placing the letters back into the chest, I closed the royal blue felt-lined lid without a sound.

"Even though I was a girl of ten and four, I well remember your mother as a beautiful, spirited young woman, Anne. Her thick, wavy black hair would sway to her French heritage music. Oh, what a free spirit she was. Her fine white teeth shining, how she loved to dance and sing—to twirl like a top. I often thought she was a bit wild ... oh, how her black eyes flashed—with passion and fire.

"I wanted to become a French woman just like her, but Papa ... Papa put a stop to all that. Bless her Anne, she held such a love for life, and how little I have dared to experience such a life!

"Oh, but your father was so taken with her, Anne. When they met, he fell desperately in love. Mama often cried, 'Our dearest James, mild, refined, quiet ... he had not finished Cambridge when he decided he could not live another day without her.'

"Dr Hathaway and your father, James, were close friends from their youth, Anne. I was a mere child then. Anthony was such a tease, I adored him so. Oh, how I love him still, Anne." She dabbed her eyes. "James and he remained quite close until ... until Anthony tried to dissuade James from marriage ... to finish school first. He pleaded actually. Oh, Anthony respected your mother, Anne, but your papa and she were such opposites.

"Mama said that James wrote her that he would soon be bringing his fiancé, Catherine Hiriart, home to meet his family. Mama and Papa were astounded at your mother's fresh laugh, her quick wit, her pure love for music; her delights in our London society.

Aunt whimpered. "I so loved James and your mother, Catherine. Your father knew Papa respected Anthony, and he begged him to vouchsafe for her, to come to Lesington Hall and plead with Papa to accept her. I must tell you, Anne, Papa hated the French—his father was slaughtered by Napoleon, and when Catherine proclaimed her noble French heritage and touted her education ... a mere governess, Papa soured."

Aunt stood and walked to the hearth. Resting her head on the mantle, she sighed. "Papa would not hear of the marriage. He was furious and forbade such a union. Anthony interceded, tried to plead with Papa, but he, along with James and Catherine, were ordered from the house. 'Never to set foot in Lesington Hall again!'

"My heart was broken. I lost my brother, Catherine, and Anthony." Turning from the hearth, Aunt's eyes brimmed with tears. "Anne, I am so sorry."

I hugged her. "But Mama and Papa married, Aunt Alice."

"James married her the following day. Papa was furious and disinherited him. Soon he was penniless. Mama funnelled as much money to them as she could without Papa knowing. At last James found a position teaching. They could afford no more than a little house in a small village, miles from Cambridge. After seeing how poor James was, I turned away from Papa thinking him a cruel heartless man. Reading the newspapers, I later learned Anthony finished his medical degree, and in time, married a fine lady.

"What became of Mama and Papa, Aunt Alice?"

Tears dropped thickly as she twirled the gold band on her finger.

"Mama and I visited them as often as we could, Anne. We found James happier than we had ever seen him, but Catherine loved the city, the music, and the wine. Oh, they were such opposites, Anne. Mama said she did not think Catherine could adjust from the busy Cambridge atmosphere to Holybourne, such a small village.

"I remember Mama's words, 'The glow on her once proud face turned pale, her smile had faded, the spark in her French black eyes dimmed, there was no music to fill her ears, no space to twirl.'

"We were grieved to learn, she delivered several stillborn children and was left with little to sing about. Your mother hid your birth from us ... apparently scared you would be taken from her after the death of your father. Oh, pity your mother, Anne. We sent her money. Oh, had we only known sooner of your existence."

Aunt folded into her chair. Holding her handkerchief to her face she sobbed. "I cannot relive another moment, Anne. Forgive me."

I patted her shoulder, not knowing what to say. Holly Berry clamoured to her side as well, whimpering, and pawing at her skirt. I tried soothing them both and patted Aunt on the head by mistake. "Forgive me, I meant to pat Holly's head ... Oh, Aunt, please do not cry so."

Holly Berry howled along with Aunt Alice.

"But I am the one who should be crying."

Glancing at me, she whimpered, "Forgive me, Anne."

I poured her a sherry. Removing my prized Miss Pramm's handkerchief from my sleeve, I handed her the drink and the hanky. "There now, Aunt, you may destroy them both."

With a giggle and trembling hand, she drank every bit of the sherry. Dabbing her eyes, she smiled. "Thank you, Anne." Taking me in her arms, she hugged me. "Believe me, love, I did not want to tell you our family history until you were older."

Glancing up, I found Sir Anthony standing in the open doorway—his eyes were teary. Kissing her cheek, I moved aside. "Aunt, tell me, after all these years, do you still love Dr Hathaway?"

Smiling through her tears, she brought the gold band up and kissed it. "I have loved him since childhood, Anne. I shall love him until the day I die."

"You would marry him, Aunt?"

She lowered her head. "He would never ask me again, Anne."

I led Holly Berry away, but just before I left the room, I heard him say, "I have loved you from the moment I met you, Alice. I shall love you until the day I die."

I stopped at Elly's door before going downstairs. "They loved each other from the moment they met, and will love each other until the day they die."

"Humph," said Elly, "I could have told you that years ago."

"Too bad about the vicar, Elly." I smirked.

She shook her head. "I must admit, I was a bit nervous betimes. Well, don't stand in the door like a wedge, Anne. Come fluff my pillows."

"Dr Hathaway was weeping, Elly." I fluffed her pillows. "If Aunt had not loved him, I surely would."

She laughed and winced for the effort. "Yes, you have always been fond of him, Anne." She tweaked my nose. "A good judge of character, so you are."

I kissed Elly's cheek. "I must now go and see Misha."

* * *

Descending the staircase, I heard Elly's cuckoo clock. "Cuckoo, cuckoo," I cried out, feeling silly, happy, and glad for Aunt Alice and Sir Anthony. Holly Berry whooshed past me as she half-ran, half-plopped down the steps. All of a sudden she growled, playfully. There at the bottom of the steps stood a replica of Sir Anthony. My mouth dropped. "Why, you must be Mr John Hathaway?" I held out my hand. "Dr Hathaway's son?"

He bowed. "Pleased, Miss Holt." His face turned pink. His hands were soft and kind. He was nervous, and though clearly a man, slight in build.

"Sir, your eyes are a deeper chocolate than your brother Edward's."

His face grew a deeper pink. "And yours the exact shade of your Aunt's."

"Really? You've met her, then?"

He half-smiled. "Not formally, Miss Holt. But, yes, your hair, fair skin ... quite a remarkable match, miss."

"Indeed." I remained a little dazed at his keen eye for detail. "Well, then, sir," my brain went blank, I flushed at his nearness, "ah, your father told me you are a student of veterinary medicine."

"Yes, miss."

"He said you might look in on my dog friend, she has been injured, sir."

He relaxed in laughter. "Dog friend? I do hope it's not a male."

Looking deeply into his handsome eyes, I melted. I could feel the blood in my body bubble, looping wildly from my toes to my nose—what an odd sensation. I had never experienced *that* before in my life. The hair on my neck prickled. "This way, sir."

Instead of skipping into the kitchen, I walked properly. Along the way, I prayed to God to please thank Aunt for Miss Pramm's most excellent class on walking with great refinement.

"Was that you I heard earlier, cuckooing, Miss Holt?"

"How many cuckoos, sir, did you hear?"

He laughed. "Well, miss, whoever she was, you must not set your watch by her."

Walking through the servants' dining area, we found Nancy, Miss North, Abigail, Franklin, and Mrs Savarin having tea in the kitchen. They all suddenly stopped chatting and watched me, intently.

"You have been hurrying about, Miss Anne?" inquired Abigail.

"No, why do you ask, Abby?" I shouldn't have asked.

"Your face is all a blush, miss."

I did not notice, right off, who snickered first, but I did spy Franklin exchanging glances with Miss North.

Dabbing my brow, I ignored them. "This way, sir. My friend, Misha, is just there."

Kneeling, John murmured, "Well, then, let me see." As he unwrapped Misha's leg with great care, she wagged her tail and licked his hand. "Easy, girl." He laid her on her back and moved each leg slowly.

Leaning down, I kissed her sweet face.

"She will become spoiled with all your affections, Miss Holt."

"Oh, I think not, sir." Sighing, I added, "There is nothing in this entire world that spoils from too much love." Holly Berry squirmed along side of me, nudging my face for the same attention.

"Indeed," he nodded with a laugh. "There now, Miss Holt, do hold her front paws for me."

I did as directed. He maneuvered Misha's leg. When she whimpered, he stopped. "Yes, I am afraid it just may be broken."

"And?"

He shook his head.

"What is it, sir? Is there is nothing else wrong?" I could sense something quite dreadful.

"I do not know, right off, Miss Holt. May I take her with me? I would like to be absolutely sure of something, and I would need to set her leg, but not here. I have not the tools or materials."

I nodded, glancing down at Misha. "Certainly, you may."

He gently touched my shoulder. "Have I frightened you, Miss Holt?"

"Yes, sir." My lips quivered.

"There now, miss." He lifted my chin. "It is difficult to love something so dearly and then lose it. I shan't lose her, I promise."

At that moment I read his thoughts. His dear mother had died, and he was still grieving. I felt terribly sad for him, his brooding and troubled mind. "Yes, I know how it is to lose one's mother. ..."

A deep silence spread about his pink, slender hands. With the greatest care, he rewrapped Misha. With his arm around her, he smiled the dearest smile. "I think we shall be the best of friends, Miss Holt."

"You may call me, Miss Anne, sir."

* * *

The following morning, the vicar stood waiting in the parlour. Entering, I shook my head solemnly. "You are too late, Mr Phillipps."

He wove back and sat, squashing his hat. "Oh, how ghastly." His face turned the colour of pasty glue. Laying back his head, he first stared at the ceiling, then closed his eyes and whispered to the chandelier. His eyes sprang open, finding me staring up his nostrils.

He hemmed, shaking his head. "I came as soon as possible. Why, it was only this morning that I heard Mrs Mills injured her ankle ... ."

"Oh, Mr Phillipps, it's nothing of *that* sort, sir. It is that my Aunt has become engaged."

Standing abruptly he turned to his hat—now shaped much like an accordion—an organ grinder and monkey accordion. Picking it up, he stared at the creases. "Engaged?" Frowns gathered at the bridge of his nose. His voice cracked, "Engaged to whom?"

"Dr Hathaway."

CHAPTER FOURTEEN

Aunt's wedding would be performed in the gardens at Lesington Hall, and though to some, it might seem a rushed affair to marry in the month of September, I knew she had waited long enough. It was a beautiful time of the year—a mild end of harvest season—fruitful and plenty. Aunt and Sir Anthony seemed thankful and expectant, contented and deliriously happy.

Mr Morse, the vicar from Sir Anthony's parish, would perform the ceremony. Mr Phillipps and his sister, Charlotte, were invited.

Glancing out to the fieldstone wall, I envisioned—buried on the other side—my mother and father, lying in wait for us all. After Aunt was officially Mrs Anthony Hathaway—Lady Alice, I would visit their graves and place my bridal bouquet on their headstones. At last I had learned the history of my Mama and Papa and felt a great release within my heart. I could feel Mama dance away in the heavens holding hands with Papa.

"There you are, Imp." Charlotte tugged at my sleeve. "You look very pretty, Anne."

"I beg your pardon?"

She tweaked my nose. "You have been daydreaming again. I said you look beautiful."

"Thank you." I whispered, "How is Professor Mandeville?"

She looked around making sure her brother wasn't near. "Your aunt wrote to me." She clasped my hand in great happiness. "Professor Mandeville will be conducting the music today." Her face turned pink. She glanced to the heavens.

Dear God, please let Charlotte Phillipps and Professor Mandeville marry. I crossed myself for good measure. "I prayed for you both, Charlotte."

"I noticed." She moved closer. "Tell me, Imp, does He grant prayers when you do that?"

"When I cross myself, He does ... most of the time. But one must not be greedy, Charlotte."

She closed her eyes and crossed herself.

"Charlotte," gasped her brother, "what, may I ask, were you doing just now?"

I spied Professor Mandeville arriving with his students. "Well, I really must be going. Good afternoon, Mr Phillipps, please excuse me."

I hurried away, not looking back—poor Charlotte. As I approached the professor, I pointed to the white tent, the makeshift music stage. "Professor Mandeville, there, sir, where the fat cat is sleeping is where you will perform."

He smiled and glanced over my shoulder, but not at the stage. Charlotte was moving toward us. He began blabbering, "Oh, Miss Anne, I cannot thank your aunt enough."

"Indeed, Professor, I shall inform her of your intentions. We have all been waiting patiently for your proposal. ..."

His face wrinkled into a question mark. "Proposal, Miss Anne?"

"Aunt Alice wishes to see your *proposal* of music before you play today, Professor." I smiled, "Oh, excuse me, sir. Why, you must be thinking of something quite different regarding matters of proposals. ..."

"Oh, Miss Anne," he smiled sheepishly, "it is you. It has been you all along who thinks of wedding proposals ... come now, admit it."

"Very well, I admit it."

"Excuse me Professor Mandeville," said Kate tugging at my braid. "Anne, look, there come Miss Pramm and Mrs Bleecher." Taking my arm, she huffed, "Hurry along, Anne, before they spy us."

Entering the house, we found Aunt standing at the window. "The weather is holding quite nice, Aunt Alice."

"Yes," she smiled glancing out at the ancient yew, "I am so thankful." Spreading her fan, she cooled her face. "It is indeed a splendid day for late September."

Kate and I stood next to her watching the wedding guests assemble. Some mingled about the lawn, while others sat in the white cloth-covered chairs, their parasols up.

"Yes," Kate squinted with a smile, "I see Miss Charlotte Phillipps is engaged ..."

Aunt sighed. "Well, that is good news. I had quite given up on the Professor."

She shot a glance back at Aunt. "Oh, no, Miss Holt, I only meant that my brother, Charles, has *engaged* her in conversation."

"Hmm," Aunt frowned, "I see."

"Elly has recovered quite nicely, Aunt Alice." I pointed. "She is hobbling about the garden with Misha traipsing at her heels."

"Oh, John Hathaway did a remarkable thing for the blessed dog. Yes," she smiled, "remarkable recovery."

Sir Anthony entered the room. "Remarkable?" He took Aunt's hand and kissed it. "You are remarkable, Alice." His fingertips brushed her blushing face.

Just then the cuckoo clock clucked. Turning, we all stared at the wooden bird as it chirped two times.

"Within the hour, Aunt Alice, you shall be Mrs Anthony Hathaway."

She nodded. "But Anthony, I do not see your son, John?"

My ears perked up, my heart perked up. I held my breath. Kate nudged me.

"I expect him to be here very soon, Alice. He wrote saying he was indeed excused from school, but had to leave us right after the service, being granted only one day, and as you know, most of that is travel."

"How cruel he cannot stay longer," Aunt frowned in sympathy.

"The Royal Veterinary College is strict, my dear. However, you will, at long last, meet Miss Elizabeth Revelt. She is John's guest. Miss Revelt enrolled at the college two years earlier than John and is doing quite well, I hear."

"Hmm," Aunt nodded and shot a quick glance at me, "indeed."

My heart sank—I knew enough about my intuitive heart that this woman, this Miss Revelt, was to play a crucial part in the future of my heart's happiness.

Sir Anthony continued, "Indeed, Miss Revelt is very bright and excellent with animals. She has been friends with Edward and John since they were youngsters. John just informed me they may team together as surgeons and open a veterinary clinic."

"Is that so, dear?" said Aunt Alice, "Interesting."

"Edward spoke of it just this morning. Indeed, he will be their accountant. But, they have a number of years yet, before deciding on that."

"I hope by fifty years, sir," I muttered, already envious of this other woman.

"I beg your pardon, Anne?" said Sir Anthony.

"Let's take the air, Anne," said Kate pulling me from the room.

Abigail flitted about the crowd, pausing to direct Nancy where to hide Gib for a few hours. "At least until the food is away."

Stopping to ask Franklin if he had seen Professor Mandeville, we were interrupted.

"Franklin," snapped Mr Phillipps, "seat us away from that dastardly yew tree."

"But of course, sir."

I glanced up and my heart stopped. John just entered the garden with Miss Revelt hanging on his arm. She looked all a fancy glitter.

"Kate," I gestured with my head, "do you really think she is all that beautiful?"

"Miss Revelt?"

I nodded.

She wrinkled her nose. "Heavens no, Anne."

"But she must be smart. You heard your uncle mention that she may be John's assistant when he opens his clinic someday."

"Perhaps," Kate sniffed the air, "but, refined ladies do not do such things. She would be thought most unladylike, I assure you."

"Very unladylike." I agreed. "Monstrous, actually." Glancing away, I sighed. "I feel pangs jabbing my heart, Kate."

"Jealousy, Anne. The *pangs* are really quite dreadful, and you have every right to feel them." She took my hand, "But, let us not judge her too harshly. Perhaps at closer inspection, you shall find Miss Revelt agreeable after all."

"I think not, Kate." I knew within my panging little heart that I did not like Miss Revelt now, nor would I ever like her for the rest of my life.

Abigail half-curtsied. "Miss Anne, your aunt wishes to see you."

"Come with me, Kate."

"Oh, Anne, I see Mama and Papa coming, I must join them, but I will find you later." She smiled, waved, and fluttered away.

"Very well," I pouted, my voice trailing into nothing.

Entering the drawing room, I found Aunt staring at herself in the hand-mirror. At second glance, I saw that her eyes were closed and I put my arms around her waist. "Praying, Aunt?"

Her eyes fluttered open. "Oh, Anne, it is you," she sighed. "No, I was just resting my eyes."

"Well, they do not look tired, Aunt." Standing back a little distance, I told her how beautiful she looked. "I am happy you are at last marrying Sir Anthony."

She kissed my forehead. "Anne, truly, I never imagined this day to ever come." With her hands on my shoulder, she gazed into my eyes. "Anne, you once said something so profound to me that it literally changed my thinking, for the better. I remember your words exactly. You and I were strolling in the garden and you innocently said, 'I think Mama's niche was marrying Papa and delivering me into your caring hands, Aunt.'

"At that moment, Anne, my life resumed its living. My purpose was once again affirmed. God works in miraculous and wondrous ways—indeed, you were sent to me."

She removed a bejewelled ring from her finger, one I had never seen before and placed in my palm. Folding my hand closed, she kissed my brow. "It was your mother's wedding ring, your grandmother Holt's. The one your father originally wanted to give her, but could not."

Staring down at the beautiful ornate filigree silver diamond ring, I stood in awe. "Oh, thank you, Aunt Alice. I shall cherish it my whole life."

Overwhelmed, and on the verge of tears, I smiled, kissed her cheek, and left the room. Not wanting anyone to find me teary-eyed, I hurried down the hall searching for the front entrance and away from the bustling guests, the chatter, the music. Head down, I rushed out the door. I felt the ring, the warm sun on my face and then—a black void, a noiseless, hollow emptiness floated about me.

"Miss Anne, are you all right?"

Staring at my empty hand, I cried, "Oh, dear me, I have lost my mother's ring!" I sat up, desperate to find it. "Oh, I have lost her ring!"

A gentle, warm hand touched my chin. John Hathaway was kneeling at my side. "Are you looking for this?"

I took Mama's ring and held it to my lips. "Oh, thank God." I took his hand. "And, thank you, sir. Thank you."

He helped me up. "Please forgive me, Miss Anne, I was standing in your way, being distracted." He pointed to Gib. "I was watching that cat creep about the food table."

I wiped my eyes. "Oh, sir, it was entirely my fault for not watching where I was going."

He handed me his handkerchief. "Are you hurt?"

"More embarrassed than hurt, sir. No, I shall be fine."

"But your tears?"

I could not share with him what finding my mother's ring meant. "Really, sir, I am fine."

He began to brush off my mud stained dress with his spotless kidskin gloves.

"Oh, sir, you must not soil your gloves. You have done quite enough in finding my ring." I brought it to my lips again, in thankful appreciation.

"Why not wear it, Miss Anne?"

I shrugged. "Well, I suppose it is too large."

"Let me see." He slipped it on my finger, smiling. "It's a little loose, but you shall one day grow into it, Miss Anne."

I love you, John Hathaway. I loved you the moment I met you. I will love you until the day I die.

Franklin issued from the porch, "Miss Anne, the ceremony is soon beginning."

Aunt was so gleeful and happy that she seemed not to notice my soiled dress. The music started and she slowly gathered at the door. I stood behind her and took in her flowery scent. "You smell like a lavender bush, Aunt Alice."

The audience, now sitting in their white wicker chairs, stood. Stepping onto the lawn, Aunt was more than beautiful in her lavender silk gown—Sir Anthony's favourite colour. Her red springy curls glistened atop her head, tiny pink paper flowers nestled in her plaits.

Lesington Hall looked spectacular. The horizon held a warm yellowish-blue haze; the ferns and greens were still verdant and lush, the lawn freshly shaven. An altar was situated beneath the yew.

The music resumed its slow tempo as we proceeded down the long, white rug. At the altar, Sir Anthony stood to the right, his sons Edward and John by his side. Elly stood on the left.

Mr Morse, Sir Anthony's vicar, stood in the middle. Still moving at a slow pace, I smiled and nodded in polite fashion to Charlotte's brother, but he remained stiff-lipped; his cowlick pointing toward the yew tree. Professor Mandeville must have made his intentions quite clear, for he and Charlotte were sitting very close to one another, far and apart from her brother.

When Sir Anthony took Aunt's hand, I moved to her left and glanced up at John. He was smiling at me. I could sense that his eyes had been upon my face for a very long time. Amazed, and in wonder of such feelings, I could not quite make out his reason, but returned his smile.

Aunt wept with so much joy during the ceremony that Sir Anthony passed her his handkerchief, Edward's handkerchief, and John's.

I offered up mine to Elly. At long last it ended, and Mr and Mrs Hathaway turned to the happy applause of the teary-eyed audience.

Edward patted his father's back. "Well done, sir."

John leaned in and kissed Aunt's cheek. "Welcome, Mother, to our family." His face was warm and kind, his eyes a bit teary and sincere. Turning from her, he took my hand. "Cousin Anne, welcome to our family."

He kissed my brow. His nearness took my breath; his hand trembled, his lips were soft and warm. Closing my eyes, I wished he had kissed my lips ... *my lips?*

You must kiss him back, Anne. You must kiss his lips! But, I cannot in front of all these people. The smitten angel pushed me—Hurry silly girl before the moment is lost! How was I to argue with such an authority? I closed my eyes, puckered my lips and leaned into him. I waited for a very long time, and then I heard his voice.

"Cousin?"

I opened my eyes. Aunt and Uncle were staring at me. Elly shook her head. Edward struggled with a grin.

"Cousin?" said John, as he tweaked my nose.

"Yes?" I replied as if awaking from a dream.

"Well," he teased, "she returns."

"The smitten angel of mercy took control of me, John," I whispered.

"And what did she have to say?" he asked with a grin.

I sighed with a shrug, "I cannot say."

Just then Miss Revelt appeared and took his arm. "John, I noticed a tray of your favourite kippers ..."

Aunt, and now my dearest *Uncle* Anthony, moved through the crowd nodding, kissing cheeks, and making polite conversation. *I must be on my way to place this bouquet of flowers on Mama and Papa's grave.* Stopping at the gate, I noticed John and Miss Revelt in jovial conversation. Seeming to sense my questioning eye, John smiled at me. I turned away.

* * *

When I returned to the garden, Uncle Anthony motioned for me to join him. "Anne, your Aunt and I have been looking for you."

"Yes, Uncle Anthony?"

"We will be sitting down to eat soon. Alice wishes you by her side."

"Oh, indeed, Uncle."

I had never seen Lesington Hall's Grand Dining Room look so beautiful. Actually, I had never seen it used before. Aunt's special beeswax candles were placed everywhere, she detested the new gas lanterns, finding them too smelly. I agreed.

Walking about under the warm flicker of candlelight, I noticed the wallpaper shone silky and warm beige. Our family's magnificent old cut-glass chandelier sparkled in silent elegance as it hung above the long black mahogany table that I had once written my name in its dust. In the centre, Aunt's most revered epergne held sprays of pink roses amongst green ferns arced in soft, kind hues. The candelabra's silver patina seemed to glow straight and narrow. Fine, gilt-edged china shone opulent and reflective. I could scarcely breathe for the beauty of the setting.

"It is an incredibly romantic room, Anne."

John Hathaway stood at my side holding two glasses of a sparkling silver liqueur of some sort. *Oh, he is heavenly.* I could feel my body tingle. Fanning myself with my prized handkerchief, I took a glass. "How kind of you, sir." *How does such a man magically appear offering me just the thing when my throat is parched? Oh, but he seems to be everywhere and at the most perfect moment—he is my destiny, surely.* I sighed.

While sipping my drink, I could feel the smitten angel flittering down my throat, her wings all a twitter as she engaged my entire body. My eyes turned teary with excitement. I inhaled heaven's sweet air about me. I just had to tell him that I loved him—would love him for the rest of my life. Would he wait until I grew up … would he marry me?

A feminine voice echoed behind us. "Oh, there you are, John." Miss Revelt joined us. She held a puzzled look. "John, where is *my* champagne?"

"Here you are, Elizabeth." He handed her his glass and winked at me.

"Thank you, but, John, where is yours?"

Realizing I took her champagne by mistake, I apologised, "Oh, forgive me, I, I assumed one was for me."

"Not to worry, I rather prefer sherry, actually," said John.

"I beg your pardon." I handed the empty glass to Abigail as she walked by.

"Life's little follies happen by-and-by," he added with a smile. "No worries."

Miss Revelt turned to me. "Oh, at last to be entertained at Lesington Hall, Miss Holt. I cannot tell you how grateful I am for the invitation." She glanced around the Great room; her eyes alit with reflective glitter. When she smiled, she was quite charming, actually. Even white teeth, shiny blond ringlets … smooth skin. Humph, she is probably wearing nasty old cotton pantaloons rather than silk, I thought, feeling smug.

"Oh, yes, Miss Revelt." I arched my brows smartly. "I am pleased, as well." I exhaled. "But, I must admit, I have never been entertained in here either."

Her brows lifted in surprise. "You don't say?"

"But Her Majesty and Prince Albert once twirled here." I fluttered my eyelashes.

She nodded. "Well, Lesington Hall is quite magnificent. Yes, I can imagine Her Majesty and the Prince moving in grand elegance this very moment."

Oh, God, how can I hate her? She is much too kind. Of course you can't hate her—you mustn't hate anyone.

"Indeed, when I first came here, it took me many weeks to learn all the rules. I cannot tell you how many times I slipped on the shiny floors. Once, I even got lost in the cellar. But I soon found the coal chute and climbed out." Now giggling, no doubt from the champagne, I continued, "I sprang up from the depths of hell all black and crusty and scared the gardener half out of his wits."

John laughed with gusto.

"Hmm," muttered Miss Revelt as she eyed me with furrowed brow, "how very odd."

"Cousin Anne, please excuse us, we must take our places at the table," said John.

Miss Revelt nodded. "Good evening, Miss Holt. John and I will leave after supper without delay, we must return to college. I do hope to see you again sometime."

I hope I never see you again.

"Perhaps I will see you again on holiday, John."

"Indeed, Cousin, I shall look forward to it."

His dark chocolate eyes rested quietly and softly upon my heart. I watched as he guided Miss Revelt to their seats at the dining table. Feeling the heat from the cavernous hearth behind me, I turned and faced the great fire. The huge pit took up half the wall. Logs the size of trees were held aloft by carriage-sized grates. The firebrick was blackened by centuries of fires such as this and held me mesmerised. Perhaps Mama once stood here in the arms of Papa. Patting my face, I felt my taut skin, the last remnants of tears drying in the warmth of this searing heat. *I wish I had a few leaves to toss in the fire, Mama. Oh, how I love you, Mama. I will never forget you, dear.* I twirled her ring on my finger.

Butlers stood at attention everywhere. Abigail, dressed in formal black and white, nodded to me as she approached. Her eyes were squinty for having her hair pulled back so severe beneath her stiff white cap. "What is it, Miss Anne?" she whispered. "Are you feeling sick?

I shrugged and glanced over at John and Miss Revelt. "Sick at heart, Abigail."

CHAPTER FIFTEEN

Elly, Abigail, Mrs Saverin, Nancy, Franklin, Holly Berry, Misha, Gib—especially Gib, were thankful to still be at our beloved Lesington Hall at Christmastime. But it was only until Aunt could find a suitable new home for herself and Uncle Anthony. Uncle Anthony had moved into Lesington Hall, leaving his home, Hawthorne House, for his sons.

I had not seen John since Aunt's wedding and Edward only upon occasion. But over breakfast, Uncle would kindly read aloud the letters John wrote from veterinary college.

"Anne, you must write to your cousin, John. I am sure he would be pleased to hear from you." Uncle patted my hand.

"I would not wish to bother him, Uncle. He must be busy studying."

"He thinks very highly of you, Anne. He asks about you in each of his letters."

I sighed deeply. "He is being polite, sir," I said taking a helping of eggs.

"I think not," added Aunt Alice, smiling. "He rarely asks about anyone else."

"Very well, if you insist, I shall write to him." *Dear John, I miss you more than you will ever truly believe or ever understand, and yes, I love you with all my ...*

"Anne?"

"Yes, Uncle?"

"You've been day dreaming again." Smoothing the folds of the letter, he continued reading aloud, "John says: 'Father, I do wish to stay at Hawthorne House at Christmas. Miss Revelt's mother and father will be away for the holidays, so I have invited her to spend them with us. She requests that we stay at 'our old home place' do you mind, Father? It is easier for her to find her way around the old Hawthorne place. We have much to catch up on. She graduates this year and has already planned the animal clinic in such great detail. What a dear, brilliant girl, she is.' "

Oh, beyond a doubt, muttered the smitten angel to me, *the dearest sparkle.*

Uncle continued: 'Do you mind, Father? Edward has been a great help to her. Together they have laid out a wonderful floor-plan for the veterinary offices, surgery room, and examination room. I feel quite like an outsider. They work so well together, one would think them brother and sister. He seldom discusses his fiancé, Miss Sprinkle. I rather suppose he is in love with someone else by now. Oh, and I must thank you again, Father, for keeping the staff on for Edward and me. Perhaps someday I shall buy the old place from you. My love and admiration to my dear stepmother, Alice, your lovely bride. When all this schooling is over, I sincerely hope to spend more time with you all.' "

Uncle smiled. "And here's a little something for you, Elly, '... a Christmas wish to Elly and Misha ... how are they getting on?' "

What about me? I stared glumly at my runny eggs.

"Oh, yes, and here, Anne ... 'and, my best to my little cousin, Anne.' "

'*Little cousin, Anne*'? *Little girl, Anne?* I felt my little breasts. Oui, oui they have stopped growing, again. I sighed.

Aunt tapped my hand. "Anne, really now, must you?"

Glancing quickly to Uncle, I found him still reading. "But, Aunt," I whispered in despair, "they have stopped growing."

Elly brought her napkin to her mouth, trying to stop laughing.

"Uncle?"

"Yes, Anne."

"Excuse me for interrupting, but did Cousin John ask about Holly Berry and Gib?"

Quickly glancing through to the end, he shook his head. "No, I am sorry, Anne. Not a mention of them."

"Very well, then, Uncle," I smiled, "then there *is* something, after all, that he will enjoy reading. I shall write to him this morning regarding their health."

"Indeed, he will be pleased to hear of it," said Aunt.

Uncle Anthony finished the letter and folded it. "John is a fine son. I cannot tell you how proud I am of him ... of both my

sons, Alice." He patted her hand. "And how they love you."
Nodding at me, he added, "And they love you, too, Anne."

I could feel my face burn. "I love ... them too, sir."

Elly put down her teacup. "Without a doubt."

* * *

I borrowed Aunt's rose scented writing paper.

December 1864 - Lesington Hall
Dear John,

Thank you for your kind letters. Uncle, Aunt Alice, Elly and I sit at the breakfast table and listen as your father reads aloud your letters. He certainly admires you.

(but not as much as I)

Of course fathers are like that. He and Aunt Alice encouraged me to write to you,

(though I cannot put in words exactly how much I miss you,)

so I shall tell you how Holly Berry, Misha and Gib are coming along. Holly Berry has grown taller by another two inches, and I measured her head, it is a full eighteen inches round. She has lost all her baby teeth now, and oh, my, how her new big white teeth sparkle. She has such a dear smile.

(Very much like yours.)

She has quit chewing since you advised Uncle to give her pigs' ears to gnaw. Misha still follows Elly everywhere.

In the last storm, Elly and I made a snow dog. We used a stick for her tail and put a scarf around her neck, coal for its nose and eyes. Gib refuses to set his paws in the cold, so we push him out. Poor darling scampers over the drifts, buries himself up to his chin—his whiskers pointy and frozen stiff. I am convinced he would get lost if it were not for Holly Berry being so fond of his tail. She drags the old fellow out of the snow ... and for her gallantry receives a prompt swipe to the nose.

Uncle and Aunt are the happiest of couples, John

(like you and I someday.)

> *Uncle must leave for a few days. He travels to Bath; Baron Henry Kerr has sent for him, a medical discomfort of sorts, Aunt will accompany him. She sends word that we will trim the Christmas tree when you and Edward are here.*
>
> **(I have run out of things to say ...)**
>
> *Goodbye for now, John. Aunt and your Papa send their love*
>
> **(along with mine,)**
>
> *Your friend and cousin, Anne*

I waved the letter about ... yes, yes, I smiled taking in the scent of roses. Would his hands carry the scent of my letter? Would he, upon occasion, take in the slightest whiff of my scent and dream of ...

"Anne?"

"Yes, Aunt Alice."

"If you wish, I will post your letter. Anthony and I are going to the lending library this morning."

"Oh, thank you, Aunt, yes."

"Miss Charlotte is coming for your lesson?"

I nodded. "Yes, Aunt, remember this will be her last lesson until she becomes Mrs Mandeville."

"I am happy for the dear girl." Pulling on her gloves, she shook her head. "What a severe brother she has."

"I should wonder how his new congregation in Liverpool finds him, Aunt?"

"In the north they are quite a different lot, Anne. But they should congregate quite nicely, I would imagine."

I handed her John's letter. "Smell it, Aunt."

She waved it about her face and smiled. "Well, who could have imagined sending a fine summer rose garden in such a snowy time of the year?"

"Thank you, Aunt." I felt my face burn again.

"I do hope you are playing the piano when we return, Anne. I find your touch on the keys ... beautiful." She kissed my forehead.

* * *

While I was reading in the library, Holly Berry rolled at my feet on the carpet, Misha slept next to her. Gib sat in the window seat flicking his proud tail, pretending he could spy the taunting little red birds that perched just outside watching him with a cautious eye.

I could never quite figure out how they knew Gib was blind. Oh, how they would dive and peck his head as he slinked about the garden, or sunned his belly in the warm summer sun.

Entering the room, Abigail carried a bucket of wood and a letter. "Be right with you, miss," she grunted, settling down the bucket. She tossed a few logs into the fire. "There now," she brushed her hands on her apron, "a letter for you, Miss Anne."

I sat up. "For me, Abigail? Are you sure?"

"Says here, Miss Anne Holt from Mr John Hathaway."

The smitten angel fluttered about my rib cage. "Thank you, Abigail, thank you." I ripped open the hard-pressed, creased letter. "He has a fine hand, does he not, Abby?"

"Oh, fine indeed, Miss Anne." She bustled from the room with a smile.

I held the letter, my throat went dry. I was more than excited to be reading my first ever letter from ...

December 1864 - The Royal Veterinary College
Dear Cousin Anne,

Thank you so much for such a jovial letter. I cannot tell you how much it made me laugh and miss home—a welcomed respite from the gruelling exams this time of year. How kind of you all to wait for me and Edward to trim the tree—ah, yes, the Christmas tree, yet another fine legacy from Prince Albert. I pray for Her Majesty— such a sad time of year for her.

(Yes, John, I, too, pray for her, and now I pray for us.)

I have already packed my things and by week's end I shall be home. Elizabeth Revelt and I have much to do.

(I have never liked the name Elizabeth)

Edward has been marvellous, I must say. I will have only a week in which to accomplish a great deal. Elizabeth is making great progress searching for a proper clinic ...

(Elizabeth, Elizabeth, Elizabeth! Monkey poop!)

I really must set my pen aside, Anne. My eyes are becoming foggy ... please write as often as you will. I sincerely enjoy hearing from you.
Your cousin, John Hathaway
By-the-by, happy birthday ...

Happy birthday? He remembered my birthday? But who told him? Yes, today I am ten and four. But I didn't feel any different this morning. I stood and glanced in the mirror. Turning sideways, I noticed. Oh, yes, they had begun to grow again. And my skin was indeed softer. I leaned in closer, yes, and fewer pimples, I noticed. Now standing in front of the long mirror, smiling, I curtsied, examining my teeth ...

"Ah, there it is," said Franklin as he walked around me, "the bucket. Abigail could not remember where she left it." Just before closing the door, he smiled sheepishly. "Happy birthday, Miss Anne. Oh, yes, lovely smile."

* * *

It was Christmas Eve at Lesington Hall. Aunt had decorated the entire house and it was festive and warm and lit by candles and decorated everywhere with fresh evergreens and handmade ornaments. Everyone in our small family would soon be arriving. I looked forward to seeing John, though I knew Miss Revelt would also come as his guest. I disliked that thought very much.

Feeling ill at ease, I wanted to be near Mama and Papa. I gathered up Holly Berry and Misha and took to the cool snow-laden pathways to the cemetery. I found that a light snow mist had deafly fallen upon Mama and Papa's grave. Looking around, everything in existence was now only a few colours— brown, grey, white; here and there swift smudges of black. The bark on the trees was soaked frozen, its branches spiked toward the heavens moving in sluggish grace to the frigid breeze.

I laid a wreath of greens tied with a bright red silk ribbon on Mama and Papa's grave. What a strange jolt of colour that lay atop the skiff of soft white virgin snow upon the leaden stone. Fondling Mama's locket, I wondered if she indeed had her shawl about her. I swept snow from their granite-etched names with my muff.

Holly Berry and Misha, now with their fluffy winter coats, chased about the drifts teasing one another. I smiled at how clumsy Holly Berry looked for her great size, yet so agile and cunning, just like Misha. This time Gib was left behind—to remain on guard in the kitchen, Mrs Savarin had earlier spied a mouse.

Misha barked toward the Great House. Glancing up, I spied an approaching carriage. Steam pulsed from the horses' noses and off their backs, their hooves tramping through the slush. The coachman's voice rang sharp, 'Hup, hup.'

All the sounds on such days were amplified—crystal and clear—much like the midnight peal of church bells.

"Come, Holly Berry, come, Misha," I called. "Don't go near the carriage ... the horses will trample you."

Holding Misha by the collar, I couldn't see who climbed from the carriage, but knew it must be either Edward or John—or both. My heart quickened. I started for the Great House. I then heard a tinkling giggle—it was the smitten angel again. She doused me in an icy bath, *look, it is Miss Elizabeth Revelt travelling with John.*

Turning away, I shook my head. "Come Holly girl, come Misha." I pouted, tossing sticks. "Let us take the long way back." Holly jumped and ran like a sprite.

'Anne.' I heard John calling me. 'Anne.' My step quickened, I kept my back to him. "Come, Holly Berry, come Misha." I chaffed her icy muzzle and hugged her. "Let him call for Elizabeth Revelt for all I care."

Misha growled. "Indeed," I softened, "but Misha, you must only growl at him with due respect. He did save your life, you know."

When reaching the servants' quarters, I brushed off the snow and hung my great coat on a peg. I then removed my boots, promptly stepping into a pond of snow that I had dripped on the floor. Holly shook-off and nosed Gib with great affection. Misha scampered into the kitchen to find, perhaps in her dish, a treat from her gruff friend, the cook.

"Any mice, Mrs Savarin?"

She shuddered. "Gib hasn't lost his touch, miss." Wiping her floured hands on her apron, she smiled at our fat cat.

"Don't ask me how he does it, Miss, but bless him, he catches 'em."

Smelling the fresh baked bread, I moaned. "Oh, when do we eat, Mrs Savarin? I am famished." I swayed, but surely not from hunger. I put my hand to my forehead and I felt warm. Cook slapped a tab of butter on a warm slice of bread and handed it to me.

I kissed her cheek. "Thank you, Mrs Savarin. How I love you."

Holly Berry whined—her begging eyes darted from my slice of bread to the rolling pin in Cook's other hand.

Mrs Savarin shook her head with a sigh, "If I would only learn not to look into her soulful eyes ..." She tossed Holly a slice of bread. Misha barked for her portion. After tossing her a piece, she pointed toward the door. "Out, all of you."

We three scurried from the kitchen, I laughing and shrieking with Holly Berry barking and jumping alongside. Misha scampered about like a wild chicken ... until we reached the vestibule. All of a sudden the drawing room doors swung open. Aunt, Uncle, John, Edward, and Miss Revelt hurried out.

"God in heaven," cried Aunt, "was that you, Anne?"

Still munching on my bread, I stopped. I could feel the snow melting from the cap on my head, now trickling down my chin. "Ah, excuse me, Aunt." I glanced at Uncle. "Excuse me, sir." Just then Gib snatched the last of my bread from my hand hidden behind my back. Miss Revelt's brows arched higher than Miss Pramm's could ever do. Edward, standing behind her, grinned. John, with a whimsical smile, seemed highly entertained. Uncle shook his head. Elly stood in the background making faces at me.

"Well, now, Anne," said Aunt, "you must dress for supper."

"Yes, ma'am, I will hurry."

Misha whined for Elly, and spying an open space between the door and Uncle's boot, hurried to her side. Recalling Miss Pramm's class on Ascending Steps (when someone is watching), I engaged my sopping wet stocking feet quite nicely. As Holly bounded ahead of me, and Gib leapt the steps two at a time beside me, I called back over my shoulder, "Happy Christmas everyone." My voice croaked. I could feel my face grow hot. Reaching the top step, I glanced back and found John smiling up at me.

"The happiest of Christmases to you, Anne," he said.

I hurried to my room, finding it exceedingly warm; I felt a chill, but my body was warm. My face burned, but it was so cold in my room. No, I thought again, patting my face. I had a fever. Shivering, I rang for Abigail.

"Abby, please have Aunt come to my room. I do not feel well."

Within minutes, I heard Aunt's familiar tap as she bustled in. "What is wrong, Love?" Feeling my brow, she frowned. "Dear me, I must have Anthony see you." Glancing up to Abigail, she directed, "Abby, bring Dr Hathaway at once."

"Yes, ma'am."

I was wrapped in my robe with coverings to my chin when Uncle entered. Abigail carried his medicine tray. I prayed, not the oil again ... I will gag.

Uncle took my temperature. "Hmm, yes, my dear Anne, you have a nasty fever." Aunt wrung her hands, Uncle patted them. "Calm down Alice, it is just a cold, my dear."

"Oh, how unfortunate," she frowned, "we were to trim the tree this evening. John and Miss Revelt, Edward ... ."

I closed my eyes. *Elizabeth, Elizabeth, Elizabeth! Who cares about her.* I shook my head in disgust.

"Oh, do not fret, love. I shall have broth sent up. After we have trimmed the tree, I shall come sit with you," said Aunt with concern.

"And I shall come, too." Uncle rubbed my hand consolingly.

"Oh, please, do not do such a thing." I glanced up at him. "You have so little time with your sons. Please, sir, stay with them, I shall see you in the morning. Surely I will be well enough for breakfast."

Feeling my forehead again, he shook his head. Looking once more into my eyes, he inhaled deeply. "Hmm, they are bloodshot already." He touched my nose. "I will be up now and again to check on you."

I couldn't remember that night, the next morning or the following week, actually. Now and again, I could feel the weight of Holly Berry jumping atop my bed, felt her lick my face, felt Gib sniff my eyes, felt Misha nudge my hand. Then, a sudden cold cloth startled me awake—Aunt was wiping my brow.

"Oh," she cried, tears sliding down her pale cheeks, "Anthony, Anthony, she has awakened."

I thought I saw Abigail hurry from the room and within what seemed only seconds Uncle was touching my face. "It has broken, Alice. The fever has broken. She will live."

"Live?" I wrinkled my nose, trying to lift my head from the damp pillow. "Was I dying?"

Aunt lowered her head in her hands, Uncle hugged her.

I couldn't hold my head up. Indeed, I was weak and dropped back onto my pillow. Aunt wiped her eyes and took my hand. Elly hurried into the room, she had been crying, too. Abigail, Franklin, Nancy, Mrs Savarin, all hovered over my bed.

I blinked. "I missed Christmas, didn't I?"

Uncle laughed. Aunt tweaked my nose; her eyes were strained and dark and red, but she managed a smile.

Elly shook her head. "I told them you wanted me to unwrap your present, but they wouldn't hear of it."

"Only one?" I said in jest.

Ushering the servants from the room, Franklin nodded. "We are all blessed, Miss Anne." Nancy winked and crossed herself as she followed the jovial Mrs Savarin from the room.

"They all love you, Anne." Aunt brushed my cheek with the back of her hand.

Elly kissed my brow. "Even me."

I took her hand. "I love you too, Elly, and you, too, Aunt." Uncle was standing by the window. "I love you, Uncle. I am sure you saved my life."

"The angel of mercy saved you, Anne."

"Oh, yes," I smiled, 'the smitten angel of mercy.' "

I knew the house was empty of our guests. John had gone back to college, Edward to Hawthorne House, and Miss Elizabeth Revelt back to wherever she belonged. I was thankful I didn't have to see her and John snuggle under the mistletoe.

"John peeked in on you, Anne." Uncle smiled. "He left you this."

It was a neatly wrapped package. "A Christmas present, Uncle?"

"No. He only said it was a belated birthday gift, Anne."

I was still weak. Holding it close to my chest, I must have fallen off to sleep, for when I next awoke, Uncle had gone. Nancy had built a nice fire for it was a sunny bank, nice and cosy. I drank the entire decanter of water that was on my nightstand, and feeling better, sat up. Though still dizzy, I was anxious to unwrap my gift from John.

Little by little, I removed each layer of fine paper. There, in a sturdy mahogany frame, an oil portrait of Holly Berry, Misha, and Gib. In the bottom right corner it was signed: John Hathaway, 14 Dec '64.

There was a note attached.

25 December 1864
Dear Cousin,
  I hope I have captured their likeness. If nothing else, I know their presence will cheer you to good health once again.
    Your friend and cousin, John Hathaway

Bringing the picture to my chest, I stared at my beautiful friends that John had tried so sweetly to capture. I knew I would cherish it for the rest of my life. It was more than adorable—Holly sitting up, smiling as Misha affectionately leaned on her, while Gib, curled within his tail, snuggled at their feet. I set the picture on my nightstand and managed a sigh.

I must send him a reply.

Now up and eating properly, my strength had returned to each of my limbs; my mind regained its clarity; my thinking sobered. I knew I must soon send a note to thank John for my wonderful painting. Oh, yes, I remembered the beautiful new stationery Aunt gave me for Christmas ... lavender scented.

10 January 1865 Tuesday
Dear John,
  Forgive this late note, but I have just regained enough strength to dine with Aunt and Uncle this evening. Looking at your portrait of my dearest friends every morning when I first wake is my greatest joy. It is more than adorable, Cousin! I shall cherish it for the rest of my life ... **(just as I will cherish you.)**
  I was disappointed to have missed Christmas with everyone. I hope you forgive me for my illness and causing any interruption with your dear friend Miss Revelt. **(Perhaps, someday, we shall meet properly and then she could disappear ... forever.)**

Thank you, your affectionate cousin, **(I love you)**
Anne

* * *

John, with the urging of his brother Edward and Miss Revelt, decided to locate their future animal clinic in Bath, where the best sort of clientele would be found—the wealthy sort. Miss Revelt would wait until John graduated and join him. Upon visits to Lesington Hall, John assured Uncle Anthony that he would relocate back to London once they had become profitable and on sound footing.

I hardly saw him, for he remained at college—eager to graduate and join Miss Revelt, I sadly supposed. At every opportunity, he and Edward stayed at their home-place, Hawthorne House, when on holiday. I rarely had a moment to gaze upon John's handsome face—and more handsome he became.

Uncle Anthony would pat my hand. "Dear Anne, I understand the sacrifices John must make in the beginning of his practice. We must be patient in our demands to spend more time with him."

I was certain neither he nor Aunt knew of my deep affections for John. But it seemed he had indeed devoted all his time to his studies to the exclusion of us all. I wanted to bark in his face just like Holly Berry does when I have neglected her. Perhaps then he would see that I was alive. It became exceeding painful to say goodbye to him after each of his brief visits, each holiday, each empty birthday. He would laugh and tweak my nose as I cried at his leaving. I quite convinced myself we would remain cousins ... could I even love another?

CHAPTER SIXTEEN

August, 1868. I had marked the days on my calendar until the day I would be presented at Court—twelve days remained. Gazing up into the warm thunderous August sky, I knew full well that once presented to my Sovereign, I would be an honest woman, *out* and eligible to marry—expected to marry.

But I knew my own heart. I could love no other than John. Though I had met many handsome young men, I didn't find that my heart beat in that peculiar way as when it did when I was near him. Indeed, my heart belonged to one man. I believe Uncle was anxious for me to be on my way in life, but Aunt was not so eager to release me.

"Oh, will it never stop raining, Aunt?" I folded my calendar and stood. "I so wanted to be out walking with Holly and Misha."

"Days such as these are when we must practice for your presentation to Court, Dearest."

"Goodness me, I am so thankful Kate will be presented on the same day. All my friends have been talking about it, Aunt. How worried and nervous they are to meet Her Majesty. The Baron Kerr's granddaughter, Sarah, will receive a kiss to the forehead by the Queen. All others are to kiss her hand."

Aunt nodded. "Indeed, *I* kissed her hand. Well, actually I kissed her thumb. She wears kidskin gloves you know. One is not allowed to actually touch Her Majesty."

"I will be satisfied to kiss her glove, Aunt Alice. Just to touch her. I pray she has come out of mourning."

Putting her arm around my shoulder, Aunt kissed my brow. "And Anne, I quite sense you have emerged from your own mourning."

I turned to her in amazement. "Why, Aunt, what a thought? Why, yes, yes, I suppose I have. Haven't I?"

"You are a beautiful young lady, Anne, seventeen and soon to be out. I cannot tell you how proud Anthony and I are of you."

I hugged her. "Was it not you, Aunt, who taught me, 'O Lord, who lends me life, lend me a heart replete with thankfulness?' " [11]

* * *

Today I was to be presented to Court, to take Her Majesty's hand. We had arrived at St. James Palace in good time and ushered into a *primping room*, where Elly picked and poked, smiled and fussed over me.

Glancing in the mirror, I adjusted the feathers at the back of my head. "Are they proper, Elly? Her Majesty must be able to see them when I enter the room."

"Oh, my yes, Miss Peacock, she will be able to find you in a crowded railway station ..."

Gathering up my train, I shook my head at the folds of material. "Elly, I cannot believe it is three yards long."

Our door creaked half open and Aunt peeked in. "Oh, there you are, Anne." She hurried in. "Goodness, I became lost." She fanned herself. "Oh, St. James Palace is monstrously large. Every door seemed the right one until I opened it." Her glance softened. "You look exquisite, my dear. Excited?"

"Oh, yes, Aunt."

"Well," she looked up, sighed, and paraded in front of the mirror. "I remember when I was presented, Anne. Yes, it was an exciting, wonderful day, all in all."

"You must have looked beautiful, Aunt Alice."

Elly stepped in front of the mirror, preening. "But not as beautiful as I when I was presented."

"Hmm, presented to *what*, may I ask, my dear Elly?"

Laughing, Elly and Aunt settled me in front of the mirror. They were tucking this, dabbing that. Suddenly my memory went blank. "Oh, say again what I am to do when I am called, Aunt."

---

[11] William Shakespeare, *King Henry the Sixth*, Part 2, Act 1, scene 1 (1591).

"As we have practiced, Anne, keep your train folded over your left arm. Just when you are to be presented to Her Majesty you will be ushered into the Long Gallery. There you will await the summons to the Presence Chamber. When the time comes, you will enter the room by the door pointed out to you. From there you shall make your way to the throne, having let down your train, which will have been spread out at once by the attendant lords-in-waiting. A card bearing your name will be handed to another lord-in-waiting, who then will announce your name to Her Majesty."

"Oh, yes, yes, of course." Dabbing my brow, I simmered. "I wonder if she will remember all the letters of condolence I wrote from Holybourne over the years?"

"Do not be disappointed if she does not, my dear. She has been in deep mourning these many years."

"Indeed, Aunt." I fanned my face. "It is very warm in this room."

Adjusting one of my peacock feathers, Elly leaned on my shoulder, adding, "Oh, Anne, it is much warmer in the Presence Chamber, my dear. I am sure you will faint straight away."

Aunt nodded. "I am convinced of it."

"But I am not so inclined to fits of weakness, *Elly*, as you are, perhaps. Do go on, Aunt."

"Oh, yes, then once in Her Majesty's presence, you curtsy until you are almost kneeling, whereupon you must kiss the Queen's hand. Then rise, curtsy once more to her and also to any other members of her family who are present, and then back out of the drawing room, not turning your face away from her."

Elly patted my hand. "That's when you will faint, Anne. I am sure of it."

"Oh, Elly, you are wrong," Aunt Alice quipped, "backing from the room is when she will trip over her train."

A tap, tap, tap came to our door. My heart thumped. I kissed Elly. I kissed Aunt. With one last glimpse in the mirror, I said aloud to myself, "Much luck, much pluck, I will waddle like a duck."

A deep, resonant voice called out, "Miss Anne Catherine Holt."

Entering the Royal Drawing Room, I could not take my eyes from Her Majesty. How remarkably beautiful she appeared. Her light brown hair was pulled straight and taut held by a small crown. Her skin seemed warm, with a tinge of pink, her cheeks puffy. Her eyes set well and dark beneath her pale brows. Though her lips curved downward, no doubt her widowed grief held such a pose.

All the letters I had written her, I had shared my love and concerns for her good health and fortune. How I loved this most gracious and honourable lady, my Sovereign, keeper of the faith, devoted wife of Prince Albert—her beloved. As I came closer, she held my gaze. Surely she could feel my love and admiration for her … a woman I held in such high esteem.

Now I was at her throne. She smiled and reached out to me. I curtsied and took her hand and kissed it. "Your Majesty." My tears fell onto her plump, firm grasp. "I have shared your grief my entire life."

"I know you have, my dear. Your many thoughtful letters have warmed my heart—indeed, they have made me smile upon many an occasion when I have not wanted to smile. I assure you."

"For that, Your Majesty, I am truly blessed." I closed my eyes in deep gratification. My heart was in my throat.

"Come. Come, my dear child." The Queen embraced me, kissing both cheeks. Closing my eyes, I kissed her hand once more. I arose and when I began to back away, she smiled. "You must continue to write, Anne."

"Indeed, Your Majesty."

* * *

"Anne," said Aunt in astounding amazement, "Her Majesty gathered you up? Spoke intimately with you?"

"Oh, yes, Aunt. You know how I have written her."

"But all the same, why, I am astounded she remembered your name." Aunt looked astonished.

"Oh, Aunt, she forgets nothing. Truly her heart is good."

"I know that it is, but still …"

"Come, Aunt, come, Elly. Look, there, Uncle Anthony awaits us."

Settling in the carriage, I sighed loudly. "It is done."

"You are now an honest woman, Anne." Aunt squeezed my hand.

"Indeed," said Uncle. "Everyone is talking at how Her Majesty took to you, Anne. Indeed, how she singled you out above all others."

"It is my unwavering devotion to her ... Uncle. Oh, how happy I am."

Aunt kissed my cheek. "Indeed, Anne. On this, your special day, we must all be happy and cheerful."

"Indeed, we shall," said Uncle Anthony. "We shall rejoice at your dinner party this evening at Lesington Hall. "Do not forget, you will have many more balls to attend."

Elly smirked, "And now that you are "out" you are free to marry—required to marry," she added with a nudge.

I want to marry only one man, John Hathaway. But a brooding premonition sank my heart ... a whisper echoed in its deepest corner. *John Hathaway is not the right one ... not the right man for you. He loves another ... prepare yourself, prepare your heart.*

"Oh, go away, dark angel of doom."

"Dark angel of gloom?" said Elly. "My heavens, what was that all about?"

"Perhaps I shall never marry, Cousin Elly."

* * *

The Hathaway carriage ambled onto our beloved Lesington Hall's fountain circle. We all climbed wearily from the carriage. As Aunt and Uncle disappeared into the house, Abigail was left holding my train.

Elly sighed. "Come along, Love. You must change and Abby must be about her other chores."

"Indeed," I sighed deeply. "It has been a wonderfully long, but exhausting day."

"With yet more this evening, dear." Elly leaned on the railing as if to steady herself.

"Careful as you go, old girl." I took her elbow. "Are you not feeling well, Elly?"

"Humph, well enough to reach the top before you." She tweaked my nose. "Such a spectacle you made of yourself today, Anne."

When Abby squealed at the banter, Holly Berry and Misha nipped at her heels. Gib traipsed after Mrs Savarin as she disappeared into the kitchen.

* * *

After I changed, and after Abby did my hair, I sat at my window seat admiring the yellow-warm beauty of the sunlight's arresting shadows on this early evening in August. Stroking Misha's soft head, I noticed her grey hair had now claimed her entire muzzle. Gazing out, I watched the footmen place torches along the drive for our guests this evening.

The fountain was not long ago scrubbed; water sprayed in soft shooting arcs; the shrubs and gardens were still quite verdant; hot and summery-soft floating air wafted about me. Holly Berry lay sleeping at my feet.

This day was a culmination of many days, and I thanked God in heaven for my blessings. I kissed Mama's locket, felt the warm gold to my lips. To my breast, beneath all folds of silk and satin, my Holybourne handkerchief, the leaves now but flakes and powder from the years of handling. And yet, it still held that special scent of my little village, of Mama, and I supposed, of my dear Papa. God bless you, Papa. How sweet and calm Her Majesty was today. Though the wrinkles of worry shone greatly on her face, her eyes remained keen and forthright; her voice soft and strong. Oh, God save the Queen.

Glancing over toward the mews, I spied a lone man riding his horse. Who could that be? I watched as he dismounted. "Is it Edward? No," I squinted, "no ..." my heart leapt in my chest, "it is John."

I smudged the windowpane with my brow. I had not seen him in ages.

How long, Anne?

Well, let me see. I watched as he handed the reins to the stable boy. *It must be six months or more. Well, if you really loved him you would know the exact number of months, days, hours ... you fickle girl. Wait, I am no longer a girl. I am a marriage proposal, a lovely young lady, and yes, perhaps fickle all the same.*

Dozens of carriages had assembled in the courtyard below. Aunt was, no doubt, fretting that I was not already by her side to welcome our guests. I hurried from my room, but first stopped at Elly's door and tapped lightly.

"Come in, Anne," came her whisper.

I found her still lying in bed, not dressed. "Are you not well, Elly?"

"The usual migraine, dear, not to worry, I shall be down later. I wouldn't miss your evening."

"Very well, Elly, but I shall have Uncle look in on you."

"No, no, just leave Misha and Holly Berry. I will simply rest my eyes, Love. Go now. I hear the carriages ... hurry along. I shall be fine."

I kissed her brow. "Very well, but I will return soon."

"No need."

I left the dogs to Elly and hurried down the stairs. Entering the drawing room, the musicians had begun their music.

"There you are, dear." Aunt's face softened. "Hurry, come."

I kissed her and Uncle's cheeks.

"I stopped by Elly's room, she has the migraine—sorry I am late."

Uncle Anthony took my hand. "Well, you look charming, Niece."

"Thank you, sir. Oh, Uncle, just awhile ago I saw John ride up."

"My John?"

I nodded.

"Oh, you quite mistake him, Anne."

But I knew it was John. I was quite convinced that it was he. "Why is that, Uncle?"

"You no doubt saw Edward. John and Miss Revelt are to come together later this evening."

"But are not Edward and Miss Sprinkle coming together, Uncle?"

Aunt glanced down. "In all the excitement of the day, we didn't want to spoil your happiness. Miss Sprinkle called off the engagement, evening last."

Why would such news spoil my day? I nodded. "Oh, yes, Uncle, Edward must be terribly upset." Which I knew he would not be, but Uncle most likely didn't know that Edward was in love with Miss Pramm, had been since my first formal tea party. I sighed. "I shall be discreet, Uncle. I will tread easy regarding matters of the heart around Eddie."

"Thank you, dearest." He smiled. "You are more than considerate. I do worry over Edward. You know how sensitive a man he is."

He no doubt broke Miss Sprinkle's heart, Uncle. That is how sensitive a coxcomb Edward is.

Franklin entered, and with a half-bow, introduced Professor and Mrs Mandeville.

Smiling, I took Charlotte's hand and kissed her cheek. "Oh, you look marvellous, Mrs Mandeville, and Professor, you are doing well?"

Smiling, he glanced at Charlotte. "Very well, Anne."

Charlotte nudged me. "I heard you kissed Her Majesty's hand today."

"Yes, it was more than I had expected." I didn't want to boast that Her Majesty embraced me warmly.

"Being presented at Court is quite beautiful, actually." Charlotte dropped her voice. "Before my family's fortune dwindled, Anne, I too, was to be presented to Court."

"It is something quite magnificent."

Franklin entered. "Mr and Mrs Charles Hathaway and Miss Katherine Hathaway."

Uncle whispered to Aunt, "Come, dear, it is my brother and Florence."

I took Kate's hand. "You look very pretty this evening."

"And you, Anne. I tried to find you today, but with all the confusion at the Palace ... well," she giggled, "we are both now out."

"Hmm and free to marry, Kate."

"Oh, yes, I have been warned by Papa to 'Start looking, young lady.' "

"And in the right houses," I added.

Kate laughed. "What about you, Anne?"

Franklin entered and announced, "Miss Pramm."

"Goodness, Anne, you invited *her*?"

"Edward is madly in love with her," I whispered.

Her mouth dropped. "Miss Pramm? Wherever did you hear that?"

"Shush ... Uncle Anthony and Aunt do not know as yet. I just found out Miss Sprinkle broke off the engagement with Eddie evening last."

"You quite mistake the match, Anne. Edward is not in love with Miss Pramm at all."

My face wrinkled in doubt. "No?"

"He and Miss Revelt are in love."

"Oh, but you are wrong. Why, it has been John and she who have all along been in love."

Kate shook her head. "John and Elizabeth have been strong and loyal friends since childhood, but never lovers. No, I wager it is Edward and Elizabeth Revelt. Mark my words."

I swallowed hard; my heart felt like wild birds were flapping their wings inside my chest. "But you are not positively exactly sure, Kate?"

"Well, not *exactly* sure, but I know Cousin Edward. He is definitely in love with Elizabeth."

"But is she in love with him?"

"Hmm." She pondered. "Yes, I do believe it. Yes, of course."

Franklin entered the room. "Mr John Hathaway." He paused. "Miss Elizabeth Revelt."

I stopped breathing. John looked so handsome with his kind sweet face, his soft manners. How he loved my Holly Berry, Misha, and Gib. Thinking of the portrait he had painted for me many years earlier, I felt tears well in my eyes. *I love you so dearly, John Hathaway.* Turning away, I wiped my eyes. I could feel my face burning.

Uncle came to my side. "Do not let Edward's broken heart trouble you, Anne. He will survive it all."

The music floated into my heart; I could not stand to watch John and Elizabeth move about the floor smiling, nodding, and laughing. *No, I could not possibly be wrong. They are meant for each other.*

"Anne," Aunt took my hand, "come, dearest, a physician friend of Anthony's would like to meet you."

"Very well, Aunt. Has Elly come down?"

"No, I will go up and see how she is feeling."

We moved through the guests and soon found Uncle.

"Anne," he smiled, "please meet my friend, Dr Waterbury."

"Sir, very pleased." I smiled. He was a sophisticated gentleman, middle aged; black hair with a flair of white along the temples, German grey eyes and a warm smile. He spoke with a clear, gentle voice. I noticed his clean, well-formed teeth beneath his black, razor-edged moustache.

"Miss Holt, your uncle tells me you were born in Holybourne?"

"Yes, Dr Waterbury, I left when I was a young girl, returning but once."

"Hmm, yes, well," he smiled again, "I am from Stanbury, a little north of Holybourne. My wife and two of my three children were born there—recently a son." He beamed.

Uncle Anthony nodded. "Indeed, an old professor at Cambridge was also from Holybourne. Might you know of a Professor Samuel Grinby, William?"

"Grinby? Samuel Pettibone Grinby?" He shook his head. "Such a coincidence, Sir Anthony, why, he is a cousin of mine."

"Oh, sir, Professor Grinby is a wonderful gentleman. He returned my late father's library to me. I shall forever be indebted to him. His most recent illness has kept him from attending my party."

"Pardon me, Dr Waterbury," interrupted Aunt with a harried look. Taking Uncle's arm, she apologised, "I must speak with my husband for a moment. Please excuse us."

Dr Waterbury nodded. "But of course, Mrs Hathaway."

Turning back to me, he smiled. "Tell me again, Miss Holt, how did you come to meet my dear cousin, Grinby?"

I explained that Professor Grinby wrote and offered to return my father's library to me, and that he also gave me a beautiful dog.

"A dog?" He chuckled. "Yes, that would be Grinby all right."

"A beautiful dog, sir." I thought again of the portrait John painted of my threesome—my doggie girls and the cat bachelor.

"Miss Holt, would you like this dance? The music is quite superb."

"Yes, I would like that, sir."

Leading me out onto the floor, he took my hand. "I am a dog fancier myself, Miss Holt."

I lit up. "Are you, sir? I know of only one other gentleman who fancied dogs as much." I glanced around for John, but with moving to the music and the dim candlelight, I could not find him. Sadness invaded my heart, blurring the music, blurring the entire day; even blurring my happiness at meeting Her Majesty. I suppose John and Miss Revelt have come and gone. My dream that he would take me in his arms and waltz me out onto the balcony beneath the stars was fast slipping away, along with the evening.

The music stopped. Dabbing his brow, the kind doctor smiled. "Where was that table with lemonade again, Miss Holt? I could indulge in a little lemon ice as well."

"Right this way, sir." I led him to the table where wine, champagne, tea, coffee, and iced lemonade were situated. "Here you are, Dr Waterbury."

"Anne," said Kate as she took my hand, "John wishes to see you."

"Cousin John?" My heart leaped in my chest. I glanced around. "But I thought he and Miss Revelt left?"

"He is standing there." She pointed and then shrugged. "Well, he was standing over there, by the balcony door."

"Hmm, well, I shall go look for him."

It was a warm evening, and even though all the ballroom doors were open, the room remained quite close. Approaching the evening air, I could feel its splendour, the evening breezes peeled cool against my skin. The music began again. I could feel my body move with its rhythm. I ran my hand across my face; it felt warm, moist and soft.

This evening, I felt wonderfully sophisticated, for the first time ... appealing. The glances I received from the men were different from yesterday's casual nods; this evening their eyes were centred and direct—they looked at me, not through me.

Walking out onto the balcony, I lifted my bare arms into the moon's silvery wash and stopped at the stone balustrade, I glanced out at the moon's white reflection in the rippling pond below. Hearing muffled voices, I glanced down—my breath caught as I watched John and Miss Revelt, arm in arm stroll toward the pond. I turned away. God, I do not want to see him kiss her. I heard Misha's eerie cry. Tears slid down my face.

"Anne," cried Aunt taking my hand, "do be quick; it is Elly."

Hurrying alongside her, I knew something was terribly wrong. The music slowed, everyone stopped dancing and stared as we rushed from the room and bounded up the stairs. Opening Elly's door, we found Uncle lifting Misha from Elly's still, quiet chest. Holly Berry hovered by his side.

Shaking his head, he whispered, "I am truly sorry, she is gone."

"Gone? Gone where? Oh, my God, no, this cannot be!" I dropped to my knees. Crossing myself, I pleaded to God to bring her back. "God, one more miracle, please." Crying, I pleaded, "Elly, you must come back. You didn't say good-bye."

Aunt knelt beside me. Uncle's arms were around us both. Misha slid from the bed and joined Holly—they were awash in the shining moonlight by the open window. Misha lifted her greying muzzle as if to bay at the moon. Holly Berry slinked to my side, I felt her nudge my arm as she squirmed in beside us. Wrapping my arms around her strong, warm neck, I cried.

Uncle situated Aunt into a chair. Waving him off, I remained with Holly Berry—numb with grief. It was only when Abigail and Franklin came in that Aunt and I finally left the room.

Solemnly we removed to Aunt's boudoir, where we said a few parting words and then I repaired to my room. Holly Berry curled atop my bed as Misha remained at the open window, staring out at the white full moon.

I remembered to say my prayers, my eyes burning, my throat raw—I wanted to hold John Hathaway in my arms. I was empty, alone, and shaken. I couldn't speak with God, He was busy working someone else's miracle. If I could only accept His decision, convinced that even a God makes bad decisions at times.

The next morning I lay awake in my rumpled evening gown, listening as everyone tiptoed about the halls, whispering, closing doors quietly rattling the cupboards gently. Even the whinny of the horses was subdued and distant. Holly Berry lifted her head to see if I was awake, Misha yawned, stretched, and licked my face.

I sat up and petted her head, petted Holly Berry. Both were now cuddled closer to me. They knew something terrible had happened in the house, and they mirrored my mood. I have often wondered how animals know these things. I rose from the bed and rang for Abigail.

She had kept my fire going throughout the night; my water basin fresh. I should not have rung for her, the poor dear was doubtless run ragged by now. But came her familiar knock. "Come."

"Yes, Miss Anne." Her eyes were red and swollen.

"I am sorry, Abigail. I should not have disturbed you. I can do for myself this morning. Go about your other work; I am sorry to have troubled you further."

"Oh, thank you, Miss Anne." She wiped her eyes. "We are doing up the parlour for Mrs Mills."

"Yes, thank you. Is there anything I might do, Abigail?"

"Only if you remember what I did with all that black crepe we bought last year, Miss Anne. I have quite forgotten where I placed it."

I thought for a moment. "Oh, yes, Elly kept it. It's in the chest, at the foot of her bed."

Abigail lowered her head.

"Stay here, Abby. I will get it for you."

"Oh, Miss Anne," she cried, kissing my cheek, "thank you."

Walking barefoot, I approached Elly's door and, without thinking, tapped lightly. Catching myself, I opened the door. I could smell her familiar rose water-bath; her fragrant soaps; the hearth was scorched black and empty. The sun was shining through a small opening in her drapes. I opened the chest at the foot of her bed and found the bolt of black cloth, though I did not look onto her bed, I knew her body was no longer there. For that I was thankful.

Leaving her room, I pulled the door closed without a sound. Tears welled in my eyes, I still could not believe this terrible black moment. Leaning against the door, I tried to get my breath, but everything was a blur. Feeling dizzy, I dropped the bolt of cloth and slid slowly to the floor. Feeling a strong, warm hand steady me, I glanced up. "John?"

"Come now." He helped me to the end of the hall and set me on Aunt's reading sofa, now awash in sunlight.

Abigail hurried to my side, patting my hand. "Oh, miss, are you feeling faint? Oh, I shall bring water."

"No, no, Abigail," I assured her, "I shall be fine. Thank you, you have done enough."

"I will get her water, Abigail," whispered John as he patted my hand. "Stay here, Anne, I'll be just a moment."

Watching him move down the hall, I warmed at his thoughtfulness. "Abby," I gestured to Elly's door, "I dropped the bolt."

"I'll get it, Miss Anne." She stayed with me until John returned.

Hurrying back up the hall, he took my hand. "Here now, Anne. Take a sip."

"I will go now, Miss Anne," Abby whispered. "If you need anything ..."

"I will remain with her, Abigail," he said holding my hand.

Holly Berry stood at my bedroom door staring at us. Patting his leg, John beckoned her, "Come." Holly first licked his hand and then curled at my feet. Misha whimpered at Elly's door, confused at why she was not allowed to enter.

I lowered my head. John hugged me. "If you feel like crying, Anne, I will hold you."

If I do, will you hold me for the rest of my life, John Hathaway—or will I hold you for the rest of your life?

"Thank you, Cousin, you are more than kind." *I feel your strength, your comfort, your compassion, your goodness. How are all these things possible? How can I simply feel them or could have known how strong and good you were before all this?*

His breath caught. I could feel him smile and feel his heart beat as mine.

He gazed down into my face. "Do you feel better, Anne?"

I nodded. "Yes." *But only when you are near me.* "If you would but walk me to my room, John."

"Very well, then." He helped me stand and slowly we headed for my room. Now standing at my door, I thanked him for his kindness. Kissing my fingers, I touched them to his lips. What an odd sensation rippled through my body. Stunned at what I had done, I blurted, "Oh, pardon me ..."

Miss Revelt suddenly appeared. "Does she need anything, John? Shall I ring for someone?"

She touched my shoulder with concern. I must admit she did have a sincere look on her face. The smitten angel snorted. *The only concern on her face is your concern for John Hathaway, miss. Move on now, silly girl. To think he would have any feelings for you other than cousinly is absurd.*

I shook my head and slipped into my room, easing the door closed behind me. *I do not wish to see her face, she is much too kind.* I felt my heart pounding so in my chest. *John's touch was wonderful, soothing, but why am I crying? I will hate Miss Revelt forever.* Lying on my bed, I buried my face in the pillows. *Elly, I am sorry to have such feelings when I should be thinking only of you.*

CHAPTER SEVENTEEN

Early the next morning, I awoke to "my girls" whining at the door. I had shut them out last night, poor darlings. Letting them in, Holly hopped atop my bed, sniffed about, scratched her shoulder and curled up.

I watched as Misha lay at the foot of my bed, gazing toward the window, I read her thoughts. "Come, Misha." Stroking her head, I kissed her muzzle. "Dear old girl, Elly has gone to heaven." She whined as if she understood. Dabbing my eyes, I heard Holly growl. Her attentions were also at the window.

Gib was sitting on the outside window ledge pawing at the pane, begging to be let in. I lifted the fat little ball of fur from the ledge. His hair was cool and moist. "Have you been there all night, ol' boy?"

He was meowing wildly so I knew he was probably hungry, but no worse for wear. "At least it didn't rain last night, Gib." I kissed his head and shuddered to think what would have happened if he tried to climb down by himself.

I heard Aunt's tap at my door, and she let herself in without announcement. She was wearing funeral black.

"Morning, Love," she whispered. Her face was pale and drawn. Her hair was swept back and severe. The rim of her eyes were pink; her nose red and swollen." Perusing my room, she found my companions and smiled warmly.

I kissed her cheek. "They are faithful, are they not?"

She tugged at my wrinkled dress and shook her head. "As you have always been to Elly, Anne." She buried her head on my shoulder. "How I loved her, Anne, and how I love you."

I kissed her forehead, hoping to sooth her spirits.

"She will be buried Thursday, Anne."

Gib sprang to her side, meowing. Gathering him in her arms, she held him to her face, talking to him as she had seen me do a thousand times. "What is it, Gib? Hmm? Ah, but of course, you want a bit of fresh air." Aunt opened the window and set him out on the ledge. "There you are now." Closing the window, she turned to me. "Well," she dabbed her nose, "I will rejoin Anthony, Anne. Do join us, dear." She kissed my brow.

"Yes, Aunt."

Gib was scratching at the window pane, looking a little befuddled.

* * *

Thursday came in a rush, and the weather held—no rain and that gave the guests something to be thankful for. But there was always that one irritating voice that found no goodness in anything or anyone:

"Oh, I think it disgraceful to have dogs chasing about sacred ground," said Mr Phillipps as he wiped his spittle-filled lips. He could no more lower his voice than cup his windy trousers.

"Calm yourself, Clarke, they are not chasing about, they are sitting still and well behaved. Now please, Brother, do lower your voice."

"No, no. I shall not lower my voice, Charlotte."

Professor Mandeville, sitting just behind him, tapped him on the shoulder with his baton—that brought blessed silence.

It was a crystal morning; worried birds chirped and flitted in and about the hedges where we had assembled. One brave, puff-chested, little brown bird perched atop Elly's coffin and eyed us with great discernment. Misha growled. We all bowed our heads as Mr Morse opened the service with prayer.

I could not hear his words. I had my own communion with God; had my own words; have always had my own words with Him. No one can offer up what is in my heart but me; no one can understand exactly my true feelings. God knew the despair that Elly's death had brought our family. Indeed, brought to Franklin, Abby, Mrs Savarin, Nancy, and dear sweet Misha. There was no bringing her back. We simply must wait our turn until we meet again.

"Amen." Mr Morse closed his Bible. Squinting into the warm light, he stepped back. Aunt, veiled in heavy black netting, and Uncle, holding her arm, walked to the edge of the open pit. Gib slithered from under a shrub and meandered to their side. Rubbing his proud tail about Aunt's skirt, he sniffed the raw moist earth and sat purring loudly.

Holding Misha aside, I took Holly by the collar and stole away without notice. I glanced back; the dark clothed assembly of onlookers, Uncle and Aunt, John and Miss Revelt, Edward, the servants, the others—stood remorseful amidst the aged firs and the damp mossy graven stones. I wanted no more of death.

I removed my heavy black net and settled it over my hat and felt the warm sun kiss my face. It was Elly's sweet touch. "She is in heaven, Misha and Holly Berry. No need to mourn."

In silence we walked down across Lesington Hall's great lawn, through the wrought iron gates and on toward Regent Street. I had planned on stopping there for a moment and then returning, giving me and "my girls" a good long walk. Visions of John's face, the feel of his touch, the strength of his hands was comforting. Then the vision of Miss Revelt's face ruined everything. Oh, the sadness in my heart, it was all too much.

I was thankful the day was at least sun-filled, a warm crispness, soothing, fresh and clean. The clip-clop of carriage horses echoed up from the side street just ahead. Parasols and moving gentlemen wavered about their ladies. Holly and Misha strained at their leashes.

"I cannot let you run free, my dears. Now approaching the end of Lesington's great lawn, I noticed the figure of a man standing very near a tree, his back to me. Misha growled. The hair on Holly Berry's neck bristled; she sniffed the air and pulled hard, growling.

"Easy girls ... easy."

When the stranger turned, he tipped his hat. It was Mr O'Leary. His hair now greyer; his face more yellow and gaunt; his hooknose shiny and drippy. Wearing spectacles, he blinked to clear his eyes, I supposed.

"Good afternoon, Miss Anne." He eyed the dogs with concern.

"I will hold them, sir. They would harm but a hare."

"That one," he pointed to Misha, "is part wolf. Is she not?"

"I have been told that, Mr O'Leary."

"You took her from Madame Pinchot, then?"

My face grew warm. I did not like his familiarity, his remembrances. He was a smart man with a smart memory. "Perhaps, sir." I could smell grief on him. His hands were hidden in his pockets and I could not tell if they shook, but mine did.

"Good day, Mr O'Leary." Pulling at the dogs, I realised Holly's fur was still bristled. Misha maintained her stance, watching him; her greying muzzle twitched into a snarl. Why, I believe she wanted to reach out and rip at him. "Come along, Misha. Come along ..."

"Just a moment, Miss Anne, I have something for you." When he opened his waistcoat Misha lunged. "Hold that monstrous dog!" He shouted and curled back.

"Misha, Misha," I cried, holding her at bay. "Stay." Both dogs held their ground, their ears perked; the hair on their necks bristled. They both had deep-throated growls, and I was not at all sure I could hold them if they decided to attack him.

"Do not reach above their heads, sir. I do not know if I will be able to control them. I have never seen them so agitated."

Brandishing an envelope, he frowned. "I will set it on the ground." Careful not to look them in the eye, he laid the envelope at the base of a tree and slowly backed away, curled like a spider.

"Nay, Mr O'Leary, you must take it back. There is nothing from you I wish to read."

I prepared to leave when he laughed. Spittle-webs stretched across the black oval of his mouth. I shuddered and closed my eyes.

"Then you will force me to speak with your aunt, Lady Alice, is it? And I do not think such a lovely young lady like you wishes to have your family's sordid details spread about London's social circle, nor around your aunt's particular friends or repeat things regarding your filthy, drunken mother. Nor would you wish it that your Uncle, Sir Anthony Hathaway's reputation be sullied by *your* faults; your sins; your dirty little secrets with me and Madame Pinchot ... eh, Miss Anne?"

He tipped his hat, coughed up and spit on Aunt's revered roses. He nodded, pulled his hat about his ears and walked away, laughing.

Stunned, shaken and speechless, I retrieved the envelope and moved back toward the Great House. I could hear carriages coming from Lesington's drive and cut through a bridle path to avoid them.

I unleashed the dogs and hurried through the open meadow with them, crying at the shame. The shame of what I had done. But what had I done? I could not remember any shame. What of Madame Pinchot? I had done nothing to her, but listen as she spoke to Papa in séance with Mama.

Was it that I now had her dog, Misha? But Professor Grinby gave her to me. Mama? What had Mama done? Crying harder now, I searched my memory as far back as I could remember and still I had not done anything wrong or shameful. I opened the envelope. It was a legal bit of writing ...

20 December 1861, Holybourne, O'Leary's Brewery ...

Be it known by all those heretofore that I, Shawn Timothy O'Leary, so assume financial responsibility for the care and upkeep of Mistress Catherine Holt and her daughter, Anne Alice Holt, in that I promise to furnish food, clothes and shelter, cows, chickens, maids to keep the child from perish as long as she lives in Holybourne, England. This being faithfully done until Anne was smuggled out of the village unbeknownst to me. I continued my financial assistance of her mother until her death. Thence I learned the truth of the matter. Herewith is a list of my rightful claims:

Under the watchful eye of the magistrate the Holt cottage and all meagre furnishings have been transferred to me. Hardly being sufficient to pay for the following, however:

206 pints of Gin – Mr Ruther, Carriage Inn
2 cows
20 chickens
1 maid, Mrs Tilly Marvel
16 geese
25 muttonchops
5 pigs
Mr Buffle's bill - the glover's shop
Bakery
Wood and coal
Madame Pinchot –

The total sum is two thousand pounds, plus interest or Anne's hand in marriage, as agreed in writing. Her own signature attests to her eager wish that I shroud her in good fortune, shelter her, guide her, tutor her in her father's library; make her the fine young lady she has become under my private tutelage.

By irony, I most recently learned from a Professor Grinby, that Miss Anne Holt resides in London as a fine young lady just presented at Court. All well and good, but I demand my investment or her hand.

I will be at the Red Lion Inn, Drury Lane, Cheapside for two days.

Yours truly, Shawn O'Leary

"Oh, God in Heaven," I cried, and took a deep breath. Holly and Misha crowded about my skirt and whined. "I will bring shame to Aunt and Uncle! Oh, Mama what have we done?"

I moved along the path far out into the meadow, my skirt brushing the field grass, snapping it, harsh and meaningful as I trudged through the field. Holly and Misha found a hare and darted off. Hearing a faint cry, I turned and spied Kate, waving. I waited amongst the hay shorn field, the pathway baked beige and dusty.

All a breath, she kissed my cheek. "I am so sorry, dear."

Taking her hand, I sighed, forcing back tears. "Thank you, Kate. Come along with us. Elly and I walked this path quite often." I inhaled, snapping a weed from its home. Wrapping it around my finger, I tried to hide my grief and shame and terror. "I can hear Elly right this minute, Kate, 'cover your face, minikin! You'll freckle so. People will think you've been standing behind a cow.' "

"Behind a cow?" Kate's brow knit. "A cow?"

"Her very words." I half-laughed, dabbing my eyes. "She would not want us to fret, to cry ... at least not too much."

Kate put her face under my bonnet. "A proper day of solemnity, then?"

"She would want it so, I believe, Kate."

We walked on a half-hour more. The church bells were pealing from a distance, a black-muzzled dog scurried about the field ahead, and spying Misha, quickly darted back into the woods. I sensed something troubling Kate. Her manner too subdued. I pinched her thumb. "What is wrong, Kate?"

"I cannot burden you further, Anne ... when you are grieving so for Mrs Mills. It would be most selfish of me."

"Elly is in heaven, Kate. Already she has spoken. She kissed my face through the warm rays of sunshine. You will not burden me, dearest." I saw her sweet, dear face pucker, sweat beaded upon her brow. Kate is such a faithful friend trudging by my side in the heat of the day. "Besides even Elly knew how selfish you are, and she still held you in great ..."

Kate shook her head. "I cannot jest on such a day, Anne. It is irreverent."

"You act as if you are in love, Kate, moping about so."

"Anne," she wiped her eyes with the long sash from her frock. "Mama and Papa are going to America in six weeks. Papa has important business of some sort in New York, and I must go along."

"How fortunate, Kate. America, New York. Think of the adventure, the suspense, the intrigue of a different continent." Thinking of now losing my sweetest friend, I lowered my head and felt like weeping all the more.

Kate put her arm around my waist. "I can assure you, Anne, I do not want to go to a foreign country."

"New York is not a foreign country, Kate." I blew my nose and gathered my voice. "America is made up of Englishmen."

"But, Anne, I will be gone almost four months."

"Hmm." I frowned. "Yes, that is a long time, Kate."

"Come with us, Anne. Mama and Papa would think it wonderful news. Why, they have already suggested it."

Not hesitating, I sighed. "Oh, Kate, how shall I leave Aunt?" The air thickened with the noon's heat, I could hear the haymakers off in the distant field. Gathering up a few apples, I spied a quaint, sitting place beneath a great elm.

"Come, Kate, let us sit in the shade." I glanced at her red face, grave as the squire's. Handing her the plumper apple, I kissed her hand. Trying to bolster my sorrowful friend and myself, I suggested, "Oh, four months is not such a long, long time, Kate."

She dashed away her tears, her normal sweet voice faltered, "Forgive me the words, Anne, but I am not at all happy with Mama and Papa for insisting I must come along."

Still holding O'Leary's envelope, I trembled thinking of what the dastardly man demanded of me. How could I come up with two thousand pounds? Feeling revulsion, my stomach lurched and I spit up.

"Oh, Anne," Kate wiped my mouth, "I have sickened you so, and on such a day. Forgive me."

I thought of John, and instead of his sweet face, Miss Revelt's face appeared by his side. I began to waver. *God Almighty, I will bring shame to John as well. I must leave England ... go to America. I would miss the opportunity of visiting John at college—his graduation. How proud he would look ...* and then the angel of gloom reminded me of the scene the other night when he and Miss Revelt walked arm-in-arm under the lush full moon.

Yes, continued the angel, *and Miss Revelt would, no doubt, walk him down the aisle at school; accepting his diploma with one hand and guiding him from the stage with the other.*

Go, go, said the angel Elly. *You will do me no good here, weeping and moping about so ... do, go, love, for my sake. You must escape all this sordid business ...*

Kate steadied herself on the tree stump. "Dear me, Anne, what did you say? Yes, yes?"

"I must escape to America, Kate."

She jumped up excitedly. "Escape to America! Yes, that's the spirit. To America with me, Anne!"

"But first, Aunt must allow such a parting. She must allow it first, Kate."

She glanced about the warm hay fields, squinting. "I think I could stand a foreign country now that you are to come with me, Anne."

"I know, Kate. I know."

She leaned down and kissed Misha's head. Look, Anne," she gestured toward the Great House, "everyone is leaving. ..."

I looked down upon Lesington Hall and sighed. "Yes, John must return at once to school." I turned away and sighed, "With Miss Revelt."

"Miss Revelt will be returning to Bath with Edward. They cannot possibly leave the clinic too many unattended days, I am quite sure of that."

Lowering my head, I offered, "I thought by now they would have come back to London to establish their business here." *But, it is just as well,* I thought. *If I cannot find the money in which to pay off my debt, I must marry O'Leary.*

"Yes." Kate shrugged. "But Edward now says they may never come back. The clinic is doing so well already. They are only waiting now for John to graduate and join them."

"Hmm, indeed, what is here to entice them?"

"Perhaps a veterinary clinic of your very own ... here in London, Anne.

"A clinic?" I looked at her in disbelief.

"You are smarter than Miss Revelt, Anne. You love animals. You have spoken often of caring for them, and wanting to go to a school of higher learning."

"Oh, Kate, I could not dare dream of such a thing."

"And why not, I ask you?"

Closing my eyes, I inhaled a deep breath. I could feel tears sliding down my throat. "I should want to remove to Holybourne and marry someone." I gagged. "That is my dream, Kate."

She took my hand. "Really, Anne? Why, you never mentioned that to me before? What is there in Holybourne, pray tell?"

"A debt of gratitude that I must repay, Kate."

CHAPTER EIGHTEEN

Later that afternoon as I sat alone in the drawing room, I read again Mr O'Leary's demands. *I will write to him—no, no. I shall go in person, but not alone—surely not alone. But what am I to tell him? I will tell him he must wait. I will repay him someday, certainly.* I thought again of his dark countenance, *I cannot marry such a man! I will beg his mercy until I find the money in which to repay him.*

"Beg pardon, Miss Anne," Franklin bowed at the open door, "Lady Alice said that you may join her now. She is in her boudoir."

Glancing up, I studied Franklin. He was always so very kind to me. He had taken me under his wing when I first came to Lesington Hall; laughed at me; even scolded me to protect me from harm. "Franklin, I need you tomorrow. Will you drive into Cheapside with me? It is quite urgent." I placed my hands over my quivering lips.

"Dear me, Miss Anne, but of course." His brow knit with concern. "What is the concern?"

"Something ... has happened. I need complete and absolute loyalty." I swallowed hard, trying to calm my voice. My hands shook so that I dropped the letter.

He picked it up and handed back to me. "But of course, Miss Anne."

"Forgive me, Franklin, I am truly beside myself. Not a word to Aunt or Uncle, Franklin, I beg of you." My voice wavered. Tears slid from my eyes.

"No, Miss Anne, I will be silent as the grave." With his usual grace, he bowed. His face was stern, in his eyes a grave concern, his brow furrowed. "Tomorrow, then, Miss Anne."

"Thank you, Franklin." I took his hand and pressed it. "I can trust you." Standing, I wiped my eyes. "Aunt is in her boudoir?"

"Yes, Miss Anne."

"Very well, then." I felt heartened. I loved Aunt's boudoir—our very special talking place where Uncle Anthony's gold band once sat upon the sill and was now wrapped around her finger.

* * *

I relayed to Aunt that I had a very special reason for securing Franklin on an errand and asked for the carriage. Of course, she never refused me. I then gently broached the subject of going to America with Kate and her mother and father.

Pacing before the hearth, Aunt wrung her hands. "Oh, Anne, I do not know. Why, four months is a very long time. I would miss you terribly." She dabbed her eyes, her brow knit in apparent meditation.

"I will not go, Aunt, if it pains you so."

"What of John's graduation and our holiday to Bath? Have you not been looking forward to it? Oh, John and Edward will be so disappointed."

"Oh, I think not, Aunt."

Surely, added the gloomy angel, *Miss Revelt will dispel his disappointment.*

"John will scarcely miss me, Aunt. Besides, I am certain Miss Revelt will be there to soften the blow."

She glanced at me, frowning. "How unkind of you, Anne. Yes, of course, Miss Revelt will be there, she is his partner. We should be joyous that a woman is succeeding in business."

"I will write and apologise in advance, Aunt. John will bid me go; you know his kind, sweet nature. He is the one who speaks so of adventures, life's follies and so forth. Beside all that, Aunt, I would welcome the diversion from Lesington Hall."

She took my hand. "Of course you would, Love. With Elly now gone, everything seems hollow and void. Bless Anthony at such a time; he has kept me busy."

"Yes, Aunt, he is most caring and thoughtful."

Shaking her head, she said, "It is only that I am too selfish, Anne. No, you must go and see a little of the world. You and Kate will have a marvellous time in America. Though I hear their civil war is far from over. You must promise not to travel anywhere near this Mason and Dixon's line. It is not far from New York. You must promise me."

"Indeed, Aunt. You may be assured of that."

"Very well, then. I shall have the Hathaways for supper tomorrow evening. Your Uncle and I will discuss the details with Florence and William." Hugging me, she smiled. "Kate is a dear young lady, Anne. It is important to have a close confidant. I am so happy you have each other."

"Indeed, Aunt." I thought of Elly and how devastating Aunt's loss. "I would not even have considered going, Aunt, had Uncle Anthony not been here with you."

"You are a dear, Anne." She kissed my brow. "Now that you will be gone, I will travel with him. That will please him and occupy my thoughts." She smiled. "Oh, I must share one more thing, my dear. I know you will keep this delicate information to yourself. This trip to America is extremely important for William's business, for the family's financial future. Though Florence is never one for extravagance, I wish it of you, dear, to be mindful over economy."

Mindful over economy? I am desperate for two thousand pounds. "Oh, dear me, Aunt." I pressed her hand. "I assure you, I will use economy wherever I go."

"I know you will, my love. I know." She touched my cheek. "Anne, this may not be the right time or place to tell you this, but do not think me vulgar for mentioning it now, but Elly left you a little money." She withdrew a package from her desk, pressed it to her heart and gave it to me.

"Money, Aunt? I thought Elly lived as a pensioner, off of you?"

"Oh, yes, yes, she did, but even pensioners are due wages, dearest. Apparently the sly girl had been saving money many years before her pension. Eleanor had no other family but us, Anne. You know how she adored you."

My heart leapt in my chest. I wept. Placing the package to my heart, the thought of any money in my purse at such a time sent a thrill of relief through my body. "Oh, Aunt, how dear of Elly. I had no idea." I wiped my eyes. *Thank you God in heaven and your gift angels.*

"Well, it is not such a huge sum of money, Anne. Most of it has been invested in the English funds, but there is a thousand pounds in notes there ... in the envelope."

"A thousand pounds, Aunt?" My voice withered, I sunk deeper into my chair. "Oh, Aunt, such relief."

"Relief, dearest?" She looked puzzled. "Whatever do you mean?"

"Ah, I mean relief, Aunt. Relief in that I shall wish to go on to school." I buried my lying face in my hands. Of course I could not tell her about O'Leary's demands.

"School?" She peeled my fingers from my wet face. "What school?"

Keeping my eyes closed, I whispered. "Perhaps, veterinary school, Aunt Alice. Miss Revelt has educated herself quite smartly. Now I will not have to worry over tuition." I dug myself a rather large hole ... without a ladder.

"I assure you, my niece will never have to fret over tuition. What made you think such a thing, Anne?" She wrapped her arms about me and hugged me.

"I do not know, Aunt Alice, why I should think of such a thing."

"Well, we shall discuss this with your Uncle. He will know exactly how to counsel you in your educational endeavours." She studied me for a moment. "I must say, I have thought all along what a marvellous animal doctor you would make."

I could not look her in the eye. "Thank you, Aunt."

She kissed my brow and sighed. "It would be a kindness, Anne, if you would write to John and explain that you are going to America."

"I will do so now, Aunt." Standing, I kept Elly's money envelope pressed to my heart. "Thank you, Aunt Alice."

* * *

18 Sept - Lesington Hall
Dear John,
 I write asking your understanding in that I will neither be attending your graduation nor vacationing with Aunt and Uncle in Bath. Rather, they have kindly given permission for me to be Kate's companion in America. Perhaps you already know that Uncle William has business in New York. We are to leave soon. 20 September and return 22 February or thereabout. I do know I shall miss everyone ... **(Perhaps I shall say that I love you now. Then, should the boat sink,**

**you will know what dwells in my heart, what has
always dwelt in my heart, from the moment I met
you at)** *... at Lesington Hall. I cannot, without tears,
consider leaving "my three" for four months. Holly Berry
shall quite forget me. Good-bye in advance, Cousin John.
I do hope you are in health and remain in health. When
you are come to Lesington Hall, please do look in on my
two girls and the ol' boy. ...*

  Yours most affectionately, AH

I kissed John's letter, sealed it, and set it along with Uncle
Anthony's other mail in his salver.

* * *

The following morning, Franklin and I stood on the steps
waiting for the carriage that would take us into Cheapside. The
thought of seeing Mr O'Leary brought alarm and great
disharmony to my soul. I was thankful Franklin was coming
with me.

Lightning zigzagged behind the thick grey morning sky.
Thunder boomed and would, for sure, make the horses jittery.
As the carriage made its way toward us, its wheels crunched
the new coat of stony pebbles Uncle had ordered just last week.

Franklin helped me up. Settling in my seat, I asked,
"Might you know where the Red Lion Inn is, Franklin?"

"Yes, Miss Anne. There is only one in Cheapside."

"If there is but one, then, yes, Franklin, we must go there."

He sat stoic, his gloved hands clasped, his gaze straight. I
handed him Elly's envelope with the money inside. My hand
trembled. "Please keep this for me. I would wish it that you
accompany me inside the inn, Franklin."

"Indeed, Miss Anne. I had no intention of allowing you
inside *that* place alone." He hemmed. "Once there, what am I
to expect?"

"Mr O'Leary, Franklin. Do you remember him?"

"Faintly, miss."

"Hmm, when I first came to Lesington Hall, I believe I
spoke about him ... maybe a few times."

"The brewery owner, Miss Anne?"

"The very one, Franklin." I clasped my trembling hands to stop their shaking. Feeling a nasty headache forming, I closed my eyes and shook my head. "It seems my dear mother and I owe him ..."

He scoffed through a frown. "How could a mere child owe a brewery master anything, I should like to know?"

"It is all true, Franklin. Apparently Mama and I owe him a considerable sum of money. I intend upon repaying him at least half of that amount today. In the envelope you are holding there are three notes totalling a thousand pounds—my inheritance from Elly."

"Repaying him half? Dear me, Miss Anne. One thousand pounds is a small fortune."

"I know, Franklin. I know. My hand in marriage is worth far more, I assure you. I did not know at the time, I was only nine when I signed a promissory note to marry him if I chose not to repay the debt Mama and I incurred. Mama was desperate, Franklin. Bless her. And now I must repay the debt."

Franklin's jaw dropped. "God in heaven, Miss Anne, I ..."

"I must hold my word, Franklin. I cannot bring shame to Aunt Alice or to Sir Anthony. You know very well that such a declaration in our society—such a history—would absolutely ruin them both. I would ruin all my cousins and their future happiness and Mr John Hathaway's new clinic. You must know that Franklin. No one must learn of this."

"No, Miss Anne, of course. You have my word."

The remainder of our ride to the Red Lion was in silence. Franklin remained his stoic, unflappable self. In a way, he calmed me. My hands were no longer trembling, the rain had stopped, but the wind picked up. The gusts howled through the tiniest spaces in the carriage windows, sounding very much like a wounded banshee.

Pulling up to the watering troth in front of the Red Lion, I glanced at Franklin. "You will stay near me, Franklin?"

"Your very shadow, Miss Anne."

"Franklin, you will keep the envelope until I beckon you to give it to Mr O'Leary."

He nodded and patted his vest pocket. "In return, you must request a written note of such payment, Miss Anne."

"Indeed, thank you Franklin. I had not thought of that. I will ask."

"You will demand it, miss."

Entering the Inn, Franklin made the arrangement to notify Mr O'Leary that I had arrived. It was within the half-hour that he met us.

"Well, well, Miss Anne," he glanced at Franklin, "I see you keep a man-servant. How wise you are. I see my lessons to you early-on have made a wise businesswoman of you."

"Sir," I retorted, "my mother and my Aunt made me what I am today, not you." I could see Franklin's chest swell. He stood next to me. From the corner of my eye I noticed how he glared at O'Leary.

O'Leary acquiesced, withdrawing with a bow. "How convenient a memory, my dear." He coughed without covering his toothless black mouth and sat heavy onto a squeezy bar chair.

"You read my letter, Miss Anne?"

"Franklin, give the gentleman the bank notes." I paused until O'Leary examined all three. He then tossed the envelope onto the table.

Of a sudden, a storm blew in, the shutters of the old inn slammed shut, darkening the already tomblike room. The single lantern sitting on his table flickered over the black hair on his knuckles making them appear as nervous little spiders.

O'Leary looked up at me. "There is only one thousand here."

"The rest, sir, will be paid when I return from America." Lifting my chin, I continued, "I have business there where I shall secure the remainder of my investments." I lied. I could feel my face burn red. He knew I was stalling for time. But, in truth, it would take time until Elly's investment in the English Funds could be converted to me.

He stroked the thick stubble on his chin. "And when will that be, Miss Anne?"

Franklin stepped ahead of me. "When she returns, sir." His voice filled every inch of cavernous room. His hat touched the ceiling as he straightened; the buttons on his waistcoat strained.

O'Leary's head tilted back as he looked up at the imposing figure. "But of course, but of course," he replied with a weak smile, his rheumy red eyelids droopy.

"March or April, Mr O'Leary." I moved in front of Franklin. "I give my word."

He stood, obviously nervous of the imposing Mr Franklin. "Oh, no trouble there my dear. I trust you. I've waited years as it is for my money, what matters a few months more? You are a respectable lady, now, Miss Anne. As well, your Aunt, Lady Alice." Removing his hat, he bowed low. "Capital, capital."

Franklin took my arm. "Miss Holt demands a receipt of the funds, now, sir."

"But of course." O'Leary smiled and dipped his pen. Scratching out the receipt, he smiled. "You see, Miss Anne, no trouble at all." He offered the receipt to me, but Franklin snatched it from his hand, read it, and put it in his vest pocket.

O'Leary's brows lifted. "Such a fine manservant you have, Miss Anne. And," he sucked in a toothless breath, "he can read, too."

"Come along, Miss Anne. This place is beginning to stink." Moving past the wench who mopped the floor, Franklin kicked open the door. Stepping out into the wind, my bonnet nearly blew off, saved by the fine bow tied beneath my chin. With one hand on his hat, Franklin resettled mine atop my head.

"Not a thing lost so far, Miss Anne." He laughed. "You've kept your head and your bonnet."

"And you yours, sir!" I kissed his cheek. "Thank you, Franklin."

CHAPTER NINETEEN

At long last, 20 September had arrived. Kate and I would sail to America! Though dawn had not yet come, I could hear the carriage waiting for me just outside—impatient stomps from the horses, nervous whinnies, and yard dogs yelping.

Abby tapped on my door and entered. "Morning, Miss Anne," she dabbed her eyes with her apron. "Have a delightful time of it."

I hugged her. "I will, Abby. Thank you."

"Franklin has already put the dogs in and of course, Gib." She glanced out the window. "They're waitin' for you, miss."

I kissed Abby's moist cheek and hurried down the stairs. Franklin stood at the bottom step, his stiff stoic self.

"Goodbye, Miss Anne," he half-bowed.

I kissed his cheek. "Thank you Franklin. When I return you and I shall take another trip to Cheapside."

"As you wish, Miss Anne."

I forced the thought of O'Leary from my mind ... tried to force him from it, but with such searing images well planted, it was most difficult. Poor Mama, how she must have suffered, and how terrified she must have been of the future—to reckon and bargain with such a scoundrel. I could not believe how stupid I was, so eager-vain to show off my fancy hand; to have signed away my virtue that day in his office years ago and to give my hand in marriage. And to think, all along, I knew how to read.

But of course you knew how to read, said Elly's angel, *but what of marriage? You were too young to even know what giving your hand meant.*

And my dear Tilly, she at least has found a good job with the kind Mr Grinby. I shall visit her when I return as well.

When we arrived at the Hathaway House, everyone was waiting in their carriage. We followed them to the dock where we were to board. Stepping from the carriage, I gasped at the stately magnificence of our ship, The Oceanic. It floated monstrously large, a hull, white on white, rising out of the choppy blue-black ocean water.

Dawn's leaden sky arrived evenly and settled around the four sailing masts, its one short funnel, black and shiny, spewed sulphur-like haze that stung my nose. In the backdrop, harbour ships sailed on the swelling waters, their gigantic smoke stacks puffed bilious dark grey clouds into the low gloom of early morn. Holly Berry had a fit of sneezes; Misha took in the air with questioning hesitation.

As a wave of fine salty spray snapped my face, Aunt pulled up my thick, navy blue wool-collared cloak and twisted its steel clasp snuggling it to my neck.

"Cover your chest, Love," she fussed, "you mustn't take a chill."

Tears welled in my eyes. The murmuring crowd of voyagers had already crowded near the swaying white-fenced entry plank. Meandering together a little distance behind them all, Aunt and I remained quiet, clutching hands.

Holly Berry kept snug to my side, Misha pulled at the leash. Gib remained in the carriage crouched atop the back seat, sleeping. Uncle patted his brother William goodbye and Florence kissed his cheek. Kate remained at the gate—smiling, but tremulous.

Pulling Aunt aside, I whispered, "Perhaps I shall not go after all, Aunt Alice."

"Elly would want you to go, Anne. You know how she loved to travel."

Though her hands betrayed her true feelings, I marvelled at her dry eyes, her calm chin. I kissed her cheek. "I love you, Aunt."

She whipped out a white pocket-handkerchief and wafted it about. "Away, now," she commanded, "your captain awaits you, sailor girl!"

I could not look at Holly; those soulful brown eyes would absolutely have done me in—I kissed her nervous muzzle. "I love you, Holly Berry." Misha squirmed in between us. Her black nose moist, her eyes were keen and serious. I read them, "Do not go."

* * *

Though it began to drizzle, Kate and I remained on deck waving good-bye. The ship's horn blasted loud and severe, reverberating through my boots. The fringe on my parasol quivered. Wincing at the noise, I watched Aunt, Uncle, and "my girls" break from the waving crowd. Now just the four of them walked along the boardwalk. There was one lone figure of a man rushing toward them. He too, was waving. Could it be John? Of course not, silly me.

I could see Aunt's white gloves busy about her face—Uncle comforting her. Above the shouts from our deck and the horn blasts, above the noise of the crew taking up anchor, I could hear Aunt saying good-bye. I could hear Holly Berry's frantic bark, demanding I return at once.

They all soon faded into tiny specks on the dock. I should not have cried so deeply. The little girl yet within me did not want to let go of Aunt Alice. I didn't want to leave England, leave Elly so freshly buried. I knew I would return quite a different person. I had yet Mr O'Leary to see once more.

"Come along, Anne." Kate wiped my eyes. "Here." She handed me her handkerchief.

"But," I looked at the fine lace-trimmed beauty, "it is your prize from Miss Pramm's?"

* * *

I wrote to Aunt every day while on the ship. Depositing my letters into the post for the ship's return within the week, I reassured her that:

> *I am doing quite well, under the circumstances, Aunt. But just because I was presented at Court certainly does not mean I am truly out in society. I still feel like a young child, Aunt Alice. Standing on the deck waving good-bye to England and everyone I know and love made me feel like raw meat being ripped off the bones of a monkey. Well, perhaps that was quite graphic, but all the same, I miss you already—and my dearest Uncle.*

* * *

10 October 1868 Evening - The Clarendon Hotel
Dear Aunt and Uncle,
*New York is quite the place. Accents are so plain
and broad. Rather enchanting. People are forever asking
Kate and me if we are royalty; the way we speak, walk
and act. I can scarcely understand why they would think
such a thing, Aunt. I thought you would enjoy this post
card instead of a letter. I love you. Please kiss Holly
Berry, Misha, and Gib for me. While in my room this
evening, I prayed John's graduation went well. I am
certain he looked quite handsome with Miss Revelt on his
arm the entire ceremony. Goodnight all, Love,*
Your affectionate niece, Anne

* * *

"Oh, Anne," said Kate breathlessly, "The Lord Mayor is giving a ball, and we are invited."

In excited wonder, I clasped my hands. "What a fine time we shall have, Kate. At last we are to meet some Americans."

"Mama says New York society is far less concerned with proper protocol and etiquette. I suppose we must do as they do." Kate shrugged. "Whatever that means, it quite escapes me."

"I suppose it means we must remain alert, eat as they eat."

"Oh, yes, the way Americans eat—a busy sort of affair as they cross-over their plates with their knives and forks."

"Indeed, Kate. It is an odd thing to watch. I do suppose they think the same of us."

* * *

15 October 1868 - The Clarendon
Dear Aunt and Uncle Anthony,
*Aunt Florence waltzed with the Lord Mayor Brimble
this evening and found him to have two left feet. She was*

*forced to sit out all the remainder of the dances—her toes
were quite raw. Kate had never heard her mother curse
before. C'est la vie. It has not rained one day since we
have been here. The weather is quite cool and not at all
smelly, Aunt. I have made several friends recently, dog
friends. Kate and I have offered to walk our hotel guests'
dogs along Fourth Avenue. Give kisses to my threesome.
I should soon be getting a letter from you, Aunt. I so look
forward to it. My love and affections to you and Uncle—
my thoughts and regards to John.*

    Au revoir, Anne

October 1868
Dear Aunt and Uncle,

    *Oh, yes, you can see by the picture on this postcard
how spectacular Niagara Falls really is! Buffalo, New
York. It is either named after an odd looking cow or the
cow is named after the city—Kate and I have asked
several people to confirm our suspicions, but we are met
with stares. Just across the river is our Canada. I dream
of everyone in England every day,* **(particularly John)**

    Love, Your affectionate niece, Anne

30 Oct - Somewhere in New York State on a train
Dear Aunt and Uncle,

    *Aunt Florence has found by reading the newspaper
that there is a wonderful play that we shall all attend
once returned to the City. The weather is turning a bit
frosty, I have noticed of late. Rolling along on the train
(clippity clack clippity clack) I think the land here is quite
beautiful, actually. Its verdant lush woods look just like
England. The trees have turned a brilliant gold, red,
yellow—stunning. The names of the villages and towns
are copies of ours, Aunt—only with New added. New
York, New Hampshire, New England, and even in some
places Old. Old Bethany, Old York, Old Towne ...
amazing. I look forward to seeing you, to reading your
letters. I do hope Edward and Miss Revelt have been
successful in their endeavours to finish the animal clinic
for Cousin John. He must be preparing at this very
moment to move in. Imagine, another doctor in the
family. Although I realise you find the practice
abhorrent, could you please find it in your heart to kiss*

*Holly Berry and Misha for me? Whisper "Anne" into
their ears at every moment, I shall die if they forget me!
Thank you, dearest Aunt. I truly love you with all my
heart.*

> *Regards and love also to Uncle Anthony …*
> *Yrs affecly, AH*

"Anne." Kate tugged on my sleeve. "That man keeps
staring at us."

Setting aside my pen, I glanced around. "The older
gentleman, there in the end seat?"

"Yes, I shall tell Papa if he persists."

I blew on my letter, drying the ink. "Indeed. But he does
not appear to have the strength to harm a gnat, Kate. His hair
is quite white, his skin pink …"

"All the same, Anne." She squirmed. "He looks rather
lecherous, all in all."

Spying the movement of something at his side, I leaned
forward and squinted. "Kate," I giggled, "the man is harmless.
Look there at his side; why he is carrying a tiny puppy in his
hat."

"A puppy?" She squinted. "That is not a puppy, Anne."

I stood.

Kate grabbed my sleeve. "Where are you going?"

"I must see for myself."

"Not alone." She grasped my hand and followed along.

As we moved slowly past the man, Kate remained
snuggled at my side. Just as we reached the door, a porter
stopped to chat with him. Leaving, he accidentally knocked
over the old man's cane. The elder gentleman flailed about
with his hands, searching for it.

I gasped. "Kate, he is blind."

"Oh, dear me, yes, Anne, so he is."

I hurried to his side and took up his cane. "Here you are,
sir."

"What?" He glanced about blankly. "An English lady, is
it?"

"Yes, sir."

His filmy, white coated eyes searched for my position.
"Why, thank you, miss."

"What is that there, sir, in your hat? That is, if you do not
mind us asking."

"Us?"

"My dearest friend, Miss Hathaway, was wondering what sort of animal you are holding, sir. It so reminded me of a puppy, but ..."

Kate nudged me.

Patting about, he found his hat and gently laid his hands on the *thing's* head. He lifted it up. I have never in my entire life seen such a skinny, bony, creature. Backing away, I watched as the poor dear animal trembled for its very life. Its round, bulging brown eyes were ever so watery; its tail was like that of a rat's.

The gentleman laughed. "Oh, miss, do not fret so. My little darling is a Mexican dog. She is a Chihuahua—a voiceless little canine specimen."

Kate drew back. "A dog that does not bark, sir? Oh, Papa would surely like her very much."

With great affection, he snuggled her nervous little body to his neck, my heart warmed. "Does she bite, sir?"

"Oh, a bit snappy betimes, but I hardly think such a tiny mouth could damage anything."

I could not remember how to pronounce its name. "I have never heard of such a breed, sir."

He nodded. "My son found her when he was out west ... Texas—won the tiny creature in a poker game. The dog descended from the ancient breed known to the Toltec Indians ... 9th century." He kissed her wet nose. "Now that is a very long time ago." He chuckled.

Kate frowned. "Well, sir, at the moment she looks to be freezing."

He smiled. "Aah, two lassies to entertain me this morning." He turned toward our voices, his rheumy eyes moist and cloudy.

"Is she cold, sir?"

"She always shivers when people fuss about her so. She hates people to stare at her, I suppose. I rather think she is self-conscious about her thinning hair," He laughed aloud, as we did.

"You travel alone, sir? How do you get about?"

"My son is with me. Allow me to introduce myself. I am Horace Fry. My little companion here," he held her up, "is called Freda."

We curtsied and he laughed. "I can hear quite well. Oh, you English are so well mannered. We have quite lost our civility here, I am sorry to say." He shook his head.

"My name, Mr Fry, is Miss Holt."

Kate smiled. "And mine, Mr Fry, is Miss Hathaway—London."

"Aah, yes, the Queen's English, yes, well-bred."

I glanced at Kate. "I once heard that when one loses one sense that the others sharpen ... your hearing is marvellous, sir."

"Oh, yes, my dear, my senses have sharpened considerably." He paused, glancing up. "Could that be my son coming now?"

Turning, we were met with a tall, sandy-haired gentleman.

A faint blush spread across his face. A scar about two inches long ran along his brow. He smelled of recent tobacco; a touch of whisky was on his breath. He removed his odd-shaped hat.

Mr Fry cleared his throat. "Allow me to introduce my son, Mr Clayton Fry."

"Miss Holt." I nodded.

"Miss Hathaway." Kate smiled.

We curtsied.

His son grinned, exposing fine white teeth. "Good morning to you, ladies. I didn't know my father was acquainted with any of the passengers on the train."

"Oh, sir," I gestured toward his father, "Mr Fry's cane fell, and then we ..."

Kate moved in front of me. "Indeed, we discovered Freda. Oh, I do love dogs so, Mr Fry. I find her more than charming, sir."

I knew Clayton fell instantly in love with Kate. I could see the tiniest heart shaped flecks dance about his eyes; the twitter of his lips; the subtle arch of his brow; the growing smile as he took in her exquisite face; his breathing increased. Backing away, I noticed his boots.

"Are you a cowboy, sir?" I interrupted their blushing.

His father sputtered, "Cowboy? Clay ... Clay, these English ladies are very astute. I warn you, son." He hee-hawed dabbing a bit of drool from his lips.

"Why, yes, Miss Holt, I *once* was."

Kate fanned herself with her Miss Pramm's handkerchief. Her eyes bulged like Freda's.

"And sir, have you ever seen a wild Indian?"

Clayton's smile widened. "Seen a wild Indian? I lived with 'em, Miss Hathaway."

Kate glanced at the ceiling and teetered backward. He, of course, steadied her. "Dear me," she said meekly, fluttering her eyelashes quite nicely, "you lived with savages?"

I wondered to myself how quickly two people fall in love. Such a natural occurrence, so it is. Pity all the waiting before one kisses one another. I thought of John and sighed. Yes, I let my opportunity slip by.

Of course you did, answered the smitten angel. *I told you to kiss him when you had the opportunity at the wedding.*

And then the other voice of reason reprimanded that silly angel girl quite soundly. *God forbid such wild behaviour. To kiss a man without first becoming betrothed ... such brazen vulgarity.*

I shook my head. *And which angel am I to believe?*

Me, said a tiny, little voice, situated between my lungs, below my throat, above my stomach. *Anne, you must steady your emotions. Let them simmer, like Mrs Savarin's stew. Not her soup, mind, but her stew.*

"Oh, yes, yes," I spoke aloud, "certainly not her eye-ball soup."

Clay glanced at me. "I beg your pardon, Miss Hathaway?"

"Soup?" interjected the kind old gentleman, "is it time to eat again?"

Kate recovered from her *bout* of Miss Pramm's verbal swooning and giggled. Taking my arm affectionately, she smiled. "Miss Holt is a dreamer, often talking aloud at the strangest moments. But I love her all the same." She affectionately squeezed my arm.

"What did I say, Kate?"

"Nothing to fret about, Miss Holt," answered the elder Mr Fry. "You were only talking about soup. One may dream about soup for hours upon end." He brought Freda to his lips kissing her muzzle.

Kate gently twirled the few straggly blond hairs that sprang from Freda's otherwise bald, little head—just looking at the hideous creature made me shudder.

"Kate, would not Holly Berry find her quite the toy?"

"Holly Berry?" offered Clay, "what is a Holly Berry, Miss Holt?"

"My dog, sir, she weighs one hundred pounds, stands near two feet at her shoulders. I have a small oil painting of her—of all my pets, it is in my room."

Kate laughed. "Indeed, Holly needs a saddle, I believe."

"A saddle?" He patted his vest pocket. Withdrawing a small leather wallet, he proudly withdrew a sketch. "My horse, Thunder."

Kate snuggled closer to him, eyeing the pencilled sketch. "Thunder? Oh, I can well imagine such a magnificent animal owning such a name! Did you ride him in a fast and furious manner, sir—through streams, perilous passages, and rocky slopes?"

He laughed, his face now flushed. "Well, Miss Hathaway, Thunder and I did ride many times in a furious manner." He rubbed the scar on his forehead. "Perhaps folks in England don't know about our Civil War."

"Oh, yes," she glanced at me. "Miss Holt and I know a great ... well, not a great deal about your war between the colonies, but our Prime Minister's opinions of such matters have been quoted in the newspapers."

"Hmm." He nodded. "Yep, well, I reckon they would."

"Mr Fry," I nervously tapped my fingers together, "I do hope we are nowhere near the line Mr Mason and Mr Dixon drew?"

"Oh, my no," piped the older gentleman, "my, no. Why, that is far south of here."

Kate nodded. "We promised our dear Aunt not to even come close to it, sir." Looking at Clayton, she fanned herself. "I do hope you understand her concern?"

"Oh, indeed, Miss Hathaway." He reverently refolded his sketch of Thunder and returned it to his wallet.

I heard Uncle Hathaway hem as he and Aunt Florence entered the lounge car. Turning, Kate fluttered to his side. "Papa, Mama, come, you must meet the most interesting gentlemen." She took her father's hand. "Papa, this is Mr Horace Fry and his son, Mr Clayton Fry."

"Indeed, sir." Nodded Kate's father. "I am Mr Hathaway and my wife."

"Very pleased, sir."

"Papa, Mr Fry fought in their Civil War. He has a magnificent steed named Thunder, *and* he has lived with wild Indians."

"Indeed, Mr Fry." Hathaway considered the young man and then eyed his doting daughter, Kate. "I fought in the Crimean War, myself." He puffed out his chest, tugging his lapels.

"Yes, sir." Mr Fry rubbed his scar again and smiled at Kate.

Aunt Florence touched her husband's sleeve. "Dear, it is time for tea."

"Oh, yes," he cleared his throat. "Excuse us, sir. Come along, Katherine. Come along, Anne."

Turning, Kate nodded with teary "I shall never see you again" eyes. She had twisted her handkerchief into a ball. I took her hand. "Good day, sirs."

The old gentleman nodded. "Good day, ladies."

Clayton kept his gaze on Kate. Smiling sadly, he nodded adieu.

Fondly rubbing Freda's head for the last time, I tried desperately to think of something, some way we could mingle in their company a little while longer—for Kate's benefit. But it was all so impossible; highly improper, for we had not been formally introduced.

Stymied, my mind raced. I had only seconds in which to make a miracle. After coming all this way, imagine the odds of finding one true love just outside of Buffalo. Oh, how I ...

"Mr Hathaway," called the elder Mr Fry.

Kate turned. Uncle William stopped, turning to his voice. "Yes, sir?"

"I was wondering, sir. Would it be possible to leave my precious dog in your daughter's most excellent hands for a few hours this evening? My son and I have been invited to a card ... a game in the next car, Mr Hathaway." His eyes blank and expressionless. "Sir, you are more than welcome to join us. I merely go for the company, of course."

"Cards?" Uncle William smiled. "Cards?" Patting his vest, he replied, "why, how kind of you, Mr Fry. Yes, I just might join you in a game or two."

"Dear," cautioned Aunt Florence in a whisper, "you know very well what the vicar says about gambling. ..."

"Florence, I have been entertaining three exquisite ladies for the last two months, and working diligently on my business affairs. I will upon occasion take a holiday, even if only for a few hours." From his vest he withdrew a cigar and sniffed it longingly.

Clayton smiled. "The Club Car, sir, where gentlemen gather for a few smokes ..."

"Indeed, Mr Fry." He winked. "I shall return within the hour and join you both."

"Thank you, Mr Hathaway." Mr Fry smiled. "My dear Freda does not tolerate smoke so very well." He snuggled her to his neck and cooed.

Uncle glanced at Kate. "Do you mind watching the little creature while your Papa indulges in serious business matters with our new American acquaintances, Kate?"

"Oh, no, Papa," she held Clayton's gaze, "why, I do not mind at all."

And that is how it all started between Mr Clayton Fry and Miss Katherine Hathaway. A love match made in New York. I wondered if they would serve buffalo stew for dinner this evening.

CHAPTER TWENTY

The train stopped to pick up passengers at a small town just this side of New York City. I noticed a man of photography standing on a platform with his camera, tri-poles, coverings, and luggage.

Suddenly, I noticed Clayton leaving the train and hurrying over to the photographer. He handed him what looked to be money, and then quickly jumped back onto the train. Pushing through the passage door, he came bustling up to us all a breath.

"Miss Hathaway, Miss Holt, hurry if you will! Come along with me and have your photograph taken."

Kate jumped from her seat. "I will, I will." She grabbed my arm. "Come along, Anne."

"Wait, Kate," I pondered the idea for two seconds. "Oh, very well, then, but we must hurry before the train leaves."

The departure whistles blew. Shouts from the conductor advised late boarders to hurry along. We scurried to the photographer's platform. The three of us stood together, Kate in the middle.

"Stand still. Do not breathe," cried the photography man, his head hidden beneath a black cloth.

Poof, poof. It was over.

The train puffed, the wheels screeched and spun. Black-capped porters blew their whistles. "All aboard!"

"Kate, may I have a picture of you, by yourself?" asked Clayton.

She ran back to the platform and stood smiling.

Poof, poof. It was over.

Clayton handed the picture man his name and address. "Send them to me, sir."

Breathless and laughing, we hopped back onto the moving train.

"Mr Fry," said Kate trying to catch her breath, "do you truly believe he will send the pictures?"

"Yes, Miss Hathaway, I do. My very life depends upon it."

Oh, I knew what he meant. Now he needed Kate's address to send her the pictures, and that he might write to her so she might write to him. What clever ideas develop when couples fall in love. What wonderful opportunities surface—to be taken advantage of in the name of amour, surely. I thought of John, but there were never any opportunities, I was simply born too late. To him I was, and would remain, nothing more than a silly child.

Well, whispered one of my angels in a snigger, *now you are a silly young lady.*

Returning to my berth, my heart felt happy for my dearest friend. After watching how sweetly Clayton made his intentions so very clear to Kate, I realised just how quickly one must seize the moment. Kate and Clayton appear to be desperately trying to grasp it. Oh, I must write Aunt and prepare Aunt and Uncle.

1 November 1868
Dear Aunt and Uncle,

Kate and I met an American cowboy! Mr Clayton Fry. He has even lived with the Indians—the Seneca Indians! We had our photographs taken. I am so excited, Aunt. I am sure he will send me a picture! Oh, yes, and we met his blind father, Mr Horace Fry, who had a tiny dog that his son won in a poker game in Texas. Oh, Aunt, the dog, Freda, is adorable ... weighs only two pounds, cannot bark ... Mr Fry says she is a voiceless dog. Uncle William loved that feature. 'Oh, if our neighbours only had such a breed!' he said. Aunt Florence was not too pleased with the Frys inviting Uncle William to the next car ... gambling, whiskey, cigars ... but Uncle William was happy when he returned. I think he won handsomely. As well, Clayton gave him a humidor full of expensive cigars from an island named Cuba. Clayton wears real western boots and his horse is named Thunder. You should see the scar on Clayton's forehead— from the Civil War. Do not worry Aunt, the Mason and

*Dixon's line is way south of where we travelled. I must
go, loveliest of Aunts and Uncles ... Kate sends her love;
she wants to know how John is doing ... I love you,*
        Kisses and affections, your niece, Anne **(Tell John I
love him)**

* * *

"Oh, Anne," cried Kate, "we will soon be back in New York
City. I just know I shall never see Mr Fry again."

"I think you will, Kate. I really think he is in love with
you." I nodded. "From the moment he laid his eyes on you. ..."

She pressed my hand. "You mustn't trifle with me, Anne,
you can be such a tease."

"Oh, I am not teasing, Kate. Why would he let your father
win at gambling and give him a fancy box—full of cigars?"

"Hmm, yes," she nodded, "you must be right. Papa is not
proficient at cards ... Mama and I beat him at nearly every
hand."

"So there you have it, dear girl, *and* you gave him your
address."

"Papa gave him our address to send the pictures ... and
more cigars."

I smiled and tweaked her nose. "I venture to say the day
you return to London your salver will be overflowing with
letters ... *love letters*, Kate."

Her face flushed, she began to cry. "Oh, Anne, it all
happened too soon. One moment I was thinking about petting
that tiny beast's nimble head and the next I was thinking of
petting Mr Clayton Fry's head. Oh, but he has marvellous blue
eyes." She sighed deeply. "How can such matters of the heart
develop so rapidly, Anne? Why," she dabbed her brow, "I had
no warning."

I thought of John at the end of the stairway the night I
met him at Lesington Hall. I hugged her. "I know, Kate. I
know."

"And tonight is our last night on the train, Anne. We will
be arriving in New York City first light."

The smitten angel piped up, *If he is serious about her, he
will find a way.*

"He will find a way, Kate."

Glancing up at me, she smiled, wiped her eyes and hugged me. "I pray so, Anne. But Mama has warned me, her exact words: 'Careful Katherine, we do not know the Frys *and* whether they are socially upstanding, morally correct—financially sound.' "

"Yes, I know, Kate, of what she speaks. But their manners are proper, their clothes quite expensive."

"Indeed, Anne. Surely I would not fall in love with a poor man?"

"Hmm." The angel of gloom tapped my forehead. *Remind her of what Miss Pramm said: 'It is just as easy to marry a rich man as it is a poor one.'*

"Kate, surely your Papa has ways to find if the Fry's are financially secure."

She sighed. "I wouldn't know how to approach the subject, Anne."

"Let me ponder the thought. Perhaps I shall find an opportunity to probe the elder gentleman Fry with a few well-placed inquiries regarding their status ... that is, if we run into them again this evening."

"Very well, Anne." She shook her head sighing. "What a pity to worry about financial trivia when love should be the utmost of concerns."

* * *

Kate and I hurried from our club-car and joined her mother and father in the dining-car.

"Well, there you two are," said Aunt Florence. "You look pale, Kate. Feeling unwell, dear?"

"Oh, no, Mama, I am very well. I really don't know what should make me look pale."

"Perhaps it is love sickness, Florence?" Uncle William chuckled as he spooned into his soft-boiled egg.

"Oh, Papa, what am I to think of you?"

"Well, think what you may, young lady." He glanced up. "Have I touched a raw nerve, Katherine? Your cheeks have miraculously regained their blush."

Sipping my tea, I sighed. "Mmm, this tea is remarkably similar to England's—for once on our journey, I am satisfied with a proper tea."

There came a voice behind us, "Oh, yes, yes, Miss Holt, it is Buffalo Tea—just what I prefer myself, actually."

Kate and I pulled the dining curtain aside. It was the elder Mr Fry, with Freda. "Good morning, sir," we said in unison.

"Good morning. Pardon me for interrupting, but I thought you would like to know what brand of tea you were drinking."

The kind Mr Fry was dining alone.

"Sir," said Uncle William, "we would be honoured if you would join us."

"Oh, thank you, Mr Hathaway, but I have Freda with me. Perhaps Mrs Hathaway would object."

She smiled. "Oh, I assure you, sir, I would do nothing of the sort. You are both more than welcome. Come, please, do join us."

Kate and I helped him resettle at our table. "Here, sir." I found another chair and took his arm. "Here, sit here, sir."

"Mr Fry, tell me, is your son not joining you this morning? Or is it too early?"

"No, Miss Hathaway, my son departed on the last stop. He had to pay an urgent visit to his fiancée."

The table grew silent, the only nasal noises being Freda's. Kate slowly swallowed her oats; her spoon dropped slightly and hovered over the bowl, frozen in space. Uncle William's face grew red. Aunt Florence's eyelashes moistened. I took Kate's hand.

Mr Fry nodded. "Forgive me for being rude, Mr and Mrs Hathaway, but what I mean is, for sharing a bit of news that is certainly none of my business, but then," he reached over and ran his hand over Freda's head, "it is my business, in a way. The happiness of my son ..."

I squeezed Kate's hand; her tears were now dripping in great profusion down her cheeks, 'round her nose cavity, onto the ski slope of her hand and splashing into her oats.

"Yes, the happiness of my son. His fiancé broke the engagement and he must confirm the details with the lady. That is why he departed from the train in haste near dawn. He said he would catch up with me in New York—the next train. I have never heard him sigh in such relief."

Uncle William's face returned to normal. Sucking an oyster from its half-shell, he nodded. "Well, then, Mr Fry, I am relieved to hear such news." He winked at Kate and swallowed.

I watched the oyster as it slid down his throat. Aunt Florence sighed and dabbed her moist eyes. Kate returned to dipping into her oats.

Mr Fry chuckled. "Indeed, Miss Hathaway, indeed. I think my son is very fortunate."

"Fortunate, Mr Fry?" inquired Aunt Florence.

He hemmed. "I mean being *released*."

"Sir," offered Uncle William, "we will remain with you in New York until your son returns for you."

"Oh, that is more than kind, sir. But I would not think of inconveniencing you over the matter. Freda and I do very well by ourselves, Thank you. I am not totally blind, sir. I can see blurs and splotches ... but if you would be so kind as to call for my carriage at the station, I would be most grateful."

"Sir, I assure you, there is no trouble in such a request."

"Indeed, Mr Fry, we will see you safely aboard your carriage, sir," said Aunt Florence. "Yes, yes." She patted his hand. "Have no worries."

"Thank you so much, madam. I shall wait for my son there. The next train is only an hour's wait."

Uncle puffed up. "Then we shall wait with you, sir. Hmm, indeed, perhaps over a hot cup of tea or sherry." He smiled at his wife.

"Oh, yes, Mr Fry," she nodded. "We should like that, *with tea*." She exchanged glances with Uncle William.

Kate looked more than thrilled. "Oh, indeed, Mr Fry, imagine a grand welcoming committee for your son when he steps from the train and finds us waiting."

"Oh, yes, we could wave flags, throw confetti ..."

Aunt Florence frowned. "That will do, Anne."

* * *

We arrived in New York City to the bustle of trains coming and going, congested streets, carriages up one side of the street and down the other; horse dung and house slop piled to the curb. Everyone complained of the lack of rain. I scarcely missed it at all, except now the city was beginning to smell a lot like London, though not quite as smoky.

Uncle inquired at the train terminal when the next train from Buffalo was due. He reported that it would be three hours. Normally it would be less than an hour, but there had been an unexpected problem with the rails.

Uncle and Mr Fry decided that we all should go back to our hotel and settle ourselves. Then, after lunch, he and the elder Mr Fry would return to the station. Kate convinced her mother and father that we should accompany them. She was beside herself with good cheer and humour.

"Oh, Anne," she fretted, "I can scarcely wait to see Mr Fry again. Help me decide what I shall wear."

"Oh, by all means wear your lavender silk, with matching hat. It worked for Aunt Alice." I thought for a moment. "However, I should wonder what sort of mood he may be in, Kate. A broken engagement might have put him in ill-humour."

"Oh, yes, indeed," she frowned, "and perhaps melancholy. Maybe I should dress more conservatively, my dark blue taffeta, then, Anne?"

"On second thought, Kate, Mr Fry would not know that we know that he has just been set free of his engagement."

"True. So I should wear my shiniest blue dress, then?"

"But, on the other hand, if he sees all of us standing on the platform waving and cheering, he will certainly figure that his father told us."

"So, I will wear my most conservative brown dress, then?"

"Hmm, but if you dress too conservatively, he will think you do not really care all that much ... one way or the other."

"Very well then, I shall wear my most brilliant lavender dress."

"Well, dear, you do not want to be too presumptuous—and scare him away."

With her hands on her hips, Kate shook her head. "Miss Anne Holt ... Imp of Satan, you are teasing me again."

"Teasing? Why, what would make you think such a thing?"

* * *

Uncle William smiled warmly when he met his daughter in the hotel lobby. "Kate, you look exquisite in that brilliant lavender."

"Thank you, Papa." Patting her coif, she added smugly, "Anne dressed my hair."

The elder Mr Fry lifted his head. "You smell like a rose garden, Miss Hathaway."

"Excuse me, sir," I hemmed. "*I* am the rose garden; Miss Kate is the lavender bush."

Laughing, we all made our way back into our carriage and off to the train station to greet the unsuspecting Mr Clayton

Fry. Freda, cupped in Mr Fry's hat, meekly peeked out over the hat's brim. Her bulging brown eyes scanned the crowd in timid wonder; her wrinkled little nose took samples from the air and then promptly sneezed.

* * *

We reached the train station in good time. Uncle found the platform, where we five took up an entire bench. Mr Fry tapped his cane this way and that; Uncle William puffed his cigar. Aunt Florence grimaced and waved the blue smoky haze away. Kate whispered sweet nothings into a vacancy of thoughtless romantic wonder.

Of a sudden, a shrill whistle jolted the docile air. Doors pushed opened wide. The busy bodies waiting within buzzed out—swarming as they hummed in unison toward the honey of the tracks.

We rose as one. I stared at the massive train's one huge light flicker off the rain-slick rails—Mr Fry teetered and I took his elbow.

"Thank you, Miss Rose Garden."

"You are more than welcome, sir."

"Not long now, Mr Fry," said Uncle, tossing his soggy cigar butt into a leafless shrub.

"I cannot thank you enough for your kindness, Mr Hathaway. My son will be overwhelmed at your generosity. I do believe he will insist on taking you to supper one evening. That is, if you do not mind?"

Kate squirmed and smiled broadly at her father.

"We do not mind at all, Mr Fry, no, not at all."

The train chugged to a stop, steam sprayed and hissed. Fog enveloped and curled about the busy walkway. I watched the passengers step down from the train, one after the other, after the other, kissing friends and relatives, passing off luggage. Children ran, shrieking; conductors checked their pocket watches; porters moved about their luggage carts ...

"Father!" Cried Clayton.

Mr Fry turned. "I hear my son," he pointed with his cane, "from that direction."

Squinting at the bustling crowd, I sorted face after face; I didn't hear Mr Clayton's call to his father, nor did I spy him hurrying to join us. It began to rain again, and though we were under a shelter, the lightning and thunder added to my confusion.

Turning back, I found Kate. She had jumped from the platform and began running—her glittering lavender silk skirt billowing wildly in the rain. I glanced a few feet in front of her and—rushing in the opposite direction—Mr Clayton Fry; his black top hat toppling about the crowd.

He gathered her up in a bolt of lightning and as the thunder boomed, he kissed her passionately ... on the mouth! In front of God, in front of her father, and in hearing range of Mr Horace Fry himself!

Tears slid down my cheeks. I know John would never have greeted me in such a wild fashion.

Because, mademoiselle, sniped the laissez-faire angel, *you would never run wildly toward him with open arms, as she did.*

I sighed, you are very right angel, you are very right. But that does not mean I love John less.

"I think my son is fond of your daughter, sir." Mr Fry smiled as he cuddled Freda huddling in his vest pocket—his bulging vest was all a tremble, poor Freda.

Uncle William hemmed. "Yes, I do believe that is your son, ah, holding my daughter." He turned and escorted Mr Fry into the station. "I will call our carriage, sir. Please do sit down, it is dryer in here."

Kate and Clayton entered the building. Both were smiling, deliriously drippy from the rain and obviously in love. On his left arm hung his umbrella, dry as a bone—Freda sniffed it.

Clayton hugged his father. "Sir, I have invited everyone to supper this evening."

"Mmm, I am mighty hungry, son. That sounds the best of plans."

Kate beamed. Taking her hand, I whispered, "Now you must be relieved that you wore your most brilliant dress." I kissed her cheek.

* * *

During supper at our hotel, in the exquisite New Yorker lounge, Clayton invited us to their home. "Once settled, of course," he added. "Will next weekend, Saturday night, suit you?"

Uncle William glanced at his wife, Florence. "Do we have any prior engagements, dear?"

"No, Mr Hathaway, we do not." Florence smiled at Clayton.

"And sir," addressed Uncle William to the elder Fry, "what do you do, sir?"

"Oh, Mr Hathaway, I am retired now and do very little; just an occasional turn about the garden with my guide, Freda." He chuckled. "Then an occasional visit from the grandchildren and my daughter and her husband." He rubbed his eyes. "However, before my eyes weakened, I was in the commodity markets, a financial advisor in the acquisition of lead, zinc, copper, and tin. My son, Clayton, now heads the firm. We were just returning from Niagara on business when we met you all."

"I must admit," said Clayton in a low tone, "I was not the perfect son." He glanced at his father. "Just after college, I travelled out West for awhile, migrated back to New York and joined the Union Army." Touching his forehead, he smiled proudly. "I was injured and returned home. Father nursed me to health." He smiled at Kate. "I have since settled. I am now, what one would call, a respectable businessman."

"Any regrets, sir?" I asked.

"None," he hesitated, "except one, Miss Holt."

Hmm, and that was, I suspected, his betrothal to whomever "she" was.

He glanced at Uncle. "Sir, I cannot tell you how pleased Father and I are that you and your family are coming to supper Saturday. Do come early, I will show you the grounds. Lincoln Park is quite spectacular this time of year."

I did no probing that evening regarding their financial and social stability. Uncle William and Aunt Florence seemed more than satisfied on that score. Kate was quiet and demure— a giggle here, and a laugh there—oh, yes, she seemed quite smitten with her rugged Clay cowboy.

* * *

Later that evening, in our room, Kate and I sat before the lovely hearth fire sipping hot cocoa. I dropped our bed coverings onto the floor, and we, giggling and silly, snuggled together, chatting before the crackling fire. It was now raining quite hard. The wind and rain pattering against the windows put me in mind of home.

"I miss England, Kate. I miss Aunt and Uncle, Holly Berry, Misha, and Gib." In my mind's eye, John's sweet face appeared. "Oh, if John only knew how much I loved him."

Kate pressed my hand. "Well, I certainly do, Anne."

"I can't hold it in a moment longer, Kate. I suppose after watching how soon you and Mr Clayton fell in love, I must now confess. I, too, fell in love with John as quickly. But that was years ago—at the bottom of our stairs at Lesington Hall. One look and I was sunk."

She set down her cocoa and took my hand. "Oh, my dearest cousin, how you must be tormented having so much love pent up in your heart for all these years."

"Pent up with very much torment as well, Kate." I shook my head. "Very tormented, indeed." I wiped my eyes on my sleeve. "I suppose I was just born too late for him, Kate. He does not look my way."

"Why haven't you shared all this with me before, Anne? I thought you were merely smitten. Or I wouldn't have teased you so."

"I don't know, Kate. I suppose I was afraid if I said the words aloud they would evaporate into thin air."

"Evaporate into thin air?" She shook her head. "I must admit I don't understand that one, dear girl."

"I have an angel, Kate—many angels, to be exact. They have taken residence in my body. Sometimes they sit on each shoulder and argue between one another—good over bad. Sometimes they flit about my heart, trickle down my windpipe. But mostly they encamp in my brain and whisper suggestions to me."

"Hmm," she nodded sympathetically, "yes, dear. I have heard of such fairies."

"No, no, Kate, these are not fairies, I assure you. I would say they are more on the order of *figments*."

"Of your vivid imagination?" She giggled.

"Oh, I would imagine so, Kate." I laughed too. "But, all in all, they are quite whimsical, sometimes naughty, and betimes, quite sly and irksome."

"Well, dear Cousin," she kissed my cheek, "the angels could not have found a lovelier, kinder, sweeter dwelling place than your heart."

"What a dear cousin you are, Kate. Thank you for understanding."

"Oh, Anne, I can certainly understand your love for John. He is the dearest of gentlemen. I now realise that it does not take a long courtship to know when two people love one another." Glancing at the snapping fire, she sighed. "I cannot express in words how much I am in love with Mr Fry, Anne."

"I know, Kate." I glanced at the flames and whispered, "How well I know."

Resting her head on her knees, she looked up at me. "Do you still believe John is in love with Miss Revelt?"

"I suppose I have always imagined that to be the case, Kate."

"*Imagined* is correct, Anne. I can assure you, he does not love her."

"Even so, I do not suppose he shall ever look my way."

"Oh, I think he has always favoured you, Anne, and wasn't your first dance at your coming out party reserved for him?"

"I thought so, but when I went to the balcony, as you suggested, in search of him, he was nowhere to be found. Then, hearing voices, I glanced down to the courtyard and I found he and Miss Revelt, arm-in-arm, strolling under a love moon. Oh, Kate," I cried, "I could not witness them a moment longer and hurried back into the ballroom."

"Silly girl, that wasn't John, it was Edward."

"What do you mean it was Edward?"

"Well, they do look so much alike, I can see where, in the dark, you could mistake him. But John was with me, Anne. He watched you dance with that handsome Dr Waterbury and he expressed his fears ... quite openly, that you had captured the heart of every man in the room, including his own."

"I had captured *his* heart, Kate? But how can that be? I could not capture anyone's heart, surely."

She took my chin, "Anne, you silly girl. You never notice how men stare at you? You are really quite exquisite. If I didn't love you so, I certainly would not want to be your companion. Why, men simply don't flirt with me when you are around."

"I don't remember any men flirting with me, Kate. Not a one."

"Let me count them, even your Aunt's butler, Franklin, goes out of his way to please you. He always has. Then there is Edward, Charles, Father, Uncle Anthony, John. They all are always commenting at your sweetness, your charm. Then there are Professor Mandeville's friends who were all gawking at you when we were at the theatre. John was quite beside himself at your coming out party." She tweaked my nose. "He said, and quite forlorn, I might add, 'For now she is an eligible woman.' "

"Oh, stop, Kate." I know my face was burning red.

It certainly is, Miss Anne. She is only saying those things because she is in the stupors of love. Giddy with euphoria of, at long last, having a man fall in love with her. Of course she gives freely of her finest compliments. Just wait until this Yankee Doodle Clayton disappoints her; then see how she talks.

I shrugged and stood. With a sigh I said, "Well, Kate, before the evening ends, I must write to Aunt and Uncle."

"Oh, Anne, I quite forgot, Papa gave me a basket full of letters this morning, most of them yours, from Aunt Alice."

"Letters?"

"Just there," she pointed, "there on the table. There is one in the mix for me, from Edward."

I sorted eight letters in all. "Aunt puts the date on the envelope, Kate. She is so wise." Sliding my finger under the seal, I read her earliest letter first:

> *Dear Anne,*
>
> *Anthony and I just returned from seeing you off. Terrible thing to do, I do not like goodbyes. John joined us at the dock. I was so surprised to see him. He waved to you, but I am sure you did not see him. He was still in Bath and by the time he received your letter, he hurried to the ship to say goodbye—the poor dear was sad for not being able to wish you well. You really must write to your dear cousin, Anne. Anthony and I are going away for a few days. I miss you.*
>
> *Love from your affectionate Aunt Alice*

Kate looked up from her letter, smiling. "Edward says John plans on opening the clinic earlier than planned. He wishes we were there for the opening ceremony. "Oh, apparently Miss Revelt has found a marvellous place in Bath in which to open their clinic."

"Yes," I laid Aunt's letters in my lap, "Kate, I missed John's graduation from veterinary college and now I will miss another important event in his life ... ."

"Anne, if there is anyone on the earth who understands situations, it is John Hathaway."

"Yes." I lowered my chin. "Yes, he would, of course." When I opened Aunt's second letter a smaller letter dropped out. I recognised the handwriting at once. It was John's. I hurriedly ripped it open.

> *Dearest Cousin Anne,*
>
> *I received your letter and had planned on joining Father and Mother at the dock to see you off, but arrived too late. Unfortunately, a horse took a nasty spill just ahead of our gig and I helped the poor creature to his feet. The old fellow should have been put to pasture years earlier, but on that aspect I could do little but lecture the driver in a severe tone. Oh, these cold-hearted, abusive people, Anne. At every visit to Lesington Hall, I pay particular attention to your "threesome." I kissed Holly Berry and Misha today in your honour, but could not find Gib. We all miss you. Do write, Cousin,*
>
> *Affectionately, your cousin, John*

"Oh, Kate," I giggled, "when John visits Lesington Hall, he tells me he kisses Holly Berry and Misha in my honour! But he could not find Gib ... he thinks the old boy is hiding from him." I hugged my knees. "Oh, how utterly delightful, Kate."

"Indeed, he is." She stroked my hair. "I think he is quite in love with you."

I shook my head. "I dare not even imagine it, Kate."

Setting my letters aside, I felt a deep pang of guilt. I should not have been roaming about New York when the finest people in the world were at home going about without me—I was such a part of their lives. Dear Holly Berry and Misha, and my Gib. There were Franklin, Nancy, Abby, and Mrs Savarin, and John, dearest, sweetest John. I was indeed a selfish prig.

Selfish, yes, Anne, that is you—beyond a doubt it is. Forever and always, thinking of what suits you; Taking Elly out into a rainy jaunt to Holybourne just so you could satisfy your whim to learn about your father; Inconveniencing

Franklin, putting yet another burden to his daily duties by going to Cheapside to meet with O'Leary. And then there is the matter of ... .

"Here, love," said Kate as she handed me a cocoa. "And?"

Looking up, I shook my head. "And?"

"What does Aunt Alice write?"

"Oh, yes." I blew the warm chocolaty vapours aside and took a sip. "Aunt and Uncle were off on holiday, she does not say where—but, no doubt, Bath." Perusing the rest of Aunt's letters, I sadly did not find another letter from John. "Everyone is quite well, Holly Berry and Misha have been following Aunt about the house like shadows—they have taken over my room." Dabbing my eyes, I continued, "Oh, listen Kate: Charlotte Mandeville is with child." Glancing up, I cried, "I quite imagine that infant will be tuneful."

Kate giggled. "And, no doubt, off key in the middle of her brother's sermons."

"We are a wicked duo, Kate."

* * *

The following weekend came ever so slowly, but Friday was our usual shopping day and we ventured out to find Kate a lovely *something* for our Saturday supper with Mr Clayton Fry, his father, and of course, Freda.

"Oh, Mama," said Kate, "I must look my very best when we dine with the Frys tomorrow night."

"Indeed you must, Kate." Aunt Florence glanced out the carriage window. "Dear me, the air is frosty already."

"It is the second week of November, Aunt Florence. I overheard the footman say the weather could turn sour at any moment."

"Sour? Indeed. Well, then, Kate, you must find a suitable cloak and hat if you wish to walk about Lincoln Park with Mr Fry." She pressed her hand. "Mind to use economy, dear. Oh, and do remember proper walking boots."

"Indeed, Mama."

Stopping at one store, I begged off. "Excuse me, but I must post these cards before noon. I shall return to the carriage and wait there."

"Very well, Love," said Aunt Florence, and they happily disappeared down Broadway.

Sorting through the stack of postcards to Uncle, Aunt, Charlotte, Franklin and a few of the other servants, I found John's card. I fondled it to my heart. Holding it aside, I reread what I had written,

November 14 - Nw Yrk
Dear Cousin John,
 It is turning cool at night. Not a lovely moon in sight, not that I could find one with all these tall buildings. Perhaps, though, I shall find one Sat eve, when we are to dine with the American at Lincoln Park ... his ancestral home. I cannot tell you how much pleasure I felt when you wrote to say you kissed Holly and Misha ... I weep at the very thought—how I truly miss everyone. Our Feb homecoming is too far away,
  Your most affec C, Anne

Walking at a brisk pace to the post, I deposited each card, until coming to John's; I absent-mindedly kissed it and dropped it into the slot. Oh, dear me. I froze. I was wearing lip rouge ... my lip imprint would be on his post card.

A voice shrieked from somewhere in my temple of thoughts, *Brazen!*

Mind your own business, I huffed, and made way back to the carriage. *What of it? There is no harm. If Kate can kiss a man's mouth, surely I can kiss a man's postcard.*

That is exactly right, Anne, Elly's angel fluttered to my side. *Besides, I venture to say that is the nudge John needs. Once he spies those lippy-love-pats it will quite set his mind to rapturous conclusions.*

Now standing at our carriage, I muttered aloud, "Oh, you are both wrong."

Startled, the coachman and footman exchanged glances. "Beg pardon, Miss Holt? Have we done somethin' wrong?"

CHAPTER TWENTY-ONE

As we approached Mr Fry's Lincoln Park Estate, that momentous Saturday evening, I just knew Kate was destined for something more than extraordinary. Sitting next to me, she looked quite like royalty though nervous and twittery. I quieted her trembling hands by covering them with mine. "He will think you more than beautiful, Kate."

"Thank you, Anne."

Why would he not? She wore a beautiful chemisette, trimmed with handmade lace and embroidery under her bodice. Her light coloured silk gown was trimmed with braid, ruche and ribbons; her skirt was full, and for wonder, beneath she wore a dozen starched and flounced muslin petticoats; around her shoulders draped a cream coloured cashmere shawl; an elegant hat sat upon her head decorated with petite silk flowers and ribbons. Inside her latest French purse, knitted with colourful silk and silver cut-steel beads was her prized Miss Pramm's handkerchief. What man could not love such a beauty?

I thought about the postcard I had kissed and sent to John.

Kate giggled. "He will like it very much, Anne."

"And how would you know what I was thinking?"

As our carriage slowed, Aunt Florence caught her breath. "Oh, my, this is a magnificent park, indeed." She glanced around in awe. "Equals every bit of London's finest, I should say."

Uncle William settled back into his seat, looking puffed up and fine. A smile lingered on his countenance.

The coachman called out to the gatekeeper and the ornate black wrought iron gates were pulled open by two, fashionably dressed, servants. The gates were well oiled and fluid, for they swung smooth and without one creak. In magnificent gold scrolling, the letter "F" was entwined in the iron latticework. The red brick pavement, porous and dull, was bordered by well-trimmed flower beds; populous planted leafless shrubbery, ribbon-like, bordered the drive before us as it curled and disappeared into a copse of ancient firs. The clatter of hooves frightened a cluster of cardinals—their brilliant red bodies glowed like lanterns amongst the long needled dark green pine.

Now moving beneath an arched carriage-porch, Clayton greeted us. Standing beneath the beautiful brownstone portico, he smiled. Behind him stood his home—his mansion.

"Lincoln Park, indeed, Kate." I pinched her.

As we stepped from the carriage, Clayton was all a flush. My, but he was a handsome cowboy. I inhaled the chill of late afternoon air, and felt a little frost nip my face. I found the New York air exhilarating, all in all.

"Beautiful, Mr Fry." I glanced around at our surroundings in awe. *Impressive* must have emanated from my eyes.

Kate's face glowed. "Oh, Mr Fry, it is beautiful here."

"Thank you, thank you both." He took Kate's elbow. "Please, shall we?"

The servants took our wraps. Fry escorted us into the drawing room with mirror-like varnished floors. The chairs and sofas covered with striped silk—blue, green and white. Why, it was more than spectacular. The walls were hung with pictures in gilt frames; porcelain ornaments clustered on the mantle piece. It was charmingly elegant.

"What a cheery room, Mr Fry." Walking to the mantle piece, Kate looked up at a portrait. "Family, sir?"

"My mother, Miss Kate." He moved closer to her. "She died many years ago."

"Dreadful, sir." Joining Kate's side, I peered up at the stately looking woman and tried to match her facial expression with her son's.

"Indeed, sir." Aunt Florence bowed her head in sadness.

"Yes," he sighed, "but I was too young to remember her."

We nodded in solemn unity.

"Father shall be down in a moment. Please do sit. A sherry all around?"

Uncle William nodded with grin. "Oh, that shall do, Fry. That shall do nicely."

Aunt Florence nudged Uncle. "Nothing for us, thank you, sir."

"On second thought," said Uncle, "I will indulge, sir." He broke from Aunt's side and helped Clayton pour. He shuddered. "Oh, on such a frosty day as this, what harm in a little sherry, I ask?" He turned to Aunt Florence and hemmed. "I repeat, Mrs Hathaway, what is the harm?"

"Tea or coffee, then, ladies?" asked Clayton.

"Very well, sir," returned Kate in a near whisper. "Perhaps a coffee would indeed warm me." She rubbed her arms briskly and smiled.

"Warm you? Dear me, Miss Kate, you must be chilled." Clayton tugged on the bell-pull and impatiently tugged again. "I shall have the fire tended immediately. May I fetch your wrap in the meantime?"

She blushed at his kind attentiveness. "Oh, no, sir, surely a cup of coffee would warm me on such a day."

The butler and two maids hurried into the room. "Sir?"

"Hurry up the fire, Wilson. And see to it the dining room is warmer than usual. One of our guests has taken a chill."

The maids scurried to the hearth. One removed the screen, another handed Wilson the logs. Within minutes, a roaring, monstrous fire blazed.

"There you are now." Clayton gestured toward a chair near the hearth. "You must try my favourite chair, Miss Kate."

She demurred. Sitting, she spread her fine silk dress in queenly fashion (Miss Pramm would have deemed the motion very fine, indeed). Moving her hands over the smooth, supple silk armchair, she leaned back and sighed. "Indeed, sir, it is more than comfortable now."

Aunt Florence broke the spell between the moon-eyed couple. "I so admire your taste, Mr Fry. It is magnificent." Continuing about the room, glancing at this and that, she added, "Yes, yes, elegant as any royal drawing room."

Just then, the elder Mr Fry entered, Freda just a few steps ahead of his cane. Her long, thin nails, snapped on the wood floor much as a rat scrambles about the rafters. She sniffed and snorted us each: one, two, three hems and uncle's shoe. Even a glittery bow about her neck did not improve that ghastly skeletal frame. If Gib should bump into *that* in the middle of the night—*Oh, dear me*, I fanned my face, *what a dreadful calamity.*

"Good evening, friends," said the elder gentleman cheerfully. "And ladies, you are in good health, I assume?"

Nodding to the elder Mr Fry, Aunt Florence replied, "Oh, indeed sir, we are, and to you, a good evening as well. And yes, I am in health, warm, and comfortable at the moment."

While Uncle William and Mr Fry exchanged pleasantries, I noticed Clayton's eyes cast about Kate's sweet fire-flushed cheeks. Aunt Florence and Mr Fry were at once engrossed in conversation over an elegant, embroidered and framed Biblical quotation that hung on the wall. I overhead him say that his daughter Julia designed it. Freda lay stretched across his feet gnawing at her bony little paws.

Sipping the last of his revered sherry, Uncle smiled. Leaning on his heels, he asserted, "Yes, sir, Clayton, if our company, Lilliard Shipping, could interest your firm in shipping supplies to England, why, I am more than confidant we could ... I beg your pardon, sir?"

I overheard just a small bit of the conversation, but watching Kate's face, I sat up. Freda lifted her head from the elder's shiny shoes, and with pricked ears, sniffed the air. Aunt Florence's words froze on her lips ... the elder Fry smiled.

Uncle set down his drink. "You wish to marry my daughter?"

*　*　*

On the ride home that evening, Kate remained quiet, love-eyed, calm and confident. For our part, Aunt Florence and I patted our tummies, marvelling over the exquisite supper the bachelor Clayton Fry had presented:

Oysters on half shell, julienne soup, baked pickerel, roast turkey, oyster stuffing, mashed potatoes, boiled onions, baked winter squash, cranberry sauce, chicken pie, plain celery, lobster salad, olives, spiced currants, English plum pudding, wine sauce, mince pie, orange water ice, fancy cakes, cheese, fruits, nuts, raisins, confectionery, and coffee.

Besides the magnificent confectionary, alas the young Clayton Fry was in love. After touring the wine cellar, even Uncle William fell in love; the wedding was promptly scheduled for the following spring. Ah, love is mighty, but a fine wine is mightier and I quote Kate's father, Mr Hathaway.

On our return trip to the Claredon, Kate sat all aglow. "Oh, Mama, I am simply overwhelmed by it all."

Aunt Florence, frowning at Mr Hathaway's snoring, patted my hand anxiously. "We do not need to repeat how much Uncle William imbibed this evening, dear Anne. Despite his love for an honest day's work, he also loves an honest day's nip."

"Do not fret, Aunt Florence." I sighed. "My dear mother could out guzzle him in a twinkling."

"Oh," she covered her mouth in disbelief. "Oh, indeed." She dabbed her lips and kicked her husband's shins. "Wake up, love, wake now, dear. We have arrived at the hotel."

* * *

18 Nov - The Clarendon, Nw Yrk
Dear Aunt and Uncle,

I must keep a secret ... a wedding in the spring. But I think it sooner, however. My heart is overflowing. Oh, Aunt to hug you at this moment. Kate is beside herself. You remember our conversation on economy? Well, Uncle William has quite secured the future of his business and security of his family. He is in such jovial mood you would scarcely know him. He mentioned just this morning at breakfast that if all goes as planned, we may cut short our trip here (Hooray!) and return home a month early. I love England, you and my family. I am weeping (joy) more so for thinking we may come home sooner rather than later. Once upon English soil, I will breathe again. Have you been whispering my name in Holly Berry and Misha's ear? Must go, Aunt. We are to dine at the Frys again for lunch ... I cannot tell you how beautiful his mansion, Lincoln Park! I have not heard a word more from John. He must be terribly busy with the new clinic ... ?

Yours most affectionately, Anne

* * *

After breakfasting with Uncle William and Aunt Florence at the hotel, Kate and I strolled about Clayton's magnificent Lincoln Park grounds. It had become a pleasant morning routine. Clayton was often gone, but if he should find time to return early, he seemed to take great delight in finding us visiting with his father and walking about the grounds.

Uncle William was away daily with his business; Aunt Florence, hating the cold weather remained at the Clarendon in front of her revered fire sipping her tea.

The weather had turned colder; snow was now at least a foot or more. Though the pathways were kept clear, dearest Freda had the worst time of it trying to do her dainty squats. This morning, as we perused the great white expanse of the Park's grounds, a beautiful red bird swooped several times and alit on a branch just above our heads. Its beady black eye focused on Freda. As two grey squirrels hopped across the frozen blanket of snow, one stopped to examine her as well, no doubt wondering if she was a mutant turn-coat—the other, leaped from limb to limb, glancing only once to titter.

Scrambling back to me, Freda danced tippy-toed until I once more secured her snugly into my muff—we have grown quite close.

"Holly Berry and Misha will quite hate her, you know," laughed Kate.

"I rather supposed they have forgotten me by now." I wiped my eyes.

"Oh, I think not, Anne."

We walked on a few steps when she offered, "But I think John may have. You have not written to him in a very long time."

"Well," I pouted, "I have not received one letter from him." I frowned. "The last being the one in which he wished me ... let me say it exactly ... he wished me: 'all good happiness in whatever decisions you make.' Now what do you suppose that means, Kate? It is certainly an odd thing to say."

"Hmm, 'All good happiness in whatever decisions you make ... ?" She shook her head. "He is a thoughtful, considerate fellow, Anne. What did you last write that could provoke such a response?"

"I didn't write anything to elicit such an idea, Kate. I spoke only of our daily walks here and Mr Fry's kind considerations. You told me it was a secret about your engagement, your plans, so I didn't mention it."

"Yes, yes, I want to surprise Uncle Anthony, Aunt Alice, and all our cousins and friends."

"So, I could not say a word, only saying how handsome Mr Fry; how beautiful Lincoln Park, so on and so forth. I merely hinted at a possible betrothal, but only said exactly what you permitted me to say, Kate. Have I said too much, do you suppose?"

"Oh, I think perhaps you have, Anne."

Reaching the end of the pathway, we turned and headed back.

"Anne, did you write your letters in a way that may have made John think *you* were in love with Mr Fry?"

Turning to her, I gasped. "Oh, Kate." I could feel Freda nervously scratch about inside my muff. I lowered my voice. "Dear words of words. Perhaps I might ... have. Oh, let me think." I exhaled, frowning. "Oh, Kate, I don't remember what I wrote exactly." I took her hand. "Come along then, you must help me write a letter right now that erases any confusion."

"Indeed," said Kate. "You must write John that it is *I* who is engaged. He will keep the secret."

Hurrying into the Great House, I handed my muff, with Freda still inside it, to the elder Mr Fry. "Excuse me, sir. I must write an urgent letter ..."

He cradled little Freda with the arms of a grandmother. "Why, certainly, Miss Anne, and you may use my stationery if you wish. I shall have you shown to the study." He rang for one of the servants.

"Oh, thank you, Mr Fry."

"Dear me," he said, groping for his cane. "I do hope it is nothing terribly serious."

"Oh, no, sir," said Kate. Freda poked her head out of the muff. Kate giggled and rubbed her head, "nothing too terribly serious ... only affairs of the heart. Anne must write her true feelings to the love of her life."

"Oh, well then," he exhaled. "Well then, by all means, hurry along."

Dipping into the ink jar, I squared the rather masculine stationery, glanced up, thought for a moment and began:

2 December - Lincoln Park
Dearest John,
    Kate is engaged to Mr Clayton Fry. I was not
supposed to say a word until we returned home. But
Kate, just moments ago, changed my mind, changed her

mind, actually. Anyway, I do not love Mr Fry, never
loved Mr Fry, will never love Mr Fry. Well, that is, not
until he is my cousin ...
      Goodbye, John,   Your affectionate cousin,   Anne

I waved it about allowing the ink to dry. "Come now, Kate.
Read it."

She snatched it from my hands. Frowning, she sighed
deeply. "No, no, Anne. You must write that you love him."

"I cannot say such a thing, Kate."

"But you must, Anne."

"I cannot. He must say it first. It would be too bold of me.
You remember exactly what Miss Pramm said regarding being
brazen and bold."

"Yes, and she is *Miss* Pramm, and will forever be a *Miss*
Pramm. You may be subtle in your declarations to John, but
you must declare them. Lead him softly to the conclusion that
you are hopelessly in love with him ... that you would accept
his proposal."

I thought for a moment, catching up at the brilliant force
of sunlight streaming about the crystal wall sconces. Rainbows
of tinkered glint dappled over my writing paper, over my
writing hand. "Very well, I shall be subtle in my declarations."

Dear John,
      I love you, I have always loved you, and I will love
you for the rest of my life.
      Love,   Anne

Kate gushed. "Oh, yes, yes, subtle enough. That shall do,
Anne."

Sealing the envelope, I held it to my heart, breathless. "I
cannot believe I have written such words."

"You have spoken from the heart—you brazen thing!"

"Oh, Kate," I giggled, "dare I post such a letter? But, oh, I
feel such relief. Why has it taken me so long to say it?"

She smiled a knowing smile. "The heart is a strange little
island, Anne, surrounded by uncertain waters."

I took her hand. "Well, it is good that we are stout
islanders of English blood, then."

"Oh, indeed."

"Come then, Kate, we must have this posted as soon as possible."

* * *

Our carriage made good time to the post office. Holding John's letter once more to my heart, I sighed before dropping my life into the letterbox. "Kate, my future is now in the hands of fate."

Kissing my cheek, she giggled. "I wager you shall hear from John before Christmas."

"Oh, I could not dare wish it, Kate. Think of the disappointment if I do not. A sudden thought froze my heart. "Dear me, Kate, what if the boat carrying my letter sinks?"

She took my hand. "Come along, dear, Mama is expecting us."

* * *

Upon awakening that snowy New York morning on my eighteenth birthday, I brought the covers to my chin. The fire had been looked after for the tending-smoke haze still floated in the room. I glanced at the ice-glazed windows and shuddered. Hearing Kate's deep breathing in the next bed, I pulled the covers over my head.

Closing my eyes, I tried to remember my life as far back as I could. I found myself in Holybourne with Mama. I remember the day I was sent to Aunt Alice's ... I could faintly remember an earlier birthday. I was possibly five or six. 14 December seemed always rainy and damp, oft times snowy. 'Fitting weather,' I remember Mama saying that as she gazed out at the dreary morning, 'your father died on such a day as this, on your birthday.'

The closing of a hotel door jolted me back to New York. I sighed away the melancholy for I had not thought of Mama like that in a very long time. My heart ached. I miss you Aunt Alice, Holly Berry, Misha, Gib ... Lesington Hall. God bless you, Your Majesty. I hope this day finds you calm. Oh, I miss England. We will be going home next month, only one month ahead of schedule. Oh, only three weeks more. Thank you God, I can scarcely wait.

To breathe the fresh English air, to walk in Elly's meadow, to visit Mama and Papa's graves—to see John—to see John. Feeling my face burn, I shook my head. He will not answer my letter. I suppose when we again meet, in his kindness, he will kiss my cheek, laugh about my silly declaration of love for him. And being the gentleman that he is, he'll no doubt pretend to have forgotten all about what I had written. Yes, that is how he shall act toward me, and I shall hold the very same countenance ... perhaps I have grown up after all, past the impetuous age of seventeen—for today I am eighteen.

"Good morning, Anne."

Sitting up, I smiled at Kate as she tossed off her quilt. "And happy birthday!"

"Thank you, Kate. You remembered my birthday—how happy you make me feel."

Yawning, she rubbed her eyes. "How could I forget my dearest cousin? After we dress, I have a surprise for you."

Tossing my covers aside, I dangled my feet over the bed and rubbed my eyes awake. "I must see it before then," I teased. "I simply cannot wait."

"Oh, no, you must first brush your hair."

"Very well." Yawning, I wiggled into my robe and tied it snug. "Goodness me, Kate, I don't feel eighteen." Walking to my toilet-table, I sighed. "Just a moment ago, while waking, I thought back to when I was a young child, odd that I could picture Mama's face in such vivid detail." Washing my face, I continued, "That's the first time I have remembered her so clearly, Kate."

"What did she look like, Anne?"

"Well," as I patted dry my hands, "Mama had long black hair, thick with curls; it was very soft. He eyes were black; her skin was a warm tan. She was always grieving for Papa, and more so, on my birthday. That was when he died. Pity how she must have suffered."

Kate began brushing my hair. "Well, it is a pity how *you* suffered, Anne," she said in a huff. "It was not fair of her to punish you. Why, you were only a child."

"Ouch, Kate, you're pulling my hair."

"I am sorry, Anne, but ..."

Sitting back, I turned and faced her, shocked. "Kate, I have never heard you speak so vehemently before."

"You are too dear of a person to have had such a nasty beginning in life, Anne. It's no wonder your angel friends speak so rudely to you—all along it has probably been her doing all the speaking."

"Her?" I was at first puzzled at Kate's inference, and then I reasoned that perhaps she meant the voices in my head were those of my mother. "No, Kate," I turned to face her, "not Mama, not her. She does not speak to me."

"Anne, I am sorry. I did not mean to hurt you, but ..."

"Say no more, Kate. Please, say no more. I want no more heart aches in my life regarding my mother. It was not her fault entirely that she died and left me, nor was my father's accident. I blame no one." Turning away, I groped for something more to say. "As to the voices, well, I will one day reason as to their meaning."

"I hope you do, Anne." Kate quietly retreated to her side of the room.

That scene made me feel even more depressed. Coming of age was not what I had dreamed it would be. The sobering truth was that maturity seemed cold, stark, bruising and unfortunate.

* * *

That afternoon, to celebrate my birthday, Kate and Clayton invited me to a party in Central Park. We were to skate on the pond, eat at my favourite restaurant, and then drive about the park in his sleigh. I had wished for a small celebration and was happy that it would be with just the three of us

However, Clayton had also invited a business acquaintance, Mr Peter Rourke, a wealthy cattle rancher from the state of Texas. Mr Rourke was in New York on a business meeting. Clayton didn't think I would mind so much if he joined us.

"Another cowboy, Anne," Kate giggled. "Clayton says he is handsome and very eligible."

Hmm, whispered Elly's angel ... *very eligible, which means he is no doubt very ugly. If he is very wealthy, then that means he is, no doubt, very fat.*

I frowned. "If he is not handsome, Kate, I will simply take Clayton's arm instead."

Kate and I were introduced to Mr Rourke in front of the Fleur de Lis restaurant, just across from the park. He was a big Irishman. Remnants of his brogue left me feeling warm and reflective. His voice rather put me in mind of Tilly. His fair eyes crinkled, his red ruddy face had a quick smile. He said Kate and I sounded like his mother; she, too, was from England.

"My father came to America twenty years ago: I was born in Dublin. Mother was from Kettering, north of London a pace or two. Don't remember anything of it, actually. Love America. No, would not go back. I'm American now, you see. My money and future are here. This great open pasture of life is fresh and wild, gold and green, lush with opportunity—maybe even," he winked, "a pot o' gold."

"Well, Mr Rourke," I interrupted, "I miss England terribly. I could no more leave it behind than leave my ..."

He nudged me with his elbow. "Couldn't leave your Ma and Pa." He snorted. "Come now, colleen, Clayton tells me today you are eighteen—old enough to separate yourself from the apron."

Apron? Suddenly I found his red ruddy face an irritant pimple—no, more to the point, a boil. His smile a goading ... let me think, *yes, a goading goat-like sneer.* That sounds it exactly. Oh, but I must remember to share that one with Kate.

"Sir, I assure you I have never tugged on anyone's apron strings, other than Mrs Savarin's. And in the future, I wish that you would not discuss such a kind-hearted woman in such a tone again."

"Beg pardon, Miss Holt?" He looked confused. "By my word, you do sound just like my mother." He laughed, slapping his fat thigh in rude fashion. "Come along then, Miss Holt, our sleigh is waiting."

Squinting in the snow's bright glare, I watched Clayton and Kate's sleigh move quickly ahead toward the snow garden. Bonfires burned along the pond edge. Dogs, chasing sticks atop the thick ice, skidded forever in retrieving their prizes. I prayed for Holly Berry and Misha; they too would be trouncing in the snow, without me. I was sure Gib was warm and snuggled in the kitchen, acting quite the Pharaoh's mousetrap for Mrs Saverin, the cook. Clasping my hands within my muff, I sighed, thinking of my most recent friend Freda. I should have brought her. John entered my thoughts in warm vapours. I felt embarrassed that he just might be reading my love letter this very moment. ...

Whistling, Mr Rourke signalled the driver to move on. "Follow Mr Fry's sleigh." While holding his hat, he nudged me in the ribs. "I'm hungry, how 'bout you, colleen?"

"I had a rather large breakfast, sir. And please, my name is Miss Holt." From the corner of my eye, I could see him examining my profile. As we whooshed along, gliding over the snow trails, over the bumpy runnels, I could hear Kate's sweet flirtatious laugh echo through the pines.

He nudged me rudely again. "Gettin' cold?" He bellowed.

Settling another blanket about my lap, I smiled. "I am fine, sir, thank you." My hair was blowing about my face, my nose was numb, and fearing it would soon drip without warning, I held Miss Pramm's handkerchief to it.

Now alongside Clayton's sleigh, Mr Rourke waved and laughed. I winced, for his laugh was considerable, actually loud and uncouth. As we passed them, Kate waved. I waved back, and to my horror, my prized handkerchief had remained stuck to my nose. Oh, God in heaven! Cupping my hand to my face, I tried to loosen it, ouch! But, it wouldn't budge. At long last, I cried, "Pull up, sir, to the nearest bonfire, at once!"

Climbing from the sleigh, I slipped and slid to the fire's crackling assembly of burning logs. Leaning into the fire, I tried wiggling the handkerchief loose from my nose. Mr Rourke remained in the sleigh gawking at me. Fanning the warm flames to my face, I turned to find Kate scrambling to my side.

"A nose bleed, dear?"

"No, it's my handkerchief, the lace, it froze, Kate." Little by little, I pulled it loose. "Disgusting bit of lace ..."

Kate cupped her mouth, giggling. "Oh, how should such a thing happen?"

"Careful, careful," I warned, "do not sneeze or you shall soon see how such a thing happens."

Adjusting her scarf, Kate turned her back to the men. "And how do you find Mr Rourke?"

I glanced over her shoulder at him. "Oh, I find him jolly enough."

"Hmm." She glanced back at him. "Yes, a jolly *large* specimen of Ireland, Anne. But fair enough, Clayton finds him a worthy and honest client."

Taking in the brisk air, I nodded. "Speaking of pork chops, I am becoming quite hungry, Kate. Will *Paddy* be joining us for supper, too?"

Rolling her eyes, she nodded. "No doubt."

Warming my hands over the fire, I shook my head. "Thank you, dearest. It is a wonderful birthday all the same."

Turning her shoulder, she whispered, "Perhaps later you and I shall take a stroll down 18th Street and walk about Union Square for a hot cup of cocoa and cream."

I smiled. "Now that sounds the best of birthday plans."

Helping me back into the sleigh, Clayton said to Mr Rourke, "Shall we make one more swing about the park and then go to dinner?"

Slapping his thigh again, Rourke huffed, "I'm so hungry I could eat a side of beef."

Clayton nodded. "Very well, very well, once more around then."

Our sleigh sped away so quickly that I soon lost sight of Kate. We melded-in with all the others, swooping up and over hills, trotting here and there slicing through the snowy pathways until eventually we found the inn.

Helping me down, Mr Rourke eyed me rudely. "Why, your nose looks like a bloomin' red rose, miss. Been blowing it hard?"

Blowing it hard? Did he say blooming red rose? Oh, I shall ignore him.

"Anne," Kate hurried to my side, "so, you tried to outfox us ... Clayton saw your sleigh disappear through the shorter section of the park."

"Oh, indeed." I took her hand. "I so wanted to watch Mr Bon Vivant consume an entire side of beef that I urged him to hurry along."

She burst out laughing. "Hmm. Yes, yes. Anne, you must not make me laugh. My lips have become quite chapped."

"Let us sup, Kate, then I shall claim a headache and you and I will steal away for a nice walk."

"Very well, Anne."

I glanced back at Mr Rourke and sighed.

* * *

I couldn't finish supper soon enough nor plug my ears from Mr Rourke a second longer. Finally, we left the table and were escorted to the lobby at the Claredon. Mr Rourke removed his hat and bowed his adieu. Kate and Clayton said their good-byes.

I aimed my feet toward the stairs as Kate scurried alongside.

"I am so sorry, Anne, that Mr Rourke was such a bore."

"Not to worry, Kate." I was about to say how much I missed the civilities of the English gentleman, but I held my tongue. Clayton was, however, every bit a gentleman.

As we entered our room, Kate giggled and slid a package from under her pillow. "I have something for you, Anne. I made it myself—a birthday surprise."

I opened the package and pulled out an elegant lavender angora neck scarf. "It is more than beautiful, Kate." I wrapped it around my neck. "Oh, it feels so luxurious." I kissed her cheek. "Thank you."

"You look so delicate in lavender with your pale skin, light eyes, red hair."

"Come then, Kate." I pulled her along. "Let me show it off."

As we left the Clarendon, snow flurries whipped about our faces. The pavement was shiny and beginning to slush. Carriages ambled by, whistles, whips and hooves struck in discordant notes. The air was fresh. Now and again I caught a whiff of bread baking; hot, sweet and butter crusty.

Snuggling with Kate, I felt happy and yet alone, what would John be doing at the moment? The shop windows were decorated with green pine garlands, rough-edged cobbled cones, and white lace crumpled and twisted about like snow. Scarlet red velvet ribbons intertwined a cross that sat amidst the scene. Christ's birthday would be soon upon us.

"I miss decorating Lesington Hall, Kate. I helped Aunt trim the tree and all ..."

"Yes, I too, miss home. New York is New York, certainly not London."

"No, certainly not London." Touching the lavender softness about my neck, I sighed. "This scarf will keep me safe and warm, Kate. I must thank you again for your thoughtfulness."

"Here we are then, Anne. They call it a soda shoppe." She opened the door and we entered. "We seat ourselves, Anne. Clayton and I were here just yesterday afternoon."

"Quite the place, Kate." I glanced about the crowded room. All the tables had white tablecloths, napkins prearranged, cups, saucers ...

Taking my hand, Kate gestured toward an empty table in the corner. "We shall sit by the window."

Sipping my hot cocoa, I nodded appreciatively. "Wonderful idea, this is delicious." Looking out onto the shiny boulevard, I caught sight of a jaunty dog crossing the street.

Kate followed my eyes. "What is it?"

"Nothing, it's just that I spotted a dog that looked like Holly Berry." I laid down my spoon.

She pressed my hand. "I know, Anne."

We finished in silence, paid for the cocoa and left the quaint, vanilla scented warm little soda shoppe.

"We have less than three weeks, Anne. I know how much you miss home."

"I thought I could survive it, but I am not doing well today." I wiped my eyes. "Forever, it seems, on my birthday I become melancholy—forgive me my selfishness, Kate."

"Your birthdays have not always been pleasant, Anne. I do understand, but I wager tomorrow you shall rise a smiling imp."

"Yes, imp, that's me exactly. Charlotte used to call me that." I laughed. "I do hope all is well with her and Professor Mandeville."

We strolled together a few blocks farther. Dusk was falling—the once billowy cumulus sky was now a hazy swirl of oranges, reds, and pinks. The gas streetlights were just beginning to take notice; the pavement was a deep shiny black; without a sound, the snow had begun to fall again. People came streaming from the shops—going home for the evening, I supposed. A spire clock rang out in the distance; street cleaners hopped off their wagons to shovel the snow, horse dung and slop ... the wind had calmed enough only to rattle loose a weary leaf or two.

"I suppose we must return to the hotel, Anne."

"Yes, I suppose, though I am enjoying the walk and the fresh air."

When we approached the Claredon, the doorman reminded me of Franklin. He stood tall and proud, I smiled and hesitated. "Go along, Kate, I wish to remain out for a while longer. The air feels cool, refreshing. It is altogether too warm inside."

"I will stay with you, dear."

"No, no, go in. I shan't be long."

"Very well."

Standing in front of the hotel, I thought perhaps I did look conspicuous standing alone. Not proper, indeed. Spying a safe, quiet place nestled amongst the hotel's gathering of potted pines, I found a quaint bench, a private, covered cosy area— where the men came to gossip to their cigars, I imagined. I needed to be alone and I sat alone taking in the sweet smell of the pines.

Closing my eyes, I thought of Elly's meadow, Holly Berry, Misha and Gib. How I had thrown snowballs at Holly, and when she caught them how they melted into a puzzling sip of water; I laughed at her silly quizzical face. I thought of Misha and how she sank in the deep runnels, and Gib, detesting the icy nip, avoided our play. A vision of Aunt Alice flashed before my eyes. How wonderful it would be to kiss her red cheeks again. Uncle, to hug him ... dare I think of John—no, I could not think about him. It pained me exceedingly. What a silly girl I had been.

I had not heard from him. This, my eighteenth birthday, I wished for a surprise letter from him, but my wishes were not to be granted. I received letters from Aunt and Uncle, and even one from Cousin Edward, but not from John. A sickening feeling beat in the strange waters of my heart and began to assault my island.

Well, I tried to warn you about writing such brazen bold words to the poor fellow, whatever his name is. ...

"Who are you?" I asked.

Let me just say a friend of Miss Pramms. Indeed, miss, for she shall remain a miss—spinsterhood does not frighten her in the least, dearie.

"I should wonder."

Wonder all you wish, but this John fellow is quite shocked at your sudden declarations of love, such a letter you wrote ... I venture to say he shall never write to you again ... you might as well find a cowboy of your own.

"Anne," said Kate as she peeked into my secluded pine tree world. "Come up." Holding a scarf over her head, she pleaded, "It is beginning to snow harder. Come, come. I have another surprise."

I took her hand and we hurried up the steps. Entering our room, Kate winked.

"Anne, wonder upon wonder, Clayton is hosting a Christmas Ball at Lincoln Park, announcing our engagement to his American friends. It was supposed to be a surprise, but he could not keep the surprise a moment longer. He just left, and Papa is very excited as well. He says a great number of important business associates will be there. Oh, Papa is very happy."

I nodded, not looking up.

"What's wrong, Anne?" Wrapping her arms around my shoulders, she hugged me. "I have been boasting; forgive me, Anne."

"Oh, no, Kate, it's not that. I could not be happier for you, believe me. It's just that I should have heard from John by now—a telegraph, perhaps. Oh, Kate, I should not have written that love letter. Surely he has found someone else."

She took my chin in her hand. "Never regret expressing love to someone, Anne. God forbid that John should find someone else, but he is a man of character. He would write and tell you if he had. He would never embarrass you, Anne, never. Nor would he have intentions to wound you."

I wiped my eyes and sighed. "Yes, you are right, Kate."

"So, which nasty angel has been talking to you again?"

"A friend of Miss Pramm's ... she would not confess her name."

"Confess? Well, there you have it, Anne. Now do you see what scoundrels lurk in the strange waters surrounding us?"

Laughing, and hand-in-hand, we joined Aunt Florence to decide just what we were to wear to Kate's grand and glorious Christmas Ball.

CHAPTER TWENTY-TWO

Though Kate's words soothed my nervous heart, I remained anxious every morning in anticipation of the mail. I even lingered in the hotel lobby as the post carrier made his delivery. I had hoped above hope that a letter from John would arrive before Kate's ball—but alas, nothing. There was, however, a letter from Aunt. Choosing an intimate corner in the lobby, I removed to seclusion and sat down. I eagerly opened it.

Lesington Hall
Dearest, Loveliest Niece,
    I received your last letter. A spring wedding? I know you are of age, dear, but I have always fancied myself that you would consult me regarding serious matters of the heart. I grieve to think you might make decisions without my advice. I so worry for your welfare, Anne. I hope this letter finds you in happy spirits. I cannot wait to see you, and your news that you will be home in January is beyond happiness! Yes, Holly Berry, Gib and Misha ask about you every day. Anthony has been very busy. The influenza has been quite nasty this season. Thank you for all your postcards, Love, and forgive me for not writing often ... I have been away with Anthony, but with you coming home soon, that shall slow.
    Love, Aunt Alice

23 December 1868 - Clarendon Hotel
Dear Aunt,

Please do not worry over the affairs of my heart. I do not think any man shall ever love me as I love him. I cannot wait until I am home, Aunt. And never will I leave Lesington Hall again as long as I live. I want to hold you, Holly Berry, Misha and Gib. ... This will be my last letter, for we leave for home 5 January. I am packing already. I love you Aunt Alice. Give my love to Uncle Anthony, and John and Edward. I hope you had a very lovely Christmas ...
Anne

* * *

It was the evening of Kate's Christmas Ball and I debated if I would go—perhaps I should not; what enjoyment would I have? No, I could not disappoint Kate so cruelly ... I knew I must go. I began to dress. I sorely missed the wise counsel of Elly, how I missed her. *Oh, Elly, I have not spoken to you in so long, what a pickle I have found myself.*

But clear as day, I heard her familiar voice: *Yes, a sour pickle dear. Go to the party, I wager you will have a delightful time of it—if you are not dancing in the arms of a handsome veterinarian, perhaps then a handsome cowboy ...*

Elly, this is no time to joke. There is only one handsome cowboy in all of New York, Mr Clayton Fry. Besides I am in no mood for a Rourke cowboy at the moment.

Very well, dress and go to the ball. Eat a bite and then beg off with a headache ... you know, as I used to do.

"Yes, yes, then, I shall. Thank you Elly."

* * *

I dressed early and after helping Kate with her last minute fusses, I went to Aunt Florence's room and sat with her. "Aunt, your hair is done-up very well this evening. You look quite festive. Nice idea with the blue velvet ribbon in your hair."

"Thank you, Anne." Primping in front of the long mirror, she sighed. "Tonight is special." Turning, she smiled, "And you also look pretty, Anne. But you always do."

"Lavender is my favourite, Aunt Florence."

"Yes, and if my memory serves me, it is your Aunt Alice's favourite, as well."

"Aah, yes," I smiled. "Lavender seems to grant wishes, Aunt."

"Is that so, Anne?"

"Oh, how splendid Aunt Alice looked in her lavender dress when Uncle Anthony paid visit to Lesington Hall one fateful night, and then her beautiful wedding dress—and Kate looking so splendid in her brilliant lavender as she dashed into Clayton's arms at the train station. Yes," I sighed, "Aunt Florence, perhaps something lavender shall happen to me tonight at the ball."

Patting my hand, she chuckled, "We are a better family since you have come into it, Anne." She kissed my forehead. "I hope all your lavender wishes come true, my dear."

Kate entered the dressing room fidgeting with the lace in her bodice. "It scratches my skin, Mama. Look, I am red from it already."

"But red and white are festive," I quipped.

Kate ripped out the irritant stiff lace and tossed it over her shoulder.

"Hmm, let me see, Kate." She spun her daughter around. "Very well, then, you may leave it out."

"Indeed, you look stunning in white, Kate. Sequins become you."

She twirled. "I am in a dream, Anne."

I pinched her cheek in fashion. "Yes, little fairy, I should think you would be."

Uncle William knocked and stuck his head around the door. "Come along my ladies, our carriage awaits."

Scurrying from the room, Kate and I followed them to the lobby. Once there, Kate whispered, "Anne, have you inquired about the mail today?"

My head was low. "No, I could not face another empty salver."

She squeezed my hand. The doors opened and an icy mist kissed my face. I noticed the walks were swept clean. The snow was light and fluffy and from the earlier spell of frigid weather this evening actually felt quite warm. The gas lamps along the boulevard were flickering, the pavement shone wet and black; clumps of shovelled snow lay in heaps about the curbstone. Something in the air smelled like burning leaves. I thought of Holybourne and pictured Mama throwing leaves into

Monsieur Pinchot's fire-pit. *What would Mama think of me now? Would she be proud of me?*

Why would she be proud of you? What have you accomplished? Nothing.

"Anne, come along now." Aunt Florence took my hand. "This way, dear."

Stepping into the carriage, I took my place next to Kate. From the lights of the Clarendon, Kate's face looked radiant. Taking her gloved hand, I smiled. "I do believe you could pass for Royalty."

Kate lifted her chin. "Do you think so, subject?"

William and Florence shook their heads.

When we arrived at Lincoln Park, the gates were open. The guard gestured for us to continue moving. All along the drive there were lit torches, lanterns in coloured glass of red and green.

"Well, well," replied Uncle William glancing out, "Clayton doesn't spare the oil."

The horse's hooves splashed thick upon the slush as they pulled under the carriage-porch. In the vestibule, fresh moist greens draped about the walls. It was snug and warm in the mansion, exacting in great detail, the scent of Christmas.

"Kate, it strikes me odd that always it is warm and comfortable wherever we visit. Think how cold, damp and drafty our homes are."

"Clayton tells me he uses a ton of coal a day to warm Lincoln Park."

Uncle William shook his head. "Freda is blessed."

Clayton greeted us. Smiling down upon Kate, his blue eyes glittery, his smile warm, he wished us all a very Merry Christmas. He took her arm. "Come, the servants will take your wraps."

Before long, they disappeared into the drawing room, Uncle William and Aunt Florence followed. Not at all excited about the affair, other than being very happy for Kate, I lingered in the hall as John lingered heavy about my heart.

Other guests bustled in, shaking snow from their garments; stomping their shoes as the servants wiped up the slush. One was busy hanging up capes, wraps, furs while another servant brushed snow from the gentlemen's hats. I watched their efficient work with a constant half-smile. Then spying Mr Rourke, panic seised me. *What is he doing here?* I dashed into the crowded ballroom and searched until I found Uncle William and Aunt Florence.

"There you are, my dear." Aunt Florence was flushed as she glanced around in a nervous flutter. "Why, this ballroom is more than magnificent, Anne."

"Indeed, Aunt, it is, it is." I was thankful the odious Mr Rourke had not made an appearance yet. "I have never seen Kate so glittery, so happy, Aunt Florence."

"Oh, I remember my engagement ball, Anne." Aunt fanned herself, holding a reminiscent smile. After a moment's pause, she took my arm. "Oh, I received a letter today from our nephew John."

My heart leaped. "John Hathaway, Aunt?"

"Yes."

"And?" My mind raced. Would she tell me what he wrote?"

"Oh, yes, long before I left England, he had asked me to find him a proper catalogue of veterinary medicines and supplies while here. New York has one of the most extensive libraries on the subject."

"Is that right?"

"Oh, yes, indeed, Anne. He wrote to remind me of the catalogue." Nodding and smiling at one of the passing guests, she continued fanning herself.

"And, Aunt Florence, did he say if he was in health?"

"He said only that he was weary and in need of rest. He didn't mention Edward or Miss Revelt. But I well imagined on that score, he would remain mute."

"Remain mute concerning Edward, Aunt Florence?"

"Oh, my no, dear," she turned to me, smiling, "regarding his dearest confidant, Miss Revelt."

"Oh, but of course." My stomach formed little knots. *Regarding his dearest confidant did not sound encouraging at all.* "Excuse me Aunt Florence." I made way for the ice bowl. Indeed, my head was beginning to pound.

So, his dearest confidant, is it? Claim your headache and go back to the hotel. You'll not enjoy this party.

Feeling a tug at my hem, I glanced down to find Freda— her bulging brown eyes, wiggly tail and trembling body pleading for a lift. My headache ceased. Picking her up, I spied the elder Mr Fry and took his hand. "It is, I, sir, Miss Anne Holt. Freda came to say hello to me."

"Oh, Miss Anne, yes, yes, I felt her scamper from my lap. She does love you so."

He grimaced, and I well imagined it was from the loud music. I glanced around and found Mr Rourke heading toward me. "Sir," I lifted Mr Fry from his chair in haste, "perhaps a stroll about the halls. I think Freda is becoming frazzled with all the commotion."

"Oh, indeed, Miss Anne." I steadied him as we hurriedly left the room. I peeked back through the door crack and found Mr Rourke stopping to visit with Aunt and Uncle.

"I must not go back in there."

"I agree, the music is a bit wild."

"Indeed, sir." Regaining my composure, I sighed. "Why, this is a wonderful hallway, Mr Fry. I wish some day you will come to England and bring Freda. She would love to meet Holly Berry, Misha, and Gib, and of course, Aunt and Uncle."

"I am looking forward to the day, Miss Anne. We are to have an English wedding in the spring, I have been told."

"Kate has wished it so, Mr Fry. All our family and friends, of course, are there."

"Indeed, our family is small. I do wish for you to meet my daughter, Julia, and her husband, Joseph, and my grandchildren. Pity the weather has not permitted them into the city for this splendid occasion, but they will sail with us to England."

"Yes," I sighed, "I have never seen Kate so taken."

"And what about you, my dear? Already I have overheard many comments this evening of your charm and beauty."

I felt my face burn. "Thank you, Mr Fry. But I have long been in love, sir. I think of no one else but him."

"Oh, indeed. He awaits you in England?"

"Yes, he awaits me, Mr Fry, but I do not believe he returns the affections."

He nodded and we continued walking arm in arm. "Hmm." He sniffed the air. "I believe there is a vine growing about the halls. Indeed: 'Yonder is a girl who lingers Where wild honeysuckle grows,' ... ."

I smiled, finishing the poem. " '... Mingled with the briar rose.' "[12]

"Exactly." He smiled and patted my arm. "He will be there when you return, my dear. He will always be there."

---

[12] H. Smith. Quoted from *Flora Domestica* by Elizabeth Kent (1825).

CHAPTER TWENTY-THREE

The final day of living in New York City arrived with an early morning knock to our door. It was Aunt Florence. "Hurry along, girls, it's time. We must not be late for the ship."

"Time?" I had been awake and packed since four. Kate, however, was in no mood to 'hurry along.' She could not put a thing into her trunk without weeping for leaving Clayton behind.

"Kate, brush you hair, I will pack your things." While I was stuffing her things into every available corner of her trunk, I assured her she would see Clay in a few months. "There now, sit on the trunk while I fasten the lock."

Teary eyed, Kate was searching about the room. "I must find them," she sniffled. "Where could I have put them?"

"*They* must be in your trunk." I grunted. "Come now, sit on it."

"But, Anne," she sighed and climbed atop the trunk, "I must have hankies."

"Use your sleeve."

* * *

Leaving The Clarenden Hotel for the last time, I confirmed in prayer that I would never set foot on this soil again. I wondered why King George III ever fretted over losing the colonies in the first place.

I was the first to board our carriage—mortified to find that Mr Rourke decided to come along to see me off. Helping me into the carriage, I inched myself between Uncle William and Aunt Florence, much to their surprise.

When we arrived at the harbour, I was first out and the first to scamper up the boarding ramp. Keeping my back to New York, I stood alongside Captain Canary as he welcomed the passengers aboard.

I was whistling when Kate stepped across the threshold, I grabbed her hand. "This way, Kate." We moved in and around the passengers until we found a place along the rails to wave good-bye. While Kate stood searching the bobbing heads below for Clayton, I remained with my back to New York. I handed Kate my handkerchief.

Accepting it, she whimpered, "It breaks my heart, Anne, to leave him." She waved, dabbed her eyes, and waved to him again. Now blowing into my prized handkerchief, her voice croaked, "Thank you, dearest, Anne."

"It will be only four months, Kate." I put my arm around her waist. "Just four months."

"I know, Anne, but it will be a wrenching four months."

She waved until the ocean splashed away the skyline. "Come along, Kate, let us find our cabin and have a nice hot cup of tea. You must write to him, you know."

"Every day I shall write, Anne."

"Maybe two would even be more appropriate, Kate."

"Yes, of course. A letter and then a post card, or perhaps ... ," she dropped her chin, "two letters ... ."

"Or two postcards and two letters ... ."

* * *

The last days of our long voyage were smooth; the waves parted from the hull like a warm knife to butter. The salt air, though frigid and biting, felt magnificent. Staring out over the white caps and foamy mist, I, more than once stopped the officers on deck, pointing, "Is that home, sir, there on the horizon? Oh, but surely it is home."

"I am sorry, miss, no, it is not, but when we spot land," he smiled, "you will know it."

The officers, now passing me by, would offer with a smile, "Not yet, Miss Holt. Not yet."

"There you are, Anne."

"Kate," I perked up at her voice, "yes, I waited for you this morning, but you would not wake up. I did not want to disturb you."

"I was up late last night, reading."

"And writing to Clayton?"

"Yes." She pulled her scarf tighter about her neck. "It is too blustery here, Anne. Come in now for breakfast, Mama and Papa have sent me to find you."

* * *

It was the following morning, 15 January, eight o'clock. I gripped the ship's wooden rail tightly staring out at the choppy waves. The glint of sun shone on the deck blinding me for an instant—though the wind was cold and blowing hard, I remained steadfast, promising myself that I would never view England from this viewpoint ever again.

"Land, ahoy!" Whistles blew, the huge stacks blasted. Feeling the reverberating power tickle my feet, I burst with tears. "Home, Oh, dear God, home."

The refined, gentle lady, who had been standing next to me in proper idle conversation, hugged me. "Yes, child, home. Home."

We both stood crying and laughing. Her little pug, snuggled in her arms, snorted and squirmed between us. Laughing like silly children, we danced about the deck crying, "Long live the Queen!"

* * *

I knew it was not ladylike to run down the gangplank, but once I spied Aunt and Uncle, Holly Berry, Misha, and Gib, I tossed my hat to the wind—weeping blindly until I was once again in Aunt's arms.

Holly Berry and Misha wagged their tails with little enthusiasm—I knew they were put out over my lengthy absence. When I bent to apologise, kissing them over and over, they soon warmed and demanded more. Gib, however, sniffed my cheek and promptly turned up his nose.

Smiling, Uncle kissed my cheek and hugged me. "Gib can be quite the snubber, Anne." Laughing, he hugged me again, "Oh, how we have missed you."

Holding her handkerchief to her face, Aunt seemed unable to speak. At long last, halfway home, she found her voice. "Anne, I would wish it that you would never leave home again."

I took her hand. "I assure you Aunt Alice, I will not."

The carriage was crowded with love. Uncle Anthony was still his kind, sweet self—understanding and pliant. Misha took residence at his feet. Holly Berry cuddled at my knee, Gib purred like a rattle upon Aunt's shoulder—sneezing now and again as the feather from her hat tickled his nose.

We were home in little time, and once setting my sights upon Lesington Hall, I assured everyone there was not a word in the dictionary to express my gratitude.

"Look there," I pointed, "there, on the porch, Franklin and Mrs Savarin. Oh, how well they look."

Once the carriage tuned into the portico, they rushed to help us from the carriage. Nancy, Mary and Abby giggled and waved from the open door.

"Home, home." I smiled. "For each of you I have a souvenir and a coin from America!"

Franklin bowed. "We received your postcards, Miss Anne—thank you."

"Oh, yes, yes. Thank you, Miss Anne." Abby took our wraps.

Sniffing the air like Gib, I smiled at Mrs Savarin.

"Indeed, Miss Anne—soup's on." She smiled her toothless grin.

After their kind welcome, I excused myself and ascended the steps to my room. Holly waited at the landing, sitting, refined and proper now—I supposed from months of shushed, quiet solitude in utmost decorum. Well, a few days running and tumbling would soon cure that. Hesitating at the landing, I ruffled her hair, and glancing back, I found Aunt and Uncle disappearing into the study, Gib at their heels. Misha was sniffing toward the kitchen. I continued toward my room, but first stopped at Elly's door. Touching her doorknob, I bowed my head. I missed you at the dock, Elly.

Oh, be about your affairs, child. Don't mind my absence. In the wink of an eye, Love, we shall be together again ... in the wink of an eye.

"Yes, I suppose so, Elly."

* * *

I had slept-in my first morning back and was awakened by a rude, cold nudge to my face. I opened my eyes. There, staring down at me was Holly, her tail wagging. Gib was sniffing at my nose; his whiskers made me sneeze. Misha was trying to snuggle her way atop my pillow, but Holly—barring her teeth—would have nothing of it and she retreated to the foot of my bed.

Sitting up, I kissed each anxious head. The bed was still, so different from the incessant rolling of the ship to which I had grown so accustomed. I could hear the crackling fire above the rain pattering against my window. *Thank you, God, for this moment—thank you for all my blessings.* Holly's thick black tail was still thumping hard upon my legs—she wanted me up and out to run.

Sitting up, I reached for the quaint pet portrait John had painted. "I kept this picture of all of you while I was gone," I said smiling to them. "I set it on my nightstand. Just before I went to sleep every night, I kissed it and prayed for each one of you."

There came a tap. "Come."

Aunt entered the room with a breakfast tray. "Dear, it is eleven o'clock."

"It cannot be, Aunt." Glancing at my mantle clock, I was shocked. "Forgive me for being such a bed bug, I ..."

"No matter, Love. I have brought you your breakfast. You must be exhausted for all the travelling. Come now, have a spot of tea."

Shooing my menagerie off the bed, she set the tray on my lap.

"Thank you, Aunt. How kind. I cannot even begin to tell you how happy I am for being in this very bed."

"I knew by your letters, dear, how homesick you were."

"They could not impart what was really in my entire heart, Aunt."

"That was what had me worried, Anne." Taking my hand, she looked deeply into my eyes. "Have you given it away, Anne?"

"Given my heart away, Aunt?"

"Your letters ..."

"Oh," I giggled, tossing each beggar a piece of toast, "not me, dearest Aunt Alice, I was hinting at Kate's betrothal—it was meant to be kept a strict secret. I could not tell you in writing, but now that we are alone—she is having a grand ball to announce her engagement to Mr Clayton Fry, the American cowboy."

"Oh, thank God," she exhaled heavily. "I was beside myself with worry. Poor dear Anthony had one emergency after the other and could not leave. I was prepared to sail to New York by myself, and then I spoke with John ..."

I lifted my head abruptly. "Cousin John, Aunt?" My face burned at the mere mention of his name.

"He is such a dear young man, Anne, a dear, compassionate young man. I read him your letters and he soothed my concerns. He reminded me of what a solid, good thinking young woman you were. 'Anne is not one to run willy-nilly into love,' he assured me. 'And if she has found someone, he must be of the highest calibre.' "

"He said all that, Aunt?"

"Indeed, Anne, and he advised me that if my worries continued, he would sail to New York and speak to you personally."

Setting the tray aside, I took her hand. "Oh, Aunt, what a sorry bit of confusion I have created." I shook my head. "Dearest John, poor darling, what must he think of me?"

"Indeed, I quite think he adores you, Anne. Though," she hemmed, "I would not say in a cousinly way ..."

"I should hope not, Aunt. I esteem him and I assure you, not in a cousinly way."

Aunt glanced up from her nervous twiddling. A faint smile began at the corners of her mouth. "Yes, yes, even as a child, Anne, you were quite fond of him." Kissing my cheek, she brushed a few curls from my face. "Oh, how often I mistook the depth of your love and devotion, Anne." She took my chin. "You are so like me, dearest—once you love, you love forever."

Burying my head to her heart, I sighed. "I have loved John for a very long time, Aunt Alice—since I was a young girl. He will not leave my heart—I dream of him only."

While dressing, I explained to her about my letters, my inadvertent kissing of his postcard, and, at Kate's urgings, how I wrote my bold confessions of love.

"Goodness me, Anne."

"Oh, Aunt, what am I to do? John did not respond."

"Well, he is too much the gentleman ..."

"I think he does not return the affections, Aunt. I shall be mortified to face him."

"Hmm," she took her chin in thought, "so, Anne, you declared your love beyond a doubt?"

"I wrote: I love you, I have always loved you, and I will love you for the rest of my life."

Nodding she hung her head in thought. "Beyond a doubt you did," she giggled. Stepping over the dogs, Aunt paced about the room—glancing at me now and again as I brushed my hair. "But, all in all, it is odd that he never once mentioned your letters to me, Anne—never once. That is more than odd. Where did you send the letters Anne?"

"Where? Aunt."

"London or Bath?"

"I sent to them to Hawthorne House, London. I didn't know his address at Bath."

"But of course! That's it!" She scooped Gib up and kissed his fuzzy head. "Maybe, just maybe," she smiled, "John has not received a one of your letters."

Dropping my brush, I tilted my head. "Dare I ask what you speak of, Aunt Alice?"

"Anthony was to see after John's mail. He went to Hawthorne House every day when John and Edward first left for Bath—many months now—but then the mail trickled to nothing. I suppose he has not seen to it for a good while. We must go and see for ourselves, Anne. I wager your letters are there collecting dust."

I touched my heart. "Oh, God, Aunt Alice!" I kissed her brow.

Thief! Screeched the angel of letter carriers. *Thief!*

"Oh, wait, Aunt. I cannot take them. That would be stealing."

She put her hands to her hip. "Well, who wrote them?"

"I did."

"Come along then, Anne. God will forgive you for stealing your own letters, just this one time."

* * *

Taking up Aunt's hand, I sighed. "Oh, how could I expect to have every letter I wrote to him safely stacked at Hathaway House unread, Aunt? I should think someone would have forwarded them."

"Mr Percival is the caretaker—he is getting on in years. Anthony was supposed to have been seeing to all that. But, as I said, for the longest time nothing had come for John or Edward. I dare say, he did not expect anything more to come and quite forgot all about the matter. Besides, I think he does not like going there so often any more, Anne."

"Yes, I should wonder."

When our carriage ambled into the Hawthorne House drive, Percival stood stoop-shouldered on the steps, squinting.

"I will wait here, Anne."

Inhaling deeply, I stepped from the carriage, shielded my eyes from the bright morning sun and nodded to the caretaker. Before entering the house, I glanced back at Aunt and smiled.

"Good morning, Miss Holt," bowed Percival.

"Yes, it is a beautiful morning, Percival. I wish to see Uncle Anthony's study.

"Indeed, miss." He gestured with his wobbly hand. "This way."

All the chandeliers and wall sconces were covered with white cloth. The furniture draped, the portraits turned ... as he led me into Uncle's study, our footfalls echoed about the cold vacant black-and-white chequered floor. He opened the study door and stood back.

"Yes, Percival, and where might the mail salver be?"

"Just there, Miss Holt, on Master's desk."

"Thank you, yes, I see it."

Standing at the open door, he held his nose quite high, all in all.

Reaching for the letters, I felt someone slap my hand.

Thief!

"Oh," I cried and dropped the salver, "but I am not a thief!"

The letters flew about the floor.

"I beg your pardon, Miss Holt?" Frowning, Percival crouched on his hands and knees and gathered them up.

Dabbing my forehead, I glanced to heaven. "Oh, God, I am not a thief, I assure you."

"Indeed, Miss Holt. I should imagine that you are not." Percival stood erect and handed the letters to me.

Hurrying from the ghostly Hawthorne House, I climbed into the carriage slamming the door behind me. "Oh, Aunt!" I dabbed my forehead.

She patted my hand. "It is such nasty business retrieving old love letters."

"Aunt?"

She giggled and cried out, "Drive on."

* * *

Away in the privacy of my room, I sorted through the letters and found the post card with my brazen red lip rouge; found the latest one declaring my love. Holding them to my heart, I sighed and put them away. Glancing upward, I assured God that I would, indeed, give them back to John. "At a later date, Sir."

What? At a later date? What sort of promise is that to the God of all gods?

I exhaled soundly. It was the postman angel again. I could hear the drumming of his fingertips atop the letterbox of all letterboxes, uniformed and proper, he stood guard.

Full of indignation, I replied, "Such a nerve to eavesdrop. For your information, sir, I will, of course, return John's letters sooner rather than later."

"Anne," said Aunt as she bustled into my room knocking but once. "An invitation has come ... from William and Florence."

"Yes, Aunt, no doubt for Kate's surprise announcement of her betrothal."

"Right you are. Oh, and there is a telegram for you."

"A telegram, Aunt?" Opening it, I smiled. "It's from Mr Clayton Fry, Aunt—oh, he will be coming to her ball after all. It is to be a great surprise!"

"Well, I should hope so. One could hardly have a ball announcing one's engagement without the fiancé being there, Anne."

"I agree, but I wager Mr Fry sacrificed a good deal of money in his business to make this trip to England."

"Oh, which reminds me, Anne, Elly's finances are now in order. I have the bank notes in your name. Uncle Anthony has them secured for you. He will give them to you very soon." She took my chin. "And just what will you do with your small fortune, my dear?"

I thought of O'Leary and knew I had to settle my personal debt, and soon. "I think I shall invest in the happiness of my future, Aunt Alice."

Gliding from my room, she blew me a kiss. "Well, that sounds the best of plans, my dear. So, I must be off. I am lunching with your Uncle Anthony. See you for dinner."

"Good-bye, Aunt." Putting aside the telegram from Clayton, I heard Aunt's muffled footfalls descend the steps. I stared out the window and watched the birds flitter about the pond; Gib was stumbling behind Nancy as she carried a pail full of milk. Early noon was settling warm with slices of orange and pink clouds swirling about the poplar and oak standing in the west. A quick thought of paying my debt to O'Leary eased my troubled mind.

Now looking to the east, dark clouds were gathering. Rumblings of thunder rolled and boomed—I thought of Kate dashing into Clayton's arms. Oh, how she will faint when she sees him enter the ballroom. She will no doubt be wearing a lavender gown, just as Aunt Alice had. Sighing, I recollected Aunt Florence's wish that all my lavender wishes would come true. Touching my lips, I felt the smile, and knew John would be there at her ball.

* * *

Over supper, Uncle Anthony set his cup onto the saucer and hemmed. "I just received a note from Edward. He and John will be at Kate's ball. That is good news, indeed."

Aunt glanced at me. "Did they mention Miss Revelt?"

"No." he responded with a shrug. "I just assumed she would be coming, she always does."

"Then we must ready Hawthorne House, dear—unless they would wish to come here."

I kicked her foot.

"On the other hand, love, I do think Hawthorne House would be more appropriate. Ah, to best suit everyone's needs. Miss Revelt, you know, rather likes it so much better."

"Hmm." He finished his coffee-mocha. "Oh, well then, yes, Alice, of course she does. After dinner, I will write them a note."

Excusing myself, I left the table. Grabbing my wrap, I removed to the dining room balcony to watch the heavens. The stars glittered brilliant in a small cloudless space in February's deep purple sky. A slight, icy breeze blew on my face and though it was cold, it felt delightful. As I closed my eyes, John's face came to me in intimate perfection—*I must soon return my letters to you, John.*

CHAPTER TWENTY-FOUR

It was the night of Kate's engagement ball. Smiling to myself, I thought of Clayton coming to the ball this evening and surprising Kate. I wondered if his father and Freda would be there. It was beginning to snow and I drew tight the drawstrings to my cape, took Uncle's hand and boarded our carriage.

As we turned off Regent Street toward Uncle William and Aunt Florence's house Uncle pressed Aunt's hand. "Alice, I am much relieved at William's business successes in America. He is back on the road to prosperity again. Thanks to Mr Clayton Fry. He must be very much in love with Kate to wager such an investment in William's business."

"Oh, Anthony, yes, I, too am pleased. Florence must be relieved of that, I am sure." Aunt tweaked my nose. "You look pretty tonight, Anne."

"Indeed," said Uncle, "there will be many eligible young men there, Anne."

"Yes, Uncle, I know."

We were the tenth carriage in line to be left off under the carriage-porch at William and Florence's home. The circular drive was posted with flickering gas lamps; from the windows of the Great House a warm orange glaze spilled onto the snow-dusted windowsills. Dog tracks led into the house—I fancied a few to be crouched beneath the food tables with begging eyes.

"Here we are, then. Uncle tugged at his gloves, "the Hathaways."

We entered the Great House to the music of Mozart—Aunt Florence's favourite. They had installed electric lights, and yet many candles burned at every nest. Holly wreaths hung at every door. Swooping in and around the banisters of the ancient oak staircase were greens—I half expected a bird to flitter by.

Remaining behind Aunt and Uncle, I surveyed everyone. Mingling about in the grand ballroom were groups of ladies in thin silks, colours of the rainbow, and gentlemen in splendid evening dress—stark and opposite they stood self-assured and handsome in black and white.

I caught sight of Aunt Florence, her lovely complexion was rose tinted as she chatted amicably with her guests. Kate was conversing with Miss Pramm, but of course. Oh, but where was John?

Little by little I inched my way to Kate's side and took her hand. "You look beautiful this evening, but I thought you would be wearing lavender?"

"Oh, no," she glanced down at her outfit, shaking her head. "I could not wear it. I am saving that particular gown for when Clayton comes."

"Oh, yes, indeed," I hugged her. "Nonetheless, you look divine, Kate."

"John is here, Anne," she said with a sly smile.

My heart leapt. I took a deep breath. Closing my eyes, I exhaled. "Where?"

"I saw him a just few minutes ago," she gestured with her head, "over by the champagne table. Shall I find him for you?"

"No, Kate," I whispered, taking in another great breath, "I really think he should find me."

"Oh, but of course." Kate shimmered in glee. "I'm so excited, have you brought the letters, Anne?"

"Yes." I glanced down at my purse. "They are in here."

She kissed my cheek. "What have the angels to say over that?"

"Well, the postman was furious that I stole them."

We laughed.

"Oh, dear me, Anne, soon I must waltz with Papa; then he will announce my engagement." She wiped her eyes. "I cannot tell you how low I feel without Clayton by my side."

"I know, Kate, but it cannot be helped. You must announce your intentions far in advance. The social calendar, you know, fills without notice."

"So it does, Anne."

The music began again. Uncle William came to Kate's side and took her hand. "Come, my dear."

She hugged me and left. I watched in awed wonder as my dearest cousin moved proudly alongside her father. Now into the centre of the gleaming ballroom floor, he bowed and took her into his arms. The music began and heads held high, they glided around the room. Above the billowy pink rustle of her gown, I heard the faint gurgle of the most unusual sort and glanced down ... there situated quite snugly inside a black hat, in the middle of the ballroom floor, huddled Freda!

The music fluted to an end, and Kate let go her father's hand. Walking toward the hat, she scooped up the trembling dog. "Why, Freda, what are you doing here?"

As Uncle William motioned for the music to resume, Clayton strolled out onto the floor behind her. "May I have this dance, Miss Hathaway?"

Watching as the two moved as one about the floor, I glanced at the open balcony doors and spied John. Our eyes met. He smiled and moved toward me. Oh, God, John. I have been waiting for you ... *Calm yourself, Anne, calm yourself.*

Indeed, said one of the calming angels, *let him come to you.*

Run to him, Anne. As Kate did to Clayton; look at what happened to them ... what more do you need? Run!

Calm down, Anne. Calm down. Miss Pramm would never run through a crowd of people ... London's society ... think of the whispers ...

I felt myself hurrying across the floor. I could not take my eyes from John. The room seemed to shimmer in the music. It was warm and perfect, absolute and perfect. Reaching out, I would take his hand. I would kiss his mouth. Thank you God for ... I closed my eyes for an instant; my body was warm and fluid; wine and roses filled my heart. I would taste his lips in my own lavender gown after all.

"Miss Holt!"

I felt a hard, brisk hand around my waist; my eyes jarred opened. I was flying, twirling, now off my feet. *Where am I?* Shaking my senses, I looked up and gasped, "Mr Rourke?"

His red-orange hair sprung up like carrots; his red bulbous freckled nose wrinkled in giddy fashion; his blue eyes crinkled; he looked like a potato stuffed with shamrocks; his whiskey breath trilled sour and strong—he laughed loud, long, and hardy.

"Sir, what are you doing? Let go of me! I did not promise this dance to you."

"Oh, I'll have none of that talk, colleen. I sailed a long ways for this dance. When we Texans stake a claim, we take it."

Twirling rudely about the room, my feet still off the floor, I tried to find John. I thought I saw him there ... no there.

"Oh, please Mr Rourke," I pleaded vehemently, "you must put me down this instant. You are creating a scene."

"Very well, colleen, one final twirl."

Spinning me like a top, his gaudy gold-nugget-California-cufflink caught my silk purse and ripped it open—my love letters spewed about the floor. Mortified, I huddled in the middle of the room. Couples continued to waltz around me. Mr Rourke stumbled back into the crowd. I tried frantically to find each letter; each postcard; my eyes filled with tears.

There were exactly ten letters, fussed the postman ... *and two postcards, Miss Holt!*

"Yes, yes, I know, I know."

"Here, Anne, I shall help you." John knelt by my side. His strong, sweet voice calmed me. In his quiet, firm manner, he put his arm around my shoulder. "Allow me, Anne. I see you have dropped your ..." Picking up the letters, he noted his name and address on each. Spying the postcard, he smiled.

"There were ten letters, John," I whispered, not taking my eyes from his, "and two postcards, sir."

"I have them all, Anne. Come, then." He took my hand and led me from the dancing.

The music played on as we slipped out onto the balcony and slowly faded into the soft, quiet snowflakes tumbling upon us.

"This way, Anne." He led me into Aunt Florence's solarium and sat me in a white wicker settee surrounded by palm fronds, fresh earth, upstart trees, and moist warm air, the music floating distant.

"It is quite beautiful in here, John." I smiled too embarrassed to look him in the eye.

"Yes, Aunt Florence spends most of her time here in the winter."

I glanced about the soft glow of electric lights. "I can well imagine."

Touching my hand, he glanced down. "I see you have grown into your mother's ring, Anne."

"You said I would, John." Kissing it, I smiled up at him.

"You remember, then?"

"I remember everything, John."

He removed the letters from his vest pocket. Now examining the post card with my red lip rouge imprinted on it, he inhaled deeply.

"You must forgive me, sir."

"Forgive you for what, Anne?"

I could feel my face burning with embarrassment. "I am a thief, sir."

"And what did you steal, Anne?"

Biting my lip, I confessed, "Those letters, John, are yours. I wrote them from New York and sent them to London ... ah, by mistake." Wringing my hands, I continued, "The mistake being, I did not know your address in Bath and I sent them to Hawthorne House instead."

He remained quiet and reflective. My heart beat madly in my chest. I wanted to touch him. No, I could not be so forward. He looked wildly handsome in black. His hair dark, his warm brown eyes—though he remained sitting quietly, holding the letters, I wanted to run my hand along his soft sweet face. *No, you must not do that, Anne.*

"I had not heard from you, Anne, the entire time you were gone to America."

I dabbed my eyes. "I know."

"When I would visit Lesington, your aunt would share her deep concerns regarding you. We were both worried over your future. We thought you had become engaged."

"I am sorry John, I sent the letters to the wrong place, forgive me. Uncle Anthony was supposed to have ..."

I could feel his gaze, now warm and steady upon my face; his eyes scanning my profile, my neck, my bare shoulders.

His tone softened. "You look exquisite in lavender, Anne. That is my favourite colour."

"I know."

Turning toward me, his words echoed soft and sweet upon my face. I closed my eyes. *Oh, God in heaven, I will kiss his mouth.*

"Yes," he whispered, "but then I told you that a long time ago."

I smiled. "I remember it exactly, John. We were walking in a field of lavender, Lesington Hall. I remarked at how magnificent the bloom, it was my very favourite flower. I was only eleven at the time, and still it is my favourite."

"And ever since, it has been my favourite, too, Anne."

My breath caught, now feeling my body tremble. "How dear of you, John, to make it so."

"Anne, you must tell me about these letters."

Wiping my eyes, I glanced at him. "I would rather you read them, sir, one by one." My voice faltered.

"Well, perhaps I shall just burn them, Anne."

I grabbed his arm. "No, you must read them, now." I wept. "I cannot endure this torture a moment longer." Tears slipped down my cheeks. "I have missed you so."

Handing me his handkerchief, he stood and walked to the wood burning stove, opened the heavy black door and tossed them into the crackling flames.

"There now, Anne," he whispered as he gathered me into his arms. "I would rather you speak those words that you wrote."

Burying my head to his heart, I held him tight. I could feel his breathing quicken.

Lifting my chin, he wiped my tears. Smiling into my face, he whispered, "I love you, Anne. I have loved you from the moment I saw you, and will love you until the day I die."